SONGS OF
LOVE & DEATH

SONGS OF LOVE & DEATH

All-Original Tales of Star-crossed Love

EDITED BY

George R. R. Martin & Gardner Dozois

GALLERY BOOKS

New York   London   Toronto   Sydney

Gallery Books
A Division of Simon & Schuster, Inc.
1230 Avenue of the Americas
New York, NY 10020

*For everyone we've loved and lost
—you know who you are.*

CONTENTS

STAR-CROSSED LOVERS

The earliest reference we can find for the phrase "star-crossed lovers" traces it to 1595, attributing it to Shakespeare's *Romeo and Juliet*, a tragedy about the doomed romance that blossoms between a young man and a young woman on the brawling streets of Verona, a romance that is destined to fail because the families they come from are locked in a deadly feud: "From forth the fatal loins of these two foes,/a pair of star-cross'd lovers take their life."

It's an astrological phrase, of course, stemming from the old belief (still held today by millions of people, as a look at any newspaper will tell you) that the position of the stars at your birth casts a supernatural influence that determines your fate. So to say that a romantic relationship is "star-crossed" is to say that the influence of the stars are working against it, that it's opposed by fate, ill-fated, "thwarted by a malign star." Not meant to be. That you're destined to be kept apart no matter how hard you struggle to be together.

In real life, even without the influence of the stars or the dread hand of Fate, there are any number of things that can doom a relationship—differences in temperament, race, religion, social status, political affiliations, being on different sides of a bitter war, philosophical dogma, degrees of affluence (or lack of it). Even simple distance can work to keep people apart, and over the centuries there must have been many lovers who stood on the dock and watched their loved ones sail off to destinations like Australia or America thousands of miles away, knowing that they'd never see them again, since in the days before modern transportation, they might as well have been sailing off to Mars. Many, many immigrants must have left someone behind them in the Old Country, as they were forced into exile or set off to find their fortunes, and most were never reunited.

This is a theme that has been eagerly embraced by fiction and folklore, and world literature is full of star-crossed lovers desperately struggling to hold on to love no matter how overwhelming the odds against them: Paris and Helen, Pyramus and Thisbe, Lancelot and Guinevere, Roxanne and Cyrano, Cathy and Heathcliff. Recently, thanks to the booms in fantasy and romance, everyone knows of Buffy and Angel, Bill Compton and Sookie Stackhouse, Edward Cullen and Bella Swan.

Which brings us down to the book you hold in your hands at this moment (unless you're using your mental powers to make it levitate or reading it off a screen), a cross-genre anthology called *Songs of Love & Death,* which explores the borderlands of fantasy and romance, stories from the heart and about the heart, tales of endangered love played out against every kind of setting, from ghost-haunted fantasy landscapes to mile-long spaceships in transit between the stars, stories where a lover's heart is put in danger, and love, life, and happiness are at risk with great odds to be overcome to achieve them. Star-crossed lovers who are *really* star-crossed, with grave obstacles to be overcome before they succeed in finding love (if they do): a wizard who must battle both a supremely powerful vampire and the hidden desires of his own heart; a man who must seduce a reluctant maiden or forfeit his family's life to the Queen of Faerie; a woman who falls in love with a superhero she glimpses hurtling toward the scene of a crime; a ghost who lusts for sex and blood long after he should be safely in his grave; a girl who must brave the wrath of an otherworldly prince to rescue the man she loves; a lonely man who falls in love with a woman he can never meet; a smuggler who dares to fall in love with the ruler of a star-spanning Empire; a soldier cast adrift from his world who will face immense hardships to return to his own time and place; a lover who may—or may not—exist; a love that persists across lives and worlds, and transcends death . . .

We've gathered for you here some of the most prestigious and widely read names in romance and fantasy, and the booming hot new field of paranormal romance, including Jim Butcher, Robin Hobb, Neil Gaiman, Diana Gabaldon, Jacqueline Carey, Carrie Vaughn, and eleven other first-class writers. Among other goodies, we are proud to offer you a brand-new Harry Dresden story, a pivotal story in the Kushiel series, a follow-up to *An Echo in the Bone,* and a new novelette set in the Farseer universe. And more star-crossed lovers, of every imaginable sort, than you can shake a stick at.

Enjoy!

Jim Butcher

New York Times *bestseller Jim Butcher is best known for the Dresden Files series, starring Harry Dresden, a wizard for hire, who goes down some very mean streets indeed to do battle against the dark creatures of the supernatural world and is one of the most popular fictional characters of the twenty-first century to date; he even had his own TV show. The Dresden Files books include* Storm Front, Fool Moon, Grave Peril, Summer Knight, Death Masks, Blood Rites, Dead Beat, Proven Guilty, White Night, Small Favor, *and* Turn Coat. *Butcher is also the author of the swashbuckling sword and sorcery Codex Alera series, consisting of* Furies of Calderon, Academ's Fury, Cursor's Fury, Captain's Fury, *and* Princeps' Fury. *His most recent books are* First Lord's Fury, *the new Codex Alera novel, and* Changes, *the new Dresden Files novel. Butcher lives in Missouri with his wife, his son, and a ferocious guard dog.*

Here he sends Harry Dresden up against one of his deadliest adversaries and also into battle with the secret desires of his heart—which may turn out to be even more dangerous.

Love Hurts

Murphy gestured at the bodies and said, "Love hurts."

I ducked under the crime scene tape and entered the Wrigleyville apartment. The smell of blood and death was thick. It made gallows humor inevitable.

Murphy stood there looking at me. She wasn't offering explanations. That meant she wanted an unbiased opinion from CPD's Special Investigations consultant—who is me, Harry Dresden. As far as I know, I am the only wizard on the planet earning a significant portion of his income working for a law enforcement agency.

I stopped and looked around, taking inventory.

Two bodies, naked, male and female, still intertwined in the act. One little pistol, illegal in Chicago, lying upon the limp fingers of the woman. Two gunshot wounds to the temples, one each. There were two overlapping fan-shaped splatters of blood, and more had soaked into the carpet. The bodies stank like hell. Some very unromantic things had happened to them after death.

I walked a little farther into the room and looked around. Somewhere in the apartment, an old vinyl was playing Queen. Freddie wondered who wanted to live forever. As I listened, the song ended and began again a few seconds later, popping and scratching nostalgically.

The walls were covered in photographs.

I don't mean that there were a lot of pictures on the wall, like at great-grandma's house. I mean covered in photographs. Entirely. Completely papered.

I glanced up. So was the ceiling.

I took a moment to walk slowly around, looking at pictures. All of them, every single one of them, featured the two dead people together, posed somewhere and looking deliriously happy. I walked and peered. Plenty of the pictures were near-duplicates in most details, except that the subjects wore different sets of clothing—generally cutesy matching T-shirts. Most of the sites were tourist spots within Chicago.

It was as if the couple had gone on the same vacation tour every day, over and over again, collecting the same general batch of pictures each time.

"Matching T-shirts," I said. "Creepy."

Murphy's smile was unpleasant. She was a tiny, compactly muscular woman with blond hair and a button nose. I'd say that she was so cute I just wanted to put her in my pocket, but if I tried to do it, she'd break my arm. Murph knows martial arts.

She waited and said nothing.

"Another suicide pact. That's the third one this month." I gestured at the pictures. "Though the others weren't quite so cuckoo for Cocoa Puffs. Or, ah, in medias res." I shrugged and gestured at the obsessive photographs. "This is just crazy."

Murphy lifted one pale eyebrow ever so slightly. "Remind me: How much do we pay you to give us advice, Sherlock?"

I grimaced. "Yeah, yeah. I know." I was quiet for a while and then said, "What were their names?"

"Greg and Cindy Bardalacki," Murphy said.

"Seemingly unconnected dead people, but they share similar patterns of death. Now we're upgrading to irrational and obsessive behavior as a precursor . . ." I frowned. I checked several of the pictures and went over to eye the bodies. "Oh," I said. "Oh, hell's bells."

Murphy arched an eyebrow.

"No wedding rings anywhere," I said. "No wedding pictures. And . . ." I finally found a framed family picture, which looked to have been there for a while, among all the snapshots. Greg and Cindy were both in it, along with an older couple and a younger man.

"Jesus, Murph," I said. "They weren't a married couple. They were brother and sister."

Murphy eyed the intertwined bodies. There were no signs of struggle. Clothes, champagne flutes, and an empty bubbly bottle lay scattered. "Married, no," she said. "Couple, yes." She was unruffled. She'd already worked that out for herself.

"Ick," I said. "But that explains it."

"Explains what?"

"These two. They were together—and they went insane doing it. This has the earmarks of someone tampering with their minds."

Murphy squinted at me. "Why?"

I spread my hands. "Let's say Greg and Cindy bump into Bad Guy X. Bad Guy X gets into their heads and makes them fall wildly in love and lust with each other. There's nothing they can do about the feelings—which seem perfectly natural—but on some level they're aware that what they're doing is not what they want, and dementedly wrong besides. Their compromised conscious minds clash with their subconscious and . . ." I gestured at pictures. "And it escalates until they can't handle it anymore, and bang." I shot Murphy with my thumb and forefinger.

"If you're right, they aren't the deceased," Murphy said. "They're the victims. Big difference. Which is it?"

"Wish I could say," I told her. "But the only evidence that could prove it one way or another is leaking out onto the floor. If we get a survivor, maybe I could take a peek and see, but barring that, we're stuck with legwork."

Murphy sighed and looked down. "Two suicide pacts could—technically—be a coincidence. Three of them, no way it's natural. This feels more like something's MO. Could it be another one of those Skavis vampires?"

"They gun for loners," I said, shaking my head. "These deaths don't fit their profile."

"So. You're telling me that we need to turn up a common denominator to link the victims? Gosh, I wish I could have thought of that on my own."

I winced. "Yeah." I glanced over at a couple of other SI detectives in the room, taking pictures of the bodies and documenting the walls and so on. Forensics wasn't on site. They don't like to waste their time on the suicides of the emotionally disturbed, regardless of how bizarre they might be. That was crap work, and as such had been dutifully passed to SI.

I lowered my voice. "If someone is playing mind games, the Council might know something. I'll try to pick up the trail on that end. You start from here. Hopefully, I'll earn my pay and we'll meet in the middle."

"Right." Murph stared at the bodies and her eyes were haunted. She knew what it was like to be the victim of mental manipulation. I didn't reach out to support her. She hated showing vulnerability, and I didn't want to point out to her that I'd noticed.

Freddie reached a crescendo, which told us that love must die.

Murphy sighed and called, "For the love of God, someone turn off that damned record."

"I'M SORRY, HARRY," Captain Luccio said. "We don't exactly have orbital satellites for detecting black magic."

I waited a second to be sure that she was finished. The presence of so much magical talent on the far end of the call meant that at times the lag could stretch out between Chicago and Edinburgh, the headquarters of the White Council of Wizardry. Anastasia Luccio, Captain of the Wardens, my ex-girlfriend, had been readily forthcoming with the information the Council had on any shenanigans going on in Chicago—which was exactly nothing.

"Too bad we don't, eh?" I asked. "Unofficially—is there anyone who might know anything?"

"The Gatekeeper, perhaps. He has a gift for sensing problem areas. But no one has seen him for weeks, which is hardly unusual. And frankly, Warden Dresden, you're supposed to be the one giving *us* this kind of information." Her voice was half teasing, half deadly serious. "What do you think is happening?"

"Three couples, apparently lovey-dovey as hell, have committed dual suicide in the past two weeks," I told her. "The last two were brother and sister. There were some seriously irrational components to their behavior."

"You suspect mental tampering," she said. Her voice was hard.

Luccio had been a victim, too.

I found myself smiling somewhat bitterly at no one. She had been, among other things, mindboinked into going out with me. Which was apparently the only way anyone would date me, lately. "It seems a reasonable suspicion. I'll let you know what I turn up."

"Use caution," she said. "Don't enter any suspect situation without backup on hand. There's too much chance that you could be compromised."

"Compromised?" I asked. "Of the two people having this conversation, which one of them exposed the last guy rearranging people's heads?"

"Touché," Luccio said. "But he got away with it because we were overconfident. So use caution anyway."

"Planning on it," I said.

There was a moment of awkward silence, and then Anastasia said, "How have you been, Harry?"

"Keeping busy," I said. She had already apologized to me, sort of, for abruptly walking out of my personal life. She'd never intended to be there in the first place. There had been a real emotional tsunami around the events of last year, and I wasn't the one who had gotten the most hurt by them. "You?"

"Keeping busy." She was quiet for a moment and then said, "I know it's over. But I'm glad for the time we had together. It made me happy. Sometimes I—"

Miss feeling that, I thought, completing the sentence. My throat felt tight. "Nothing wrong with happy."

"No, there isn't. When it's real." Her voice softened. "Be careful, Harry. Please."

"I will," I said.

I STARTED COMBING the supernatural world for answers and got almost nothing. The Little Folk, who could usually be relied on to provide some kind of information, had nothing for me. Their memory for detail is very short, and the deaths had happened too long ago to get me anything but conflicting gibberish.

I made several mental nighttime sweeps through the city using the scale model of Chicago in my basement, and got nothing but a headache for my trouble.

I called around the Paranet, the organization of folk with only modest magical gifts, the kind who often found themselves being preyed upon by more powerful supernatural beings. They worked together now, sharing information, communicating successful techniques, and generally overcoming their lack of raw magical muscle with mutually supportive teamwork. They didn't have anything for me, either.

I hit McAnnally's, a hub of the supernatural social scene, and asked a lot of questions. No one had any answers. Then I started contacting the people I knew in the scene, starting with the ones I thought most likely to provide information. I worked my way methodically down the list, crossing out names, until I got to "ask random people on the street."

There are days when I don't feel like much of a wizard. Or an investigator. Or a wizard investigator.

Ordinary PIs have a lot of days like that, where you look and look and look for information and find nothing. I get fewer of those days than most, on account of the whole wizard thing giving me a lot more options—but sometimes I come up goose eggs anyway.

I just hate doing it when lives may be in danger.

Four days later, all I knew was that nobody knew about any black magic happening in Chicago, and the only traces of it I *did* find were the miniscule amounts of residue left from black magic wrought by those without enough power to be a threat. (Warden Ramirez had coined the phrase "dim magic" to describe that kind of petty, essentially harmless malice.) There were also the usual traces of dim magic performed subconsciously from a bed of dark emotions, probably by someone who might not even know they had a gift.

In other words, goose eggs.

Fortunately, Murphy got the job done.

Sometimes hard work is way better than magic.

Murphy's Saturn had gotten a little blown up a couple of years back, sort of my fault, and what with her demotion and all, it would be a while before she'd be able to afford something besides her old Harley. For some reason, she didn't want to take the motorcycle, so that left my car, the ever-trusty (almost always) Blue Beetle. It's an old-school VW Bug which had seen me through one nasty scrape after another. More than once, it had been pounded badly, but always it had risen to do battle once more—if by battle one means driving somewhere at a sedate speed, without much acceleration and only middling gas mileage.

Don't start. It's paid for.

I stopped outside Murphy's little white house, with its little pink rose garden, and rolled down the window on the passenger side. "Make like the Dukes of Hazzard," I said. "Door's stuck."

Murphy gave me a narrow look. Then she tried the door. It opened easily. She slid into the passenger seat with a smug smile, closed the door, and didn't say anything.

"Police work has made you cynical," I said.

"If you want to ogle my butt, you'll just have to work for it like everyone else, Harry."

I snorted and put the car in gear. "Where we going?"

"Nowhere until you buckle up," she said, putting her own seat belt on.

"It's my car," I said.

"It's the law. You want to get cited? 'Cause I can do that."

I debated whether or not it was worth it while she gave me her cop look. And produced a ball-point pen.

I buckled up.

Murphy beamed at me. "Springfield. Head for I-55."

I grunted. "Kind of out of your jurisdiction."

"If we were investigating something," Murphy said. "We're not. We're going to the fair."

I eyed her sidelong. "On a date?"

"Sure, if someone asks," she said, offhand. Then she froze for a second, and added, "It's a reasonable cover story."

"Right," I said. Her cheeks looked a little pink. Neither of us said anything for a little while.

I merged onto the highway, always fun in a car originally designed to rocket down the autobahn at a blistering one hundred kilometers an hour, and asked Murphy, "Springfield?"

"State fair," she said. "That was the common denominator."

I frowned, going over the dates in my head. "State fair only runs, what? Ten days?"

Murphy nodded. "They shut down tonight."

"But the first couple died twelve days ago."

"They were both volunteer staff for the fair, and they were down there on the grounds setting up." Murphy lifted a foot to rest her heel on the edge of the passenger seat, frowning out the window. "I found skee-ball tickets and one of those chintzy stuffed animals in the second couple's apartment. And the Bardalackis got pulled over for speeding on I-55, five minutes out of Springfield and bound for Chicago."

"So *maybe* they went to the fair," I said. "Or maybe they were just taking a road trip or something."

Murphy shrugged. "Possibly. But if I assume that it's a coincidence, it doesn't get me anywhere—and we've got nothing. If I assume that there's a connection, we've got a possible answer."

I beamed at her. "I thought you didn't like reading Parker."

She eyed me. "That doesn't mean his logic isn't sound."

"Oh. Right."

She exhaled heavily. "It's the best I've got. I just hope that if I get you into the general area, you can pick up on whatever is going on."

"Yeah," I said, thinking of walls papered in photographs. "Me too."

THE THING I enjoy the most about places like the state fair is the smells. You get combinations of smells at such events like none found any-where else. Popcorn, roast nuts, and fast food predominate, and you can get anything you want to clog your arteries or burn out your stomach lining there. Chili dogs, funnel cakes, fried bread, majorly greasy pizza, candy apples, ye gods. Evil food smells amazing—which is either proof that there is a Satan or some equivalent out there, or that the Almighty doesn't actually want everyone to eat organic tofu all the time. I can't decide.

Other smells are a cross section, depending on where you're standing. Disinfectant and filth walking by the Porta Potties, exhaust and burnt oil and sun-baked asphalt and gravel in the parking lots, sunlight on warm bodies, suntan lotion, cigarette smoke and beer near some of the attendees, the pungent, honest smell of livestock near the animal shows, stock contests, or pony rides—all of it charging right up your nose. I like indulging my sense of smell.

Smell is the hardest sense to lie to.

Murphy and I got started midmorning, walking around the fair in a methodical search pattern. It took us all day. The state fair is not a rinky-dink event.

"Dammit," she said. "We've been here for hours. You sure you haven't sniffed out anything?"

"Nothing like what we're looking for," I said. "I was afraid of this."

"Of what?"

"A lot of times, magic like this—complex, long-lasting, subtle, dark—doesn't thrive well in sunlight." I glanced at the lengthening shadows. "Give it another half an hour and we'll try again."

Murphy frowned at me. "I thought you always said magic isn't about good and evil."

"Neither is sunshine."

Murphy exhaled, her displeasure plain. "You might have mentioned it to me before."

"No way to know until we tried," I said. "Think of it this way: maybe we're just looking in the exact wrong place."

She sighed and squinted around at the nearby food trailers and concession stands. "Ugh. Think there's anything here that won't make me split my jeans at the seams?"

I beamed. "Probably not. How about dogs and a funnel cake?"

"Bastard," Murphy growled. Then, "Okay."

I REALIZED WE were being followed halfway through my second hot dog.

I kept myself from reacting, took another bite, and said, "Maybe this is the place after all."

Murphy had found a place selling turkey drumsticks. She had cut the meat from the bone and onto a paper plate, and was eating it with a plastic fork. She didn't stop chewing or look up. "Whatcha got?"

"Guy in a maroon tee and tan BDU pants, about twenty feet away off your right shoulder. I've seen him at least two other times today."

"Doesn't necessarily mean he's following us."

"He's been busy doing nothing in particular all three times."

Murphy nodded. "Five-eight or so, long hair? Little soul tuft under his mouth?"

"Yeah."

"He was sitting on a bench when I came out of the Porta-Potty," Murphy said. "Also doing nothing." She shrugged and went back to eating.

"How do you want to play it?"

"We're here with a zillion people, Harry." She deepened her voice and blocked out any hint of a nasal tone. "You want I should whack him until he talks?"

I grunted and finished my hot dog. "Doesn't necessarily mean anything. Maybe he's got a crush on you."

Murphy snorted. "Maybe he's got a crush on *you*."

I covered a respectable belch with my hand and reached for my funnel cake. "Who could blame him?" I took a bite and nodded. "All right. We'll see what happens, then."

Murphy nodded and sipped at her Diet Coke. "Will says you and Anastasia broke up a while back."

"Will talks too much," I said darkly.

She glanced a little bit away. "He's your friend. He worries about you."

I studied her averted face for a moment and then nodded. "Well," I said, "tell Will he doesn't need to worry. It sucked. It sucks less now. I'll be fine. Fish in the sea, never meant to be, et cetera." I paused over another bite of funnel cake and asked, "How's Kincaid?"

"The way he always is," Murphy said.

"You get to be a few centuries old, you get a little set in your ways."

She shook her head. "It's his type. He'd be that way if he was twenty. He walks his own road and doesn't let anyone make him do differently. Like . . ."

She stopped before she could say who Kincaid was like. She ate her turkey leg.

A shiver passed over the fair, a tactile sensation to my wizard's senses. Sundown. Twilight would go on for a while yet, but the light left in the sky would no longer hold the creatures of the night at bay.

Murphy glanced up at me, sensing the change in my level of tension. She finished off her drink while I stuffed the last of the funnel cake into my mouth, and we stood up together.

THE WESTERN SKY was still a little bit orange when I finally sensed magic at work.

We were near the carnival, a section of the fair full of garishly lit rides, heavily slanted games of chance, and chintzy attractions of every kind. It was full of screaming, excited little kids, parents with frayed patience, and fashion-enslaved teenagers. Music tinkled and brayed tinny tunes. Lights flashed and danced. Barkers bleated out cajolement, encouragement, and condolences in almost-equal measures.

We drifted through the merry chaos, our maroon-shirted tail following along ten to twenty yards behind. I walked with my eyes half closed, giving no more heed to my vision than a bloodhound on a trail. Murphy stayed beside me, her expression calm, her blue eyes alert for physical danger.

Then I felt it—a quiver in the air, no more noticeable than the fading hum from a gently plucked guitar string. I noted its direction and walked several more paces before checking again, in an attempt to triangulate the source of the disturbance. I got a rough fix on it in under a minute, and realized that I had stopped and was staring.

"Harry?" Murphy asked. "What is it?"

"Something down there," I said, nodding to the midway. "It's faint. But it's something."

Murph inhaled sharply. "This must be the place. There goes our tail."

We didn't have to communicate the decision to each other. If the tail belonged to whoever was behind this, we couldn't let him get away to give the culprit forewarning—and odds were excellent that the man in maroon's sudden rabbit impersonation would result in him leading us somewhere interesting.

We turned and gave pursuit.

A footrace on open ground is one thing. Running through a crowded carnival is something else entirely. You can't sprint, unless you want to wind up falling down a lot and attracting attention. You have to hurry along, hopping between clusters of people, never really getting the chance to pour on the gas. The danger in a chase like this isn't that the quarry will outrun you, but that you'll lose him in the crowd.

I had a huge advantage. I'm freakishly tall. I could see over everyone and spot Mr. Maroon bobbing and weaving his way through the crowd. I took the lead and Murphy followed.

I got within a couple of long steps of Maroon, but was interdicted by a gaggle of seniors in Shriners caps. He caught a break at the same time, a stretch of open ground beyond the Shriners, and by the time I got through, I saw Maroon handing tickets to a carnie. He hopped up onto a platform, got into a little roller-coaster style car, and vanished into an attraction.

"Dammit!" Murphy said, panting. "What now?"

Behind the attraction, advertised as the Tunnel of Terror, there was an empty space, the interior of a circle of several similar rides and games. There wouldn't be anyone to hide behind in there. "You take the back. I'll watch the front. Whoever spots him gives a shout."

"Got it." Murphy hurried off around the Tunnel of Terror. She frowned at a little plastic barrier with an Authorized Personnel Only notice on it, then calmly ignored it and went on over.

"Anarchist," I muttered, and settled down to wait for Maroon to figure out he'd been treed.

He didn't appear.

The dingy little roller coaster car came wheezing slowly out of the opposite side of the platform, empty. The carnie, an old fellow with a scruffy white beard, didn't notice—he was dozing in his chair.

Murphy returned a few seconds later. "There are two doors on the back," she reported, "both of them chained and locked from the outside. He didn't come out that way."

I inhaled and nodded at the empty car. "Not here, either. Look, we can't just stand around. Maybe he's running through a tunnel or something. We've got to know if he's inside."

"I'll go flush him out," she said. "You pick him up when he shows."

"No way," I said. "We stay with our wing"—I glanced at Murphy—"person. The power I sensed came from somewhere nearby. If we split up, we're about a million times more vulnerable to mental manipulation. And if this guy is more than he appears, neither of us wants to take him solo."

She grimaced, nodded, and we started toward the Tunnel of Terror together.

The old carnie woke up as we came up the ramp, let out a wheezing cough, and pointed to a sign that required us to give him three tickets each for the ride. I hadn't bought any, and the ticket counter was more than far enough away for Maroon to scamper if we stopped to follow the rules.

"Sir," Murphy said, "a man we're looking for just went into your attraction, but he didn't come out again. We need to go in and look for him."

He blinked gummy eyes at Murphy and said, "Three tickets."

"You don't understand," she said. "A fugitive may be hiding inside the Tunnel of Terror. We need to check and see if he's there."

The carnie snorted. "Three tickets, missy. Though it ain't the nicest room you two could rent."

Murphy's jaw muscles flexed.

I stepped forward. "Hey, man," I said. "Harry Dresden, PI. If you wouldn't mind, all we need to do is get inside for five minutes."

He eyed me. "PI, huh?"

I produced my license and showed it to him. He eyed it and then me. "You don't look like no private investigator I ever saw. Where's your hat?"

"In the shop," I said. "Transmission gave out." I winked at him and held up a folded twenty between my first and second finger. "Five minutes?"

He yawned. "Naw. Can't let nobody run around loose in there." He reached out and took the twenty. "Then again, what you and your lady friend mutually consent to do once you're inside ain't my affair." He rose, pulled a lever, and gestured at the car. "Mount up," he leered. "And keep your, ah, extremities inside the car at all times."

We got in, and I was nearly scalded by the steam coming out of Murphy's ears. "You just had to play along with that one."

"We needed to get inside," I said. "Just doing my job, Sergeant."

She snorted.

"Hey, Murph, look," I said, holding up a strap of old, worn leather. "Seat belts."

She gave me a look that could have scoured steel. Then, with a stubborn set of her jaw, secured the flimsy thing. Her expression dared me to object.

I grinned and relaxed. It isn't easy to really get Murph's goat and get away with it.

On the other side of the platform, the carnie pulled another lever, and a moment later the little cart started rolling forward at the blazing speed of one, maybe even two miles an hour. A dark curtain parted ahead of us and we rolled into the Tunnel of Terror.

Murphy promptly drew her gun—it was dark, but I heard the scratch of its barrel on plastic as she drew it from its holster. She snapped a small LED flashlight into its holster beneath the gun barrel and flicked it on. We were in a cramped little tunnel, every surface painted black, and there was absolutely nowhere for Maroon to be hiding.

I shook out the charm bracelet on my left wrist, preparing defensive energies in case they were needed. Murph and I had been working together long enough to know our roles. If trouble came, I would defend us. Murphy and her Sig would reply.

A door opened at the end of the little hallway and we rolled forward into an open set dressed to look like a rustic farmhouse, with a lot of subtle details meant to be scary—severed fingers at the base of the chicken-chopping stump, just below the bloody ax, glowing eyes appearing in an upstairs window of the farmhouse, that kind of thing. There was no sign of Maroon and precious little place for him to hide.

"Better get that seat belt off," I told her. "We want to be able to move fast if it comes to that."

"Yeah," she said, and reached down, just as something huge and terrifying dropped onto the car from the shadows above us, screaming.

Adrenaline hit my system like a runaway bus, and I looked up to see a decidedly demonic scarecrow hanging a few feet above our heads, bouncing on its wires and playing a recording of cackling, mad laughter.

"Jesus Christ," Murphy breathed, lowering her gun. She was a little white around the eyes.

We looked at each other and both burst into high, nervous laughs.

"Tunnel of Terror," Murphy said. "We are *so* cool."

"Total badasses," I said, grinning.

The car continued its slow grind forward and Murphy unfastened the seat belt. We moved into the next area, meant to be a zombie-infested hospital. It had a zombie mannequin, which burst out of a closet near the track, and plenty of gore. We got out of the car and scouted a couple of spots where he might have been but wasn't. Then we hopped into the car again before it could leave the set.

So it went, on through a ghoulish graveyard, a troglodyte-teaming cavern, and a literal Old West ghost town. We came up with nothing, but we moved well as a team, better than I could remember doing with anyone before. Everything felt as smooth and natural as if we'd been moving together our whole lives. We did it in total silence, too, divining what each other would do through pure instinct.

Even great teams lose a game here or there, though. We came up with diddly, and emerged from the Tunnel of Terror with neither Maroon nor any idea where he'd gone.

"Hell's bells," I muttered. "This week has been an investigative suck-fest for me."

Murphy tittered again. "You said 'suck.'"

I grinned at her and looked around. "Well," I said. "We don't know where Maroon went. If they hadn't made us already, they have now."

"Can you pick up on the signal-whatsit again?"

"Energy signature," I said. "Maybe. It's pretty vague though. I'm not sure how much more precise I can get."

"Let's find out," she said.

I nodded. "Right, then." We started around the suspect circle of attractions, moving slowly and trying to blend into the crowds. When a couple of rowdy kids went by, one chasing the other, I put an arm around her shoulders and drew her into the shelter of my body so that she wouldn't get bowled over.

She exhaled slowly and did not step away from me.

My heart started beating faster.

"Harry," she said quietly.

"Yeah?"

"You and me . . . why haven't we ever . . ." She looked up at me. "Why not?"

"The usual, I guess," I said quietly. "Trouble. Duty. Other people involved."

She shook her head. "Why not?" she repeated, her eyes direct. "All these years have gone by. And something could have happened, but it never did. Why not?"

I licked my lips. "Just like that? We just decide to be together?"

Her eyelids lowered. "Why not?"

My heart did the drum solo from "Wipe Out."

Why not?

I bent my head down to her mouth, and kissed her, very gently.

She turned into the kiss, pressing her body against mine. It was a little bit awkward. I was most of two feet taller than she was. We made up for grace with enthusiasm, her arms twining around my neck as she kissed me, hungry and deep.

"Whoa," I said, drawing back a moment later. "Work. Right?"

She looked at me for a moment, her cheeks pink, her lips a little swollen from the kiss, and said, "Right." She closed her eyes and nodded. "Right. Work first."

"Then dinner?" I asked.

"Dinner. My place. We can order in."

My belly trembled in sudden excitement at that proposition. "Right." I looked around. "So let's find this thing and get it over with."

We started moving again. A circuit around the attractions got me no closer to the source of the energy I'd sensed earlier.

"Dammit," I said when we'd completed the pattern, frustrated.

"Hey," Murphy said. "Don't beat yourself up about it, Harry." Her hand slipped into mine, our fingers intertwining. "I've been a cop a long time. You don't always get the bad guy. And if you go around blaming yourself for it, you wind up crawling into a bottle or eating your own gun."

"Thank you," I said quietly. "But . . ."

"Heh," Murphy said. "You said, 'but.'"

We both grinned like fools. I looked down at our twined hands. "I like this."

"So do I," Murphy said. "Why didn't we do this a long time ago?"

"Beats me."

"Are we just that stupid?" she asked. "I mean, people, in general. Are we really so blind that we miss what's right there in front of us?"

"As a species, we're essentially insane," I said. "So, yeah, probably." I lifted our hands and kissed her fingertips. "I'm not missing it now, though."

Her smile lit up several thousand square feet of the midway. "Good."

The echo of a thought rattled around in my head: *Insane . . .*

"Oh," I said. "Oh, hell's bells."

She frowned at me. "What?"

"Murph . . . I think we got whammied."

She blinked at me. "What? No, we didn't."

"I think we did."

"I didn't see anything or feel anything. I mean, *nothing*, Harry. I've felt magic like that before."

"*Look* at us," I said, waving our joined hands.

"We've been friends a long time, Harry," she said. "And we've had a couple of near misses before. This time we just didn't screw it up. That's all that's happening, here."

"What about Kincaid?" I asked her.

She mulled over that one for a second. Then she said, "I doubt he'll even notice I'm gone." She frowned at me. "Harry, I haven't been this happy in . . . I never thought I could feel this way again. About anyone."

My heart continued to go pit-a-pat. "I know exactly what you mean," I said. "I feel the same way."

Her smile warmed even more. "Then what's the problem? Isn't that what love is supposed to be like? Effortless?"

I had to think about that one for a second. And then I said, carefully and slowly, "Murph, think about it."

"What do you mean?"

"You know how good this is?" I asked.

"Yeah."

"How right it feels?"

She nodded. "Yeah."

"How easy it was?"

She nodded energetically, her eyes bright.

I leaned down toward her for emphasis. "It just isn't fucked up enough to really be you and me."

Her smile faltered.

"My God," she said, her eyes widening. "We got whammied."

. . . .

WE RETURNED TO the Tunnel of Terror.

"I don't get it," she said. "I don't . . . I didn't feel anything happen. I don't feel any different now. I thought being aware of this kind of thing made it go away."

"No," I said. "But it helps sometimes."

"Do you still . . . ?"

I squeezed her hand once more before letting go. "Yeah," I said. "I still feel it."

"Is it . . . is it going to go away?"

I didn't answer her. I didn't know. Or maybe I didn't want to know.

The old carnie saw us coming and his face flickered with apprehension as soon as he looked at us. He stood up and looked from the control board for the ride to the entranceway to the interior.

"Yeah," I muttered. "Sneaky bastard. You just try it."

He flicked one of the switches and shambled toward the Tunnel's entrance.

I made a quick effort of will, raised a hand, and swept it in a horizontal arc, snarling, "Forzare!" Unseen force knocked his legs out from beneath him and tossed him into an involuntary pratfall.

Murphy and I hurried up onto the platform before he could get to his feet and run. We needn't have bothered. The carnie was apparently a genuine old guy, not some supernatural being in disguise. He lay on the platform moaning in pain. I felt kind of bad for beating up a senior citizen.

But hey. On the other hand, he did swindle me out of twenty bucks.

Murphy stood over him, her blue eyes cold, and said, "Where's the bolt hole?"

The carnie blinked at her. "What?"

"The trap door," she snapped. "The secret cabinet. Where is he?"

I frowned and walked toward the entranceway.

"Please," the carnie said. "I don't know what you're talking about!"

"The hell you don't," Murphy said. She leaned down and grabbed the man by the shirt with both hands and leaned closer, a snarl lifting her lip. The carnie blanched.

Murph could be pretty badass for such a tiny thing. I loved that about her.

"I can't," the carnie said. "I can't. I get paid not to see anything. She'll kill me. She'll kill me."

I parted the heavy curtain leading into the entry tunnel and spotted it at once—a circular hole in the floor about two feet across, the top end of a ladder just visible. A round lid lay rotated to one side, painted as flat black as the rest of the hall. "Here," I said to Murph. "That's why we didn't spot anything. By the time you had your light on, it was already behind us."

Murphy scowled down at the carnie and said, "Give me twenty bucks."

The man licked his lips. Then he fished my folded twenty out of his shirt pocket and passed it to Murphy.

She nodded and flashed her badge. "Get out of here before I realize I witnessed you taking a bribe and endangering lives by letting customers use the attraction in an unsafe manner."

The carnie bolted.

Murphy handed me the twenty. I pocketed it, and we climbed down the ladder.

WE REACHED THE bottom and went silent again. Murphy's body language isn't exactly subtle—it can't be, when you're her size and working law enforcement. But she could move as quietly as smoke when she needed to. I'm gangly. It was more of an effort for me.

The ladder took us down to what looked like the interior of a buried railroad car. There were electrical conduits running along the walls. Light came from a doorway at the far end of the car. I moved forward first, shield bracelet at the ready, and Murphy walked a pace behind me and to my right, her Sig in hand.

The doorway at the end of the railroad car led us into a large workroom, teaming with computers, file cabinets, microscopes, and at least one deluxe chemistry set.

Maroon sat at one of the computers, his profile in view. "Dammit, Stu," he snarled. "I told you that you can't keep coming down here to use the john. You'll just have to walk to one of the—" He glanced up at us and froze in midsentence, his eyes wide and locked on Murphy's leveled gun.

"Stu took the rest of the night off," I said amiably. "Where's your boss?"

A door opened at the far end of the workroom and a young woman of medium height appeared. She wore glasses and a lab coat, and neither of them did anything to make her look less than gorgeous. She looked at us and then at Maroon and said, in a precise, British accent, "You idiot."

"Yeah," I said. "Good help is hard to find."

The woman in the lab coat looked at me with dark, intense eyes, and I sensed what felt like a phantom pressure against my temples, as if wriggling tadpoles were slithering along the surface of my skin. It was a straightforward attempt at mental invasion, but I'd been practicing my defenses for a while now, and I wasn't falling for something that obvious. I pushed the invasive thoughts away with an effort of will and said, "Don't meet her eyes, Murph. She's a vampire. Red Court."

"Got it," she said, her gun never moving from Maroon.

The vampire looked at us both for a moment. Then she said, "You need no introduction, Mr. Dresden. I am Baroness LeBlanc. And our nations are not, at the moment, in a state of war."

"I've always been a little fuzzy on legal niceties," I said. I had several devices with me that I could use to defend myself. I was ready to use any of them. A vampire in close quarters is nothing to laugh at. LeBlanc could tear three or four limbs off in the time it takes to draw and fire a gun. I watched her closely, ready to act at the slightest resemblance of an attack. "We both know that the war is going to start up again eventually."

"You are out of anything reasonably like your territory," she said, "and you are trespassing upon mine. I would be well within my rights under the Accords to kill you and bury your torso and limbs in individual graves."

"That's the problem with this ride," I complained to Murphy. "There's nothing that's actually *scary* in the Tunnel of Terror."

"You did get your money back," she pointed out.

"Ah, true." I smiled faintly at LeBlanc. "Look, Baroness. You know who I am. You're doing something to people's minds, and I want it stopped."

"If you do not leave," she said, "I will consider it an act of war."

"Hooray," I said in a Ben Stein monotone, spinning one forefinger in the air like a New Year's noisemaker. "I've already kicked off one war with the Red Court. And I will cheerfully do it again if that is what is necessary to protect people from you."

"That's irrational," LeBlanc said. "Completely irrational."

"Tell her, Murph."

"He's completely irrational," Murphy said, her tone wry.

LeBlanc regarded me impassively for a moment. Then she smiled faintly and said, "Perhaps a physical confrontation is an inappropriate solution."

I frowned. "Really?"

She shrugged. "Not all of the Red Court are battle-hungry blood addicts, Dresden. My work here has no malevolent designs. Quite the opposite, in fact."

I tilted my head. "That's funny. All the corpses piled up say differently."

"The process *does* have its side effects," she admitted. "But the lessons garnered from them serve only to improve my work and make it safer and more effective. Honestly, you should be supporting me, Dresden. Not trying to shut me down."

"Supporting you?" I smiled a little. "Just what is it you think you're doing that's so darned wonderful?"

"I am creating love."

I barked out a laugh.

LeBlanc's face remained steady, serious.

"You think that *this*, this warping people into feeling something they don't want to feel, is *love*?"

"What is love," LeBlanc said, "if not a series of electro-chemical signals in the brain? Signals that can be duplicated, like any other sensation."

"Love is more than that," I said.

"Do you love this woman?"

"Yeah," I said. "But that isn't anything new."

LeBlanc showed her teeth. "But your current longing and desire is new, is it not? New and entirely indistinguishable from your genuine emotions? Wouldn't you say, Sergeant Murphy?"

Murphy swallowed but didn't look at the vampire. LeBlanc's uncomplicated mental attack might be simple for a wizard to defeat, but any normal human being would probably be gone before they realized their mind was under attack. Instead of answering, she asked a question of her own. "Why?"

"Why what?"

"Why do this? Why experiment on making people fall in love?"

LeBlanc arched an eyebrow. "Isn't it obvious?"

I sucked in a short breath, realizing what was happening. "The White Court," I said.

The Whites were a different breed of vampire than the Reds, feeding on the life essence of their victims, generally through seduction. Genuine love and genuine tokens of love were their kryptonite, their holy water. The love of another human being in an intimate relationship sort of rubbed off on you, making the very touch of your skin anathema to the White Court.

LeBlanc smiled at me. "Granted, there are some aberrant effects from time to time. But so far, that's been a very small percentage of the test pool. And the survivors are, as you yourself have experienced, perfectly happy. They have a love that most of your kind seldom find and even more infrequently keep. There are no victims here, wizard."

"Oh," I said. "Right. Except for the victims."

LeBlanc exhaled. "Mortals are like mayflies, wizard. They live a brief time and then they are gone. And those who have died because of my work at least died after days or weeks of perfect bliss. There are many who ended a much longer life with less. What I'm doing here has the potential to protect mortal kind from the White Court forever."

"It isn't genuine love if it's forced upon someone," Murphy said, her tone harsh.

"No," LeBlanc said. "But I believe that the real thing will very easily grow from such a foundation of companionship and happiness."

"Gosh, you're noble," I said.

LeBlanc's eyes sparkled with something ugly.

"You're doing this to get rid of the competition," I said. "And, hell, maybe to try to increase the world's population. Make more food."

The vampire regarded me levelly. "There are multiple motivations behind the work," she said. "Many of my Court agreed to the logic you cite when they would never have supported the idea of strengthening and defending mortals."

"Ohhhhh," I said, drawing the word out. "You're the vampire with a heart of gold. Florence Nightingale with fangs. I guess that makes it okay, then."

LeBlanc stared at me. Then her eyes flicked to Murphy and back. She smiled thinly. "There is a special cage reserved for you at the Red Court, Dresden. Its bars are lined with blades and spikes, so that if you fall asleep they will cut and gouge you awake."

"Shut up," Murphy said.

LeBlanc continued in a calmly amused tone. "The bottom is a closed bowl nearly a foot deep, so that you will stand in your own waste. And there are three spears with needle-sized tips waiting in a rack beneath the cage, so that any who pass you can pause and take a few moments to participate in your punishment."

"Shut up," Murphy growled.

"Eventually," LeBlanc purred, "your guts will be torn out and left in a pile at your feet. And when you are dead, your skin will be flayed from your body, tanned, and made into upholstery for one of the chairs in the Red Temple."

"Shut up!" snarled Murphy, and her voice was savage. Her gun whipped over to cover LeBlanc. "Shut your mouth, bitch!"

I realized the danger an instant too late. It was exactly the reaction that LeBlanc had intended to provoke. "Murph! No!"

Once Murphy's Sig was pointing elsewhere, Maroon produced a gun from beneath his desk and raised it. He was pulling the trigger even before he could level it for a shot, blazing away as fast as he could move his finger. He wasn't quite fifteen feet away from Murphy, but the first five shots missed her as I spun and brought the invisible power of my shield bracelet down between the two of them. Bullets hit the shield with flashes of light and sent little concentric blue rings rippling through the air from the point of impact.

Murphy, meanwhile, had opened up on LeBlanc. Murph fired almost as quickly as Maroon, but she had the training and discipline necessary for combat. Her bullets smacked into the vampire's torso, tearing through pale flesh and drawing gouts of red-black blood. LeBlanc staggered to one side—she wouldn't be dead, but the shots had probably rung her bell for a second or two.

I lowered the shield as Maroon's gun clicked on empty, lifted my right fist, and triggered the braided energy ring on my index finger with a short, uplifting motion. The ring saved back a little energy every time I moved my arm, storing it so that I could unleash it at need. Unseen force flew out from the ring, plucked Maroon out of his chair, and slammed him into the ceiling. He dropped back down, hit his back on the edge of the desk, and fell into a senseless sprawl on the floor. The gun flew from his fingers.

"I'm out!" Murphy screamed.

I whirled back to find LeBlanc pushing herself off the wall, regaining her balance. She gave Murphy a look of flat hatred, and her eyes flushed pure black, iris and sclera alike. She opened her mouth in an inhuman scream, and then the vampire hiding beneath LeBlanc's seemingly human form exploded outward like a racehorse emerging from its gate, leaving shreds of pale, bloodless skin in its wake.

It was a hideous thing—black and flabby and slimy-looking, with a flaccid belly, a batlike face, and long, spindly limbs. LeBlanc's eyes bulged hideously as she flew toward me.

I brought my shield up in time to intercept her, and she rebounded from it, to fall back to the section of floor already stained with her blood.

"Down!" Murphy shouted.

I dropped down onto my heels and lowered the shield.

LeBlanc rose again, even as I heard Murphy take a deep breath, exhale halfway, and hold it. Her gun barked once.

The vampire lost about a fifth of her head as the bullet tore into her skull. She staggered back against the wall, limbs thrashing, but she still wasn't dead. She began to claw her way to her feet again.

Murphy squeezed off six more shots, methodically. None of them missed. LeBlanc fell to the floor. Murphy took a step closer, aimed, and put another ten or twelve rounds into the fallen vampire's head. By the time she was done, the vampire's head looked like a smashed gourd.

A few seconds later, LeBlanc stopped moving.

Murphy reloaded again and kept the gun trained on the corpse.

"Nice shootin', Tex," I said. I checked out Maroon. He was still breathing.

"So," Murphy said. "Problem solved?"

"Not really," I said. "LeBlanc was no practitioner. She can't be the one who was working the whammy."

Murphy frowned and eyed Maroon for a second.

I went over to the downed man and touched my fingers lightly to his brow. There was no telltale energy signature of a practitioner. "Nope."

"Who, then?"

I shook my head. "This is delicate, difficult magic. There might not be three people on the entire White Council who could pull it off. So . . . it's most likely a focus artifact of some kind."

"A what?"

"An item that has a routine built into it," I said. "You pour energy in one end and you get results on the other."

Murphy scrunched up her nose. "Like those wolf belts the FBI had?"

"Yeah, just like that." I blinked and snapped my fingers. "*Just* like that!"

I hurried out of the little complex and up the ladder. I went to the tunnel car and took the old leather seat belt out of it. I turned it over and found the back inscribed with nearly invisible sigils and signs. Now that I was looking for it, I could feel the tingle of energy moving within it. "Ha," I said. "Got it."

Murphy frowned back at the entry to the Tunnel of Terror. "What do we do about Billy the Kid?"

"Not much we can do," I said. "You want to try to explain what happened here to the Springfield cops?"

She shook her head.

"Me either," I said. "The kid was LeBlanc's thrall. I doubt he's a danger to anyone without a vampire to push him into it." Besides. The Reds would probably kill him on general principle anyway, once they found out about LeBlanc's death.

We were silent for a moment. Then stepped in close to each other and hugged gently. Murphy shivered.

"You okay?" I asked quietly.

She leaned her head against my chest. "How do we help all the people she screwed with?"

"Burn the belt," I said, and stroked her hair with one hand. "That should purify everyone it's linked to."

"Everyone," she said slowly.

I blinked twice. "Yeah."

"So once you do it . . . we'll see what a bad idea this is. And remember that we both have very good reasons to not get together."

"Yeah."

"And . . . we won't be feeling *this* anymore. This . . . happy. This complete."

"No. We won't."

Her voice cracked. "Dammit."

I hugged her tight. "Yeah."

"I want to tell you to wait a while," she said. "I want us to be all noble and virtuous for keeping it intact. I want to tell you that if we destroy the belt, we'll be destroying the happiness of God knows how many people."

"Junkies are happy when they're high," I said quietly, "but they don't need to be happy. They need to be *free*."

I put the belt back into the car, turned my right hand palm-up, and murmured a word. A sphere of white-hot fire gathered over my fingers.

I flicked a hand, and the sphere arched gently down into the car and began charring the belt to ashes. I felt sick.

I didn't watch. I turned to Murphy and kissed her again, hot and urgent, and she returned it frantically. It was as though we thought that we might keep something escaping from our mouths if they were sealed together in a kiss.

I felt it when it went away.

We both stiffened slightly. We both remembered that we had decided that the two of us couldn't work out. We both remembered that Murphy was already involved with someone else, and that it wasn't in her nature to stray.

She stepped back from me, her arms folded across her stomach.

"Ready?" I asked her quietly.

She nodded and we started walking. Neither of us said anything until we reached the Blue Beetle.

"You know what, Harry?" she said quietly, from the other side of the car.

"I know," I told her. "Like you said. Love hurts."

We got into the Beetle and headed back to Chicago.

Jo Beverley

New York Times *bestselling author Jo Beverley is the author of thirty-two novels of historical romance, including* Something Wicked, Dangerous Joy, Tempting Fortune, An Unwilling Bride, A Lady's Secret, Lord of Midnight, Lord Wraybourne's Betrothed, *and many others. She's the winner of five RITA Awards for best novel, and is a member of the Romance Writers of America Hall of Fame. Her most recent novels are* The Secret Wedding, My Lady Notorious, The Secret Duke, *and* The Stolen Bride. *She lives with her family in England.*

Here she tells the story of a man wooing a very reluctant maid—with his life and the lives of all his relatives in the balance, all doomed to die if he can't overcome her resistance. Which is not going to be easy.

The Marrying Maid

1

IT WAS AS if a new song entered his world, or a new taste, or a new sense—and yet one instantly recognized.

Rob Loxsleigh turned to look around the park, striving to make the movement casual to his chattering companions, so noisy in their silks and lace, but already fading under the power of his new awareness.

There.

He smiled, with delight but with surprise.

The woman in gray? The one strolling through the park at the side of another woman just as ordinary, wearing a plain gown with little trimming and a flat straw hat?

She was his destined bride?

He'd been told he'd know, and for years he'd sought the unignorable. Sometimes, with a particularly pretty girl or fascinating woman, he'd tried to believe his desire meant that his quest was over. A kiss had quickly proved him wrong.

Now, however, he *knew*. She alone seemed real in an unreal world and his body hummed with a symphony of need, not just desire, but a hunger for everything she would bring.

Now, within weeks of disaster, Titania had sent his marrying maid.

. . . .

A PRICKLE ON the neck.

When Martha Darby turned, she saw a man looking at her. A London beau in silk and lace with powdered hair and a sword at his side. A peacock in company with other birds of fine plumage, their bright laughter and extravagant gestures indicating that they'd escaped the gilded cage of court in the nearby Palace of St. James. But why was one of them staring at her, a very sparrow of a spinster?

He turned back to his companions. She'd imagined his interest, but now she couldn't help staring at him. He seemed somehow brighter than his glittering companions. Merely the effect of a suit of peacock blue silk, she told herself, but he did seem perfectly made and he moved with such grace, even in ridiculous shoes with high red heels.

"Such extravagance in their clothing, and a shower of rain would ruin all."

Martha turned to her mother, smiling at the practical comment. "I'm sure chairmen would rush to carry them to shelter. Let us admire nature instead. Trees welcome the rain."

They strolled on their way.

Martha and her mother were enjoying the park, but also, it must be admitted, some glimpses of the follies of the great. Martha had certainly seen nothing like those courtier peacocks in York. But then, in York, she'd lived quietly for so many years, helping her mother nurse her father through a long, distressing illness. This visit to a relative in London was to help them regain their spirits and be ready to pick up life, but Martha wondered what form her life could take. She was too accustomed to quiet and routine and too old for adventures.

Unless . . .

She was looking at that man again! She quickly turned away. "Let's walk toward Rosamund's Pond, Mother." Away from temptation.

Temptation?

Ridiculous. Lord Peacock was a wastrel courtier and she was the virtuous daughter of a canon of York Minster and at twenty-four, long past the age of folly.

Yet she looked again.

Just to be sure she was safe, she told herself.

Safe? Did she think he would pursue her? Laughable . . .

But then she realized that he *was* looking at her again. He smiled.

She turned her back, heart pounding. Lud! Had he caught one of her glances and taken it as admiration? Even as lewd encouragement? Heaven defend her! The court was notoriously licentious. She urged her mother to walk more quickly, but plump Anne Darby was never energetic. Her strolling involved many pauses to admire a vista, or yet another pelican. For some reason this park was full of them. Pelicans and peacocks . . .

"Come, Mother. We must hurry."

"What? Why?"

Martha came up with the only possible excuse. "I need to piss."

"Oh dear, oh dear. Yes, very well." Her mother did walk faster and gradually Martha's panic simmered down. They were safe and she would not come here again.

"Ladies."

Martha froze, then would have walked on if her mother hadn't already turned, incapable of being cold or discourteous. Thus she must turn too, already knowing who had spoken. By logic, surely, not by a frisson on the back of her neck and a strange tension deep inside.

He stood mere feet away, his silk suit embroidered with silver thread as well as colors. The lace at throat and wrist would have cost a fortune, and his neckcloth was fixed by a gold pin that sparkled in the sun, as did rings on his fingers and the jeweled hilt of his sword. As did his eyes, as green as a summer leaf. His handsome, lean face was painted to give him fashionable pallor and then to restore color with rouge on cheeks and lips.

He was ridiculous, but Martha was powerfully aware of being dressed in mourning gray with only a silver pin for ornamentation, and of never having let paint touch her face. She should have been disdainful, but instead the peculiar sensation within could almost be awe.

He was smiling directly at her now and holding out a handkerchief. "I believe this is yours, ma'am?"

Martha glared at the linen, ferociously irritated that the handkerchief was indeed her own, marked by the embroidered forget-me-nots in one corner. How had it come to fall out of her pocket?

Before she could lie, her mother said, "Oh, see it is, Martha! How kind of you, sir."

He bowed to them both in the most extravagant manner imaginable, dancing the handkerchief in little curlicues. "I am in heaven to be of service to so enchanting a lady."

Martha plucked the fluttering linen from his fingers. "My thanks to you, sir."

He put hand to chest. "No, no. Thank you, ma'am, for providing me the opportunity to do this small kindness."

Providing? Was the wretch implying that she'd dropped her handkerchief on purpose? It was a well-known device of foolish women, but she would never stoop so low!

She sent him an icy look, but he'd already turned another bow on her mother. "Robert Loxsleigh, ma'am, at your service."

Sensible Anne Darby curtsied, blushing, flustered and delighted. "So kind, so kind. Mistress Darby, sir, of York, and this is my daughter, Miss Darby."

More bowing and greeting, and all of it mockery. If only her mother hadn't been inveigled into exchanging names.

"May I hope to encounter you again in London, Mistress Darby?"

Martha quickly answered. "Alas no, sir. We leave tomorrow."

Her mother began to protest, but Martha shot her a ferocious glare.

"Thus Town is left desolate. But York will soon rejoice. A charming city. I know it well, as my home is near Doncaster."

Martha could have groaned. That he was also from Yorkshire would make her mother regard him as a friend.

"We really must go, Mother," Martha said with meaning, reminding her of her spurious need.

"Oh, yes, sir, I'm afraid we must. I do hope we will meet again one day, in York, perhaps?"

He bowed to both of them, but was looking at Martha when he said, "I'm sure of it, ma'am."

"Oh, my," said her mother, watching him walk back to his friends, so lithe and elegant despite uneven ground and those shoes.

"Oh, what idiocy," Martha said, steering away at speed.

That was the end of that—except that she was holding her handkerchief as if it were precious. She screwed it up and thrust it into her pocket.

"Why did you say we were leaving Town, Martha? We are to stay three more days."

"Because I thought him up to no good."

"Truly? But . . ." Her mother sighed. "We can't be liars, can we, so we must leave. All for the best, perhaps. We can stay longer with your Aunt Clarissa in Newark."

And thus I am punished, Martha thought. Aunt Clarissa was a very silly chatterer. It was all the peacock's fault. Mr. Robert Loxsleigh had been playing a game for the amusement of his idle friends and fecklessly upset her life.

And yet—and yet—as she resisted an almost overpowering need to look back, Martha knew she would never entirely forget an encounter with a peacock in St James's Park.

ROB RETURNED TO his companions, protecting Miss Darby from their curiosity by letting them assume he intended a seduction. It was no lie. If Miss Martha Darby seemed likely to succumb, he'd bed her tonight.

She was the one, the one, the one, his marrying maid, which meant that at first kiss his talent would awake, and when they lay together, it would roar into full power. He would be at last a true trouvedor of Five Oaks, and his family would be saved.

Rapid seduction was unlikely, but a kiss? Perhaps if he pursued her now. Not to do so was like refusing water when parched, but she seemed to be prim to a fault. Perhaps even a Puritan. His very appearance would have counted against him and any boldness could ruin everything. No, he must resume simple dress and manners and then court her carefully.

There was so little time, though. Just two weeks to his birthday.

To doomsday.

But he'd found her at last, and she would be willing to be wooed. Faery would make it so.

Zounds! They left Town tomorrow. He separated from his companions, suppressing panic. He needed to untangle himself from court, say farewells, settle bills—

The Darby ladies would travel the York road, however, and surely on the public coach. He could follow post chaise and catch them in days.

As he walked toward his rooms, he wondered how Oberon had hidden Martha Darby for so many years? He visited York quite often.

That didn't matter. Titania had prevailed. The heir to Five Oaks had found his marrying maid with time enough to woo and win her. It was always so. The dark Lord of Faery had never won this fight, not in five hundred years.

2

MARTHA SLEPT BADLY and spent the first hours on the crowded York coach braced for pursuit. What—did she think Mr. Peacock Loxsleigh was racing after on horseback, intent on dragging her from the coach for ravishment?

Such scenes, alas, had featured in her dreams. How could a lady's mind produce such things? She had never even flirted, for a canon's daughter should not. She'd had a few suitors over the years, all clergymen, but her mother and sick father had needed her, and truth to tell, none had truly appealed.

Now she was free, and returning to York to live a full life. She was emerging from a chrysalis, but too old, dull, and dry to become the simplest sort of butterfly.

Except that . . .

No! She would not allow that man in her mind.

She did have a suitor. A perfectly eligible suitor.

Dean Stallingford had been a good friend to her family in recent years and had expressed his interest just before this journey, saying that he wished to make his intentions known before she was exposed to London's temptations. Martha knew she should have committed herself then, but for some reason the words had stuck in her throat. He was fifteen years her senior, and a widower with three young children, but that was not to his discredit.

Very well. She would accept him when they returned and become a married woman with house and family to manage and a place in York society, but she was aware that he sparked no excitement within her. Robert Loxsleigh had created sparkles in a moment.

Such madness must be why women succumbed to seduction, racing fecklessly to their ruin. She was in no danger of that, but she wished the coach had wings. She wished they weren't to stay for days at Aunt Clarissa's. Once in York, she would become Mistress Stallingford as quickly as was decent, and be safe.

She repeated that like a litany over two long days of travel, and as they climbed out of the coach in Newark. They were soon in Aunt Clarissa's modern brick house, awash with her chatter. Clarissa Heygood was a childless widow, having lost her soldier husband early to war, and enjoyed visitors very much. That evening they took a stroll around the town, eventually taking a path by the river. Martha enjoyed the exercise after so much sitting, but she dropped behind for relief from her aunt's endless flow of gossip.

Her own company, however, gave space for dismal thoughts. Marrying Dean Stallingford would mean remaining part of the chapter of York Minster, and that felt . . . cloistered. Even York itself held no savor. She had few friends there because her time had been so taken up with her father's care.

She was frowning at some innocent ducks when a man said, "Heaven is before me. 'Tis the lady of the forget-me-nots."

Martha turned, heart pounding, and indeed it was the peacock. Except now he was a much more ordinary bird—if such a man could ever be ordinary. He wore riding breeches and boots with a brown jacket and his hair was unpowdered. Hair of burnished gold.

Stop that. It was a russet shade catching the setting sun.

"Alas," he said, those green eyes laughing at her, "she has betrayed her handkerchief and forgotten me."

"I certainly have not!" Regretting that, Martha walked on to catch up with her mother and aunt, alarmed by how far they were ahead.

He kept up without effort. "You remember my gallantry, Miss Darby?"

"I remember your impudence." Heavens, when had she ever been so rude? Cheeks burning, she walked ever faster.

He stayed by her side. "For returning your handkerchief? A harsh judgment, ma'am."

Good manners compelled. She stopped and dipped a curtsy. "I apologize, sir. That was kind of you."

He smiled. "Then may I call on you at your inn?"

Martha thanked heaven she could say, "We stay in a private home, sir."

"How pleasant for you. The home of the lady ahead?"

She could do nothing about it. He outpaced her with ease and made his courtesies to her mother, who of course introduced him to Aunt Clarissa, who was in ecstasies to give him carte blanche to call at her house whenever he wished. Martha was in danger of grinding down her teeth, and when he left with an invitation to sup at Aunt Clarissa's within the hour, she could have screamed.

But what protest could she make? Both the older ladies thought him charming and were not immune to his good looks, either. Then, as they hurried home to make preparations for a guest, Aunt Clarissa stopped to exclaim, "From Five Oaks! Why, he must be a son of Viscount Loxsleigh. And by the stars, I do believe he has only one. Lud, we will have a future viscount to sup!"

She almost raced on her way. Martha trailed after. He was a lord? A future one, but it came to the same thing. He was as far above her as the stars, and for some strange reason that caused a deep pang of loss.

When Martha entered the house, her aunt was already calling frantic instructions to her cook. Martha's mother said, "The heir to a viscountcy. And I believe I saw him look at you in a most particular way, dear."

"Mother, for heaven's sake. What interest could such a man have in a woman like me?"

Her mother sighed. "I suppose that's true. But his company will make an agreeable evening."

Martha considered claiming a headache as escape, but for some reason she couldn't say the words. She went to her room to tidy herself, and slowly her good sense returned. It was ridiculous to imagine Mr. Loxsleigh was pursuing her, but she would be chaperoned by her mother and aunt.

She would enjoy the novelty, she decided, tying a fresh cap beneath her chin. She'd met no man like him before, and likely wouldn't in the future. If he did attempt a seduction, that would be the most novel experience of all. She was not the tiniest bit vulnerable to his sort of tinsel charm, but watching his attempt could be diverting.

Loxsleigh did not attempt to seduce her, and indeed how could he when both her mother and aunt fluttered around him like adoring moths to the flame?

He entertained them with the wonders and follies of the court. He pretended interest in Anne Darby's impressions of London, and even in Aunt Clarissa's chatter about Newark. His sympathetic manner soon drew out the story of Canon Darby's long illness, and of Aunt Clarissa's old tragedy. He mentioned his own mother's death three years ago with tender feeling.

Where was the artificial peacock? This might be a different man.

All the same, beneath easy manners, he was *intense*. A strange word, but the only one Martha could find. And his intensity was centered on her. When their eyes met, she felt its power. That must be a skill of practiced seducers, and on a weaker woman it might work, for it created the illusion that she was special, that she was important to him.

When he invited them all to dine at his inn the next afternoon, Martha agreed with as much pleasure as the rest. It appeared he might plan an attempt on her virtue. Perhaps dry spinsters from the provinces were a new dish for such as he, and she looked forward to seeing what other skills he would bring into play. Would he attempt to get her alone? He'd fail, but it would be like watching a play, and the performance of this leading actor should be a wonder to behold.

However, the price for her amusement was more embarrassing dreams, and others even odder. Where did the woodland scenes come from? She'd spent her life in a city, but in the night she visited dense woodlands and glades woven through with a hauntingly beautiful song, where strange creatures danced, loved, and quarreled.

Quarreled over her.

An exquisite lady in iridescent draperies and a lord in dark velvet prowled and snarled. Over her . . .

When she awoke to her sunlit bedchamber, Martha felt as if the misty greenwood still surrounded her, but by the time they left to walk to the Crown Inn, she was sensible again.

She could wish Aunt Clarissa so. That lady was in alt at Loxsleigh's high station and had spent the morning making inquiries of her friends, which also allowed her to spread the word about her interesting new acquaintance. "He *is* the heir," she'd told Martha and her mother. "And the family is famously rich!"

As soon as they were seated at the inn, she said, "I understand your home at Five Oaks is most unusual, sir. Famous for its antiquity."

"It is, ma'am."

"A part of it dates back to the thirteenth century!"

"A small part," he said as soup was served. "Only the old great hall and some rooms above it."

"Five hundred years old!" Aunt Clarissa declared.

"Is it not rather uncomfortable?" asked Martha's practical mother.

He turned his smile on her. "Which is why it's hardly used, ma'am."

"Are there five oaks?" Martha challenged.

"Of course, Miss Darby."

"Trees die, even oaks. There cannot always be five."

Her sharpness did not cut him. "There can if one counts saplings. But yes, there have always been five mature oaks." Before she could debate that point, he added, "Or so legend says. There are certainly five now. Perhaps you would care to visit and see for yourself?"

He addressed it nicely to both Martha and her mother, but she knew it was intended for herself. So that was it. He wanted her in his home, under his power . . .

Before she could forestall it, her mother had agreed, and then she made it worse.

"I hope we'll be able to return your hospitality soon, sir, and serve you a dinner when next you visit York. Perhaps we can show you some entertainments. We will soon be out of mourning. Dear Martha missed so much of her youth while helping me nurse Mr. Darby that I look forward to her enjoying parties and assemblies."

"I'm past the age for such frivolities, Mother."

"Why say that, dear? I declare I am not. I intend to dance when asked, and enjoy many entertainments."

"And so you should, ma'am," Loxsleigh said. "I will certainly ask you to dance."

He addressed her mother, but Martha felt the message was to her. She found her hand tight on her knife and fork as if she'd need to fight him off.

Talk turned safely to musical evenings and assemblies, but then both Martha's mother and aunt shared stories from their youth that implied more liveliness than Martha had imagined. Her mother had flirted with a number of suitors, and even slipped aside from a dance for a kiss? And not with the future Canon Darby, either. In their recollections, the older ladies became more youthful, brighter-eyed, rosier-cheeked, while Martha remained herself, dull and lacking memories to share.

Did everyone dance and flirt their way into their twenties except her?

She became aware of hunger, and not for soup.

She hungered for touches and dances and teasing and flirtation. All the things the older ladies remembered with such pleasure. All the things she'd missed and feared never to experience, especially in Dean Stallingford's embraces.

Good heavens. She'd never let her imagination go so far, and now the idea revolted her.

She caught Loxsleigh looking at her and immediately envisioned embraces that would not revolt her. How was he doing this to her?

She seized her wineglass and drank. He also raised his glass, but sipped, his eyes remaining on her, bright as fire. Heat rose through her body. She began to sweat.

This wasn't a play, and it wasn't harmless. She would *not* go to Five Oaks. She would return directly to York and marry Dean Stallingford and be safe.

The meal seemed to take an age, and when they rose to take their leave Martha gave thanks that the torment was over. However, Loxsleigh insisted on escorting them back home and walked beside her as they left the inn. She could feel his presence, perhaps even a vibration. She welcomed fresh air and the hubbub of ordinary life—people in the street, vendors calling their wares, a line of chairmen offering transport.

"I feel quite fatigued," said Aunt Clarissa. "I do believe I'll take a chair."

Loxsleigh summoned a sedan and paid the men. "Mistress Darby? Would you, too, care to be carried home?"

"I confess the idea appeals, sir. Don't feel obliged to join us in laziness, dear," she said to Martha. "I know you enjoy a walk and Mr. Loxsleigh will ensure your safety."

If Martha's senses were any guide, Mr. Loxsleigh planned the exact opposite, but she took a sudden resolve. Even if she refused to visit his home, he could follow her to York. The only way to put a stop to this was to directly dismiss him.

"Yes," she said. "I should like to walk. It's a lovely afternoon."

3

As soon as the older ladies were carried away she turned to him. "And now, Mr. Loxsleigh, we will talk plainly, if you please."

He extended his arm. "I will be delighted, Miss Darby."

Martha didn't want to touch him, but propriety compelled. She curled her hand around his arm and they set off down the street. Even through gloves and sleeve, she felt that vibration again and it rippled into her. She twitched and glanced around. Had she heard that song again? The one from her dream . . .

"Plain talk, Miss Darby?" he prompted.

"I wish to know, plainly, sir, why you are pursuing my mother and myself. We can hardly be amusing to you after court."

"Court is a constantly repeating play. Its charms soon wear thin."

She gave him a look. "So we are a new play, a novelty?"

"As I am for you, I'm sure."

"I'm certainly not accustomed to such elevated company." She was launched on an argument about their different stations, but he said, "I assume you meet the archbishop now and then."

"That is hardly the same."

"But extremely elevated. Where does the Archbishop of York come in the order of precedence? Closely after royalty, I believe, and far, far above the heir to a viscountcy."

Jaw tense, Martha said, "I have very little to do with the archbishop."

"But would not reject his company as unsuitable. Come, Miss Darby, why are you so prickly? What have I done to offend?"

She glared at him. "Do you pretend that you encountered us in Newark by accident?"

"It is on the North Road, which we both must take. But I confess that I wanted to meet you again."

"Why?"

Martha suddenly realized that they'd taken a shortcut through the churchyard. It was the route her party had walked to the inn, enjoying the tranquillity. Now the leafy quiet seemed dangerous.

She released his arm and stepped away. "Why?" she demanded again. "What interest do you have in us?"

"In *you*. Your mother is delightful, but you are the lodestone."

"Lodestone?" But that was best ignored. "I insist you leave us be, sir. There is no connection, and can never be."

"There was a handkerchief," he said whimsically. "My dear Miss Darby, my intentions are completely honorable."

"Honorable?" She was becoming an echo, but he'd opened the way to an attack. "That sounds as if you intend to propose marriage."

She waited with relish for him to show panic, but instead he smiled. "I believe I do. But first I must kiss you."

"*What?* You wretch, to make fun of me. And to suggest something so wicked!"

"A kiss is wicked? Then the whole world is destined for hell. Including you. With such tempting lips, you must have been kissed many times."

"Certainly not!" Martha snapped, but instantly regretted the admission. "My father's illness . . . Mourning . . ."

He sobered. "As your mother said, you have missed much." He captured her hands. "Allow me to introduce you to the kiss."

He didn't wait for permission, however, but pulled her beneath a tree. And kissed her.

A mere press of lips to lips, yet sparkles started there and spread throughout her body—into her chest, down her spine, right to her fingers and toes. She almost felt that her tight-pinned hair crackled.

She tried to step back, but that brought her hard against the tree's trunk and he pressed over her, his hot mouth claiming hers hungrily, destroying both conscience and will. She gripped his jacket, lightning-struck and helpless, until a deep, urgent ache awoke her to peril.

She pushed him away with all her strength. He crushed closer, as if he might force her . . .

But then he put hands to the tree and thrust violently backward, as if breaking bonds, breathing hard, eyes bright and wolfish in their hunger.

A hunger that pounded in herself.

He went to one knee. "Miss Darby, will you marry me?"

She stared, then snapped, "Of course not!" from an instinct as sharp as that which snatches the hand from a burning pot.

His eyes still shone. "You must, you know."

Martha backed away, but the infernal tree blocked her. "*Must?* From a *kiss*. A kiss forced upon me? I fear you're mad, sir!"

And he looked it, with those wide, burning eyes and flushed cheeks.

"I will be if you reject me. Why do you refuse?"

"Why? My father was a canon. Yours is a viscount. You will be a viscount one day. I have an extremely modest portion to bring to a marriage and no idea of how to behave at court."

"I don't live at court," he said, rising to his feet. "And I don't need your portion, but in fact you bring a dowry of immense value." He stepped forward. "Let me kiss you again."

Martha pushed him away. "Stop that! I know what you're about. You're trying to seduce me."

"I'm trying to marry you."

"I don't believe you."

He sighed and looked up. "I thought an oak would have some power."

"What?"

He took her hand—"Come"—and dragged her toward the church.

"What are you doing? Stop this!" Martha stumbled along, unable bring herself to scream. They turned a corner, and there at last were people—two gravediggers, chest deep in the ground. "Sirs!" she cried.

"I want to marry this lady," Loxsleigh interrupted. "Will you stand witness?"

The men grinned, showing crooked teeth. "If you wish, sir."

"I do." He tossed them both a coin. "Come." He dragged Martha onward.

She grabbed a headstone. "You're drunk, sir. You must be. It would serve you right if I took up your offer."

He stopped, beaming. "Do, please, my marrying maid."

"Your what?"

"You, my dear, my darling Miss Darby, are my marrying maid. I have sought you high and low, long and far, despairing of ever finding you in time. But here you are, and here I am, and all is wondrous!"

He grasped her waist and swung her around in the air. Nothing so alarming, so wonderful, had ever happened to Martha Darby before. She swatted at his head, beat at his shoulders, and when her feet touched the ground again she exclaimed, "You're mad, or drunk, or both!"

"Not a bit of it!"

But then he swooped down to dig his fingers into the long grass by the edge of the path.

Mad, Martha thought, tears gathering in her eyes. Tragically, the man was mad.

"See." He straightened, showing her a small golden earring as if it were a wonder of the orient. "Is it not wonderful?"

"You must return it to its owner," Martha said gently.

"Of course, but it's proof, you see."

"Proof of what?"

"That you're my marrying maid. How soon can we be wed?"

"Mr. Loxsleigh, I am not going to marry you."

He shook his head, as if she were a moonling.

Martha reached for the only weapon she had. "I'm promised to another."

That did cloud his sun. "Do you love him?"

Martha couldn't quite lie. "We are very well suited," she said and set off along the path toward the street, toward people. Sane people.

He passed her and spoke walking backward. "You *don't* love him. Of course you don't. A marrying maid wants no other. I wonder why I didn't find you years ago."

"Perhaps," she said tightly, "because we belong in different spheres and still do."

"Ah! Your father was a canon. Did you live close to the Minster?"

The safety of the street lay ahead, but he blocked her way. "Yes."

"And in the long years of caring for your father, did you mostly stay at home?"

"Of course."

"That explains it, then. Faery powers can't work in powerful Christian spaces."

Fairies. He was a worse case than she'd feared.

He turned and opened the gate for her. "If I try to explain, you'll never believe me."

"Quite likely I won't," she said, safe at last on the street.

"Martha, my dear, just say yes."

She looked him in the eye. "No."

"Come to Five Oaks."

"No."

"What harm can it do?"

"Said the spider to the fly." She marched on. Aunt Clarissa's house was in view. Martha had never been so glad to see it.

"Come to Five Oaks," he persisted. "It will change your mind. But if it doesn't, I'll bother you no more. And that is a painful promise for me to make."

Martha was struck by his sincerity and slowed her steps. "Why?"

He didn't immediately answer and seemed to be calculating her reaction. "If you don't marry me," he said at last, "I will die."

"Die of love? We hardly know each other!"

"Simply die. And not just me. Many others."

Mad, mad, but she was suddenly unable to abandon him. If she went to his home, she would be with her mother. Aunt Clarissa would know where they went. Perhaps his father didn't realize how sad a case he was. There might be some way to help him.

"Very well," Martha said at last. "I will visit Five Oaks."

He beamed, all that bright light shining, but the song came from elsewhere, as did the burst of ethereal laughter. Martha looked around even as she knew neither was anything to do with the here and now.

Was insanity infectious?

4

BY MORNING MARTHA had second, third, twentieth doubts about the wisdom of her decision, especially in light of her dreams. That one kiss had unleashed wickedness beyond comprehension, and even more vivid images of impossible things.

Mr. Loxsleigh arrived, and though he was striving to appear normal, his eyes revealed that madness still rode him. Not dangerous madness, she assured herself. What was more, he'd brought a luxurious traveling carriage drawn by six horses, which meant three postilions who would hardly allow evil.

She guessed he intended rash speed, however, and said, "We will travel only as fast as is reasonable, sir."

He handed her into the carriage. "We must reach Five Oaks today."

Martha paused in the doorway. "Why?"

She caught him staring into nowhere, but then he was with her again, smiling. "My impatience to see you there, Miss Darby. But my word on it, we'll travel no faster than is safe."

With yet more misgivings, Martha took her seat at her mother's side, facing the horses. It was difficult to be a well-bred lady who never behaved improperly, and did not upset arrangements.

"How lovely to travel post," her mother said. "So kind of you, Mr. Loxsleigh."

He took the opposite seat. "It is you who are kind, ma'am, agreeing to come to Five Oaks."

As the carriage moved off, Martha gripped her hands together. She forced them to relax. She was safe. Any other impression was a lingering effect of her dream.

Or proximity to a man. The seating put her far too close to Loxsleigh. Their knees almost touched. Unless she chose to look outside all the way, she must look at him, be aware of how he looked at her with eyes that now seemed to gleam emerald bright.

She turned away as if fascinated by the sight of the castle over nearby houses.

He said, "Our road is good according to those coming south."

In other words, he claimed speed was safe. To prove it, as soon as they left the town the horses picked up their pace. It did not jolt over ruts, however, so Martha couldn't reasonably complain.

Extravagantly, they halted for new horses in an hour, and then again.

They would have continued that way till dark if Martha hadn't prompted him to stop to dine at gone two o'clock. He agreed, but though he smiled and conversed, he hurried them through their meal and out again to the carriage. Even Martha's mother commented on it.

"Is there urgency, Mr. Loxsleigh? Do you have bad news from home?"

"No, ma'am. I'm merely anxious that we arrive before dark."

"If it becomes dark," Martha said, "we must stop."

He looked at her with something like rage and she shrank back, wishing there was some way to escape with propriety. He instantly smiled, so that she might have believed she'd imagined the reaction, but she didn't.

He turned to her mother. "There's a family legend that might interest you, ma'am, as it concerns the oldest part of Five Oaks. May I relate it to pass the time?"

"By all means, Mr. Loxsleigh."

"Long, long ago," he began, "an ancestor, also called Robert Loxsleigh, traveled the land, seeking to do his knightly duty and defend the weak. One night, he became lost in dense woodland despite the fact that it was a full moon. When he came into a clearing he saw a beautiful woman being assaulted by a man. He leaped from his horse, drew his sword, and rushed between them. The lady fell on his chest in gratitude, but the man was furious. He declared Sir Robert was his prisoner for entering a Faery circle under the full moon. You see the warring couple were Titania and Oberon, Queen and King of Faery."

"As in Shakespeare!" Anne Darby exclaimed. " 'Ill met by moonlight.' How interesting."

"Ill met, indeed," Loxsleigh agreed, but when he turned to Martha, that fire of intensity burned. Worse, she felt it in herself now, as if she had urgent need to race to his home, but it fought with a desperate need to turn away from the course.

"Sir Robert sought to escape, but his horse had disappeared, as had his squire and all the woodland except for the five gnarled oaks that circled him. He knew of faery ways, and knew that a mortal who invaded a faery circle at full moon was their prisoner. He believed himself lost to our world, but Titania took him under her protection and declared that he should go free, and would even receive a reward. One wish."

"What did he wish for?" Anne Darby asked.

"Remember, ma'am, he was a truly noble knight. He asked for some talent that would enable him to help the poor and helpless even more than before."

"Ah, the good man."

"What talent?" Martha asked, hearing her tension make it harsh.

Loxsleigh looked at her. "The ability to find lost gold."

"Lost?"

"Coins, salvers, jewelry."

"Such as an earring?"

Their eyes were locked. "Quite possibly." But then he turned to her mother. "Anything already mined and formed by man. Gold is a mystical metal, valued everywhere. Some believe it also has mystic and healing powers. It serves us well and shouldn't be lost. According to this story, faery has the task of ensuring that lost gold is found and returned to use. Have you ever heard the story of the gold at the end of a rainbow?"

Martha clung to silence, unable to understand why she felt such threat. Her mother seemed unaffected and asked to know more.

"That legend appears in many places. It says that if a person can find the place where a rainbow touches the ground, they will find gold. Thus it is a way for faery to put some of their trove back into human hands. Or, sometimes buried gold is brought to the surface to be exposed by the plough, or coins hidden in a wall are revealed when someone is inspired to break it down."

"I have heard of such cases," Anne Darby declared, wide-eyed.

"It's only a legend, Mother."

That caused Loxsleigh to look at her again. "You doubt, Miss Darby, and therein lies the problem. Once, the fey folk lived close to humans, dwelling in the dense woodlands that surrounded every village and manor, interacting with people according to their whim. But much of that woodland has been cut down and the land put to agriculture, and modern thought has made skeptics of us all. Nowadays faery lives among us only in their mystic havens. To continue the work, Titania made Sir Robert her deputy, enabling him to find lost gold and put it to use to benefit the poor."

"Then why," Martha asked, "are his descendants so rich?"

"Martha!" her mother protested.

But Loxsleigh smiled. As if she'd opened a door.

"Queen Titania wished Sir Robert to found a line that would continue this work, so she bound him with rules. He must keep a seventh of the value of any trove and use it for his own health and prosperity. He must marry and sire children, so that an eldest son would carry on the work, and so must his heirs for all time. Those with the talent must do the work. If he or his descendants broke these rules there was a penalty—they would die within the year. Not just the trouvedor, for thus the gold finders are called, but all Robert's descendants to that day."

"Over five hundred years?" Anne Darby exclaimed. "That could be a vast number!"

"Faery is not benign, ma'am. We are as moths to them, dead in a moment."

And that rang deadly true. Martha desperately tried to make sense of this, but she remembered him saying that if she did not marry him, he would die. He could *not* be claiming that this story was true, that he possessed a fairy gift!

"Those are easy enough conditions, Mr. Loxsleigh," Martha said with deliberate flippancy. "To live a comfortable life and marry."

"Martha," her mother said again, becoming distressed.

Loxsleigh still smiled, but Martha was more and more aware of dark tension all around him. "As you say, Miss Darby. Except that Oberon does his best to thwart his queen."

The coach lurched into an inn then for a change of horses, breaking the moment. Almost breaking a spell.

Was that it? Was she under a spell? Was that why she'd agreed to this mad journey?

But that would mean it was all true. Fairies. Gold finders.

He climbed down to inspect the new horses and pay the fees. She watched him, remembering the earring. His bright burning exultation. Him sweeping her up in that mad whirl. A predictor of this mad whirl. But she'd been alive then. Alive as never before.

No, she would have none of this. She was a rational Christian woman. The man was mad, and she could only pray he wasn't dangerously so.

He climbed back in and the coach moved on.

Martha's mother said, "You mentioned Oberon, sir. Do tell us more."

Martha saw that he wanted to tell her, intended to tell her, and could do nothing to prevent it.

"You will remember that Oberon had reason to hate Robert Loxsleigh, but by faery law he could not deny his lady's gifts. Titania had already imposed rules and a dreadful consequence, however, so he set out to make obedience difficult. He decreed that Robert Loxsleigh and his heirs would not achieve their talent until they married, and that they must marry a woman that he would choose, and before their twenty-fifth birthday.

"Titania insisted that the woman must be healthy, and of a suitable age and station, but she and her husband enjoy their battles, so she made no more attempt than that. Thus—if we are to believe my family lore— there will always be a destined bride for the Loxsleigh heir, but Oberon will make her hard to find." He turned to Martha. "When found, how-ever, there will be no doubt. On either side. We call the bride his mar-rying maid."

Martha inhaled, clenching her fists.

How old are you?

She would not ask, she would not. She turned away, looking outside, and noticed gathering clouds. Rain often turned the roads to mud and she prayed for it. She didn't want to reach his house, and with delay perhaps she could escape.

"What a charming story," Anne Darby said.

Martha turned to her mother. *"Charming?"*

"Fairies, noble knights, and brides."

"And threat of death for many, if there was any truth in it."

"But there isn't, is there, dear?"

Martha forced a smile. "No, of course not. I was swept away by it for a moment. The weather looks ominous, sir. We should stop at the next stage."

"We can reach Five Oaks today, I promise," Loxsleigh said.

Martha didn't argue. If she was any judge, the clouds would do her work for her.

Her mother asked, "Does the name Five Oaks come from that legend? From the oak trees in the glade?"

"It does, ma'am. In fact, the legend says that the old part of the house was built in that very glade, as you will see for yourself within hours." He looked out at the gathering clouds, however, and frowned.

"Do you have any other stories, Mr. Loxsleigh?" her mother asked.

Martha closed her eyes briefly, wondering what more there could be.

"I do have one more, ma'am, which is very whimsical. We left Sir Robert with his faery gift, and once he married his marrying maid, he used his talent but kept the seventh, thus obeying the rules. However, he began to find it harder to distribute the gold to the poor. His generous charities were beginning to cause comment. He tried leaving gold for people to find, as faery had done, but it offended him when it was found by rascals or the rich.

"He traveled farther to escape attention, and when returning from a benevolent journey he was set upon by outlaws. The leader took his purse and made a play of him having donated the purse to the poor. That gave Sir Robert an idea. He set up a trap and captured that leader and put a proposition to him. If he would give up his thievery, Sir Robert would protect him and his companions and provide money for them to live on. In return, Robin Ahood and his men would pass on the gold, claiming that they'd stolen it from the rich to give to the poor."

"Robin Hood!" Martha exclaimed. "Now I see you play with us."

"I did say it was whimsical, Miss Darby."

"And many people think Robin Hood was real," her mother said. "Especially around Yorkshire and Nottinghamshire."

"They think fairies real, too," Martha scoffed. "Or magic wells, or that eleven days were stolen from them when the calendar changed."

"Oh, I remember that," said her mother. "Such a furor. Even rioting. There are some still convinced that their lives will be shorter." She turned to Loxsleigh. "One neighbor in York whose birthday was on the tenth of September that year insists to this day that she's a year younger than she truly is."

Loxsleigh didn't respond. In fact, he looked dumbstruck. He looked outside at the gathering gloom, and then at Martha, eyes wide.

"Robin Hood," Martha said sharply, hoping to bring him back to reason. "That device could only have lasted a while. Men die."

He blinked as if her words made no sense, but then said, "No, of course. I mean yes." He shivered. "A legend can live forever. The Robin Hood stories are spread over centuries, you know, and from Nottinghamshire to Yorkshire. To Barnsdale, where Five Oaks lies. One version links to the Loxsleigh name, though spelled differently. It could be true."

It was a good attempt, but close to babble.

"How interesting," said Martha's mother, but he continued to look at Martha.

"You disbelieve all?"

"Robin Hood might have existed," she said, "but fairies certainly do not."

"Pray God you're right," he said and turned again to study the weather as if willpower could change it.

5

ROB DIDN'T KNOW how he was presenting a normal appearance. If he was.

The change of calendar! How could he have ignored it? How could his father?

Five years ago the calendar had been corrected by going from the second day of September to the fourteenth. As Mistress Darby said, many of the simple folk believed that eleven days had been stolen from them. There had been riots demanding their return. People with birthdays during the eleven days had fretted about how old they were.

He'd regarded all this with amusement. Why hadn't he realized?

No one could tell how faery viewed such human matters as dates and calendars, but if the rules applied to the old date, it would explain the gathering storm—and not the one visible in roiling clouds. At first it had been a dark chanting in his head, but that had turned into a cacophonous chorus that flogged him toward Five Oaks. Hurry, hurry, hurry.

Over the past hours he'd become aware of them around him. Gleeful Oberon and furious Titania. No wonder. If the rules kept to the old calendar, his birthday wasn't the twentieth day of June, eleven days away, but the ninth.

Tomorrow.

If he didn't bed Martha Darby before tomorrow, perhaps before eleven in the morning, his hour of birth, Oberon would be free to finally exact his revenge on the line of Sir Robert Loxsleigh.

That left no time for niceties and wooing. By kind means or cruel, he must have her in the next twenty hours. He tried to compel calm. They would be at Five Oaks in hours, even with the worsening weather. Oberon's work, he was sure. Once he took Martha to the old hall, where faery energy burned so fiercely, she would have to believe, have to agree to anticipate the wedding. Even she, the prim daughter of a canon of York.

If not?

Damnation. Oberon had chosen well and done his mightiest, but he could not be allowed to succeed.

But then the rain swept toward them, sheeting down, pounding the rough ground of the road.

"We must stop at the next inn, Mr. Loxsleigh," Martha said. "We risk becoming stuck in the mud."

"The road's sound," he said desperately, "and it's not far now. Perhaps only an hour." The coach had slowed, however, and he could feel the labor of the horses. The postilions would be miserable, but they must press on. Then the wheels sank and the coach stopped.

He opened the door to jump out. "We must lighten the load!"

The coach lurched forward then, the wheels finding new purchase. He fell back into his seat.

"This is folly!" his bride declared. "Look, I see lights ahead. We must stop. We can't climb out to lighten the load in this weather. My mother could catch her death."

He wanted to rail at her, but every word was true. They could not go on.

"Very well," he said, desperately seeking solutions. "My apologies."

The lights turned out to be a small inn, but called the Maid Marian. Was that a hopeful sign or a twisted joke? It had two tiny bedchambers for them, but they would have to take their supper in the common room. That didn't matter. He made his plans.

He ordered supper for them and hot punch, making sure it had plenty of honey and spices. When it arrived, he strengthened it with the flask of brandy he had in his valise.

Mistress Darby declared it excellent and drank two glasses. Martha drank well of it, too. He topped up her glass when she wasn't looking and saw her drain it again.

Mistress Darby began to nod off. She started. "Oh, my, the long journey has tired me out. I'm for bed."

She left the room somewhat unsteadily. Martha rose and he saw her steady herself on the back of her chair. "I, too, am tired. You set too hasty a pace, Mr. Loxsleigh."

"Perhaps I did. I am simply impatient to see you in my home."

He watched her struggle to focus. "I am *not* going to marry you."

"You must. You know the story now. Remember Oberon's revenge."

"Fablesh . . ." She frowned. "Fables for the credulous."

He grabbed her and shook her. "Why am I cursed with such an impossible woman!"

She fought him off. "Cursed. *Cursed.* Because I will not sin in your bed I'm a curse?"

"I want to *marry* you!"

"*I don't want to marry you!*" she yelled, inhibitions shattered by drink. She was magnificent. But adamant.

"You're mad, Mr. Loxsleigh," she said with the careful precision of the drunk. "It's sad, but I will not bind myself to a madman."

A man laughed, deep and dark.

Martha looked around, almost losing her balance again. "Who was that?"

"Oberon. Anticipating victory. Martha, listen to me. My birthday isn't twelve days away, it's tomorrow. We need to go to bed together. Now."

She blinked at him. "That is a most improper statement, sir."

"I know. Very well, we need to go on to Five Oaks. Now."

"Mad, mad, mad."

"We could ride."

"I cannot ride."

"We could share a horse." He desperately wanted her willing. "Martha, if we don't . . . wed by tomorrow I will die. My father will die. All the descendants of Sir Robert Loxsleigh, wherever they may be, will die within the year."

She swayed slightly. "It is impossible for us to marry by tomorrow, sir. Banns . . . and I do believe that you have made me drunk."

He approached again. "Certainly you are affected by the punch, Miss Darby. Permit me to escort you upstairs."

She swatted at him. "Keep away from me, you . . . you . . . *horny goat.*"

That came so improbably from her lips that he laughed.

A mistake. She backed away, muttering, "Mad, mad, mad. Keep away from me. And I will *not* go to your home. Not tomorrow. Not ever!"

He watched her steer carefully toward the door. Some were made docile by drink, and some quarrelsome. Clearly Martha Darby was the latter. Some were made lusty, but he'd never trusted to that.

He followed at a distance, ready to save her if she stumbled on the narrow stairs. Halfway up her legs betrayed her and she sat down, leaning her head against the wall, muttering, "Drunk. I'm drunk. Oh, the shame . . ."

Then she slipped into a stupor.

Rob went to where she slumped and touched her prim cap. "Martha, my love, I wish it had been otherwise. Pray God you forgive me."

He gathered her into his arms, aware of Titania's exultance and Oberon's fury and hating both equally. Titania's lilting voice approved. But then Oberon changed his tone to coaxing.

Will you rape her? it murmured. *Despoil her limp body? What will be the result when she regains awareness and understands what you have done?*

She'll love you, argued Titania. *She's your marrying maid. It is her destiny to love you just as it is your destiny to love her. Do it now, my knight. Do it now so you and your line can live.*

Do it now and eat bitter bread forever. Perhaps it is not necessary. Perhaps I will allow your birthday to be as your worldly custom designates.

Rob carried Martha up to his bedchamber where he laid her on the bed. He untied the stings of her cap and took it off, then unpinned her hair. He spread it, astonished by its silky thickness, aroused by it and hungry. He leaned down and pressed his lips to hers . . .

Which were slack and unresponsive.

He inhaled, straightening. "I cannot," he said. Titania screamed at him; Oberon laughed.

Where was virtue and vileness here? Where was right and wrong?

There was one last hope.

6

MARTHA WAS FIRST aware of a throbbing head, and then that she was cold and wet. Then that she was not in her bed, but being carried. Was this another odd dream?

She struggled feebly and realized she was trapped in something. In heavy cloth.

"Hush, love, we're home. I'll soon have you warm."

"Home?" She forced her eyes open and saw a distant starry sky. Closer, she saw Loxsleigh's shadowed face.

"What have you done?" Her mouth was almost too parched for speech.

"Brought you to Five Oaks. It was the only way."

"No . . ." He was going to rape her, and here in his house there would be no noble Sir Robert to stand between. She felt her own hot tears on her cold cheeks.

He kissed them. "Don't be afraid, love. I won't harm you. But I had to bring you here. I had to try."

He put her down on the steps to open the door, but only for a moment and still swaddled, so her feeble struggles achieved nothing. They entered total darkness, but he must know it well. Of course he did.

Then wild candlelight showed a high, painted ceiling. "My boy, my boy! You're home and with your bride. Praise be to God!"

Martha turned her head and saw a tousled-haired man in a night robe, candle in hand.

"Welcome, my dear, welcome. Oh, happy day. But why such a journey? The poor girl must be chilled through. Bring her up, bring her up. She can lie in my bed for now."

"No!" Martha cried. Not the father, too.

"No," Rob Loxsleigh said. "I must take her to the old hall."

"The old hall? She'll catch a lung fever."

"I hope she'll catch credulity." Already striding across the entrance hall, he called, "The calendar change. It changed my birthday. We have no time! Bring brandy and water. Rouse the servants to prepare her a bed."

"Please," Martha cried. "Please, don't."

But he rushed forward into darkness, struggling to open doors, leaving them wide behind him, and all around her a cacophony of voices swelled—high voices, low voices, merry and angry, coaxing and threatening, tangled up in a song. In that song. Her nightmare song.

A man growled, "He plans to rape you. Fight, mortal creature, fight!"

She tried, but was helpless.

Then Loxsleigh stopped. Small-paned windows let in a trace of light and Martha's eyes were accustomed to the dark. They were in the ancient part of Five Oaks. And the nightmare song and creatures whirled around.

A dream. This had to be a dream!

He put her on her feet, supporting her still.

The lady was there, the one in iridescent robes. She smiled like a Madonna, but with blank eyes. Titania.

The man paced around them like the panther she'd seen in the Tower of London. "He cannot rape you. He's too puny for that. You have only to resist."

Titania pressed close in a cloud of woodland perfume. "Dear child, you have only to surrender to Rob, to that which you most desire." Her hand brushed Martha's forehead and the dull throb there faded. The room seemed brighter by the moment, and all her senses heightened. The song turned sweet.

"You love Rob Loxsleigh," whispered the Queen of Faery. "He loves you. You were destined from birth. And the threat is real, dear child. Refuse and my lord will have his way."

"Then stop him."

"I have brought you together. Now it lies in your hands."

"You demand that I sin!"

Titania laughed. "I demand nothing. It will annoy me if my lord wins this little contest, but there are many others."

Faery, Rob Loxsleigh had said, are not benign.

Martha realized that whether the light came from a magical glow or from the fey folk themselves, she could see. The room was long and low and paneled in dark oak, but held no furniture. Rob stood nearby, wild haired and grim, watching her, but prepared, she understood, to abide by her decision.

Here, now, she could not deny the reality of the threat. It showed in Titania's heartless smile and in handsome Oberon's simmering anticipation. He waited to exact revenge for an offence half a millennium old. Others flowed around the room and in and out of the dark walls, watching and chattering. They were enjoying the show, as people watch animals fight to the death simply for amusement.

The unearthly song swelled—sweet, yes, but chanting both love and death.

Martha turned to Rob. "They are vile. We must deny them both."

He took her hands. "Martha, Martha, they are as wind, wave, and lightning. Deny them if you will, but you will still die. Or rather I will, and my father. My uncle and aunt, my cousins and my cousin Cecilia's newborn child. Who knows how many others carry Sir Robert Loxsleigh's blood? Trust me, love. There is only one way. Come to my bed and lie with me. We will be married as soon as may be, but Oberon will be thwarted only if we love each other tonight."

"It would be wrong," the dark lord growled in her ear, "and you know it. What good can come from that?"

"We can pledge ourselves now," Rob argued. "We can say our vows. I will keep them, as will you. There can never be any other for you or me."

"By your beliefs, it must be in a church," Oberon argued. "Think of the scandal. Your reputation . . ."

It was as if all around held their breath, as if the very room, the old house, the one built by Robert Loxsleigh in a faery glade guarded by five oaks, held its breath. Even the song stopped. But Oberon had misplayed his hand. Martha's morals still quailed, but to let innocents die for her reputation would be vile.

She looked into the man's eyes. "I will lie with you tonight, Rob Loxsleigh, my husband in all but the ceremony."

The chorus burst into song again, a song of wild rejoicing that clashed with thunderous rage. Rob took her hand and raced her out of the ancient part of the house, back to the entrance hall, lit now by a branch of candles. The noises faded and then stopped.

Martha knew that the faery had gone. Gone on to other entertainments.

Rob took her into his arms, holding her tight and close, burying his head in her hair.

Her loose hair, Martha realized, as it had never been except between brushing and pinning.

He separated and kissed her, a gentle, reverent kiss. "You will not regret this."

"No, I don't believe I will." But she swallowed before saying, "Do we do it now?"

He smiled. "We have all night. You're damp in places and wet in others. Come up to your room and be comfortable."

She went up with him, hand in hand, but still embarrassed. She could hear servants around, woken from sleep and talking softly. About her. They would all know . . .

But she would not sacrifice hundreds to her discomfort.

He led her to a room where three maidservants worked, still in their nightwear with tied shawls atop. They cast her looks, but smiling ones. Did they know? Did everyone here know?

The room was lit with candles and warmed by the flickering flames of a new-laid fire. Two of the servants were running warming pans through the bed. The other was spreading a nightgown over a rack before the fire.

"I'll leave you in their care," Rob said, smiling down at her.

She could do nothing but smile back. "I'm all awhirl."

"I know. Be comfortable. I'll return later."

The subject still embarrassed her too much for speech, but she nodded.

He left and she surrendered to the maids' care. They gave her small beer to slake her thirst, and stripped off her damp outer clothing. Martha wouldn't let them strip her naked. She retired behind the screen to take off her shift and put on the nightgown.

The maids toweled dry her hair and then settled her into the warm bed with a cup of chocolate and a sweet cake. There was a plate of fruit as well, but Martha could eat nothing.

The servants left. She sipped the chocolate, which was richer than any she'd tasted. And she waited.

All awareness of faery had gone, making her realize how it had lived in her for days, ever since that encounter in the park. Instead, there was a growing peace, a growing certainty that all was now right, despite the lack of church and clergy.

She was drinking the last of the chocolate when Rob came to her, shining and handsome again, in a rich, blue robe.

"My peacock, I see."

"At your command," he said, crossing the room to her. "Always."

He extinguished the candles until only fire lit the room and came into the bed beside her. "I'm sorry it must be this way, my love, but it will be holy."

He was naked and she had to look away, even though she said, "I know it."

Wildly she thought, *It would never have been like this with Dean Stallingford!*

He took her hand and she felt his warm lips on her knuckles. "Look at me, Martha."

She turned her head shyly, but he'd pulled the covers up to his neck. There was nothing to embarrass her except that he was here, a man in her bed.

He took her hand, her left hand, and slid a ring onto her third finger. "My pledge to you, dear heart."

Martha raised her hand and saw a complex ring of gold, set with small, smooth stones.

"I've carried that for years, love, as I sought my marrying maid. Come, let me love you now."

He gathered her into his arms and kissed her, and there was all the magic she remembered from that other kiss, so long ago, a day ago. Heat and sparkles danced through her and this time she felt no need to resist. Shyly, she kissed him back. Her hands encountered his skin and she laid her hands on him, uncertainly but with growing pleasure.

She moved against him, her whole body twining with his so they seemed one. Especially when he raised her nightgown high, then took it off. She stared up at the bed canopy as he put hands to her naked breasts. And then his mouth. But then she was lost to anxiety and swept up into his passion, her need building so that when he thrust inside her, she cried out as much in satisfaction as in pain.

The pain was short and soon forgotten. The pleasure built until she thought she'd die of wanting more. Until it came, and she didn't die, but ended up hot and sticky in his arms, laughing softly at the splendor of it. "So that," she said, "is magic."

He chuckled into her hair. "If it's magic, it's a magic available to everyone, love." He nuzzled and kissed her there. "Thank you, my dear, my darling, my marrying maid. We will be gloriously happy—"

But Martha suddenly sat up. "Mother!"

Laughing, he pulled her back down. "Someone's already been dispatched to bring her here safely on the morrow. The explanations may be delicate, but I think she'll be mollified by our wedding." He cradled her face. "Any regrets?"

Martha shook her head. "None. This is right and true."

"We'll follow faery's rules and all will be well, and when our son is of marrying age we'll work with him to circumvent Oberon's wiles."

A distant look came into his eyes, and Martha said, "What? More trickery from them?"

He focused on her again. "No, love. But I'm aware of the gold now. After the kiss, it was a whisper, and all I've found is nearby pieces. Now, it's a symphony on the air, a choir in my mind, from near and far. Tomorrow, will you come with me to find lost gold?"

She snuggled into his chest, also hearing this new, sweet song. "I will, husband. And right merrily."

Carrie Vaughn

Bestseller Carrie Vaughn is the author of a wildly popular series of novels detailing the adventures of Kitty Norville, a radio personality who also happens to be a werewolf, and who runs a late-night call-in radio advice show for supernatural creatures. The Kitty books include Kitty and the Midnight Hour, Kitty Goes to Washington, Kitty Takes a Holiday, Kitty and the Silver Bullet, Kitty and the Dead Man's Hand, Kitty Raises Hell, *and* Kitty's House of Horrors. *Vaughn's short work has appeared in* Jim Baen's Universe, Asimov's Science Fiction, Subterranean, Wild Cards: Inside Straight, Realms of Fantasy, Paradox, Strange Horizons, Weird Tales, All-Star Zeppelin Adventure Stories, *and elsewhere. Her most recent books are* Voices of Dragons *and a new Kitty novel,* Kitty Goes to War. *She lives in Colorado.*

In the clever tale that follows, she demonstrates that the line between dreams and reality can be a thin one—and that sometimes it's hard to tell if you've crossed it.

Rooftops

T he wires were obvious, strung with LED lights that switched on
the moment the hero launched upward, illustrating the fact that no
one had yet figured out how to get a real flight-capable superhuman to
act in a play or movie or anything.

"Well?" Otto Veck, acclaimed director, looked at Charlotte.

The stage was a mess. A chain-link fence formed the backdrop, supposedly suggesting the shadows of a forest. A pile of stuffed black gar-
bage bags made a castle shape. A woman in a white bustier, panties,
fishnets, and a black garter with a cute little bow clinging to her thigh
lay at the foot of the tower of trash as if she had just thrown herself off
it, to her death. Nearby another body lay, a twisted man dressed in a
three-piece suit with a tire iron sticking out of him, suggesting a sword
at the end of a duel. The hero, a handsome man with a clean-shaven
face, wearing an alluring amount of leather, had been kneeling beside
the woman, hand to his chest, overcome by the wretchedness of the
world. Then he flew away, straight up into the rigging overhead, vanishing into the heavens.

The scene was supposed to look a mess, but it didn't match the picture Charlotte imagined. She winced. "Can we make it a little more . . .
I don't know . . . pretty?"

Otto tilted a thoughtful head, as if regarding the stage from a slightly
different angle. It was Marta, the actress, who sat up, appalled. Fred,
who played the fiendish villain/bureaucrat, stood and set aside the tire
iron as he stretched muscles and groaned. Harry, who played the tragic
hero too late to save his lover, but not too late to exact revenge on the

fiendish villain/bureaucrat, slowly descended, hanging passively in his harness as the stage crew lowered him back to earth. Out of character now, he looked tired.

"Pretty? You want this to be pretty?" Marta said. "What happened to the terrors of modernity? There's nothing *pretty* about modernity." She had her hands on her hips and glared with the air of an offended artist. The truth was, she looked good in the lingerie and knew it, and was probably afraid that "pretty" meant putting her in a floor-length gown.

Charlotte thought she had said something along the lines of wanting to recast classic gothic narratives as a vehicle for alienation—the terrors of postmodernity expressed as the sublime. They had the terrors of postmodernity down pat but seemed to be missing the sublime.

The last dress rehearsal was a little late to be rethinking the project. Was it too late to cancel the whole thing? It had all seemed so much more clever when she wrote it.

"Never mind," she said. "It's fine. It's all fine."

"Maybe the lighting," Otto said, trying to be helpful. "More of a halo effect upstage." He put on his headset. "Bob, is it too late to change that last lighting cue?"

She sat in her squishy velvet seat in the middle of the house and pondered. This was supposed to be her big break. Her jump from the bush leagues to the big-time, with a director like Otto, an award-winning actress like Marta starring, in a theater that didn't seat its audience in folding chairs. Charlotte couldn't help but feel that her career was already over.

Her phone rattled, and she dug in the pocket of her jeans for it.

The screen showed Dorian's text: "Wrk late, won't make dinner, sry, make it up to you."

She quelled her disappointment and instead decided to admire Dorian's dedication. An up-and-coming assistant DA like Dorian Merriman didn't win cases like the one against the Midnight Stalker by going on dinner dates with struggling playwrights.

Otto and the three actors were all looking at her, and she might have blushed.

"Everything okay?" Otto said.

"Fine," she said, putting her phone away.

"Are we done, Otto?" Harry said.

"We're done. Call's at five tomorrow." Otto and the actors disappeared backstage.

Part of her wanted to curl up right here for the next twenty-four hours, until it was all over. Maybe she could sleep through it.

Instead, she found her coat and bag and went to catch a bus home. It was early summer, still daylight, still warm. She could have walked the whole way, scuffing toes on the sidewalk and thinking of everything that could go horribly wrong tomorrow night. She didn't even have to go on stage and she was terrified.

As an alternative to going home and stewing, she decided to take herself to dinner. Just because Dorian couldn't go out didn't mean *she* had to stay home. She had to celebrate either the beginning of her career or mourn its incipient demise. She had a favorite place, a hillside café with a rooftop patio, perfect for watching the urban neon sunset. And it arranged its wine list by price, which she thought was postmodernly classy.

SHE DIDN'T PLAN for the jewelry store next door to the café to get robbed while she was there.

She had just ordered a salad and a glass of zinfandel. Something to take the edge off while she stared at the hazy city sky and reminded herself that she was lucky and she had a great boyfriend when he was around, and her dream was coming true and the play really was okay and no one was going to write wretched reviews calling her names. Everything was going to be *just fine*.

Alarms started ringing, clanging mechanically, vibrating through the floor. The police sirens joined a minute later. A dozen customers and waitstaff crowded along the patio rail to see what was happening. Charlotte was already sitting there and had a pretty good view of the street. But like many others, she also looked up and around at the sky and rooftops, wondering which hero would swoop in to save the day: Breezeway? The Bullet? Captain Olympus himself?

The police sirens approached, howling, then a half dozen Commerce City PD squad cars roared up the street and screeched to cinematic halts, skidding to angles that blocked the intersections. Uniforms bounded out and pointed guns at the building. Out came the bullhorn, and one of the officers called through it, "Come out with your hands up!"

Shouting echoed up the stairwell that led to the roof. Six men wearing purple Kevlar vests, fatigues, and ninjalike masks appeared. Two held heavy metallic briefcases, no doubt filled with something nefarious and stolen. Four held what had to be ray guns—plastic, streamlined, with parabolic dishes where the barrels should be. They made quite an impression.

They must have planned to jump to the next rooftop and keep running until they found a ladder to shimmy down while the police were still racing up the stairs after them. The police were a little too fast, and the thieves were a little too desperate, because they went for hostages.

The two gunmen pointed their weapons and yelled, "Freeze!" which nobody did. Instead people screamed and tumbled out of the way, covering their heads, falling to the floor, scrambling on top of each other. It was a pretty good strategy, because if they stayed in a mob and the gunmen fired, it would probably be somebody else who got shot.

Astonished, Charlotte just kept sitting there, back to the railing, instead of fleeing with the others. So one of the guys grabbed her, arm around her throat, and held her against the rail, purple parabolic dish to her temple.

Her captor shouted the obligatory "Nobody move!" She thought the other gunman was standing at the top of the stairs, pointing his weapon at the oncoming cops, preventing rescue. So much for a nice evening out.

Staring back at the gun, which had become very large in her vision, she wondered if the weapon would incinerate her or simply make her vanish in a stream of light. She wondered which one would hurt more. Maybe she wouldn't have to go through opening night after all. Maybe Dorian would avenge her, after standing forlornly over her poor broken body. Would he feel guilty for missing dinner with her?

The tableau froze: heroine and villain, random crowd huddling like a Greek chorus, henchmen wreaking chaos. Time stopped, her heartbeat stilled to a moment of perfect silence, a universe holding its breath.

She didn't know where the newcomer entered from, but the gun left her head and pointed at something else, and there he was in the middle of the patio, hands on his hips. He was also wearing a mask, and that may have been what set the gang of jewel thieves most on edge. One more variable must have been too many to handle.

The thieves had an out, and they took it: Her captor tipped her over the railing.

Charlotte gasped a breath as the sky spun past her feet. She was falling—then she wasn't. She jerked to a stop, hanging two stories over the sidewalk. She didn't even have time to scream.

She wasn't sure how it happened, but she could see how it ended up:

The masked man, the hero, gripped her hand and held her dangling thirty feet up. She swayed and came to rest against the concrete wall. His other hand held the railing. He must have dived over the edge as she fell, faster than a heartbeat, faster than a blink. He must have grabbed her, grabbed the railing, and stopped her mid-plunge. Her shoulder throbbed with the pain of being wrenched. His must have felt worse. Now they hung there, looking at each other.

"I'll need you to climb up," he said, voice tight with strain.

"What?" she squeaked.

"I'm fast. Not all that strong," he gasped.

He lifted her partway until she could grab hold of his jeans, then his shirt, then his shoulder, panting and panicked, too shocked to be scared, unbelievably remembering not to look down. She used him as a ladder, until she put her arms around his shoulders. He swung his leg up to hook it over the railing, shrugged to hint that maybe she should make her way to the railing as well. She meant to dig her fingers more tightly around his shirt, but she got the muscle of his shoulder. He only flinched a little. She managed to slide over, hook her elbow over, then her leg, and the two of them rolled onto the patio together.

The ray gun–toting thieves had used the distraction to flee.

Charlotte and her rescuer looked at each other. He was nondescript, but the mask made all the difference. Without it, she'd have glanced at him once, maybe admired the muscled shoulders under the almost-too-tight T-shirt. No uniform, just T-shirt and jeans, plain black boots, well worn. But he wore a mask, a length of black cloth with eyeholes over his head and tied in back. She stared at his eyes, brown, rich. With the mask, it was like looking at someone through a window. She wasn't sure she could really see him. He held her arms—maybe she looked like she was going to faint, falling backward, making him rescue her all over again.

Imagine it—her, rescued at the last second by a real-life hero! Just like one of her plays. Unbelievable. Thrilling.

He was breathing hard. The feat hadn't been easy for him; sweat shone on his neck.

"Are you all right?" she asked.

"I should be asking you that," he said, smiling. He had a very nice smile.

"No . . . well, yes . . . but you—that was amazing." She sounded a little breathy. "I'm fine. Are you?"

"Just fine," he said. He never stopped smiling.

Then, just as a crowd of police trooped up the stairs, he ran—and yes, he was fast. He sped to the other side of the roof, to the back of the building, where a fence gave him a chance to jump off, climb down, flee, and vanish—all in seconds. She couldn't see movement, arms and legs pumping, just this shape that flowed away. Then it was dusk, and she couldn't see anything.

"AND YOU HAVE no idea who he was?" the detective asked again.

"No. I have no idea." When she arrived at the police station, someone put a blanket over her shoulders and a cup of coffee in her hands. Then she started shivering. She hadn't realized she was cold.

The detective stared at her, annoyed, because she was clearly making his job more difficult. Sighing, he pulled over a three-ring binder, opened it in front of her, and started turning pages. "Are any of these the guy who rescued you?"

This looked almost like the binders the theater got from agents—catalogs of actors. The first round of cattle calls. Instead of headshots, the detective's pictures mostly showed blurry full-body action shots of the masked vigilantes. She recognized a lot of them from news clips and reputation: the Invincible, dressed in red, white, and blue, who as far as anyone could tell really *was* invincible and could fly to boot; Black Belt, who dressed like a ninja and could shoot laser beams from his hands; Quantum Girl, a woman in a silver leotard and spike-heeled boots who could teleport; and more. There were maybe two dozen of them—more than she'd realized. No one knew much about them, where they lived or what they did when they weren't out fighting crime. Maybe they had secret identities. Maybe they had secret hideouts, like Gothic castles. Maybe they were robots who only emerged when there was crime to be fought.

In her play, she had assumed that her hero was a person with a heart to break like everyone else.

She flipped through the whole book and shook her head. "He wasn't anybody I recognized. He didn't even have much of a costume, just a mask. Shouldn't you be going after the thieves instead of him?"

"I need all the information I can get for the report," the detective said flatly.

She finished making her statement, which she couldn't see being very useful to any investigation. All she had seen was a swarm of masked men running around performing some mystery play.

"Charlotte!"

Dorian Merriman, hot-shot assistant DA, on the fast track after that Midnight Stalker trial—front-page stuff. She hadn't called him about what had happened. He had just known, probably through one of his connections in the police department.

He rushed to her side, heroically even, but she was a little too wrung out to be impressed by the feat.

"Are you all right? What happened? I came as soon as I heard. Are you hurt?" He turned to the detective. "Is she hurt?"

"She'll be fine," the man said. He straightened the pages on his desk, signaling that they were done.

"Hi," she said, her smile weak.

He knelt by her side, smoothed back her hair like she was a child, and she beamed back at him. "Now let's get you home," he said.

Dorian had brown eyes.

Reporters had arrived at the police station, snapping pictures and demanding answers. Word had gotten out about the masked man, a new rooftop hero in the city, and they kept asking: What was his power? His name? Had he talked to her? What did he say? They already knew who she was; a witness at the restaurant had told them everything. She wondered what the papers would make of it; she'd been right there and she didn't know what had happened. The detective told her not to say anything, so she didn't.

In Dorian's car on the way to her apartment, she got a second wind.

"You should have seen it; it was amazing, I don't know who this guy was, and the way the cops were talking I'm not sure if they want to catch the thieves or him. You know, I'd have expected him to be wearing some suit or armor like the other ones do, at least maybe spandex, but no, just jeans, and you know how you joke around because you don't think those flimsy masks would really hide anyone's identity? But I can't for the life of me remember what he looked like. I just saw the mask."

"You weren't scared?" He glanced at her.

"Well, yeah, sure." But she let the thought fade. She only wanted to remember amazing.

Charlotte shared an apartment with several other starving-artist types in too small a space, an arrangement that worked because most of them were gone most of the time, at their theaters or band rehearsals or projects or day jobs. The place was in a part of town that in another ten years would be hip and gentrified, and they were all hoping they'd have made their fortunes by then so they could afford to stay.

He guided her inside, made her put on pajamas, tucked a cup of tea in her hands, and apologized.

"I have to get back to work. I want to tell the DA about this. We'll get those guys. We won't let anything like this happen again."

Well, that wasn't nearly as romantic as him rushing to the police station to tend to her emotional wounds. But Dorian was a very dedicated assistant DA. She didn't feel quite right complaining.

"But . . . but I'm not sure I want to be alone right now."

He gave her a quick kiss on the forehead. "I'm sorry, I wouldn't leave if it wasn't an emergency. Call me if you need anything, anything at all."

And there he went, saving the city again. She sighed.

She couldn't sleep, so she made another cup of tea and sat in a chair by the bedroom window. She half expected to see a shadowed figure running across the rooftops, pausing to strike a heroic pose against a backdrop of city lights. She fell asleep, wrapped in a blanket and leaning against the window, dreaming strange dreams, until one of her roommates came home, nudged her awake, and put her to bed.

HER PHONE RANG early. She had to scramble for it; it was still in the pocket of her jeans, on the floor somewhere.

"Hello?"

"Have you seen the news? Was that really you? Are you okay?"

"Otto?"

"Charlotte, are you all right?"

Muzzy-headed, she rubbed her face. Hadn't it all been a dream? "Wait a minute. What? How did you—I mean, yeah, I'm okay. How did you hear about what happened?" It was the only conceivable reason Otto would be calling this early in the morning.

"It's all over the news, hon," he said. "They've been calling the theater. You're a genius, Charlotte."

"What are you talking about?"

"As publicity stunts go, this is over the top. I love it."

"But it wasn't—"

"I know. I'm teasing. You're really all right?"

"I—I think so."

"I know it's opening night, but if you're not up to coming out, don't sweat it."

Opening night. Almost as terrifying as dangling off a roof. "I'll be there, I think. I gotta go."

She clicked him off and went to the computer, to find two roommates already there, ogling over her. And Otto was right, the story was everywhere. Someone had gotten a cell phone picture of the guy in the mask—and Charlotte, looking flustered and windblown. It was all fairly dramatic. The more sedate Web sites had facts and figures, what had been stolen—a shipment of loose diamonds—and what the police knew, sparsely delivered news. Including Charlotte's name, her association with the theater, and her profession—playwright. There it was in the news; it had to be true, right?

Her phone rang three times in five minutes, friends wanting to know if she was okay, *really* okay. She put them off as quickly as she could, which probably convinced them that she really wasn't all right. They'd call again in an hour.

Then Dorian called. "Honey, are you okay?"

"I think so. Hey, do you have time for breakfast or lunch or something?" Anything?

"Well, not really, I'm afraid. I talked the DA into giving me the case. At least, when there is a case, I'll get it. Isn't that great? I have to get to the precinct and find out what they're doing. They'd better not screw this up. This could make my career."

I almost died, she wanted to mew. Her phone beeped to tell her of another incoming call. She checked—it was her mother this time. She canceled the call. "But you'll be there tonight, won't you?" she said to Dorian.

"Tonight?"

"The play, opening night." It must have seemed like such a small thing to him.

"Oh, right. Of course I'll be there. I'll meet you at the theater."

"And don't forget about the party afterward. Otto rented out Napoli's."

"Of course I'll be there."

After Dorian hung up, the phone rang again, a reporter this time. She told the woman to call the police. Then the police called, telling her to tell reporters to call the police, which was a relief.

Mostly, though, she read everything she could find about what had happened.

. . . .

THE MOST HELPFUL source was a Web site called "Rooftop Watch."
It tracked superhumans and masked vigilantes and villains, recorded
sightings, and gleefully spread all manner of gossip. *Her* masked man
had been seen two previous times. In both cases, he'd foiled residential
robberies by racing in, shining a high-powered flashlight at the would-
be burglars as they were breaking into the back doors of houses, then
racing out before the thieves could react. Their cover blown, the burglars ran, and so did the masked man, but by then the owners were
awake and on the phone with the police.

They were calling him Blue Collar, which seemed rude. It was a commentary on his wardrobe rather than his powers or personality. Nothing
like Speed or Blaze or Comet. There was a lot of speculation about who
he was, what he was doing. Most commentators in the know figured
he was new and starting small, foiling robberies and break-ins. He'd
work up to bigger feats—like snatching young playwrights from certain
death. Maybe he'd even get a real uniform someday.

The cell phone picture of him standing with Charlotte was too good
not to post all over the Internet a billion times. She hoped someone was
getting rich off it. The possibility of prosecuting the case was certainly
making Dorian happy.

She arrived at the theater two hours early and crept backstage, unsure
if she should gather everyone together for a manic pep talk or hide in a
closet. Unable to decide, she paced along an out-of-the-way section of
wall backstage, while stagehands and tech crew bustled.

She'd gotten her dress at a fancy consignment shop, which meant she
looked much richer than she actually was. Red, sleek, slinky, strapless.
She'd even found the heels to go with it in the right size. She'd been in
one of her good moods, thinking of the glamorous life and her possible
place in it. Now she felt a bit like a dyed poodle. Unnatural, vaguely
humiliated.

She'd been in a good mood when she met Dorian at a fund-raising
party for an arts-in-the-schools organization. She was there helping run
the party, and he was there to rub elbows, see and be seen, and all that.
She liked to think that they swept each other off their feet with their
mutual romantic notions.

The actors swooped in, Marta last of all, carrying on, and backstage
got loud after that.

Marta even rushed over to stage-hug her. "Charlotte, I can't believe you're even here after what happened! My God—what happened? Are you all right? If it were me, my nerves would be shot, I'd be traumatized, I'd be in bed for a week, how are you even here? Oh, where'd you get that dress? Nice. Oh my God, what time is it—" And she rushed off again.

Charlotte wondered—should she be more traumatized by what had happened? It really did seem like a dream.

Otto had slipped in earlier, unseen, phantomlike, working his director magic backstage. When he found Charlotte he asked, "Are you all right? Are you *really* all right?" She glared.

"You look great, by the way."

She still glared.

A half an hour before curtain, she didn't dare peek into the house to see if anyone was actually there, if anyone had actually deigned to come. And Dorian was going to be late. She had his ticket. They were supposed to sit in the back, cuddled together, watching her big debut. She'd had it all planned out.

But she couldn't honestly be surprised when her phone buzzed, showing Dorian's number.

"I'm really sorry, I'm going to be stuck at work for at least another hour. I'll come see the show another night. I'll make it up to you."

"Can you at least come to the party? It probably won't start till eleven or so."

"Sure, I'm sure I can make the party. I'll meet you there. Napoli's, right?"

"Right." And he hung up.

Ten minutes before curtain, Otto ran from the wings, beaming. She nearly stumbled away, the sight was so shocking.

"It's all right," he said, coming up and taking her hand. "It's going to be all right."

"What? What is?"

"We've sold out. The house is full. It's your adventure last night. You're famous. They're here because of you."

That didn't make her feel any better.

Otto continued backstage to the dressing rooms to tell the cast and jolt them into more spirited performances. Or greater heights of anxiety.

She couldn't stand it anymore, so she crept to the edge of the curtain and peeked out. And it was true. The house was full, only a handful of empty seats left scattered as the last people filtered in. And those two empty seats in back meant for her and Dorian. The murmurs of the crowd hushed over her.

The theater was full. But what if no one liked it?

Because she couldn't bear to watch, she waited backstage, pacing. Everything went well, she supposed, but all she heard from the faint voices reciting her lines on stage were the mistakes, awkward phrasing she should have fixed a long time ago, bad delivery that she couldn't do anything about. From backstage, applause sounded muted and lackluster.

Then it was all over. At last. Otto came at her, grinning and nearly shouting. "There you are! Come on, get out front!"

"What?"

"For the curtain call!" He took her hand and dragged her.

Opening night, of course the director and playwright would come out on stage as well.

"Smile!" he hissed. She scrounged together what poise she could.

Then they were under the stage lights, the cast around them applauding. Otto gestured, offering Charlotte to the audience, or the audience to her. They were on their feet, the whole audience on its feet, clapping and cheering. Someone pressed long-stemmed roses into her arms. She cradled the bundle like it was an infant.

They must have liked it.

She was still dazed as the curtain closed at last and the cast fell to laughing and embracing. Champagne appeared and Marta herself popped the cork—after shaking the bottle—letting the contents spray everywhere. The stage manager wouldn't be happy about that. People came to hug Charlotte, and she held them off with the shield of roses and tried to be gracious. She was suddenly exhausted. All that pacing backstage. But everyone else was buzzed and manic as squirrels, and the night was just starting.

She realized that she hadn't thought this far ahead. It was enough to have her play finished and actually staged, and she hadn't dared think any further than that, except to assume that it would all be a dismal failure. But, by all appearances, the play was a success. Shouldn't she be happy?

IF THE PLAY had been a failure, the invitation-only opening-night party would have been a wake, and they could have mourned in peace without having to talk to anyone but themselves. Since the play had been successful, it would be the most sensational and sought-after party of the month. Tonight would be a celebration. Charlotte tried to ignore a growing sense of foreboding.

Otto had reserved the restaurant, but Marta had rented the limo for them all to arrive in, them being Marta, the actors, Charlotte, Otto, and Otto's young actress wife, Helen. Part of why Otto was a good director was because he didn't automatically cast Helen in everything he did.

"Where's your handsome lawyer? I didn't see him at the theater," Helen asked, and Charlotte blushed.

"Working late."

Helen acknowledged this happily enough, but Otto gave her a sympathetic, almost pitying smile.

Otto had Helen on one arm and Marta on the other as he swept them up the sidewalk to the door of Napoli's. Harry and Fred tried to sweep Charlotte the same way, but she resisted, extricating herself from their grips in the restaurant's lobby.

"Dorian's meeting me here," she said, faking confidence.

"Wait for him inside," Harry said, pouting.

"Just another minute."

More and more people arrived, passing through the restaurant's lobby, checking their coats, hugging and kissing cheeks. Many were already drunk, all of them cheerful. There were reporters here, and photographers. Otto would get all the publicity he could hope for. It was fabulous. Charlotte paced. Her steps dragged, and the maître d' kept asking if he could get her anything. She almost gave up. She almost lost faith.

Then there he was, in his sweeping overcoat and intense face, a man with purpose. He held a bundle of roses.

"You came!" she said, maybe a little too brightly.

"Of course I did. You look wonderful." He pressed the roses into her arms and leaned in for a quick kiss on her cheek. He'd rushed, she could tell. He was still catching his breath and a faint sheen of sweat lay on his neck. "I'm sorry I missed the play. I'll make it up to you. How did it go?"

She took a deep breath. The thrill was finally starting to build. "It was amazing. It was brilliant, it was—" She sighed. "Come inside, help us celebrate." She took his hand and tried to urge him in.

"Honey, that's wonderful. But I'm not sure I'm up for a late night with all your theater friends. Wouldn't you rather have a quiet evening? We could celebrate in private, just the two of us."

Her heart melted at that, a little. But she might only ever have one big successful opening-night party. She couldn't be expected to pick between her dashing boyfriend and her opening-night party, could she?

"Just for a little while. Please?"

He finally slipped off his coat and gave it to the check clerk. Charlotte held the roses with one arm and him with the other as they entered the main dining room.

The room was full. She hadn't realized so many people were here— the cast and crew and all their significant others didn't account for everyone. How many invitations had Otto given out? He probably hadn't expected everyone to come. But the show was a success. They were hip and cool. Who knew? She recognized a handful of celebrities, the deputy mayor, a popular news anchor. And was that the masked hero Breezeway, in uniform, posing with some of the cast? Maybe her own rescuer would be here. But she looked and couldn't see him.

She could smell champagne as if it flowed from fountains. The place was in chaos, people sitting on tables, shouting across the room, accosting waitstaff bearing platters of finger food. No one should have noticed Charlotte and Dorian slipping in late. But they did.

"Charlotte!" Otto called from across the room, where he held court at a round table covered with a red satin cloth and a dozen champagne bottles. He was loud enough to draw the attention of the others, who turned to look.

"To our playwright! To the genius!" Otto raised a glass.

Marta, at her own table with a dozen fawning admirers, took up her own glass. "To the genius!"

And everyone raised glasses and cheered and applauded all over again. This was more than Charlotte had expected, more than she had imagined. She could only bask, silent. The playwright, wordless.

Beside her, Dorian looked at her and smiled. He put his arm around her shoulders and pulled her close.

"Congratulations," he whispered, posing for pictures with her, making sure the reporter spelled his name right.

The party went until dawn, but they left early. He brought her home to his place this time and made love to her more attentively than he had since their first weeks together.

BY MORNING, TEN different people had e-mailed Charlotte a photo going around the news Web sites of the masked hero on surveillance footage thwarting a convenience store robbery yesterday evening, the same time she'd been pacing backstage. The photo was black-and-white, grainy, and showed him standing with one foot on a guy who sprawled in front of the checkout counter. A gun could be seen nearby, as if it had fallen and skittered away from the would-be robber's gloved hand.

Is this the same guy? everyone wanted to know, and how would she know because all she saw was the mask. But she thought it was the same guy. He kept himself busy. She tried to put him out of her mind.

But she recognized the convenience store, on a corner a few blocks away from the theater. He'd been right there, almost.

The reviews of the play were all right, which was more than she'd hoped for, and while they didn't sell out again after the opening, the house was mostly full every night. Maybe that first night had sold out because of the novelty of her instant fame, if people were just coming to see the play written by that woman who was rescued by that Blue Collar vigilante. But if that was all the play offered, ticket sales would have bombed soon after. Which meant that maybe she knew what she was doing, and maybe everything was going to be all right. Weeks passed, and the play continued its respectable run.

Then people starting asking, "How is the next play coming along?"

And it wasn't. She stared at her laptop for hours, took her notepad to the park, the coffee shop, the library. She thought she had characters— another woman, another hero, another subversion of traditional gothic narratives, etcetera. But every line she wrote sounded just like what she'd already done, and the words didn't fit anymore.

She'd sit in her chair by the window all night—even the nights she spent at Dorian's—make notes in her notebook, and watch the sky grow light. If she was at Dorian's, he'd wake up, see her sitting wrapped in a blanket, staring instead of writing, and try to be helpful.

"You'll get there," he said. "You did it before, you can do it again." Like it was just a matter of arguing a case.

One morning at Dorian's, she'd made it to bed and was still there when he was nearly ready for his day.

"The DA wants to come see your show. I told him I could get him tickets." Looking in the mirror, he straightened his tie. "You can get tickets, right?"

"Sure," she said, emerging from blankets. "For when?"

"For tonight."

"That might be kind of tough."

"Come on, honey, surely you have some pull. You guys always hold a few tickets back, right?"

Maybe, but she didn't run the box office. She still had some of her comp tickets left for the run, but there might not be anything for tonight. "I'll see what I can do, but I'm not a superhero."

"Great. Text me when you get them, all right? Don't forget to lock up on your way out."

"Have a good day, Dorian." He gave her the appropriate kiss on her forehead and then was gone.

THE BOX OFFICE did have a pair of tickets for that evening. They were even decent seats. Charlotte was very apologetic, promising she'd have more notice next time, and that this was an emergency, and she was very grateful. On the other hand, the box office manager outdid herself apologizing in return, making sure the tickets were the best ones possible, and thanking her for the opportunity to be of service.

Dorian would have known what to do in this situation. The problem wasn't that Charlotte didn't have pull. The problem was she didn't know what to do with it.

The manager filed the tickets with Will Call, she texted Dorian, and went to her favorite coffee shop to write.

Then she saw him.

She was at a sidewalk table, chin resting on her hand, staring at the traffic moving along the tree-lined street, because staring somewhere else wasn't any less productive than staring at a blank page. She caught movement. It might have been the flickering of a set of leaves at the top of one of the trees, but it wasn't. It was a person on the roof across the way. Jeans, dark T-shirt, and a mask.

He seemed to realize that she saw him. He stood and ran, disappearing to the back of the roof.

She stood, jostling the table and tipping over her coffee, which streamed to the edge and dripped to the sidewalk. Grabbing her notebook and satchel, she ran across the street, dodging cars like a creature in a video game. At the first alley she came to, she ran to the back of the building to look, but of course he wasn't there. Just trash that hadn't made it into the Dumpsters and puddles from the last rain filling cracks in the asphalt. The back doors of various businesses, shut and blank.

Maybe if she waited here until after dark, she'd get caught by muggers, and the masked man would come to rescue her. She didn't want to leave, she didn't want to pretend that he was a ghost, that it hadn't happened, that she could move on.

"Hello?" she called. Her voice rattled in the empty space and no one answered.

DORIAN WAS WORKING late again and asked her to bring dinner—Thai takeout—to his office.

"He's a crazy superhuman vigilante. You know what they're like," he said when she told him the story.

She felt the need to defend the superhero. While not offending Dorian. "You're both working so hard to catch these guys, maybe you should work together. Pool your resources. Collaborate." That was a theater word. She should have used another.

He gave her a look, appalled and amused at once. A "yeah, right" and "don't be ridiculous."

That night, back at her own apartment, she tried to sleep, couldn't. She collected her notebook and sat by the window. Still didn't write a word, but sitting with a pen in hand at least made her feel productive. The moon was full; she could see every detail of the street, the apartment blocks, the row of shops and Laundromats with steel grates pulled over the doors; at night, all the colors washed out to various degrees of half-tone shading.

On the roof of a row of shops, a figure moved. Monochrome, like the rest of the scene. Black T-shirt. Charlotte couldn't see his face.

He was watching her. He was. And her heart fluttered at the thought.

SHE HAD SEEN him at all hours. Mostly on rooftops. She couldn't predict where he'd be, unless maybe she staged a convenience store robbery. But the odds of that ending badly were very, very high, so she didn't.

Instead, she went to the top of a parking garage on the fringes of downtown with a set of binoculars and scanned the surrounding rooftops. She might have become a vigilante herself, searching for crime, because if she found crime, she'd find him. She didn't see anything.

For another night, she sat at her bedroom window, wrapped in a blanket, waiting for a shadow to race across rooftops and strike a dramatic pose.

And she started writing. Just a few lines in her notebook.

Dorian took her to a charity banquet and introduced her to the mayor. She wore the red dress she'd worn on opening night, met the mayor, accepted compliments from the DA, and Dorian beamed. The evening was a strange echo of the first night they'd met, but different. *She* was different. An accessory instead of a novelty. She should have been thrilled—this was part of her dreams of a glamorous life, wasn't it? But she was distracted. It all seemed shallow.

For real drama, some disaster would strike the banquet. Some villain or group of thieves—maybe the same gang that had robbed the jewelry store—would storm the hall, divest the women of their jeweled necklaces and the men of their gold cufflinks, along with wallets and platinum cards and stock portfolios. They would take Charlotte hostage. The red dress made her stand out.

Then *he* would arrive, an epic battle would ensue, there'd be flames and bullets, she'd be trapped behind a burning door and he would—

"What are you looking for?" Dorian asked her.

"Oh. What? Nothing. Nothing." She'd been craning her neck, looking at the doors and windows for impending drama.

"You writers," Dorian said, squeezing her hand.

SOME NIGHTS, SHE went to the theater to take in the atmosphere, but avoided Otto because he always asked about the next play. She watched the old play from the house once, but otherwise sat backstage, well out of the way, and made notes. She was like an observer on a rooftop.

The text messages from Dorian continued. "Sry. Work ran late. Will make it up to you. xoxo."

So again, she took herself to dinner, to the same favorite café with the rooftop patio. It was raining, but she asked to sit on the patio anyway.

"But it's raining," the host said.

"I have an umbrella," she said.

She dried off a chair with a napkin and sat in a sheltered spot near the wall that housed the main part of the café, under her umbrella, drinking coffee. The petunias and daisies in the large planters at each corner drooped, and the sky grew grayer.

And there he was. He didn't seem to mind the rain. The T-shirt molded to him a little more, and water dripped off his arms and the edges of his mask. Quickly she stood, then thought maybe she shouldn't—she didn't want to scare him off. But when he didn't run, she didn't sit down.

"Hi," she said.

A moment passed. "Hi."

He seemed nervous; he kept looking away. So he was shy. That made sense. He had secrets to hide, no one could know who he was—it was all very romantic, she was sure. Beautiful, even right down to his jeans, to his ungraceful boots.

Then he said, "I have to go—"

"Wait!" But for what? For *her*? How did she talk a masked avenger into waiting for *her*? "Who are you?" She winced. So obvious.

He gave her a lopsided smile. "I can't say."

"But—" And what excuse would she give, about why she was different? Why was she any different, except that he'd once plucked her out of the air? "Why are you following me?" she said, surprised to say anything, even the first thing she thought of. She'd expected to let him flee.

"To make sure you're safe. That gang—they could come after you again."

"Really?"

He averted his eyes. So the answer was no. She hadn't thought so.

"If you're looking for them, trying to catch them, you should talk to Dorian. He's my—" She didn't want to say the word. She didn't want to shut the door. "My friend, he's an assistant DA, he's got the robbery case if it ever goes to trial. He's working with the police. He may have information you can use. Maybe you could work together." It seemed reasonable.

"I don't think so."

"Is it just because of the mask? Because you'd have to tell them who you are? I mean, do you really have to hide who you are?"

"It's traditional," he said, and now he sounded apologetic. The only expression she could see under the mask was a flat-lipped frown, a gaze somewhere between determined and resigned.

"I'm sorry, I shouldn't pry, but it's just—I'm sorry." It's just that he was strange, and she wanted to help him.

"I saw your play," he said then.

She wondered, How? Was he in the audience? In the rafters? How had she missed him? But what she asked was, "What did you think?"

"I liked it." What a sweet smile. He turned bashful again. "I'd never seen a play before."

"Really? *Really?* Oh my God, mine shouldn't have been your first play ever! How could you have never seen a play?"

"I guess I don't get out much," he said, which seemed ironic.

They just kept standing there in the rain. She lifted the umbrella and stepped closer to bring him under the shelter—he stepped back, as if afraid.

She tried not to be hurt. Tried not to take it personally. She swallowed her pride.

"I don't know anything about you." A statement containing all her questions. "I mean, where do you live? What do you do? Do you have a day job? A . . . a girlfriend? What's your name?"

He might as well have been an alien, a character, a face on a billboard. He seemed uncertain, pain in his eyes—biting his lips. He seemed to consider. When he returned, taking back the step he'd moved away, closing the distance between them, she thought he'd tell her everything. He moved quickly, with the reflexes that had saved her from crashing to the pavement. Touched her chin with gentle, calloused fingers.

She closed her eyes, waiting for that kiss, and so didn't see him run away. Only felt a draft on her face where there should have been warmth.

"Wait!" She saw a shadow fleeing through the mist, then he was gone, and she was alone, the only one stupid enough to stay on the rooftop in the rain.

THE NEXT EVENING, Dorian's text message about working late came later than she expected, but it came. It rained again, and Charlotte imagined the masked man out there in it. She watched the news for an hour, looking for signs of him. But he didn't seem to be busy tonight, or if he was, the network wasn't showing it. They were more interested in the flashier heroes, the Invincibles and Red Meteors, who had a sense of style and public relations. And she thought of Dorian in his courtroom attire, which was just as alluring as a vigilante costume, in its own way.

Then she wondered. Dorian had been so busy lately.

The masked man had brown eyes, Dorian had brown eyes. They were about the same height, and their chins—chagrined, she realized she couldn't say that she had ever noticed Dorian's chin before. It was a nice chin, average. She noticed the hero's chin because the mask drew attention to it.

The masks were deceptive. They seemed like they shouldn't be able to disguise anything, but it was more than a mask, it was a distraction. She had never, ever seen Dorian in jeans and a T-shirt. His version of casual involved Dockers, polo shirts, and loafers. Boating or golf attire. He always had a bit of polish because, as he said it, he never knew when he might run into someone who needed impressing. She could never imagine him standing out in the rain, wearing a T-shirt and a goofy smile.

Maybe that was the point. She had seen Marta in half a dozen shows, playing ingenues and dutiful daughters, unrecognizable from one role to the next.

Later that week, they didn't meet for dinner, but she came over to Dorian's place anyway, late, to spend the night. Dorian was in the kitchen, pouring himself a tumbler of scotch.

"You've been working late a lot," she said, watching for his reaction.

"Yeah," he said, in a mock long-suffering tone.

"What exactly do you do?" She winced because it sounded accusing.

"Paperwork, mostly, believe it or not. I meet with people all day so the paperwork gets put off. And the police work late. I like to keep track of them."

"Ah. I guess I've never had a sense of what goes on in a real job." She quirked a smile, trying to make it a joke.

"That's why you have writer's block. You need to get out in the real world and then you'd have something to write about."

She tried to remember how the masked man had smelled. She'd been close enough to smell his skin, his sweat. Maybe she could tell if he and Dorian smelled the same. But all she remembered from him was the smell of rain on fabric, and the sensation of warmth when he touched her.

Get out in the world so she'd have something to write about. Yeah.

WHILE DORIAN SLEPT, Charlotte was about to go sit by the window when Dorian's phone rang.

He seemed to be ready for it. "Hello? Yeah?" He rolled out of bed and took his phone into the next room. Sitting very still, she could hear.

"You got them? They're cornered and not surrendering . . . Of course I want to be there. Give me fifteen minutes." He came back into the bedroom and dressed quickly—he didn't even bother with a tie.

"What?" she said.

"Never mind. Go back to sleep. It's all right."

"But—"

He was out the door. He'd never even turned on the lights.

Something was happening. Or was about to happen.

Charlotte got up and went to the next room to turn on the TV, but whatever was going on, the news hadn't picked up on it yet. Dorian's laptop sat on the desk, and she went there next, fired it up, and checked "Rooftop Watch."

A dozen updates had been posted just in the last ten minutes. "It's those jewel thieves, the cops are there." "Any supers?" "On the lookout for supers." "The police seemed to be centered on 21st and Pine."

She was turning into one of those superhero stalkers who haunted Web sites like this and posted conspiracy theories. She didn't care.

Then she read the latest post: "Blue Collar's been sighted! Just for a second!"

Charlotte found her phone and called Dorian. Waited, and waited, but got no answer. And maybe that was her answer. She called a cab while getting dressed, reached the curb just as it pulled up, trundled into the backseat, and told the sleepy-looking driver the address.

"And hurry!" she said, like this was some spy movie. He sighed.

They didn't get there. The police cordoned off the area a block away. A dozen squad cars parked, flashing lights reflecting off the concrete walls of body shops and warehouses, red, white, and blue, fireworks and Christmas at once.

The driver glared at her like it was her fault. She paid him and left.

She ran, just to see how far she'd get until someone stopped her, which turned out to be pretty far, because no one was looking out to the streets for crazy women. They were all looking inward, to the unfolding drama. She joined the inner circle, the edge of the stage, and watched.

Six masked jewel thieves sprawled in a heap on the ground, their purple outfits streaked with dirt, their ray guns in a neat pile a few feet away, as though someone with superspeed had snatched them away and placed them there.

And there he was, her rescuer, standing over them and looking worn out rather than particularly heroic. His arms hung at his sides, and he seemed to be trying to catch his breath. A couple of suited men who might have been detectives stood across from the thieves, who seemed like prey that he'd caught and delivered to them. Also with the detectives was Dorian. Dorian and the masked man were looking at each other.

Then the masked man saw Charlotte. When he turned to look, so did everyone else. The jig was up.

Dorian called, "Charlotte! What are you doing here?"

The uniformed cops on either side of her looked her over and glared.

She didn't say anything, hardly noticed that the tableau had unfrozen, and police were now collecting the thieves, putting handcuffs on them, and shoving them into cars. That left Dorian, the vigilante, and Charlotte.

"I told you you guys should work together," she said lamely.

"Charlotte—" Dorian exclaimed again, a word that was a question, demanding explanation.

"Are you having an affair?" she asked him, because it was the only other thing she could think of.

"What? No! For God's sake, what gave you that idea?"

He was indignant enough that she believed him, but she also wasn't sure she'd be able to tell if he was lying. She watched actors on stage all day, and actors on stage did nothing but lie while convincing her they were telling the truth.

"It was all those late nights," she said, and tried to explain all at once, to both of them. "All those broken dates and the evasions and I thought, I thought something must be going on. Then I met *him*"—and she still didn't know his name—"and I thought, I don't know what I thought. You both have brown eyes."

He looked at the masked man, looked at Charlotte, and sounded a little forlorn when he said, "I told you, I was working late."

"And how many men have said that to how many women? It's like something out of a bad play." She stopped. Here they were, three on the stage at the close of the curtain, a gothic postmodern shambles. The police lights flashed and didn't seem real. She knew exactly what gels would make those colors on stage.

She walked away, upset at how disappointed she was and how foolish she felt. This all seemed so plain, so messy. Couldn't we make it . . . prettier, she had said to Otto.

She got to the end of the block when the masked man appeared in front of her. That was what it looked like, he just appeared, after a blur of motion.

"The thing is," he said, "I can't take you out to dinner. I can't be there for the openings of your plays. I can't answer the phone every time you call. I can't do any of that. But I can still . . . I can still try."

She could have a hero, or have someone who was always there to take her to dinner, but not both.

He took off his mask, and she didn't know him. He seemed young, but the faint stubble and even fainter crow's-feet—laugh lines—gave him rough edges. He was handsome. He was sad. She knew nothing about him.

One thing he could do, though, was stand over her broken body, striking a pose and looking tragically bereft before he flew off into the night. And it would be pretty, dramatically speaking.

She leaned in, hand on his chest. He stood still, body tense. She felt his heart racing—much faster than a normal person's. Faster than Dorian's. He still smelled like rain. She brushed her lips against his, which trembled in response. Barely a kiss. More like an apology.

Then she walked home, and nobody tried to mug her. She was almost disappointed.

CHARLOTTE AND DORIAN split up. Dorian prosecuted the jewel thieves and talked to the press about putting in for DA in a couple of years. He started dating a painter whose gallery shows were making news.

Charlotte finished the next play. Otto liked it. Marta liked it. It needed some work. She would have been worried if it hadn't.

This one was straight realism, which was a departure for her, and which meant not stringing the wires with lights when they flew the heroes in and out. She still had to have heroes, but this time she imagined what they said to each other when they sat on rooftops looking for jewel thieves. She imagined they talked about the weather and the girls they liked and how to avoid getting ID'd by the cops. The only non-superhero character in the play was the cop who was trying to figure out who they were. She never did.

A week into rehearsals, she sat on a chair at the edge of the stage, watching Otto block actors, listening to lines, following along in her copy of the script, making notes when she thought something else would sound better. She'd think something else would sound better long after the play had had its run and closed.

Otto had been on the same page for half an hour and was on his fourth try, arranging actors, repeating lines. In a minute he'd do something off the wall and unexpected and that would be the version that worked. All she had to do was wait, and wonder how it would all turn out.

Leaning back in her chair, she looked up into the rails, ropes, chains, and lights of the fly system, distant ladders and rafters lost in shadow, and saw a masked face looking back at her, smiling.

M. L. N. Hanover

New writer M. L. N. Hanover is the author of Unclean Spirits and Darker Angels, *the first and second in the Black Sun's Daughter sequence. An International Horror Guild Award winner, Hanover lives in the American Southwest.*

In the hard-edged story that follows, Hanover shows us that not only can obsession persist through a lifetime, but can perhaps sometimes last a little longer than that . . .

Hurt Me

There weren't many three-bedroom houses that a single woman could afford. 1532 Lachmont Drive was an exception. Built in the 1930s from masonry block, it sat in the middle of a line of houses that had once been very similar to it. Decades of use and modification had added character: basement added in the 1950s, called "finished" only because the floor was concrete rather than dirt; garage tacked on to the north side that pressed its outer wall almost to the property line; artificial pond in the backyard that had held nothing but silt since the 1980s. The air smelled close and musty, the kitchen vent cover banged in the wind, and the air force base three miles to the north meant occasional jet noise loud enough to shake the earth. But the floors were hardwood, the windows recently replaced, and the interiors a uniform white that made the most of the hazy autumn light.

The Realtor watched the woman—Corrie Morales was her name— nervously. He didn't like the way she homed in on the house's subtle defects. Yes, there had been some water damage in the bathroom once. Yes, the plaster in the master bedroom was cracking, just a little. The washer/dryer in the basement seemed to please her, though. And the bathtub was an old iron claw-footed number, the enamel barely chipped, and she smiled as soon as she saw it.

She wasn't the sort of client he usually aimed for. He was better with new families, either just-marrieds or first-kid types. With them, he could talk about building a life and how the house had room to grow in. A sewing room for the woman, an office for the man, though God knew these days it seemed to go the other direction as often as not. New families would come in, live for a few years, and trade up. Or traffic from the base—military people with enough money to build up equity and flip the house when they got reassigned rather than lose money by paying rent. He had a different set of patter for those, but he could work with them. New families and military folks. Let the other Realtors sell the big mansions in the foothills. Maybe he didn't make as much on each sale, but there were places in his territory he'd sold three or four times in the last ten years.

This woman, though, was hard to read: in her late thirties and seeing the place by herself; no wedding ring. Her face had been pretty once, not too long ago. Might still be, if she wore her hair a little longer or pulled it back in a ponytail. Maybe she was a lesbian. Not that it mattered to him, as long as her money spent.

"It's a good, solid house," he said, nodding as a trick to make her nod along with him.

"It is," she said. "The price seems low."

"Motivated seller," he said with a wink.

"By what?" She opened and closed the kitchen cabinets.

"Excuse me?"

"Motivated by what?" she said.

"Well, you know how it is," he said, grinning. "Kids grow up, move on. Families change. A place maybe fits in one part of your life, and then you move on."

She smiled as if he'd said something funny.

"I don't know how it is, actually," she said. "The seller moved out because she got tired of the place?"

The Realtor shrugged expansively, his mental gears whirring. The question felt like a trap. He wondered how much the woman had heard about the house. He couldn't afford to get caught in an outright lie.

"Well, they were young," he said. "Just got hitched, and they had all these ideas and plans. I don't like selling to newlyweds. Especially young ones. Too young to know what they're getting into. Better to go rent a few places, move around. Find out what you like, what you don't like."

"Bought it and didn't like it?"

"Didn't know quite what they were getting into," he said.

The sudden weariness around the woman's eyes was like a tell at a poker table. The Realtor felt himself relax. Divorced, this one. Maybe more than once. Alone now, and getting older. Maybe she was looking for someplace cheap, or maybe it was just the allure of new beginnings. That he was wrong in almost every detail didn't keep him from playing that hand.

"My wife was just the same, God rest her," he said. "When we were kids, she'd hop into any old project like she was killing snakes. Got in over her head. Hell, she probably wouldn't have said yes to me if she'd thought it through. You get older, you know better. Don't get in so many messes. They were good kids, just no judgment."

She walked across the living room. It looked big, empty like this. Add a couch, a couple chairs, a coffee table, and it would get cramped fast. But right now, the woman walked across it like it was a field. Like she was that twenty-year-old girl with her new husband outside getting the baggage or off to work on the base. Like the world hadn't cut her down a couple times.

He could smell the sale. He could taste it.

"Lot of rentals in the neighborhood," she said, looking out the front window. He knew from her voice that her heart wasn't in the dickering. "Hard to build up much of a community when you're getting new neighbors all the time."

"You see that with anything near the base," he said, like they were talking about the weather. "People don't have the money for a down payment. Or some just prefer renting."

"I can't rent anymore."

"No?"

"I smoke," she said.

"That's a problem these days. Unless you've got your own house, of course."

She took a deep breath and let it out slowly. The Realtor had to fight himself not to grin. Here we go.

"Wrap it up," she said. "I'll take it."

MR. AND MRS. Kleinfeld had lived at 1530 Lachmont Drive for eight years, making them the longest-standing residents of the block. To them, the U-Haul that pulled up on Sunday morning was almost unremarkable. They ate their toast and jam, listened to the preacher on the radio, and watched the new neighbor start unloading boxes. She wore a pair of old blue jeans, a dark T-shirt with the logo of a long-canceled television show across the front, and a pale green bandana. When the breakfast was over, Mrs. Kleinfeld turned off the radio and cleaned the plates while Mr. Kleinfeld ambled out to the front yard.

"'Morning," he said as the new woman stepped down from the back of the truck, a box of underpacked drinking glasses jingling in her hand.

"Hi," she said with a grin.

"Moving day," Mr. Kleinfeld said.

"It is," she said.

"You need a hand with any of that?"

"I think I'm good. Thanks, though. If it turns out I do . . . ?"

"Me and the missus are here all day," he said. "Come over anytime. And welcome to the neighborhood."

"Thanks."

He nodded amiably and went back inside. Mrs. Kleinfeld was sitting at the computer, entering the week's expenses. A trapped housefly was beating itself to death against the window, angry buzzing interrupted by hard taps.

"It's happening again," Mrs. Kleinfeld said.

"It is."

It took her the better part of the day to put together the basics. Just assembling the new bed had taken over an hour and left her wrist sore. The refrigerator wouldn't be delivered until the next day. The back bedroom, now a staging area, was thigh-deep in packed one-thing-and-another. There was no phone service except her cell. The electricity wasn't in her name yet. But by nightfall, there were clothes in the closet, towels in the bathroom, and her old leather couch in the living room by the television. She needed to take the U-Haul back, but it could wait for morning.

She walked briskly through the house—*her* house—and closed all the blinds. The slick white plastic was thick enough to kill all the light from the street. The new double-glazed windows cut out the sounds of traffic. It was like the walls had been suddenly, silently, transported someplace else. Like it was a space capsule, a million miles from anything human, cut off from the world.

She turned on the water in the tub. It ran red for a moment, rust in the pipes, and then clear, and then scalding hot. She stripped as the steam rose. Naked in front of the full-length mirror, she watched the scars on her legs and elbows—the tiny circles no bigger than the tip of a lit cigarette; the longer, thinner ones where a blade had marred the skin—blur and fade and vanish. Her reflected body softened, and the glass began to weep. She turned off the water and eased herself into the bath slowly. The heat of it brought the blood to her skin like a slap. She laid her head against the iron tub's sloping back, fidgeting to find the perfect angle. She had soap, a washcloth, shampoo, the almond-scented conditioner that her boyfriend, David, liked. She didn't use any of them. After about ten minutes, she turned, leaning over the edge to reach for the puddle of blue cloth that was her jeans. A pack of cigarettes. A Zippo lighter with its worn Pink Martini logo. The click and hiss of the flame. The first long drag of smoke curling through the back of her throat. She tossed cigarette pack and lighter onto the floor, and lay back again. The tension in her back and legs and belly started to lose its grip.

Around her, the house made small sounds: the ticking of the walls as they cooled, the hum of her computer's cooling fan, the soft clinking of the water that lapped her knees and breasts. Smoke rose from her cigarette, lost almost instantly in the steam. The first stirrings of hunger had just touched her belly when the screaming started, jet engines ramping up from nothing to an inhuman shriek between one breath and the next. Something fluttered in her peripheral vision, and she scrambled around, dropping her cigarette in the tub and soaking the floor with water.

Something moved in the mirror. Something that wasn't her. The condensation made it impossible to see him clearly. He might have had pale hair or he might have been bald. He might have jeans or dark slacks. The shirt was white where it wasn't red. The movement of balled fists was clearer than the hands themselves, and somewhere deep in the airplane's roar, there were words. Angry ones. Corrie yelped, her feet slipping under her as she tried to jump clear.

The noise began to fade as suddenly as it had come. The rumbling echoes batting at the walls more and more weakly. The mirror was empty again, except for her. She took a towel, wrapping herself quickly. Her blood felt bright and quick, her heart fluttering like a bird, her breath fast and panic-shallow. Her mouth tasted like metal.

"Hello?" she said. "Is someone in here?"

The floor creaked under her weight. She stood still, waiting for an answering footstep. The water pooled around her feet, and she began to shiver. The house had grown viciously cold.

"Is anyone here?" she said again, her voice small and shaking.

Nothing answered her but the smell of her spent cigarette.

"All right, then," she said, hugging her arms tight around herself. "Okay."

"Mom. *Listen* to me. Everything's fine. We're not breaking up," she said, willing her voice to be more certain than she was.

"Well, you move out like this," her mother said, voice pressed small and tinny by the cell connection. "And *that* house? I think it's perfectly reasonable of me to be concerned."

Corrie lay back on the couch, pressing the tips of her fingers to her eyes. Sleeplessness left her skin waxy and pale, her movements slow. She had taken the day off work, thinking she would finish unpacking, but the boxes were still where they had been the day before. Afternoon sun spilled in through the windows, making the small living room glow. The refrigerator had arrived an hour before and hummed to itself from the kitchen, still empty.

"It's just something I need to do," Corrie said.

"Is he beating you?"

"Who? David? *My* David?"

"People have habits," her mother said. She raised her voice when she lectured. "They imprint. I did the same thing when I was young. All my husbands were alcoholics, just like my father was. I like David very much. He's always been very pleasant. But you have a *type*."

"I haven't dated anyone seriously since Nash. I don't have a type."

"What about that Hebrew boy? Nathaniel?"

"I saw him a total of eight times. He got drunk, broke a window, and I never talked to him again."

"Don't turn into a lawyer with me. You know exactly what I mean. There's a kind of man that excites you, and so of course you might find yourself involved with that kind of man. If David's another one like Nash, I think I have a right to—"

Corrie sat up, pressing her hand at the empty air as if her mother could see the gesture for *stop*. The distant music of an ice-cream truck came from a different world, the jaunty electronic tune insincere and ominous.

"Mother. I don't feel comfortable talking about the kind of man that does or doesn't excite me, all right? David is absolutely unlike Nash in every possible way. He wouldn't hurt me if I asked him to."

"Did you?" her mother snapped.

"Did I what?"

"Did you ask him to hurt you?"

The pause hung in the air, equal parts storm and silence.

"Okay, we're finished," Corrie said. "I love you, Mom, and I really appreciate that you're concerned, but I am *not* talking about—"

"You are!" her mother shouted. "You are talking about *everything* with me! I have spent too much time and money making sure that you are all right to pretend that there are *boundaries*. Maybe for other people, but not for us, *mija*. Never for us."

Corrie groaned. The quiet on the end of her cell phone managed to be hurt and accusing.

"I'm sorry," she said. "I understand that you're scared about this. And really, I understand why you're scared. But you have to trust that I know what I'm doing. I'm not twenty anymore."

"Did you or did you not ask David to hurt you?"

"My sex life with David has been very respectful and loving," Corrie said through gritted teeth. "He is always a perfect gentleman. The few times that we've talked—just talked—about anything even a little kinky, he's been very uncomfortable with including even simulated violence in our relationship. Okay? Now can we *please* drop—"

"Is that why you left him?"

"We're not breaking up."

"Because that's the other side, isn't it?" her mother said, talking fast. "You find someone who isn't your type, and you put yourself with him because he's good and clean and healthy, and then there you are being good and clean and healthy. Like eating wheat germ every meal when you really want a steak."

"All right, I'm lost now," she said, her voice taking on a dangerous buzz. "Are you saying that David's an abusive shit, or that he's too good for me? What's your argument?"

She could hear her mother crying now. Not sobs. Nothing more than the little waver in tone that meant tears were in her eyes.

"I don't know why you're doing this," her mother said. "Why you moved out of David's apartment. Why you're in that house. I'm afraid you've gone to a very dark place." The last words were so thin and airless, Corrie had to take a deep breath.

"Maybe I have," she said, drawing the words out. "But it's all right. I'm not scared anymore."

"Shouldn't you be? Is there nothing to be frightened of?"

Corrie stood. It was only four steps to the bathroom door. With the lights off, the full-length mirror showed her in silhouette, the brightness of day behind her, and her features lost in shadow. There was no other shape, no man with balled fists or knives. No promises that the damage was a sign of love. No cigarette burns or dislocated fingers or weekends of sex she was afraid to refuse. It was just a mirror. She was the only thing in it.

Is there nothing to be frightened of?

"Don't know," Corrie said. "I'm finding out."

"OH," MR. KLEINFELD said, suddenly off his stride. "So you *knew* it was . . ."

"Haunted?" the new neighbor—Corrie, her name was—said. "Sure. I mean, just in general terms."

Mr. Kleinfeld smiled, but his eyebrows were crawling up his forehead. Across the table, his wife poured out cups of tea for the three of them; her smile might have meant anything.

"Is that how you heard about it?" Mrs. Kleinfeld asked. "You're one of those 'ghost hunters?'"

Sunlight pressed through the still air along with the distant chop of a helicopter formation. The new neighbor took the proffered cup and sipped at it. His wife put two small silver spoonfuls of sugar into his, stirred it twice neatly, and handed him his cup.

"Not really," the new neighbor said. "It was just one of those things you hear about, you know? In the air. I don't even know where I stumbled onto it the first time, but the Realtor was pretty up-front."

"Was he?" Mr. Kleinfeld said. That had never happened before either.

"Sure. I mean, there weren't a lot of gory details. I asked about why the price was low, and he said something about ghost stories and the old tenants getting freaked out and leaving."

"The women," Mrs. Kleinfeld said. "It doesn't seem to care about men, but it *hates* women."

"It?" the new neighbor said, and Mr. Kleinfeld watched his wife settle back into her chair. The first part of the meeting might not have gone along its usual path, but they were back in familiar territory now.

"There is a restless spirit in that house," Mrs. Kleinfeld said. "Has been since before we came. It never bothers the men. They never see it."

"The *girls*, though," Mr. Kleinfeld said, shaking his head the way he always did. "I could make a list of the young women we've had banging on our door in the middle of the night, scared out of their wits. It's not a fit house for a girl to live in. Especially alone."

He sipped his tea, but it was still scalding. He blew across its surface.

"Weird," the new neighbor said. "Any particular reason anyone knows about? Ancient Indian burial ground?"

His wife nodded slowly, the steam rising from her teacup swirling around her face. The chop of the helicopters grew gradually louder. Mr. Kleinfeld shifted back a degree in his chair. His part was done for now, and just as well. The missus was better at getting through to people than he was. She always had been.

"There's a story," she said. "I don't know how much of it's true and how much of it's fancied up, but I've never heard or seen anything to contradict it. Twenty years ago, there was a couple of young people moved into that house you're in today. Young man and his wife. Well, it wasn't long before the wife started showing up at the grocery store in big sunglasses. Wearing long sleeves in the middle of the summer. That sort of thing."

"Lots of domestic abuse in the world," the new neighbor said. "Doesn't make for a million haunted houses." Her tone was light, but Mr. Kleinfeld heard something strong under it. Maybe skepticism. Maybe something else.

"He was an *evil* man," Mrs. Kleinfeld said. "People used to hear them fighting. They say he used to try to hide the worst of the screaming under the jet noise, but the whole neighborhood knew. One fellow who lived on the other side, where that nice Asian family is now, tried to make an issue of it, and the man threatened to cut his nose off. And then one night they were gone. Man and wife both, vanished from the face of the earth like they'd never been. A few months later, her people came and packed up all the furniture and put the place up for sale. Rumor was that the wife was in some sort of asylum out West, with her mind all gone to putty, talking about demons and Satan. She never did get out of that place."

The new neighbor was caught now, her expression sharp as a pencil point. Mrs. Kleinfeld had to stop for a moment while the helicopters passed overhead, the blades cutting through the high air with enough violence to drown out their words. Or their screams, for that matter.

"Next people who moved in were an older couple with a girl just in high school," she said, her voice loud enough to carry over the falling racket as the copters flew on. "Six months they were there. Not more. The mother said she'd have tried to stand it, but the spirit started coming after the daughter too, and that was that. Sold the place at a loss and moved across to the other side of the base. Only time the place has had the same owner for more than a year since then was five years back when there were four young men sharing the place, and even then, I saw their girlfriends leaving in the middle of the night, crying too hard to stop."

"What does it do to them?" the new neighbor asked. The hardness was still there, but it wasn't skepticism. Something more immediate, more demanding. Something like hunger.

"It *comes* for them," Mrs. Kleinfeld said, "and thank God they can feel it. No one's ever stayed long enough to know what it would do if it caught them, but there are nights I can feel it hating all the way over here. I'm in my bed at night saying my prayers, and it's like someone put ice against the wall. You couldn't pay me to stay a night in that place. Not for a million dollars. Something lives in that house, and it hates women."

The new neighbor nodded, more, Mr. Kleinfeld thought, to herself than to him or his wife. There was a brightness in her eyes. Not fear. Maybe even pleasure. The new neighbor's smile disturbed him more than his wife's story ever did. He cleared his throat, and she seemed to wake up a little. Her smile widened and became less authentic.

"Have you seen anything yet?" he asked. "Anything out of the ordinary?"

"Me? No," she said. "Not a thing."

THE COLD FRONT came on Friday, almost a week later; vicious winds blasting down from a cloudless sky. Gritty air ripped at the trees, stripping off leaves that were still turning from green to yellow and red and gold; the glories of autumn cut short and shredded. The low Western sun turned bloody as it fell, and Corrie wheeled her car into the undersized garage like a child pulling up a blanket. The thin walls were less protection than the idea of them. Every new gust battering against the house made the garage creak. Dust settled from the frame roof. She scurried from car to kitchen, hunched against the sound of the wind.

Once she got into the house itself, she unfurled. The wind still threw handfuls of dirt against the windows, the thick plastic blinds shuffled and clicked in the drafts, but the masonry walls seemed beyond any violence nature could contrive, solid and sober as a prison. Corrie turned on every light as she walked through the house. She examined each room in turn: the broken-down boxes in the spare bedroom, the legal pads and laptop docking station in her makeshift office, the sheets and blankets in the linen closet. In the kitchen, she counted the knives on the magnetic rack and checked the oven. In her bedroom, she squatted, her eye on a level with the unmarked bedspread. She took her shotgun from its place under the bed, counting out the shells under her breath as she unloaded it and loaded it again. In the bathroom, she lingered in front of the mirror for over a minute, her fingertips on the glass, eyes unfocused and attention turned inward. Nothing had moved. Nothing was missing. Even the raging wind hadn't so much as rolled a pencil.

She microwaved a plate of lasagna, poured herself a glass of wine, and sat down on the couch. A few bites, and she was up again, pacing. Restless. Frustrated. Outside, the sun slipped lower.

"I know you're here," she said to the empty air. "I know you can hear me."

The wind shrieked and murmured. The window blinds shuddered. The air smelled of tomato sauce a little, but burned at the edges— acid with a touch of smoke. She stood in the middle of the room, jaw clenched. Silent.

The moment lasted years before the hint of a smile touched her mouth and a mad, reckless light came into her eyes. She walked back to the couch, picked up her plate, and took it to the kitchen. She ate two more bites standing at the sink, and then dropped the plate onto the brushed steel with a clatter. The faucet swung easily, cold water drowning the food. Reddened bits of meat and pale sheets of pasta swum in a cold, ugly soup and then settled, clogging the drain. She looked at the mess and deliberately stepped back, leaving it there. Her chin rose, daring the emptiness around her.

Something within the house shifted. Walls that had been only block and plaster and paint turned their attention to her. The windows hid behind their blinds like closed eyes. She kicked off her shoes, chuckling to herself. The floor felt colder than it should have. The glass of wine still rested on the coffee table; she scooped it up, taking her purse in the other hand. The furnace kicked on, blowers roaring a thousand miles away.

In the kitchen, she leaned against the counter beside the sink. Goose bumps covered her arms and thighs. Her breath was coming fast and shallow and shaking a little. She lit a cigarette and then sipped the cool, astringent wine, rolling it in her mouth, feeling the alcohol pressing through the soft, permeable membranes of her flesh. When she swallowed, her throat went a degree warmer. She set the cigarette between her lips and stretched out a hand, lifting the half-full glass. Red trembled for a moment, as she slowly, deliberately, poured it out, the wine spilling over the floor and staining the tiles. She dropped the glass into the sink with her ruined dinner and stepped forward, grinding the soles of her feet into the puddle.

The storm outside sounded like a warning. She shifted her hips, twisted at the waist, dancing in the mess. She rolled her weight back and forth, humming to herself, and raised her arms over her head. Her joints loosened, her belly grew warm and heavy. Her nipples hardened and her breath became visible and feather-white in the sudden arctic chill. Voices came from somewhere nearby, raised in anger, but distant.

Still dancing, she pressed one hand to her belly, took the cigarette between her fingers, and drew the smoke back into her. The taste of it was like drinking fire. She flicked the ash, watching the soft gray fall down, down, down into the wide red puddle at her feet.

Not wine.

Blood.

He stood framed by the basement door. A young man, and ageless. His shoulders were broad as a bull, his pale hair cut close to the skull. The dark slacks she'd seen in the mirror were tight and strained across the hip, as if designed to point out the thing's barely restrained erection. With every deep, heaving breath, blood sheeted down his body from the hole where his heart should have been. She had the impression of corrupted meat beneath that pale skin. His lips curled back in wordless rage, baring teeth too sharp to be human.

The warmth within her was gone. Her face was pale, and the electric shock of fear turned her dance to stillness. The man shook his head at her once, slowly back and forth. When he opened his mouth and howled, she retreated two quick involuntary steps, the countertop digging at the small of her back. Hatred radiated from him. Hatred and malice and the promise of violence. The tiles between them were the slick red of fresh slaughter.

When she spoke, her voice trembled. It sounded very small, even to her.

"Don't like it, huh?"

The ghost shifted his head side to side, neither nod nor shake, but stretching. Like an athlete preparing for some terrible effort. A clearer threat than balled fists.

"W-what," she tried to say, then crossed her arms and took a fast, nervous drag on the cigarette. She lifted her chin in defiance. "What're you gonna do about it?"

His eyes moved across her body like she was something he owned. The hissing sound of his breath came from everywhere.

"So, what? You want to hurt me? Come on, then," she said, her voice taking on a little strength. "If you're gonna do it, *do* it!"

He stepped into the room, filling the doorway. The death-blood, slick on his belly, glittered. He bared his teeth, growling like a dog.

"You want to hurt me? Then hurt me," she yelled. "*Hurt me!*"

The ghost screamed and rushed across the room toward her. She felt its rage and hatred surrounding her, swallowing her. She saw its hand rising to slap her down, and she flinched back, her eyes closed, and braced for the blow. Every scar on her skin tingled like someone had touched them with ice. Filthy water poured into her mouth, her nose, corrupted and sour with decay. She felt the spirit pressing against her, pushing into her skin. Its rage lifted her like a wave.

And then it was gone.

She stood in the kitchen, her body shaking and her ragged breath coming in sobs. She was terribly cold. The wine on her toes—only wine—was half-dried and sticky. Storm wind battered at the windows, the walls. The furnace rumbled, fighting against the frigid air. She sank slowly, her back against the cabinet, and hugged her knees. A stray tear fell down her cheek and she shuddered uncontrollably twice.

Then, between one breath and the next, her mouth relaxed. Her body released. The breaking tension was more than sexual.

She started laughing: a deep, satisfied sound, like the aftermath of orgasm.

SUNDAY MORNING BROUGHT the first snow of the season. The thick, wet flakes appeared just before dawn, dark against the bright city back-splash of the clouds, and transformed to a perfect white once they had fallen. After the morning's toast and tea and sermon, Mr. Kleinfeld, wrapped in his good wool overcoat, lumbered out after breakfast, snow shovel over his shoulder. He cleared his walkway and his drive, then the stretch of sidewalk in front of his house. The trees all around were black-barked and frosted with snow, and very few cars passed, the tracks of their tires leaving white furrows and never digging so deep as the asphalt.

Finished with his own house, he made his way through the ankle-high snow to his neighbor's. No lights glowed in the house, no tracks marked her walk. Her driveway hadn't been used. He hesitated, not wanting to wake her, but it was almost midday. He rang the bell, and when no answer came, mittened manfully on the door. No one came. He shook his head and put himself to work. The clouds above were bright as the snow when he finished, the air not yet above the freezing point, but warmer all the same.

His wife met him at the door with a cup of hot cocoa, just as he'd known she would. He leaned the snow shovel by the door, took the warm mug, and kissed his wife's dry cheek.

"I don't think our new neighbor made it home last night," he said. He sat in his chair. "I figure she's seen it. Won't be long now before she moves on."

It was a conversation they'd had before, and he waited now for his wife's agreement, her prediction: two more months, another month, a week. The missus was better at judging these things than he was. So he was surprised when she stood silent for a long moment, shaking her head.

"I don't know," she said. "I just do not know . . ."

DAVID'S APARTMENT STILL showed the gaps where she had been. His clothes still hung in only half of the bedroom closet, the hangers moving into the emptiness she had left only slowly, as if hoping that her blouses and slacks and dresses might come back. The corner where her desk had once been was still vacant, the four hard circles that the legs had pressed into the carpet relaxed out a little, but not gone. The kid upstairs was practicing his guitar again, working on power chords that had driven her half-crazy when she'd lived there. They seemed sort of cute now.

"He's getting better," David said.

She rolled over, stuffing the pillow under her head and neck as she did. A thin line of snow ran along the windowsill—the first of the season. David, beside her, nodded toward the ceiling.

"He made it all the way through 'Jesus of Suburbia' last week," he said.

"All five parts?"

"Yep."

"Kid's going places," she said.

"Please God that it's places out of earshot."

She brushed her fingertips across his chest. His skin was several tones darker than hers, and the contrast made her hand seem paler than she was, and her scars as white as the snow. He had his first gray hair in among the black, just over his ear. His dark eyes shifted over to her, his smile riding the line between postcoital exhaustion and melancholy. Quick as the impulse, she rolled the few more inches toward him and kissed his shoulder. He raised his eyebrows the way he always did when he knew that she was nervous.

"What's your plan for the day?" he asked.

"Housework," she said. "You?"

"Get up early and hit the Laundromat," he said.

She nodded.

"And since that didn't work?"

"Do an emergency load in the sink to get through work tomorrow," he said. "I've got to meet up with Gemma at three to get back my scanner."

"You'll need to get hopping. It's past noon now."

"Another few minutes won't make a difference," he said, putting his hand over hers. He wasn't pretty—his face too wide, his nose bent where it had broken as a child and never been put right, his jaw touched by the presentiment of jowls. Handsome, maybe, in an off-putting way. "Is there something to talk about?"

"Is," she said.

He took a long, slow breath and let it out slowly. Not a sigh so much as the preparatory breath of a high diver. Or a man steeling himself for bad news.

"I think you should come over tonight," she said. "Take a look at the place. Bring your laundry, too."

He sat up. The blankets dropped to his lap. She looked at him, unable to read his expression.

"You're changing the rules?" he said. Each word was as gentle as picking up eggs.

"No, I'm not. I always said that the not coming over part was temporary. It's just . . . time. That's all."

"So. You really *aren't* breaking up with me?"

"Jesus," she said. She took the pillow from under her head and hit him with it lightly. Then she did it again.

"It *is* traditional," he said. "Girl gets a house without consulting her boyfriend, moves all her stuff out, tells him he can't come over. Says she's 'working through something' but won't say what exactly it is? It's hard not to connect those dots."

"And the part where I tell you in simple declarative sentences that I'm not breaking up with you?"

"Goes under mixed signals," he said.

She took a deep breath. On the street, a siren rose and fell.

"Sorry," she said. She got up from the bed, pulling one of the sheets with her and wrapping it around her hips. "Look, I understand that this has been hard. I've asked for a lot of faith."

"You really have."

"And given that I don't have an entirely uncheckered past, and all," she said. "I see why you would freak. You and my mother both."

"Your mother?"

"She's been reading me the riot act ever since she heard about it. She really likes you."

He leaned back, surprise and pleasure in his expression.

"Your mother *likes* me?"

"Focus, sweetheart. I'm apologizing here."

"And I don't mean to interrupt," he said.

Relief had left him giddy. Between his brave face and her attention being elsewhere, she'd managed to ignore the sadness and dread that had been seeping into him. Now that it was lifting a little, she saw how deep it had gone. She found her pants in a heap on the floor, sat down at the dressing table and lit a cigarette. The taste of the smoke helped her to think. When she spoke, her voice was lower.

"I've had a rough ride this life, you know? I used to be ashamed of that. I used to think that after Nash I was . . . broken. Damaged goods. Like that. And feeling like that has . . ."

She stopped, shook herself, laughed at something, and took another drag.

"Feeling like that has *haunted* me," she said, with an odd smile.

"And this house is part of not feeling that way?"

"It is."

"Then I already like it," he said. "Sight unseen. If it helps you see yourself the way I see you, then it's on my side."

Corrie chuckled and shook her head.

"That might be going a little far," she said. "But anyway. I want you to come over. I want you to see it. You should bring a sweater. It gets kind of cold sometimes."

"I'm there."

"*And* I want you to think about whether you'd like to move in."

"Corrie?"

"There's enough room. The neighborhood's a little sketchy, and the jet noise sucks, but not worse than the jukebox hero practicing all the time."

"Corrie, are you saying you still want to live with me?"

Her smile was tight and nervous.

"Not asking for a decision," she said. "But I'm opening negotiations."

He slipped to the side of the bed, slid to the floor at her feet, and laid his head in her lap. For a long moment, neither of them moved or spoke; then Corrie wiped her eyes with the back of her hand.

"Come on, silly," she said. "You've got to get ready for Gemma. Go get that scanner back."

"I do," he said with a sigh. "Come shower with me?"

"Not today," she said. And when he raised his eyebrows, "I want to smell like you when I get home."

1532 LACHMONT DRIVE seethed around her. Every noise—the hum of the refrigerator, the distant roar of the furnace, the ticking of the wooden floors as the push-pull of heat and cold adjusted the boards— had voices behind them, screaming. The faintest smell of hair and skin burning touched the air. She knew they were meant to be hers.

Corrie hung her coat in the closet. A shape flickered in the basement doorway, dark eyes and inhuman teeth. She set a kettle on the stovetop and smoked a cigarette while it heated. When the clouds outside broke, the doubled light of sky and snow pressed in at the blinds. The kettle whistled. She took a mug out of the cupboard, put in a bag of chamomile tea, and poured the steaming water in. When she sat down, there was blood on the floor. A bright puddle, almost too red to be real, and then a trail as wide as a man's hips where the still living man had been dragged across to the basement door. When she looked up, the air had a layer of smoke haze a foot below the ceiling. It might have been her cigarette. It might have been gun smoke. She sipped her tea, savoring the heat and the faint sweetness.

"Fine," she said.

She stood up slowly, stretching. The stairs down to the basement were planks of wood painted a dark, chipping green. The years had softened the edges. The basement had none of the brightness of the day above it. Even with the single bare bulb glowing, the shadows were thick. The furnace roar was louder here, and the voice behind it spat rage and hatred. She followed the trail of blood to the corner of the basement, where washer and dryer sat sullen in the gloom. She leaned down, put her shoulder to the corner of the dryer, and shifted it.

The metal feet shrieked against the concrete. The scar under it was almost three feet wide, a lighter place where the floor had been broken, taken up, and then filled in with a patch of almost-matching cement. She sat down on the dusty floor. There was blood on her hands now, black and sticky and copper-smelling. A spot of white appeared on the odd concrete and began to spread: frost. She put her hand on it like she was caressing a pet.

"We should probably talk," she said. "And when I say that, I mean that *I* should talk, and you, for once, should listen."

Something growled from the corner by the furnace. A shadow detached from the gloom and began pacing like a tiger in its cage. She sipped her tea and looked around the darkness, her gaze calm and proprietary.

"It's funny the things they get wrong, you know? They remember that you threatened Joe Arrison, but instead of his cock, you were going to cut off his nose. They know I went to the Laughing Academy, but they don't remember that I got out. Apparently, I was going on about Satan or something. 'Mind gone to putty.'"

She stroked the concrete. The frost was spreading. A dot of red smeared it at the center, blood welling up from the artificial stone.

"And you really screwed me up, you know?" she said. "Shooting you really was worse than I thought it would be. I was *so* scared that someone would find you. I had nightmares all the time. I'd see someone who looked a little like you or I'd smell that cheap-ass cologne you liked, and I'd start panicking. I even tried to kill myself once. Didn't do a very good job of it.

"I was one messed up *chica*. Every couple weeks, I'd do a search online. I just *knew* that there was going to be something. Bones found at 1532 Lachmont Drive. So what do I find instead? Ghost stories. There was one that even had a drawing of you. And so I *knew*, right?"

The shadow shrieked at her, its mouth glowing like there was something burning inside it. The blood at the center of the frost became a trickle. Corrie let the icy flow stain her fingers.

"I was so freaked out," she said, laughing. "I spent years putting myself back together, and here you still were. I don't think I slept right for a month. And then one day, something just clicked, you know? I've got a job. I can buy a house if I want."

She sipped at her tea, but it had gone cold. She was sitting in a spreading pool of gore now, the blood spilling out to the corners of the room. More blood than a real body could contain. It soaked her pants and wicked up her shirt, chilling her, but not badly. The shadow hunched forward, ready to leap.

"David's coming over tonight," she said. "I wasn't going to let him until I was sure it was safe. But tonight I'm going to make him dinner, and we're probably going to get a little high, watch a DVD, something like that. And then I'm going to fuck him in your bedroom. And you? You're going to *watch*."

The blood rushed up. It was almost ankle-deep now, tiny waves of red rising up through the basement. Corrie smiled.

"You'll really hate him," she said. "He is everything you could never be, and he really, really loves me. And you know what? I love him too. And we're going to be here, maybe for years. Maybe forever. And we're going to do everything you couldn't. And we're going to do it right. So, seriously. How's that for revenge?"

The shadow screamed, rising up above her, blotting out the light. She could almost feel its teeth at her neck. She scratched.

"You're *dead*, fucker," she whispered to the darkness. "You can't hurt me."

Blood-soaked, she picked up her teacup and walked to the stairs. The ghost whipped at her with cold, insubstantial fingers. It screamed in her ears, battering her with anger and hatred. Corrie grinned, a sense of peace and calm radiating from her. The voice grew thinner, more distant, richer with despair. With each step she took, the visions of blood faded a little more, and by the time she stepped into the winter light, she was clean.

Cecelia Holland

There's a cost for everything, but here we learn that sometimes the cost can be much too high, no matter how glittering and wonderful the prize is—or seems to be.

Cecelia Holland is one of the world's most highly acclaimed and respected historical novelists, ranked by many alongside other giants in that field such as Mary Renault and Larry McMurtry. Over the span of her thirty-year career, she's written almost thirty historical novels, including The Firedrake, Rakóssy, Two Ravens, Ghost on the Steppe, The Death of Attila, Hammer for Princes, The King's Road, Pillar of the Sky, The Lords of Vaumartin, Pacific Street, The Sea Beggars, The Earl, The Kings in Winter, The Belt of Gold, *and more than a dozen others. She also wrote the well-known science fiction novel* Floating Worlds, *which was nominated for a Locus Award in 1975, and of late has been working on a series of fantasy novels, including* The Soul Thief, The Witches' Kitchen, The Serpent Dreamer, *and* Varanger. *Her most recent books are the novels* The High City *and* Kings of the North.

Demon Lover

She slept, and in the dark it came on her, heavy and sweaty, its weight all along her body. Its mouth quested greedily after hers and she rolled her head away, sick. She felt its nakedness prodding and poking against her thighs. Her body roused; even as she fought it, a gritty, shameful lust to submit coursed through her blood. Deep inside some ancient itch woke, longing for penetration. Her hips rolled, arching upward, her knees parting, and she heard its horrible, triumphant laugh.

She jolted awake, drenched with sweat. In the dark room around her, the other girls were still sleeping. None of them made outcries. None of them moaned in her dream. Fioretta slid quietly up off the pallet, her nightdress sticking to her, her long hair dripping down her shoulders. One tress had wrapped itself around her neck. She fumbled her way to the water basin, and washed her face; she felt dirty, all over.

The day was coming. Light began to filter into the room. Behind her now the others were waking. She kept her back to them. She did not want to see them, to know their faces. They bustled around her, whispering and yawning; without asking, they peeled off the damp nightdress, they brought her a clean shift, a fresh gown. They murmured around her like a crowd of bees. She did not look at them, afraid they would see the dream in her eyes. Afraid of what she would see in their eyes.

They hated her. She had felt that at once, behind their cooing, their simpering words, "my lady this, my lady that," and their rigid smiles. They pulled and slapped at her, dressing her, yanking on the brush as they did her hair, tugged the necklace into her skin when they clasped it. One pinched her so hard she jumped. They slid golden slippers on her feet, and in their midst she went down to court.

They left the room on a cold stone stair, but as they went down the step smoothed under her feet, the space widened, the swelling light struck on burnished walls. The girls around her began to laugh and giggle. Ahead of them were tall white doors figured with gold, and as they approached the doors burst open and on a rising excitement they swept through into the brilliant, merry bustle of the court.

The room was full of young and beautiful people, in satin and lace, their faces smooth as silk. As she came in, they swooped toward her and bowed. Their eyes glittered, eager—or desperate. She went through them toward the throne at the far end, lifting her skirts in her hands; and the wizard-king stood up, his hand out. Tall and lean, he was dressed head to foot in a straight plain white gown, his hair hidden under a cap. His beard was a narrow dark fringe, his face with its long eyes and straight narrow nose chiseled as if from walnut.

He said, "Ah, my beauty. My darling one, today I shall call you Marguerite, for you are a pearl." She could not speak; her breath choked in her throat, her skin creeping. He looked so well, but she knew now. Her eyes downcast, she went up the steps to the chair beside his. He laughed, as he had in the dream, triumphant.

FROM THE BEGINNING she had known there would be a cost.

She had been born in the village at the foot of the mountain. Her mother died when she was only a child, and her father was a drunkard, so they were very poor, but Fioretta was pretty and clever and worked hard, and as she grew into a handsome girl many young men thought well of her. She was getting ready to choose one to marry when her father, blind with drink, set the house on fire. She dragged him out of it, but the fire scorched her face and burned her leg so badly she needed a crutch to walk. The wound on her face faded, but the scar caught one corner of her eye, so she seemed to squint a little.

After that, the young men thought less well of her, all but the bailiff's younger son, Palo, who was cross-grained anyway, his family's black sheep. He was round and plain, a daydreamer, a stutterer. While her father went around drinking up everybody's sympathy, Palo came to Fioretta and demanded that he marry her.

Fioretta stopped short. He had been waiting for her by the riverbank, down from the bridge, where she often went searching for herbs. She propped herself on her crutch, hostile, quick to sense pity. "What did you say?"

He stood there, squat and round, his hands on his hips, his blue eyes intense, and said again, "Y-You ought to m-m-marry me. This is a great f-f-favor to you, you know."

At that she went hot with temper. She burst out, "What makes you so wonderful? You're a fat, pompous oaf."

He sneered at her. "You're a c-c-cripple. And you're poor. Your father's the village d-d-drunk."

She flounced off, tossing her head. "You're a fool, then, to want me."

"You're a sh-sh-shrew, then, to turn down what you should gratefully accept," he said, in pursuit.

She wheeled to confront him. "You're pocky-faced. You're shorter than I am and you smell."

"You've got a tongue like a v-v-v-v—" He put his hands on his hips again. "You squinty gimp, you don't even have the wits to kn-n-now what I'm offering you."

"At least I have the wit to know to reject it."

He flung his hands up, his face bright red, and stormed off.

At that she was suddenly very lonely. She sat down on the riverbank, exhausted. She had nowhere to go—she was sleeping in the church, and she would only eat if she found herbs and mushrooms and housewives in the village to buy them. The next day would be the same. She thought regretfully of Palo. Even fighting with him was better than being alone.

There was a convent in the village on the other side of the mountain; she could go there. Her gaze rose to the river rushing by. Or she could just throw herself in. Bitterly she wished the world were different.

"Good morning," said a strange voice, beside her.

She looked up, startled, at the old man standing there. He wore a long gray hooded cloak, which shadowed his face, but his eyes shone bright and clear. His hands were tucked away in his sleeves.

"What are you doing here?" she blurted. "What do you want with me?"

"I have been watching you," he said. "For a while."

"Me." A shiver went through her. She struggled up onto her feet and braced the crutch under her armpit. "Why would you wait for me? Who are you?"

He shrugged. The gray cloak obscured him, as if he went wrapped in a faint mist. Half turning away, he mumbled into his hand, "Call me Goodman Green'm, that's near enough. Don't remember." Then he turned back toward her. "What is your name, child?"

"Fioretta," she said.

"Ah," he said, "such a lovely name. And so harsh a fate, as I have seen, for such a lovely girl." His bright eyes glimmered inside the shadow of his face. "Fate is too cruel, isn't it? But what if I told you there is a place nearby where you could be made whole, and beautiful again? More beautiful than ever."

A ripple of yearning went through her, almost overwhelming. Resisting that, she gave a snort of disbelief. She said, "I would think you were a great fool."

"Well," he said. He began to drift off, like a mist, moving along the riverbank. "But the castle is just up the mountain. Only a mile or so on. You're going that way anyway." His eyes gleamed at her from the darkness of the hood. "Come," he said. "Take the right path." And went off.

She stared after him, her mouth open; she watched him until he disappeared in the busy crowd by the bridge. She rubbed her eyes with her hand, thinking, people shouldn't say such things, that's cruel. She saw ahead of her only the world, cruel and cold.

There was the convent. If they would not let her take the veil, since she had no dowry, they would give her work, and keep her. That was all she could hope for now. In fact, if she got less, she would not be hoping too much longer for anything. She started off toward the bridge.

The crutch dug under her armpit; her leg ached. But she had hours before sundown. One of a dozen people, she clumped across the bridge and turned onto the path up the mountain.

The other travelers soon turned off, and she was alone as she climbed. The path wound steadily upward, rockier and narrow between tall pines. The crutch slipped on the stones and she almost fell. She should try to walk without it; her leg seemed to get stronger when she used it. But it hurt more too, to walk without the crutch.

Far behind her, someone called out. She shivered. The voice was too far away to tell who it was but in her heart she knew it was Palo.

She could stop. Go back. Take whatever he deigned to give her. He wasn't so bad, quick-tongued and sometimes funny. She imagined the drudge work of keeping house while he lay around, as her father had. Then the drudge work in bed at night. She hobbled along; he was far behind; he would give up soon. The path narrowed still more and turned a sharp bend around a boulder, and she stopped, startled.

Ahead of her the path divided in two. The left-hand way wound on up the mountain, paved with jagged rocks and overhung with scrawny trees.

The right-hand side led off through what seemed a glade, where the sun streamed in through tall, fair oaks and lit the flower-dappled grass between them, and the path led easily downward, smooth and wide.

She gulped. She had been up this road before, not often, but enough to know this right-hand path had never been here before. The old man's words came back to her.

A place where you could be made whole, and beautiful, and happy again—

Behind her, closer, Palo called.

Uncertainly she took a step forward, into the right-hand path.

The air was warmer here. The sunlight touched her face. She walked on, hitching along on her crutch, the ground deep with leaves, soft underfoot. The trees seemed to spread their arms over her, like a ceiling overhead, so she walked down into a dark tunnel. The wind blew through their leaves and they whispered like voices, too soft to hear the words.

A wave of uncertainty broke over her: She should go back. She turned and saw, far up at beginning of the path, where the sunlight shone, Palo's dark shape against the afternoon sky. Then, coming up the other way, she heard the bustle and laughter of a crowd of people.

She turned toward them, wondering where they had come from. They gamboled toward her, bright and pretty as a flock of butterflies, girls and men in beautiful clothes, gathering up armfuls of wildflowers as they passed through the grassy glade at the far end of the tunnel of oaks. Fioretta drew aside, to let them go by, but they did not. They gathered around her, mirthful and bright-eyed, and took the gathered flowers and wreathed her in them. She stood, too amazed to move, drenched in buttercups and violets and sprays of yarrow, and the crowd around her parted.

Through the gap came the old man. He had shed the gray cloak. He looked much younger, his beard darker. He wore white, head to foot, a gown, a peaked cap. He said, "Welcome home, Fioretta," and took her by the hands, smiling.

She could not speak; glad, and grateful, she let herself be drawn forward, into the midst of these fair and merry people. They hurried her down the road. The trees ahead parted, and across a flowery meadow, a castle tower streamed a red pennant against the violet sky. That was where they were going, that white spire above the forest.

She thought suddenly of Palo, and turned and looked back, but he was gone. Good, she thought, relieved, and turned forward, toward the wonders that awaited her.

She had known, even then, that there would be a cost, but then she had not cared.

FROM THAT MOMENT on, she had been beautiful. Her legs were quick and her feet sure, her hands graceful, with delicate fingers; her hair was like spun silk, braided with ribbons and jewels. She wore a satin gown that glistened with embroidered figures and on her feet were soft leather shoes. That first day she sat on a raised dais beside the wizard-king, looking out over his great pillared gilded hall, and watched his glittering, exuberant court flirt and laugh, dance and declaim before them.

The hall was wide, and yet full of light, from lamps standing everywhere. Round golden pillars held the roof up high above them. The crowd whirled and dipped across the floor in a constant gaiety. And she was their queen. One by one they all came and bowed down before her. Servants brought trays of bread and fruit and cheese and she ate until she was stuffed.

She put her hand to her face; the scar was gone, her cheek as soft as a rose petal. Her leg was straight again; she was whole again.

Before her passed a constant stream of amusements. There were jugglers and tumblers, which made her laugh, and singers who played so tunefully she held her breath to hear them. She turned to the man on the throne beside her, and he smiled, and patted her arm. She wondered what to say to him, how to thank him, but he only nodded, and gestured toward some new fancy. She wondered how long this would last.

A clown in red pants brought out a bear, which turned in circles, smirking. Girls wearing almost nothing commanded monkeys in little red hats to ride dogs, and the dogs to run in circles, and then stand on their hind legs and yap, the monkeys clinging tight.

Three men rushed out bearing on their arms a host of brilliant birds that shrieked and flapped their wings, deafening. She put her hands over her ears at their screams, and beside her the wizard-king gave her a sharp look and waved his hand and said something, and abruptly they were ponies.

A little group of musicmen sat down below the dais, tuned their lutes and patted their drums, and the court began to dance. The wizard turned to her. "Dance, my dear one," he said to her. "Let me see you merry."

"With you?" she asked, shy; he seemed so solemn, too majestic to dance, and in spite of her gratitude, she did not really want to touch him.

"No, no," he said, with a smile. "I will watch." He gestured her toward the round dance forming on the floor. "Show me your grace and beauty, my queen."

She stood, delighting in her nimble legs. She ran out neat-footed as a goat to the spreading circle of girls in the center of the hall. Without thinking, she knew every step perfectly, and she whirled and dipped so elegantly everybody else stopped and gathered to see it. The music was beautiful. The dance was a song her newly perfect body sang. But when, out of breath, she went back to the edge of the floor, to let someone else have a place, she heard the wall behind her murmur.

She turned her head, looking out of the side of her eye. The wall was of pale stone, the surface carved intricately into vines and leaves. At first she saw nothing, but then, in the spaces between the leaves, eyes appeared.

Desperate, gleaming with tears, they turned on her, and through a crevice between the stone vines a hand reached out.

She jerked herself forward again, her heart pounding, and stepped out a little into the middle of the floor. Out of reach. She would not see this misery. She was too happy. She could dance, and she had never eaten so well, and she was beautiful. That was what mattered. She made her way back to her place by the wizard-king.

But now she saw bits of people everywhere, eyes in the columns, too, hands, and feet, and the tables, she saw, had human legs, and the braziers were the bottom halves of people, with their open bellies full of fire. The lamps were long thin girls, all gilded, their hair aflame. When she looked down, she thought she saw the floor was made of twisted bodies jammed together. Yet it was smooth and hard as stone. She lifted her gaze to the happy whirling courtiers around her, and her heart froze.

She stood beside him, and said, too loudly, "I loved the dancing."

The wizard said, "You were the most beautiful dancer there, my Queen Maeve."

Then from the crowd suddenly a woman strode forward who was not joyous and not laughing. Her eyes flashed with anger. She cried, "No! I won't have this—I was there, yesterday—"

Fioretta stiffened, her mouth falling open. She turned toward the wizard, and he gripped her arm, leaning toward her. His gaze turned on the angry woman. "Be warned," he said, in a deep, harsh voice. "Remember what you were before."

The woman flung her arms out to him. She was beautiful, tall and shapely, with long black hair and red lips. Her clothes were magnificent, sheets of silk and silver cascading from the glowing purple calyx of her bodice. Her hands reached toward him, pleading. "Please, my lord—I did everything you wanted, I—"

"Rosa," the wizard said, and made a gesture.

Fioretta gasped. Before them the woman writhed a moment, shrinking. Her clothes shed from her like the petals of a blown flower, to leave behind a withered crone, her hair stringy and white, her arms with the skin hanging like bags off the bones. From the court looking on there went up a cry of disgust and contempt. Fioretta's arm was still tight in the wizard's grasp. The hag in the middle of the floor sank to her knees, sobbing, and then from all sides the others pelted her with food and hats and shoes.

Fioretta spun toward him. "No," she said. "Don't punish her so. I beg of you."

The wizard smiled at her. His hand on her arm did not ease its grip. He said, "Sit down, my fairy queen, my Gloriana. Remember, I am master here." His voice turned smooth. "Are you not happy here? What else can I bestow upon you? Only let me make you happy. That is all I wish."

Fioretta stood rigid under his eyes; she tore her gaze from his. Down there they were dragging off the beaten woman Rosa. Another flower. His hand on her arm tugged commandingly. Then, where all the others were moving, her gaze caught on one who did not go with the others, who stood where he was, staring at her.

He wore a red tabard and spurred boots, a gold-hilted sword at his side, and a hat with a plume. She swallowed. He was tall, with brawny arms and legs, and a proud tilt to his head, but she knew those blue eyes.

Palo had not escaped after all. Another tug, and this time, weak-kneed, she sat down. Beneath her, the chair shifted and sighed, and she sat as lightly as she could.

NOW IN THE night the horrible thing groaned over her, it slobbered over her lips, and poked at her body, and she wanted, she wanted to receive it. She wanted even its loathsomeness. She thought of the walls, and what Rosa had said, but she thought most of Palo. What a fool, to follow her. Yet it was her fault he was trapped here. She clenched her body against the dream and forced herself to waken in the dark.

The incubus was gone, when the dream was gone. She pried herself up from the bed. Six other girls slept around her, all deep in their slumber. She threw a cloak around her and went quietly among them to the door and out. She would find Palo, and she would help him escape.

She went down the great main stair in the dark, to the hall. There was only this one tower, and the hall; Palo had to be here somewhere.

The wizard was here somewhere also, and she dreaded meeting him. But she had to find Palo.

Even before she reached the hall she heard the sounds of voices. The two tall doors were wide open but no light shone beyond, only a faint blue glow, like moonlight. When she came to the last step, the broad, dim room before her was empty. Yet it was noisy with calling, sighing, weeping, cries, and curses. She stood on the step and saw, from every wall, from the columns, the hands reaching out, the fingers stretching out into the air, struggling toward the open. The tables trudged back and forth groaning and mewling, and the braziers and lamps sat slumped on the floor.

She could not bear this, and she could not find Palo anywhere. There was no sign either of the wizard, who was perhaps out prowling, as he had been when he caught her. She ran back up the stair to the next landing, below the tower room where she was supposed to be sleeping. On the far side of the landing was the narrow arched opening to another stairway, and she followed it.

This one spiraled around and down, darker with every step, soon pitch dark. The steps grew rough under her feet. Then ahead, below, the darkness yielded to a faint red light, shining on the rock.

She went around a bend into the full brightness, and stood on the edge of a kitchen, made all of fitted stone, where a fire burned in a great hearth, huge pots lined the walls, and spoons and forks hung in hooks from the ceiling. At a table in the middle sat a woman, her wispy gray hair only half-covered by a scorched linen cap, who was kneading a mass of brown floury dough.

Fioretta stopped. The woman lifted her head and gave her a gappy grin. "Well. It's been long since anyone came to see me."

"Who are you? What are you doing here?"

The woman wiped her wrist across her forehead.

"Why, I'm the cook, of course. Without me, you wouldn't eat."

Fioretta went farther into the kitchen, into the warmth and the good smells. She felt suddenly much better. The cook's arms went back to her work, the dough constantly swelling, and her hands constantly kneading it down again. Fioretta said, "You aren't—his?"

"You mean the one upstairs." The woman's arms thrust and beat on the dough. "We have an agreement. I don't poison him and he doesn't turn me into a toad."

"Who is he? How can I get out of here?"

The cook's eyes twinkled at her. "His name is written down around here somewhere. Can you read?"

"No."

The cook shrugged. "Neither can I."

She turned to the hearth, with her burly arms poking and turning the fire, and the flames shot up. The light and the heat flooded the room. Behind her on the table the dough seized the chance to grow into a wild floury puff as tall as a man. The cook came quickly back, and punched it flat again.

Fioretta came to the edge of the table. "Is there any way out—back to the real world?"

"I don't know. This is a haunted place, and since he came nothing is what it seems."

"How did you get here?" Fioretta asked.

The cook looked startled. "I—" Her eyes widened, and she peered around as if she had just noticed where she was. "I've always been here, haven't I? That's why it's . . ." Her gaze returned to Fioretta. "Maybe the question is, who are you?"

"I—" Fioretta stopped, not sure what to say.

The cook smiled at her, and then, on the stair, the young man in the red tabard came down around the corner.

"He's come for you," the cook said.

Fioretta got up. The young man stood there on the last step, his blue eyes on her, and without a word she went past him, up the stair, around the curve. He followed her, and when they were out of sight of the kitchen she faced him.

With the light behind him she could not see his face. He was taller, with brawny arms and chest. He said, "Well, here we are," and it was Palo's voice.

"It is you," she said.

He said, "Yes. Not so changed as you are. I would not know you, had I not seen it happen." His voice quivered. "You are so beautiful, and so graceful."

He put out his hand to her, and she knocked it aside.

"Why did you come?" she cried. "You must get away, somehow, you must see what becomes of people here."

"I knew you'd need help," he said. His voice twinged with sudden anger, and he put his hands on his hips, as he was used to do. "You've really gotten yourself into something this time."

"I do not need help!" But she was glad he was here, familiar even with his new good looks, his tall and broad-shouldered body. "There has to be some way out of this place."

"I've looked," he said. "I can't find any doors that open out of the castle. At night everything falls asleep; I almost did too, and in a few more days I probably will." He yawned, veiled in the half-dark, the light brimming him like a nimbus. "What are you doing out of bed, anyway?"

She blurted out, without thinking, "Looking for you."

"Well," he said. "Here I am." He reached for her hand.

"No," she said. "Don't touch me. He'll know."

He gave a sharp twitch, as if she had struck him. He backed away, and slid his hands behind him. "Oh," he said, in a different voice. "That's how it is. I guess you have what you want already. You'd better get back where you belong, then, hadn't you."

She grew hot with shame. He thought she had yielded to the wizard. In a way, she thought, she had, coming here. His voice changed, almost wistful now, softer. "You are so beautiful. You were pretty before, and clever and brave, and after the fire I thought I'd have a chance with you, but now you are so much beyond me—Go on." Brisker. "I can't bear to think what could happen to you, if—"

The worst would be that he would see me again as I really am, she thought. Gimp. Squinty-eyed. The idea drove a sort of panic through her, and then a rising resolve: She would be happy, as long as she could, as long as this lasted. But she would try to get Palo out of it. She turned and went quickly up the stair.

IN THE MORNING, she came down to the hall, and the whole court bowed down before her, and the wizard stood to greet her. "You are as glorious as the sunrise," he said. "Wherefore today I call you Io, my darling." He led her to the chair beside him, and as he sat beside her, he said, under his breath, "I have done my part." His eyes drilled into her. "Don't you think you owe me something?"

She lowered her gaze; she began to feel guilty, ungrateful. A quiver went along her nerves; she felt herself weakening, dissolving into the illusion.

He said, "Or perhaps you need some additional persuasion? What do you think of my new knight here—the one who came in with you?"

She licked her lips. "I was alone."

"There was someone else. What was his name—Buffo, Salo—"

He was playing with her, his eyes glittering. She looked away. Then a brassy blast of horns made her start.

Down the center of the hall walked a tall man dressed in black. Two trumpeters preceded him, blasting shrill challenges on their horns; after him came two more men, carrying a sword and a shield. He stopped before the wizard.

"I am here to claim your place, king of the wood! Send out your champion, and we will decide the issue now!"

The flock of courtiers had divided to let him through; now in one breath they cried out in scorn, and pressed closer. Fioretta sat up, her hands in her lap and her heart in her throat; she glanced at the wizard, wondering what this meant.

He did not look troubled. His mouth curved in a smile, and he never looked at the black knight, his gaze steady on her; she realized this was a trap.

"Name your champion," cried the black knight. He turned to his squires and drew a long gold-fitted sword from the scabbard.

From the crowd, one man after another leaped forward. "My lord, name me!" "No, me!" "Me, my lord."

The wizard's look, heavy with meaning, never left Fioretta. He stood, lifted his hand, and pointed toward the mass of the court. "You, my newest knight, you shall prove yourself today." She looked where he was pointing, and saw Palo.

Her breath stopped in her throat. If anything happened to him it would be her fault. The red knight came forward uncertainly, into the middle of the hall, took hold of his own sword, and drew it out of the scabbard, so awkward he almost dropped it. Fioretta clenched her teeth. She knew he was no fighter. The wizard watched her and she forced herself to look away.

The wizard said, "You don't care for combat, my lovely one?"

She gave a cracked laugh. "I prefer the music and the dancing."

"Ah," he said, "but this is more amusing. Watch."

The two men faced each other, and began to trade blows. The wizard paid no heed to them, his gaze steady on Fioretta. She glanced at the two men stalking around each other, slashing with their swords; Palo slipped and missed and almost dropped his. Inside the handsome body he was still the chubby boy who stuttered. Her hands fisted in her lap. Suddenly she longed for him to be that chubby boy again, back in the village, safe.

"Not much of a swordsman, this one," the wizard said. He laughed, with a glance at her. "Perhaps I should let him lose."

She said nothing. Her heart was hammering. If she said the wrong thing she was destroyed. Palo was destroyed. Out there the red knight staggered backward away from the black knight, inches ahead of the slashing blade.

"Well," the wizard said. "Does he die? Or will you save him?"

She said, "Do as you will, my lord," and stared off at the wall. Palo dodged behind one of the pillars. The watching court laughed, and the black knight with a roar pursued him.

Palo darted around the pillar, came up behind the black knight, swung the sword flat, and swept the other man's legs out from under him. The knight sprawled on the floor, his sword clattering away.

Palo stood back, letting him up. The wizard said, under his breath, "What, a Galahad?" His voice had a rough edge, as if the red knight's gallantry annoyed him.

Fioretta's heart leaped. He was brave, after all, Palo, and good. And in the wizard's annoyance she sensed some weakness. She pretended an interest in one of her hands, admiring the perfect fingernails, and watched from the corner of her eye.

The black knight rolled to his feet and snatched up his sword again. He rushed at Palo, flailing his blade from side to side. Palo backed up, stumbled, and went to one knee, and the knight raised his sword for the final blow.

The wizard said, "Shall he die, my Io?" He was watching Fioretta, not the fight. Fioretta bit her lip. But the knight, perhaps waiting for the wizard's command, had paused, and now Palo rolled away across the floor and leaped up, out of reach of his enemy. The black knight yelled, and chased him, but Palo held his ground, and as the other man plunged recklessly toward him, brought his own sword up with both hands and struck the other man's weapon sending it flying.

The black knight staggered back, his arms up. "Mercy," he cried. He went down on one knee.

The wizard stood. "Enough of this. Kill him. As you are my knight, I command it."

Palo came forward toward the throne. "My lord, grant him mercy." His handsome new face was solemn. He never looked at Fioretta. "Let him have time to regret his inadequacy."

The wizard gave a harsh laugh. He shot a quick glance at Fioretta beside him. "I give no mercy here."

"My lord," Palo said, "for your greater glory and the glory of your queen."

The wizard's teeth showed. When he spoke, it was clearly against his will. "You shall have his life, then. Go."

The black knight knelt on the floor, his hands raised, imploring. "My lord—"

The wizard jerked his hand up in command and the black knight's men hauled him off. Palo bowed and backed away into the crowd. The courtiers in their satins and gilt and jewels flooded back onto the floor, dancing and laughing again, as if nothing had happened.

She thought, *Nothing did happen, really.* He made it all up, to catch me. But somehow Palo had escaped. Had won, against the wizard's will. He had found the edge of the wizard's power. She dared not look at him, lost now anyway in the mass of merry, dancing people.

She thought, *He has found a place here. Like me.*

She looked down at her beautiful clothes. A servant was offering her a fine flaky pie and a cup of wine. The hall filled with laughter and chatter.

Maybe this is good enough, she thought. But something in her had divided, and the pieces didn't quite match anymore.

Except for the wizard, there was no one to talk to. The other people were only shells, without conversation; they laughed, and said how happy they were, and whirled away from her into the general dance. It all looked the same as yesterday: Maybe it was all the same day. Then, at sundown, when they were all going off to bed, she saw Rosa again.

The fallen favorite had become the lamp beside the door. Her body was thin as a pole, glistening gold, her arms clasped across her middle; her white hair stood straight up, glowing. Only her eyes moved, sleek and hopeless, watching Fioretta. Wanting to be there again, to be what Fioretta was. Fioretta went swiftly up to the bedchamber, and let them undress her and put her to bed, but she lay stiff on the pallet, biting her lips and pinching herself to stay awake, until the others were all asleep.

Then she rose, threw a cloak around her, and went out.

SHE WENT STRAIGHT down into the kitchen, where she found the cook stirring a great cauldron, and the red knight, sitting on the steps.

He gave her a glancing look, his face stern. She sat beside him.

"You did very well," she said. "I didn't know you could fight."

"When it's your life," he said, not looking at her, his voice cold, "you learn fast. You should go back. He'll catch you."

She said, "He's already caught me." She looked at the cook again, beseeching. "Tell us how we can escape."

The cook was slicing onions, the knife so fast it was a blur. "You came here of your own will. You must stay until the castle falls."

She groaned. Palo was watching her curiously. "You don't want to stay—where you are so beautiful and so cherished?"

She put her hand on his arm. "You were so brave. And you were good, when he wanted you to be wicked. You defied him when you did not kill the black knight, and he had to accept it. You gave me some reason to hope I can keep on resisting him." He had turned toward her, at her touch, and she looked into his eyes. "That was wonderful," she said, and she kissed him.

He flung his arms around her and kissed her back. She shut her eyes, reveling in the strength of his arms, the sweetness of the kiss. If the wizard destroyed her tomorrow she would have this one real, true moment, this one real, true knight. Palo's hand stroked her hair and she laid her head on his shoulder.

"I love you," he said. "I will always love you."

"You have saved me, so far—without you, I think I would already have given in to him."

"You haven't. Thank God you haven't."

"I don't know how long I can fight him off. I'm afraid—"

"Sssh," he said. "I'll think of something—hush, my darling one." He kissed her again.

The cook was watching them, smiling. Fioretta made herself draw back. The memory of Rosa flooded her mind. "That's not good enough. I don't know if we have much time."

He said, "No—stay—" and grabbed for her hand.

She held herself away from him. "At any moment he can ruin us. I saw him—you saw what he did to that other woman. If he finds out—"

She faced him, her heart pounding. She had found a wonderful man to love but she could never have him. She turned and ran up the stair, a sinking feeling in her heart that in fact the wizard already knew.

SHE HAD TO sleep, and when she slept, the demon came on her, whispering. "Kiss *him*, will you? Want him and not me, will you? After all I've done for you, you heartless whore!" It ground itself on her, pinching and tugging at her breasts, poking her between the legs, stirring her to a thick, greedy lust. She struggled against her own body, which longed so for the consummation. Palo, she thought. Palo.

She knew that to give in would doom her and Palo both. But her lecherous body yearned for the coupling, for the demon's thrust; she could not hold out too much longer. Between her legs was damp and thick with heat, and an evil voice inside whispered, "Let him. He'll keep me. I will be queen forever. He'll love me, and I'll be different from the others." She thought, *Palo. Palo.* She made herself see him in her mind—as he had been before, the round untested boy. With a wrench she woke up, and lay there struggling to stay awake until the dawn came.

In the morning, the other women dressed her, and they hurried down to the court, to the senseless merry laughter and the endless wild dancing. When she came in, the wizard rose, as he had before, but this time he was scowling at her.

"Behold, the adulterous one! I name you Helen, Queen of treacherous women!" She stopped before his throne, and the court fell silent.

The wizard sneered at her. "I ask one act of gratitude, and instead I am traduced. You shall not sit by my side today, slut." Then Palo stepped up out of the crowd.

"Wizard." He walked between her and the throne, and his voice rang out, loud and brave. "I challenge you for this woman!"

"Ho ho," the wizard said. "You do, do you?" He came down from the throne and paced around Palo, the hem of his white gown sweeping on the floor. "You think you can fight me, you fool? Hah!" He flung one hand up. "Go back as you were, Palo!"

Fioretta cried out. Palo seemed to buckle. His red tabard flew off, and he shrank, and grew wider. His handsome face bloated into the plain round pock-marked face of the bailiff's black sheep son. He gave a yell, and drew his sword, and the blade melted away to nothing.

The court let out a lustful howl. All at once they rushed forward, snatching off their hats and shoes to throw. Fioretta leaped forward toward the wizard, her hands pressed together.

"No. Let him live—I will do what you wish—only, let him go!"

The wizard seemed to grow taller and his eyes blazed. His voice hissed out. "Too late for that, hussy. Too late, Fioretta!"

She staggered. She felt her beautiful clothes fall away, and she stumbled on her bad leg; she put her hands to her face and felt the slick ugly scar. A shoe hit her shoulder. The crowd of the court pressed closer, their eyes glowing, their faces ugly with hate. Palo wheeled, his arms out, trying to shield her.

"Fioretta—"

Her name. She understood, suddenly, in a gust of memory, how the wizard had only spoken her name twice, and each time changed her. Something else hit her on the cheek. Palo jerked his arms up to fend off a hail of missiles. She had heard the wizard's name, once—what was it—

He stood there, laughing. Palo clutched her, as hard things rained down on both of them, and she flung her arms around him to stay on her feet.

She shouted, "Goodman Greenough, Greengood, Greenman, Greenham, Godham—"

The wizard laughed, disdainful. She sagged under the weight of the attack.

"Greenam, Goodman, Goodgreen—"

The wizard laughed again. But he was slowly turning, spinning around in place. His white robes flew off; what they had covered was not as tall, was lumpy, green, damp, covered with leaves or feathers or scales. It spun faster and faster, and the court besetting Palo and Fioretta let out a screech.

Their target had changed. The walls and columns erupted hands, legs, bodies. The great throne behind the wizard reared up into a scrawny old man and two brawny boys, who hurled themselves on the whirling green demon. The floor burst up into waves of bodies, wild hair like spume, and the arch of shoulders rising. In pieces and as one, the prisoners of the castle flung themselves past Fioretta and Palo and onto their tormentor. Fioretta cried out. Something struck her from above, and she looked up; the roof was sagging down, as legs and hands and heads rained down from it. The floor was rising around her, breaking into a tumble of arms and legs, buttocks, elbows. She clutched Palo's hand. In the door, through the thickening downpour of the collapsing roof, she saw the cook, laughing.

"Run," Palo shouted in her ear. "Run!"

She turned and hobbled after him. He caught her hand and held her up. They struggled against the tide of bodies rushing at the wizard. The air was thick with some kind of damp hot green mist and she could see nothing, but she followed blindly where he drew her. Her leg hurt. Palo's hand in hers dragged her on through the confusion. She could not breathe. The ground under her was falling away.

Then under her feet was the rocky forest floor. Suddenly she could see again. She limped along, gasping for breath, her hand in Palo's, along the mountain path. Turning, she looked back.

Back there the last of the castle was vanishing into a clump of trees clinging to the mountainside. The screaming and howling faded. She slowed, panting, her bad leg caving in, and he slid his arm around her waist.

He said, "G-g-g-ood enough?"

She turned to him, to his plain, pocky face, smiling at her. Her one true, brave knight. He had always been there, but neither of them had known. A gust of love swept over her, warm and sweet. She still held his hand and she squeezed it tight. "Good enough," she said, and kissed him.

Melinda M. Snodgrass

Here's a compelling drama set in deep space that reunites lovers long parted by rank, social status, and circumstance—although, as they both soon come to realize, it may not reunite them for very long . . .

A writer whose work crosses several mediums and genres, Melinda M. Snodgrass has written scripts for television shows such as Profiler *and* Star Trek: The Next Generation *(for which she was also a story editor for several years), written a number of popular science fiction novels, and was one of the co-creators of the long-running* Wild Cards *series, for which she has also written and edited. Her novels include* Circuit, Circuit Breaker, Final Circuit, The Edge of Reason, Runespear *(with Victor Milan),* High Stakes, Santa Fe, *and* Queen's Gambit Declined. *Her most recent novel is* The Edge of Ruin, *the sequel to* The Edge of Reason. *Her media novels include the* Wild Cards *novel* Double Solitaire *and the* Star Trek *novel* The Tears of the Singers. *She's also the editor of the anthology* A Very Large Array. *She lives in New Mexico.*

The Wayfarer's Advice

We came out of Fold only twenty-three thousand kilometers from Kusatsu-Shirane. "Good job," I started to say, but was interrupted by blaring impact alarms.

"Shit, shit, shit," Melin at navigation chattered, and her fingers swept back and forth across the touch screen like a child finger painting. Our ship, the *Selkie*, obedient to Melin's sweeping commands, fired its ram jet. My stomach was left resting against the ceiling and my balls seemed to leap into my throat as we dropped relative to our previous position.

A massive piece of steel and composite resin, edges jagged and blackened by an explosion, tumbled slowly past our front viewport. It had been four years since I'd been cashiered from the Imperial Navy of the Solar League, but the knowledge gained during the preceding twenty years was still with me.

"That was an Imperial ship," I said. My eye caught writing on the hull. I had an impression of a name, and my gut closed down into an aching ball. It couldn't be . . . but if it *was* . . . I had to know. I added an order. "Match trajectory and image-capture."

Jax, the Tiponi Flute, piped through the breathing holes lining his sides, "Not good news for Kusatsu-Shirane if the League has found them." The alien had several of its leafy tendrils wrapped around handholds welded to the walls, and his elongated body swayed with the swoops and dives of the ship.

"I'd call that the understatement of the year," Baca grunted from his position at communication.

Three hundred years ago, humans had developed a faster-than-light drive and gone charging out into our arm of the Milky Way galaxy. There we had met up with a variety of alien races, kicked their butts, and subjugated them under human rule. But two hundred years before the human blitzkrieg began, there had been other ships that had headed to the stars. Long-view ships with humans in suspended animation, searching for new worlds.

Most of these pioneers were cranks and loons determined to set up their various ideas of utopia. Best guess was that probably eighty percent of them died either during the journey or shortly after locating on a planet. But some survived to create Reichart's World, and Nirvana, and Kusatsu-Shirane, and numerous others.

The League called them Hidden Worlds, and took a very dim view of human-settled planets that weren't part of the League. In fact, the League rectified that situation whenever they ran across one of these worlds. The technique was simple and brutal: The League arrived, used their superior firepower to force a surrender, then took away all the children under the age of sixteen and fostered them with families on League planets. They then brought in League settlers to swamp the colonists who remained behind.

But it hadn't worked this time, because there were pieces of Imperial ships orbiting Kusatsu-Shirane. Something had killed a whole battle group. Whatever it was, I didn't want it destroying my little trade vessel.

"Contact orbital control, and tell them we're friendlies," I ordered Baca.

"I've been trying, Tracy, but nobody's answering. Worse, the whole planet's gone silent. Nobody's talking to nobody."

"Some new Imperial weapon to knock out communications?" Melin asked.

"Are you picking up anything?" I asked.

"Music," Baca replied.

We all exchanged glances; then I said, "Let's hear it."

Baca switched from headphone to speaker, and flipped through the communication channels from the planet. Slow, mournful music filled the bridge. It wasn't all the same melody, but they all had one thing in common. Each melody was desperately sad.

Something terrible had happened on Kusatsu-Shirane, and judging by the debris, something equally terrible had happened in orbit. Periodically, Melin fired small maneuvering jets as she dodged through the ruins, but despite her best efforts the bridge echoed with pings and scrapes as debris impacted against the hull.

"Not the safest of neighborhoods, Captain," came my executive officer's voice in my left ear, and I jumped. Damn, the creature could move quietly! I gave a quick glance over my shoulder, and found myself looking directly into the Isanjo's sherry-colored eyes. Jahan had settled onto the back of my chair like Alice's Cheshire cat.

"We'll grab an identification and get out," I said.

Jahan wrapped her tail around my throat. I couldn't tell if the gesture was meant to convey comfort or a threat. An Isanjo's tail was powerful enough to snap a two-by-four. My neck would offer little challenge.

As if in answer to my statement, the screen on the arm of my jacket flared, adjusted contrast, and the name of the ship came into focus: *Nuestra Señora de la Concepción.* My impression had been correct. It had been *her* ship. I gave the bridge of my nose a hard squeeze, fighting to hold back tears.

"Holy crap, that's a flagship!" Baca yelped as he accessed the computer files.

"Under the command of Mercedes de Arango, the Infanta who would have held the lives of countless millions of humans and aliens in her hands once her father died," Jax recited in his piping tones. His encyclopedic memory baffled me. I had no idea how that much brain power could reside in something that looked like an oversized stalk of bamboo.

"Instead, she precedes him into oblivion," Jahan said.

The attention of my crew was like a pinprick, the unspoken question hung between us. "Yes, I was at the Academy with her," I said.

"So, did you *know* her?" Baca asked.

"I'm a tailor's son. What do you think?"

Baca reacted to my tone. "Just asking," he said sulkily.

A fur-covered hand swept lightly beneath my eyes. "You weep," Jahan said, and I was glad she had used her knuckle. An Isanjo's four-fingered hand is tipped with ferocious claws, capable of disemboweling another Isanjo or even a man. She leaned in closer and whispered, "And I note you did not actually answer the question."

"Twelve ships were destroyed here. Six thousand starmen died. If things had fallen out differently, I might have been among them," I said loudly. "Of course I'm upset."

"They came here to do violence to the people of Kusatsu-Shirane," Jax tweeted.

"It wasn't a duty they would have relished."

"But they would have done it," Jahan said. "The Infanta would have ordered it done."

I shrugged. "Orders are orders. I cleared a Hidden World once. When I was a newly minted lieutenant."

"And now you trade with them and keep them secret," Jahan said.

"Making me a traitor as well as a cashiered thief." I changed the subject. "We need to find out what happened down the gravity well."

"It will take a damn lot of fuel to set the ship down," Jax tweeted. Flutes were famous for their mathematical ability, and Jax was no exception. He was our purchasing agent, and I was pretty damn sure he was the reason the *Selkie* ran at a profit. He counted every Reales and squeezed it twice.

"I'll take the *Wasp*," I said, referring to the small League fighter craft we'd picked up at a salvage auction. The cannons had been removed, but it was still screamingly fast and relatively cheap to fly.

Melin had given us enough gravity that I could grip the sides of the access ladder, and slide down to the level that held the docking bay. Even so, Jahan, using her four hands and prehensile tail, reached the lower deck before me.

"I take it that you're coming along," I said as I hauled a spacesuit out of a locker.

"I will need to report to the Council."

"Chalking up another human atrocity," I said with black humor.

"It's what we do," the creature said shortly and she removed her suit from its locker. Isanjo suits always looked strange. They were equipped with a tail because the aliens used their tails for their high-steel construction work.

"And what happens when the ledger gets filled?" I asked as I stepped into the lower half of my suit.

"We will act," she said, and I knew that she was speaking of all the alien races. "There are a lot more of us than there are of you."

"Yeah, but none of you are as mean as us." I shrugged to settle the heavy oxygen pack onto my shoulders.

"But we're more patient."

"You've got me there."

I reflected that Isanjos now built our skyscrapers and our spaceships. Under human supervision, of course, but my God, there was so much opportunity for mischief if the aliens decided that it was time for them to act! I had a vision of skyscrapers collapsing and ships exploding.

I thought about the Hajin who worked as servants in our households. How easy it would be to poison a human family.

And the Tiponi Flutes did our accounting. They could crash the economy.

Humans were fucked. Good thing I worked on a ship crewed mostly by aliens. Maybe they liked me enough to keep me around.

We secured each other's helmets, and headed for the *Wasp*, which sat in the middle of the bay. Even sitting still, it looked like it was moving a million miles an hour. The needle nose and vertical tail screamed predator.

I took the front seat, and Jahan settled into the gunner's chair. The canopy dropped, I flipped on the engines, instruments, and radio, and called to the bridge. "We're ready."

For a few seconds, we could hear the air being sucked out of the bay and back into the rest of the ship. No sense wasting atmosphere. It cost money to make, as Jax frequently pointed out. Once the wind sounds died, the great outer doors swung slowly and ponderously open. Our view was dominated by the curving rim of the planet. Green seas and a small continent rolled past us. Beyond the bulk of the world, the stars glittered ice-bright. I sent us out into space, and immediately dodged a piece of broken ship.

"Do mind the trash," Jahan said.

Something was niggling at me. Something missing in the orbital mix—but I was too busy negotiating the floating debris to figure it out. Instead of heading directly to the planet, I took the time to explore the expanding circle of debris that had been the *Nuestra Señora de la Concepción*. We soon saw bits of floating detritus that had once been people. I studied each frozen face haloed with crystals of frozen blood.

"She's dead," Jahan said.

"I know," I said. But I couldn't accept it. She was the heir to the League. There may have been added protection for Mercedes. There had to have been. She could *not* be gone. Twenty minutes later, I admitted defeat, took us out of the debris field, and headed toward the planet.

We were passing relatively close to a small moon—Kusatsu-Shirane had five but the others weren't presently in view—when I heard it. A distress beacon, sending its cry into the void. We locked on and followed it. The life capsule had clamped itself limpetlike to the stony surface of the moon. The tiny computer brain that controlled the capsule had rightly figured that it was safer for the occupant not to be floating in a battle zone, and found refuge.

I landed the *Wasp*, popped the canopy, and pushed out with such force that I almost hit escape velocity from the tiny planetoid. Jahan's tail caught my ankle, and pulled me back.

Moving with a bit more caution, I approached the body-shaped container resting in a small crater. The black surface was etched with messages in every known League language, urging the finder to contact the navy headquarters on Hissilek. There was also a dire warning to any that might stumble upon the body that the DNA of the human inside was not to be harvested or touched in any way.

I brushed away the layer of fine dust and ice that covered the faceplate of the life capsule. It was Mercedes. Placed into a deep coma by drugs injected by the capsule. Her long dark brown hair, streaked now with silver at her temples, had been braided, and the braid lay across one shoulder. A few strands of hair had come loose, and caught in her lips at the moment that the capsule had slammed shut around her. I wanted to reach out and brush them away. I studied the long, patrician nose, the espresso-and-cream-colored skin. She was so beautiful—and she was alive.

"Hmm, I thought a princess would be prettier," Jahan said.

"She's beautiful!" I flared.

"Ah, I see now. You're in love with her."

WE RETURNED TO the *Selkie*. There was no way to fit the capsule inside the *Wasp*. I reprogrammed the clamps and secured Mercedes to the hull. It made me uncomfortable treating her in such a disrespectful way, but I couldn't open the capsule in vacuum and I had no suit for her.

"That was a quick trip." Baca's voice filled my helmet.

"We found a survivor," I radioed back as I brought us in through the bay doors and dropped the Wasp onto the deck.

It was the work of minutes to unclamp the capsule from the side of the *Wasp*, and blow the seals. I eyed the tangle of IV tubes and the pinpricks of blood that stained her arms and legs where the needles had driven through her clothes and into her veins. While I was trying to figure out how to remove them without causing her pain, the capsule sensed warmth and atmosphere, and withdrew the needles that kept her in a deathlike coma.

I slid my arms beneath her and picked her up. I'd like to say that I swept her into my arms, but at five feet eight inches tall, she was not much shorter than me, and I had to work to carry her.

"You could have waited for a stretcher," Jahan said as she listened to my panting breaths, and noticed the way I braced myself against the wall of the lift. I shook my head, not wanting to waste the air. "And have you considered that you have put us all at grave risk by bringing her aboard? We were smuggling to a Hidden World. The League will not only imprison us for that, they will assume we know the location of other such worlds, and they won't be gentle in trying to elicit that information."

"I couldn't just leave her there."

"Because you're in love with her."

I summoned up a glare. I didn't have the breath for a response. We reached the fourth deck level, and I carried Mercedes into our small, but well-equipped, sick bay.

DALEA WAS WAITING for us. I wasn't sure if Dalea had a medical license, but whatever her training was, she was very good. There had to be a story about why she'd signed aboard a ship, because she was Hajin, and the herbivores weren't common in space, but I hadn't managed to worm it out of her yet.

Her coat was white with streaks of red-brown, and a thick shock of chestnut hair curled across her skull and ran down her long neck and even longer spine to disappear beneath the waistband of her slacks. Somewhere along the evolutionary chain, a creature like a cross between a zebra and a giraffe had stood upright, the front legs had shortened to become arms, and the split hoof that passed for feet developed a third digit that served as a thumb.

I laid Mercedes on the bed, and Dalea began her examination. I was jiggling, shifting my weight from foot to foot, waiting. Finally, I couldn't contain my anxiety any longer.

"Is she hurt?"

"Bumps, bruises." Dalea filled a hypodermic. "She took a pretty good dose of radiation, probably when the flagship blew. This will help."

She gave Mercedes the injection. A few moments later there was a reaction. Mercedes stirred and moaned. I laid a hand on her forehead.

"She's in pain. What was in that shot?" I asked, suddenly suspicious of my alien shipmate.

"Nanobots that will repair her damaged DNA. That's not why she's moaning. She's coming out of a rapidly induced coma, and she's got that feeling of pins-and-needles in her extremities."

Dalea exchanged a glance with Jahan, who shrugged and said, "He's in love with her. What else can you expect?"

"Would you stop saying that," I said, exasperated.

"So stay with her," said Dalea. "I'm assuming that if you love her, you must know her, and she should wake up to a familiar face."

The two alien females left the sick bay. I broke the magnetic seal on a chair, pulled it over to the bedside, and sat down. I took Mercedes's limp hand where it hung over the side of the bed, and softly stroked it. It was her left hand, and the elaborate wedding set seemed to cut at my fingers.

She should wake up to a familiar face. What would that have been like? To sleep next to this woman? To have her scent in my nostrils? To have her long hair catch in my lips? Once, twenty-two years ago, I had experienced only the last of those fantasies. We had violated lights out at the Academy and met on the Star Deck. We had kissed, and her hair, floating in free fall, had caressed my face.

I was lost in a daydream, tending toward an actual dream, when Mercedes sighed and her fingers tightened on mine. My eyes jerked open, and I shot up out of the chair. She looked up at me, smiled, and murmured,

"Tracy. I dreamed I heard your voice. But you can't actually be here."

"But I am, your highness."

She frowned, and reached up. I leaned forward so she could touch my face. She looked around the tiny space, and she accepted the truth. "Once more you rescue me," she murmured.

WALKING ONTO THE bridge, I was met with three conversations all taking place simultaneously.

"Why are we still here? No trade, no money," from Jax.

"Are you going down?" from Baca.

"I think I know what killed the Imperials," from Melin.

I answered them in order of complexity. "Because I say so. Yes. What?"

Melin picked the question out of my surly and laconic reply. "Kusatsu-Shirane only has three moons now."

I sat down at my post. "They blew up two of their moons?"

"Yep. Apparently, the Imperials closed with the planet in their normal arrowhead formation. Given the regularity of the moons' orbits, the folks on Kusatsu-Shirane picked the two moons closest to the ships to destroy. The resulting debris went through the ships like shotgun pellets through cheese. *Boom!*" Melin accompanied the word with an expressive gesture.

"That would imply that the other three are booby trapped too."

"Most likely."

"*Madre de Dios!* I landed us on one of the remaining moons." I wiped away the sweat that had suddenly bloomed on my upper lip.

"I think it took a person with a finger on the trigger to set off the explosions," Melin offered. It was comfort, but not much.

"New plan. Let's stay away from the remaining moons," I said to our navigator.

"Good plan," she said, and turned back to her console.

Baca spoke up. "Then why the dirge from the planet? They won a mighty victory."

"But short term," Jahan said. I jumped. Damn it, she'd done it again. Her fur tickled my left ear.

I nodded. "What Jahan said. The battle group's course was filed with Central Command on Hissilek. When they neither call home nor come home, the League will come looking for them. Kusatsu-Shirane is going to be discovered."

"Tracy's right."

Mercedes's voice had always had this little catch in it. Very endearing and very sexy. I stood and turned around. She was on the platform lift, and she looked shaky. I hurried to her side, and assisted her into the chair Baca hastily vacated. He was staring like a pole-axed bull. I couldn't blame him. How often did an ordinary space tramp meet the heir to an empire?

"Uh . . . hello, ma'am, Luis Baca, communications. I'll get a message off to Hissilek."

"Where are you bound for next?" she asked me.

"Cuandru."

"A message won't reach League space faster than this ship. There will be military ships at Cuandru." She was right about that; Cuandru was the largest shipyard in the League. Mercedes smiled at me, but I noticed that the expression never reached her eyes. They were dark and haunted. "You're the captain."

"I am," I said.

"Congratulations. You finally made it."

"On a trading vessel." I hoped that the resentment didn't show too badly.

"Believe me, it's better than being an admiral," Mercedes said softly.

"I'll have to take your word for it."

"So why are you still in orbit?" she asked.

"We have no communication from the planet," Jax trilled. "We are uncertain if there is anyone to trade *with*."

"Tracy was on his way to the planet when he picked up your distress signal," Melin said.

"Did they evacuate?" Mercedes asked.

"It's possible, but not likely. There were close to a million people on Kusatsu-Shirane," I said.

Mercedes stood. "Then let us go and find out what has become of them."

"I'm not sure that's a good idea."

"I'm not asking. You're still my subject."

The final words came floating back over her shoulder. I followed her onto the lift.

THE WIND WHISPERED down the deserted streets of Edogowa. There were no vehicles parked on the streets. It was all very tidy and orderly. It was near sunset, and to the west magnificent thunderheads formed a vibrant palette of blues, grays, reds, and golds. Two long but very narrow bands of rain extended from the clouds to the chaparral below. The bands looked like sweeping tendrils of gray hair, and where the rain hit the ground, the dust on this high desert plateau boiled into the air like milk froth.

"Where is everybody?" Baca asked. His eyes darted nervously from side to side.

Jahan came scrambling down the wall of a four-story office building. "Nobody's there. Lights are off. Computers shut down. It's like everybody's taken a holiday."

Mercedes shivered. I started to put my arm around her shoulders, but thought better of it and drew back. "Let's go to a house," she said.

"Why?" Jahan asked.

"When you think something terrible is about to happen, you want to be with your loved ones," Mercedes answered.

We had ended up landing the *Selkie* at the small spaceport. The *Wasp* could only comfortably carry two, and the melancholy music and the lack of human voices had me jumpy. I wanted backup. Jahan radioed our plan back to Melin, Jax, and Dalea.

Our footfalls echoed on the sidewalk and bounced off the sides of the buildings. I realized that something else was missing besides the people: the smell of cooking food. There were hundreds of restaurants in Edogowa. Most business was conducted over a meal, and deals were sealed with alcohol. Food was a ritual on Kusatsu-Shirane. But now all I smelled was that pungent mix of dust and rain and ozone as the storm approached.

The business district gave way to small wood houses with shoji screens on the windows, and graceful upturned edges on the roofs. Now we found vehicles, carefully parked at the houses. The clouds rolled in, dulling the color of the flowers in perfectly groomed beds. Overhead, thunder grumbled like a giant shifting in his sleep.

We picked a house at random and walked up to the front door. I knocked. Silence. I knocked again. Mercedes reached past me, grasped the knob and opened the door.

"Trusting kind of place," Baca muttered.

"They want us to come in. To see," Mercedes said in a hollow tone.

No one asked the obvious *see what* question. It had taken me longer, but I had finally come to the same point as Mercedes in my analysis. Japanese-influenced culture, imminent loss of their children and their way of life—for the people of Kusatsu-Shirane there was only one possible solution.

The family was in the bedroom. The children lay in their mother's arms. Her lax hands were still over their eyes. She had a neat hole in her forehead. The children had been shot in the back of the head. The father slumped in a chair, chin resting on his chest. Blood formed a bib on the front of his shirt. The pistol had fallen from his hand.

Mercedes remained stone-faced as we toured more houses. It was the seventh house before she finally broke. A sob burst out, she turned toward me. My arms opened, and she buried her face against my chest. She was crying so hard that in a matter of moments, the front of my shirt was wet. It made me think of the father in the first house, his shirt wet with blood. I closed my arms tight around Mercedes, trying to hold back the horror.

"*Why?* They would have had a good life! Especially the children. Why would they do this? They're insane!"

"Because the life we offered wasn't the life they wanted," I said softly. "This was the last choice they could make for themselves, and they made it. I'm not saying it's a good choice, but I can understand it."

"They killed their *children*," Mercedes whispered. "Thousands of children." She broke out of my embrace, dragged frantic fingers through her hair. "Why? To keep them from us? We're not monsters!"

"That depends on where you're sitting in the pecking order," Jahan said in her dry way.

There was a silence for several long moments. Mercedes stood in the living room, surrounded by the dead. She looked lost and terribly frail. I stepped to her side and put my arm around her.

"Let's go," I said softly. "There's nothing here."

"Ghosts," she whispered. "They'll be here."

MELIN PLOTTED OUR course for Cuandru, the Isanjo home world. We boosted out of orbit, heading for open vacuum between the planets before we entered the Fold.

I left the bridge and went to visit Jax in his office/cabin. He was standing in a wading pool of water rehydrating his leaves, and holding a computer while he ran figures. Nervous whistling emerged from the sound valves that lined his sides. Each valve emitted a different, discordant tone. It was like a dentist drilling.

"How bad?" I asked.

"Bad. We didn't sell the low-tech farm equipment on Kusatsu-Shi-rane, which meant we didn't pick up loads of lacquer knickknacks to sell to your jaded ruling class on League worlds. We must hope for a big reward for rescuing the Infanta," Jax concluded.

"That's it? That's your only reaction to the death of a million people? We couldn't make the sale?"

The seven ocular organs around the alien's head swiveled to regard me. "What was it one of your ancient dictators said? One death is a tragedy; a million is a statistic. And, bluntly, they were not my kind, nor is it a choice I can condone."

And that's why they call them alien, I thought as I left. I decided not to ask the other alien members of the crew how they felt.

The bizarre philosophical discussion had meant that I hadn't voiced my real concern: that the League would decide we were somehow behind the destruction of the fleet and slap us in prison. It would be a black eye for the navy and the Infanta if the government had to admit that the citizens of a Hidden World had destroyed a battle group. Better to blame a slightly shady trading vessel commanded by a disgraced Imperial officer. I decided that it couldn't hurt to clear things up with Mercedes.

I had given her my cabin. It was slightly larger than the crew cabins, and the bed could actually hold two assuming they were friendly. Privacy on ships is the opposite of what one might expect. You'd think that people living in close confines inside a tin can would want the closed door and a private place. Instead I found that crews tended to live in a constant state of togetherness, like a group hug. We walked in and out of each other's cabins. When we weren't on duty we played games that involved lots of people. I think it's because space is so vast, so empty, and so cold that you want the comfort of contact with other living things.

Which is why I just walked in on Mercedes. She was kneeling in front of the small shrine I maintained to the Virgin, and she was saying the rosary. The click of the beads set a counterpoint to the bass throb of the engines, and I was startled when I realized she was using my rosary. But of course she would have to. Hers had been reduced to dust and atoms along with everything else aboard the *Nuestra*.

She gave me a brief nod, her lips continuing to move, and the familiar prayer just the barest of sound in the room. I sat down on the bed and waited. She wasn't that far from the end.

I closed my eyes and took the opportunity to offer up a prayer for my father, still laboring away in the tailor shop on Hissilek. A stroke—brought on, I was convinced, by my court-martial and subsequent conviction—had left him with a crippled right leg, but he still worked, making uniforms for the very men who had ruined me. Sometimes it felt like the most personal of betrayals, and I hated him for it, but in more rational moments, I realized that he had to eat, and that he had spent a lifetime outfitting the officers of the Imperial Navy. It wasn't like he could become a designer of ladies' fashion at age sixty-eight.

I jumped and my eyes flew open when I felt cool fingers touch my cheek. Mercedes was standing directly in front of me, and so close. She jerked back her hand at my startled reaction. I didn't want her to take my response as a rejection, so I reached out and grabbed her hand.

"It's all right; you just startled me," I said.

While at the same moment she was saying, "I'm sorry. You just had such a hurt and angry look on your face."

"Memories." I shrugged. "They're never a good thing."

"Really? I have some nice ones of you."

"Don't." I stood up and brushed past her. "All this proves is that the universe is a bitch and she has a nasty sense of humor."

"We were very good . . . friends once."

"Yes, but that was years ago, and a marriage ago." I couldn't help it. I looked back, hoping I'd hurt her, and was embarrassed when I realized I had.

But it was hard, so hard. She had married my greatest enemy from the Academy. Honorius Sinclair Cullen, Knight of the Arches and Shells, Duke de Argento, known to his friends and enemies as BoHo. He was an admiral now, too. I touched the scar at my left temple, a gift from BoHo, and his mocking tones seemed to whisper in the throb of the engines. *Lowborn scum.*

Mercedes sank down on the bed. "We all do what we must. That must be what the people on Kusatsu-Shirane thought." There was an ocean of grief in her dark brown eyes.

I walked back and sat down next to her. Sitting this close, I could see the web of crow's-feet around her eyes, and the two small frown lines between her brows. We were forty-four years old, and I wondered if either of us had ever known a day of unadulterated happiness.

"Has it been so bad?"

She looked down at her hand, twisted the wedding set, and finally pulled it off. It left a red indentation like a brand on her finger. "The palace makes sure his affairs are conducted discreetly, and they vet the women to make sure they aren't reporters or working for political opponents, and thank God there have been no bastards." She paused and gave me a rueful smile. "Unfortunately, no legitimate children either. If I don't whelp soon, my father may remove me from the succession."

There was a flare of heat in my chest. If she wasn't the Infanta, wasn't the heir, she could live as she pleased. Maybe even with a tailor's son. There was also a bitter pleasure in learning that BoHo was sterile.

"But look at you. *Captain* Belmanor. How did you come by this ship?"

"I won a share of it in a card game. It seemed great at first. Then I discovered how much was still owed on the damn thing. Sometimes I think Tregillis lost deliberately."

Mercedes laughed. She knew me too well. "Admit it. You love it. You're a captain, you go where you please, no orders from highborn twits with more braid than brains."

"Yes, but I wanted to stay in the navy. To prove that one of my kind could be an effective officer."

There was a silence; then she asked, "Were you guilty?"

"No."

"I thought not. But the evidence against you was—"

"Overwhelming. Yes. That should always be a clue that someone's being framed." I sat frowning, shifting through all the old hurts and injustices.

She hesitantly touched my shoulder. "I'm sorry. I thought about doing something."

"So why didn't you?" And I realized that I was less angry than honestly curious.

"I was afraid . . ."

"Of—?" She held up her hand, cutting off the rest of my question.

"There would have been whispers." We sat silent for a few minutes. The memory of the Star Deck returned. "Have you married?" she suddenly asked, pulling me back to the present.

"No. I never met anyone I wanted to marry."

"Liar." Her look challenged me. I realized that our thighs were touching, shoulders brushing. Her hair was tickling my ear and cheek. She smelled of sweat and faded perfume and woman.

"Mercedes, I'm . . . um . . ."

"You saved my life," she said softly, and she took my hand and laid it on her breast.

I jumped up and looked down at her. "No. Not because you're *grateful*. That would be worse than never having you."

"You loved me once."

"I still do." She had tricked me, and I had said it. I fell back on the only defense and the source of my greatest pain. "And you're another man's wife."

She stood. "Damn your middle-class morality! My life has been bound by expectations, rules, and protocol. I married a man I do not love. I became a military leader because of my father's frustration over his lack of a son. And now I've led my fleet to destruction, and the very thought of me and what I represent has driven the population of an entire planet to commit suicide! But I'm forced to live on with all the loss and regret. Can't I have one moment of happiness?" The agony in her voice nearly broke my resolve.

She turned away, hiding her tears. I gently took hold of her shoulders. "See if you still feel this way after a night's sleep. I don't want to add to those regrets."

I left before temptation overcame scruples.

WE TOOK THE *Selkie* out to an area of open space, well away from any planetary bodies in the solar system, and folded. The ports now showed the strange gray filaments, like spiderweb or gray cotton candy, which was the hallmark of traveling past light-speed. I checked the watch implanted in the weave of my shirt. Midafternoon. I decided to check on Mercedes. There was no response to my gentle knock. Concerned, I slipped into the cabin and found her asleep, but there were traces of tears on her cheeks. She murmured disconsolately and her fingers plucked at the sheets. Feeling like a voyeur, I quietly left.

And was caught by Baca, who with unaccustomed seriousness said, "I was thinking about saying a Kaddish for the people, but I realized it was more Masada than Holocaust, and then I had to wonder if it was a righteous choice. To die rather than submit. Is that noble, or is it more noble to survive and persevere? What do you think?"

I looked at this stranger in Baca's body, and tried to compose an answer. We had stood at the edge of a massive graveyard, and I couldn't grasp it. All I knew was that this burden of guilt rested on the shoulders of the woman I loved. I couldn't do anything for the battle group or for Kusatsu-Shirane, but maybe I could do something for Mercedes.

She joined us that evening for supper. With Mercedes, it was a tight fit around the small table in the mess, but we all squeezed in. Jahan had prepared a slow-simmered stew of rehydrated vegetables and lamb for the omnivores, and there was a vegetarian dish for Dalea and Jax. Like all Isanjo food, it was highly spiced, so I drank more beer than normal. Perhaps it was due more to sitting so close to Mercedes.

Once the plates were cleared, Melin brought me a reader. I was embarrassed to display this silly ship custom in front of Mercedes. I hedged. "I don't remember where we were."

"The chapter entitled 'Wayfarers All,' page 159, second paragraph," Jax offered helpfully. I mentally cursed the creature for its perfect recall.

"What is this?" Mercedes asked.

"We read aloud after the final meal of the day," Jahan said. "Each one of us picks a book from our species. You never really know a culture until you've heard their poetry and read their great literature."

"An interesting way to spread understanding," Mercedes said thoughtfully.

"Yes, you don't allow it in your human schools and universities," Dalea said.

Mercedes blushed and I glared at the Hajin.

"And what human book did you select?" Mercedes hurriedly asked me, to cover the awkward moment.

"The Wind in the Willows."

Mercedes shifted her chair so she could better see me. "Please, do read."

I was embarrassed, and cleared my throat several times before starting, but after a few sentences, the soft magic of the story and the music of the words made me forget my special listener.

"She will clothe herself with canvas; and then, once outside, the sounding slap of great green seas as she heels to the wind, pointing South! And you, you will come too, young brother; for the days pass, and never return, and the South still waits for you. Take the Adventure, heed the call, now ere the irrevocable moment passes!" My voice cracked on the final words. I coughed and reached for my beer and finished off the last sip. "That's all the voice I have tonight," I said.

There were a few groans of disappointment, but the party broke up, some of the crew to return to the bridge, others to their cabins to sleep. I escorted Mercedes back to the cabin.

We stopped at the door, and an awkward silence fell over us both. "I've slept a night," she finally said quietly.

My collar suddenly grabbed my throat. I ran a finger around it. "Ah . . . yes, you have."

"I believe I'll take the wayfarer's advice," she murmured, and she kissed me.

I had enough wit, barely, to lock the door behind us.

LATER, WE LAY in the narrow bed. I liked that it was narrow. It meant that she had to stay close. Her head was on my shoulder, and I twined a strand of her hair through my fingers. I was very aware of the scent of Mercedes—the deep musk of our sex mingling, the spice and pine smell of her hair—her breath, which seemed to hold a hint of vanilla. I kissed her long and deep, then pulled back and smacked my lips.

"What?"

"You taste like vanilla too," I answered. She blushed. It was adorable. She ran a hand through my dishwater blond hair. "I know, I'm shaggy. I'll get a haircut on Cuandru."

"I like it. It makes you look rakish. You were always so spit and polish."

"I had to be. Everyone was waiting for the 'lowborn scum' to disgrace the service."

She laid a hand across my mouth. "Don't. Forget about them. Forget the slights."

"Hard to do."

"Don't be a grievance collector," Mercedes said. She changed the subject. "Lot of silver in there."

I stroked the gray streaks at her temples. "Neither of us is as young as we used to be."

"Really? I would never have known that if you hadn't told me." She pulled my hair, and we laughed together.

I was on the verge of dozing off when she suddenly rested a hand on my chest and pushed herself up. Her hair hung around her like a mahogany-colored veil. My good mood gave way to alarm, because she looked so serious.

"Tracy, do something for me?"

"Of course."

"Don't report that you've found me. Not just yet. I want a little more time."

I did too. So I agreed.

Late in the sleep cycle, I was awakened by her cries. Tears slid from beneath her lashes and wet her cheeks though she was still asleep. She thrashed, fighting the covers. I caught her in my arms, and held her close.

"Mercedes, *mi amor*. Wake up. You're safe."

Her eyes opened and she blinked up at me in confusion. "They're dead." She gave a violent shiver, and covered her face with her hands, then looked in surprise at the tears clinging to her fingers. "I see those houses. The children. I killed them."

I rocked her. "Shhh, hush, you didn't." But it was only a half-truth and she knew it. And she was only mentioning half the dead. There was no word of the battle group. The men she'd commanded, and who had died no less surely than the people of Kusatsu-Shirane.

Eventually, she fell back to sleep. I lay awake, holding her close and wondering when the full trauma would hit.

SINCE THERE WAS an Imperial shipyard at Cuandru, I came out of Fold at the edge of the solar system. I didn't want the big point-to-point guns deciding that we were some kind of threat. I ordered Baca to tight beam our information—ship registry, previous ports of call (excluding the Hidden Worlds, of course), and cargo—to the planetary control. My radio man gave me a look.

"We're not mentioning the Infanta?"

"Not yet. Her orders," I answered, striving to sound casual. Melin and Baca exchanged glances, and Melin rolled her eyes. I felt the flush rising up my neck, into my face, until it culminated at the top of my ears. Not for the first time, I cursed my fair complexion.

"Then she better be a crew member," Jahan said. "Otherwise, they'll think we're white slavers and we kidnapped her."

"She's not young enough," I said.

"Oh, boy," Baca muttered.

"Better not let *her* hear you say that," Jahan said.

"What?" I demanded.

Melin said, "Captain, somebody's got to take you in hand and teach you how to be a boyfriend."

"I'm not her boyfriend. She's married. We're friends."

"Okay. Then you got a lot to learn about being a lover," Melin said.

At that moment, I hated my crew. I made an inarticulate sound and clutched at my hair. "Get her on the crew list." I stomped off the bridge.

I DECIDED TO take us in to dock at the station. I shooed Melin out of her post, and she proceeded to hover behind me like an overanxious mother. Through the horseshoe-shaped port, we could see the big cruisers under construction. Spacesuited figures, most of them Isanjos, clambered and darted around the massive skeletal forms. Against the black of space, the sparks off their welders were like newly born stars.

There was a light touch on my shoulder. I glanced up briefly. It was

Mercedes, and sometime in the past few hours, she had cut her hair, dyed it red, and darkened her skin. Dalea loomed behind her.

"What's this?" I asked, hating the loss of that glorious mane.

"We had to do something to keep her from being recognized," Dalea said.

"I'm sure the port authorities will be expecting to find the Infanta aboard a tramp cargo ship," I said sarcastically, as I tweaked the maneuvering jets.

Jahan, seated at my command station, said "Tracy, her face is on the *money*."

And so it was. She graced the twenty Reales note. The picture was taken from an official portrait that had her wearing a tiara, long hair elaborately styled, and a diamond necklace at her throat. Now she wore a pair of my stained cargo pants, and one of Melin's shirts.

Jax came rustling onto the bridge. Now the entire crew and Mercedes were watching, but I wasn't nervous. I knew I was good. With brief bursts of fire from alternating jets, I took us through the maze of trading ships, station scooters, racing yachts, and military vessels. With a final burst of power from the starboard engines, I spun the ship ninety degrees and brought us to rest, like a butterfly landing on a flower, against a docking gantry at the main space station.

There was a brief outburst of applause. Mercedes leaned down and whispered, "You were the best pilot of our class." The touch of her lips and the puff of her breath against my ear sent a shiver through me.

She straightened, and addressed the crew. "So what now?"

"We try to find someone to buy the farm equipment, and we pick up another cargo," Jax fluted.

Melin stretched her arms over her head. "I want a martini and a massage. And maybe not in that order. Or maybe both at the same time."

Jahan uncoiled from the back of the captain's chair. "I'm going home to see my mates and kids."

"If the captain will give me money, I'll replenish our medical supplies," Dalea said.

Mercedes smiled at Baca. "And what about you?"

He blushed. "I'm gonna find a concert. Maybe go to the opera, depending on what's playing."

Mercedes tugged my hair. "And you need a haircut."

"I take it we're going planetside?" I asked.

"Oh, yes," Mercedes assured me.

Dalea's makeover worked. The guards glanced briefly at my ship papers, and waved us through and onto a shuttle to the planet.

IT WAS FOOLISH, crazy even. I planned to check us into an exclusive hotel, a place frequented by aristocrats and famous actors. It was going to take most of my savings, but I wanted . . . I wasn't sure exactly what I wanted. To make sure she was comfortable. To show her that I could be her equal. Fortunately, Mercedes was wiser than me. When I outlined my plan, she took my face between her hands and gently shook my head back and forth.

"No. First, you don't have to prove anything to me, and second, I'm likely to be recognized, red hair or no, and third, I've spent my life with these people. Let me have another life. A short time where I don't have to remember . . ." But she didn't finish the thought.

Jahan advised us, and we ended up in an Isanjo tree house hotel that sprawled through an old-growth forest on the outskirts of the capital city. To accommodate the occasional human visitor, there were swaying bridges between the trees, which Mercedes and I used with white-knuckled effort. As we crept across the swaying bridges, the Isanjo traveled branch to branch, and crossed the intervening spaces with great soaring leaps. The Isanjo were good enough to deliver meals to our aerie, so we spent our first day planetside in bed.

Wind whispered and then roared through the leaves as it brought down a storm from the mountains. It set our room to swaying. Lightning flashed through the wooden shutters, and thunder growled with a sound like a giant chewing on boulders. We clung to each other, torn between terror and delight. The rain came, hammering on the wooden roof, forcing its way through the shutters to spray lightly across our bodies. It broke the heat, and we shivered and snuggled close.

It would have been perfect except for her nightmares.

The next day, Mercedes took command. We went to explore the city, and to find a barber. Mercedes and the Hajin hairdresser discussed every cowlick, natural part, and the consistency of my hair before she would allow the alien to cut. Between them, they decided I should wear bangs. It felt strange, and I kept pushing them off my forehead, only to have my lady reach out and muss my hair each time I did.

We strolled through the Old Quarter, and I bought Mercedes a string of beads that she'd admired. We moved on, strolling along the river walk. Everyone seemed to be taking advantage of the good weather. Families spread blankets on the grass, children tussled like happy kittens, babies cried. Mercedes and I sat on a bench at the water's edge, listening to the water gurgle and chuckle while we shared an ice cream cone.

We ate dinner at an outdoor café. The Isanjo, being almost complete carnivores, know how to cook meat. Our steaks arrived running blood, tender, and subtly flavored by having been stuffed with cheese. We polished off a bottle of deep red wine between us, and talked about books and music and the wonderful things we'd seen during the day. She scrupulously avoided all talk of the empire, the navy, or Kusatsu-Shirane. We shared a dessert, a lighter-than-air concoction of mangos, some local fruit, cream, and pistachio nuts. I drained my coffee, and steeled myself for a conversation that had to happen.

"Mercedes."

"Yes?"

"You need to talk to someone. About what happened."

"I will. This policy can't stand. Not if it's going to lead to mass suicide," she said.

I shook my head. "Stop deflecting. You need to face what's happened, and figure out why you're identifying more with the people on Kusatsu-Shirane than you are with your own battle group."

"That's not fair."

"Tell me I'm wrong." She stayed silent. I left it there. "So, shall we go?"

"Yes."

I left money on the table, and we walked out onto the street. The air was soft after the tumultuous storms of the night before. The restaurants were still busy, and the many voices and many languages wove into something that was almost music. Then we heard real music. Dance music. Mercedes turned to me.

"Do you like to dance?"

"No," I said.

She grabbed my hand. "I love to dance." And I came along like the tail on her kite. There was a small band playing on a pier that thrust out into the river. Multicolored lanterns hung overhead. The Isanjo danced on the narrow wires that supported the lanterns. The humans, earthbound and awkward, danced on the wooden pier. I felt graceless and stupid. There had been no deportment and dance lessons in my youth, but Mercedes was gifted with grace and rhythm. She made me look good.

The dance ended, and we went off to the small bar to buy drinks. She took a long sip, and then kissed me. I tasted rum and basil.

"So, I'm forgiven for poking at you?"

"At least you notice when I'm crazy," she said.

"You're not crazy. The people on Kusatsu-Shirane were crazy."

"Were they? No one got to force them into a life—"

But she didn't get to finish the thought because there were murmurs from the crowd. Everyone was looking up. We followed suit and watched pinpricks of light appear and flash like brilliant diamonds in the night sky.

"That's a fleet coming in," I said.

Mercedes gripped me tightly. "Take me home."

It was a misnomer. We had no home, but I understood what she wanted. The comfort of bed, bodies pressed close, a roof to shut out the image of duty and responsibility now orbiting overhead.

We returned to the hotel and our lovemaking had a desperate quality. She clung to me, clawed at me as if she wanted to crawl inside my skin. Finally, I had nothing more to give. I lay gasping, body sweat-bathed, blood pounding in my ears.

Mercedes was curled up in a ball. I put an arm around her waist and spooned her. "Tracy." It was barely audible.

"Hmmm?"

"Let me stay. Really be a member of your crew." Tension and desperate longing etched every word, and her fingers clung like claws to my wrist. She turned over suddenly, her face inches from mine. "They think I'm dead. We can go away. Be together."

For an instant, I was giddy at the prospect. I thought of the worlds we'd visit together. Nights in my cabin. Listening to her read to the crew. But reality returned.

"No, love, they know you survived. Your capsule was beaming out continuous messages. When those signals stopped, they know you were found and the capsule opened. They would search for us, and they could never admit that you joined us voluntarily."

"And they would kill you," she said, her voice flat and dull.

"And beyond personal concerns, what happens if you don't take the throne? You know BoHo will try to rule in your place." She shuddered at the prospect. "We've had this moment. We couldn't expect it to last."

"It will last. At least until morning."

We didn't sleep. It would have wasted the time we still had together.

SHE WANTED TO say good-bye to everyone. I called them, and the crew assembled at a popular, if low-rent, diner. I ordered *huevos rancheros* because I could stir it together and no one would notice that I hadn't eaten. There was a brittle quality to our laughter, and only at the end did we discuss what lay between us.

Mercedes encompassed them all with a look. "Thank you all for your kindness. I'll never forget you and what you did for me. I also wanted you to know that there are going to be changes when I take the throne. There won't be another Kusatsu-Shirane, and I'll see that there's a review of the alien laws."

The parting took a while because Dalea wanted to "make sure her patient was fit." Mercedes and the Hajin retreated to the bathroom. Jahan joined me and stretched out her claws.

"Will you survive?"

"I'll have to," I said with forced lightness.

Mercedes and Dalea returned. Mercedes had an indescribable expression on her face. I briefly took her hand. "All good?" I asked.

"Yes. Oh, yes," she said in a faraway voice.

Our next stop was the hair salon. My hairdresser from the day before stripped the red from Mercedes hair, and restored it to its lustrous dark brown. Once he was finished, the Hajin studied her closely. Mercedes went imperious on him.

"All you've seen is a remarkable resemblance."

He stepped back, extended a front leg, and gave her a dignified bow. "Quite, ma'am."

We took a cab to the League Embassy. Barricades and guards surrounded the building. The driver cranked around to look at us. "They won't let me any closer than this," he said.

"That's fine," I said.

Mercedes and I looked at each other. Mercedes's eyes were awash with tears. I swallowed hard, trying to force down the painful lump that had settled in my throat.

"Good-bye," she said. She started to reach out a hand, then threw herself into my arms and pressed her lips to mine. She pulled away, opened the door, and got out.

I got out too, and watched as she walked quickly toward the elaborate gates of the embassy. She didn't look back. There was a flurry of reaction from the guards. The door of the embassy opened, and a flying wedge of men, led by BoHo, rushed out. Medals and ribbons glittered on the midnight blue of his uniform jacket, and the sunlight glinted off his jet-black hair. He was still handsome, though middle age had softened the lines of his jaw.

He went to kiss her, and Mercedes turned her face away.

MY THREE ALIEN crew members found me in a bar late that night.

"Go away."

Jax shuffled closer. "The ship's note's been paid off, so we own her free and clear. And we got a reward. A most generous reward. The Infanta meets her obligations. And I've procured a new cargo. We're ready to leave whenever you are."

Jahan curled up on the bar stool next to me. "The fleet has withdrawn. They're rushing back to Hissilek. Apparently, the emperor's had a stroke."

That pulled me out of my rapt contemplation of my scotch. I met those alien eyes, and I had that cold sensation of being surrounded by hidden forces that were plotting against humans.

"How . . . convenient," I managed.

"I think she'll be a good ruler," Jahan said. "Now the final bit of news." She gestured to Dalea.

"The Infanta is pregnant." I gaped at the Hajin. "Congratulations," Dalea added.

I'm going to be a father. My child will be the heir to the Solar League. I will never know him or her.

And I realized that maybe none of us ever gets to choose our lives. Our only choice is to live the life that comes to us, or go down into darkness.

I drained my scotch, and pushed back from the bar. "Let's go see what tomorrow holds."

Robin Hobb

New York Times *bestseller Robin Hobb is one of the most popular writers in fantasy today, having sold more than one million copies of her work in paperback. She's perhaps best known for her epic fantasy Farseer series (*Assassin's Apprentice, Royal Assassin, *and* Assassin's Quest*), as well as the two fantasy trilogies related to it: the Liveship Traders (*Ship of Magic, Mad Ship, *and* Ship of Destiny*) and the Tawny Man (*Fool's Errand, Golden Fool, *and* Fool's Fate*). The last one was reprinted in 2009. She is also the author of the Soldier Son trilogy (*Shaman's Crossing, Forest Mage, *and* Renegade's Magic*). Her early novels, published under the name Megan Lindholm, include the fantasy novels* Wizard of the Pigeons, Harpy's Flight, The Windsingers, The Limbreth Gate, The Luck of the Wheels, The Reindeer People, Wolf's Brother, *and* Cloven Hooves; *the science fiction novel* Alien Earth, *and, with Steven Brust, the novel* The Gypsy. *Her most recent books as Robin Hobb are the novels* Dragon Keeper *and* Dragon Haven.

In the poignant story that follows, she shows us that although love can build bridges across the widest of chasms, those bridges can be swept away by a flood of troubles—but that sometimes, with luck and persistence, they can be built again.

Blue Boots

She was sitting on the splintery landing of the rickety wooden steps that led up to the kitchen servants' quarters. The sun had warmed the steps and it was her free day. Timbal had an apple, crisp from the tree, and she was swinging her boots and watching the swooping swallows as she ate it. Summer was winding to a close and soon the birds would be gone. Idly, she wished she were going with them, then just as quickly changed her mind. Life at Timberrock Keep was good to her; she should be thanking the goddess Eda for such a pleasant day, not wishing for more.

Azen the minstrel came out of the kitchen door. As he passed her, he casually reached up and knocked on the bottom of her boots. "'Morning, blue boots," he said, and walked on. She sat, apple in hand, staring after him as he made his long-legged way down the winding gravel path. His trousers were blue, his jacket a deep gold. His head was a tangle of loose black curls that jogged as he strode along.

In that moment, Timbal fell in love with him.

It does not take that much to fall in love when you are seventeen and alone in the world, and Timbal was both. Her father's death had cut her adrift; she knew she'd been lucky to find a post as a kitchen girl at one of the lesser keeps in Buck Duchy. It was much better than the inn where she'd first found employment. Here, she had daily work, hot food, and her own room and bed. There was a future for her here; most likely was that she'd keep working year after year and that eventually she'd become a cook. Less likely was the prospect of getting married and becoming a wife to one of the other Timberrock servants.

A handsome minstrel had no place in either future. Traditionally, minstrels never wed or settled down. They were the wandering record keepers of the Six Duchies, the men and women who knew not just the larger history of the world, but the details of inheritances, the bloodlines of the noble families, and many particulars of agreements among the small holders and even the business of the many towns and cities. They wandered where they would, supported by the largesse of titled families and innkeepers and patrons, slept where and with whom they pleased, and then wandered on. There were minstrels' guilds in the larger cities and informal associations in the lesser towns where orphans and the bastards of minstrels might be raised to follow in their trade. It was a high and artistic calling that was not at all respectable or secure.

In short, handsome, melodic Azen was the worst possible sort of fellow for a girl like Timbal to fall in love with. And so, of course, she had.

She had seen him before the morning he knocked on the soles of her boots and she opened her heart to him. In the evenings, when the day's work was mostly done, all the folk of Timberrock Keep were welcome to gather in the lord's hall to listen to music and tales while they finished whatever chores could be done inside of an evening. Stable boys mended harness, housemaids stitched torn sheets or darned socks, and kitchen maids such as Timbal could bring a big basket of apples to core and slice for the next day's pies. And so she had seen Azen, standing in the late-evening light from the open doors and windows, singing for Lady Lucent and her husband Lord Just.

For Lord Just, long crippled from a fall during a hunt, Azen chanted tales of ancient battles or songs about deeds of daring. Lord Just had been a muscular fellow before his fall, she had heard. Confined to a chair, his body had dwindled, and his black curls were starting to turn gray. When he thudded his fist on the table and sang the refrains to some of the old songs, he reminded Timbal more of a small child banging with a spoon than a man enjoying a drinking song. The strength of his lungs and depth of his voice had diminished along with his body. Yet when he sang along, often as not, Lady Lucent would set her hand on his bony shoulder and smile at him, as if remembering the man he had once been to her.

For Lady Lucent, Azen sang romantic ballads or recited in dramatic tones the tales of love prevailing against all odds, or failing in heart-rending circumstances. When Azen performed for her, Lady Lucent's eyes never left the minstrel's face. Often she kept her kerchief to hand, for more than once his songs wrung tears from her eyes. She was not alone in that. On her very first evening in the hall, Timbal had been surprised to find her own eyes overflowing with tears at Azen's tale of a wandering warrior who finally returned home to discover he was too late; his lady love was in her early grave. Timbal had been a bit embarrassed to weep at such a sad and sentimental song; it was evidently a familiar favorite to many at the keep, for they hummed along and kept at their tasks, some whispering to one another, untouched by his words. She had no kerchief and was reduced to wiping her cuff across her streaming eyes.

And when she lowered her wrist from her face, she realized that Azen was staring straight at her. As their eyes met, perhaps a small smile quirked at the corner of his mouth. Not a mockery, but his pleasure at her response to his song. His eyes had said the same, and she had dropped her gaze back onto the potatoes she was slicing, confused and embarrassed to be noticed by him. Long minutes later, she lifted her eyes again, and was relieved to find the minstrel singing directly to Lady Lucent, as if she were the only listener in his world. Timbal managed to sit through the rest of his performance without letting her emotional responses to his songs be too obvious. Surely it wasn't appropriate for her to weep like a child at a simple song. A tender-hearted lady might break down at such a thing, but not a kitchen maid.

When evening was deep and the minstrel announced with regret that he must give his voice a rest, Lady Lucent spoke softly to Lord Just, and the man beckoned the minstrel forward. A little purse of red fabric tied with a gold cord appeared on the table at the lord's elbow. His lady might have readied it and passed it to him; Timbal hadn't seen. The minstrel thanked them both profusely, sweeping a low bow to the lord and going down on one knee to kiss the lady's hand. Timbal, relatively new to such goings-on, watched curiously; so this was how things were done in a keep! She wondered if she had blundered into a special performance on her first evening here or if this was a nightly occurrence. The minstrel rose gracefully from his obeisance and made his way out of the room. She looked up at him from her seat on the floor as he passed close by her. He looked down at her. And winked.

Or blinked, perhaps. He was gone and she was left wondering what, if anything, she had seen. The conclusion of the minstrel's performance had signaled the end of socializing in the hall. All around her, people were packing up their work. On the dais, the queen was bidding good evening to the aristocratic couple who were currently visiting at the keep, while the four stout men who carried the king's pole chair were standing by to await his orders to move him. Timbal gathered up her empty bucket, her knife, and her basin of cut potatoes, and carried them back to the kitchen. Her bundle was still in the corner where she had left it. She gathered it up and waited until the cook had a free moment, and then asked him, "Please, sir, where may I sleep tonight?"

He scowled briefly, and for one terrifying moment, she wondered if he remembered that earlier that day he'd offered her room and board in return for her labor in the kitchen. Then he said, "Out that door, to the left, up the wooden stairs two flights. I think there's a room or two empty up there. Whatever's left in the room, you can use. If it's empty, well, manage as well as you can tonight, and tomorrow I'll see who can spare what. Good night, girl."

She'd found an empty room, as he suggested, and was fortunate that it had a mattress stuffed with rather musty straw, and a simple but well-made table, and even a basin and ewer. That night, she'd taken the time to draw wash water for herself, but had slept on the mattress as it was.

In the days since then, Cook had learned her name, and she'd freshened the mattress with clean straw, and been given a rag rug and some empty sacking that had become curtains for the small window in the room. Most of the other kitchen help kept their shutters closed, winter and summer, but Timbal judged the fresh air worth the nuisance of flies in the day and mosquitoes at night. Her extra apron and servant's robe hung on a hook at night, her shoes beneath them. Her personal clothing hung on a separate hook, with the blue boots her father had bought for her arranged neatly beneath them. She knew they would not last forever, and so she wore them only on her days off and when she wasn't working in the kitchen.

There was little enough left of her former life; she'd make the boots and the memory of her father presenting them to her last as long as they could. They'd been tinkers while he was alive, and fairly good at that. Her mother had left them years ago, but she and her father had managed well enough, moving from town to town to find enough trade to keep them busy. Some months had been fat ones, with meat in the cook pot or a meal at an inn, and some months had been hard, with little more than mushrooms, roadside greens, and the occasional trout from a stream. But they had been happy, and more rare still, known they were happy with their simple life. Each night when they made their beds, her father reminded her to thank gentle Eda, goddess of the fields and farms, for her kindness to them.

In one town, they'd done exceptionally well, mending all the pots at a rich man's manor. At the next town, her father had bought her a soft shawl of gray wool, and the pair of blue boots. The boots were well made, cut trimly to her foot, and came almost to her knee. They were an indulgence and she knew it, especially the rich blue dye that the cobbler had applied to the leather, just for her. She'd hugged her father tight when he'd given them to her, and he'd told her they were no less than she deserved for being the best daughter a man could ask.

A month later, she was an orphan. Even now, when she thought about it, the events jumbled in her mind. The robbers had come to their campfire one night, brandishing clubs and an ugly knife. Coward that she was, when her father shouted at her to "Run, run!" she'd obeyed him. She fled and climbed a tree in the darkness and clung there, shaking and weeping silently until dawn grayed the sky. Then she'd crept back to their campsite, or tried to. It was noon before she found her way back to the road, and thence to where they had camped. The wagon and team, the tools of her father's trade, their clothes and supplies, all were gone. Her father lay as they had left him, his face battered and his arm broken with the bone jutting out. It had made her feel queasy even to look at it, but she had sternly mastered her horror and fear. Her father's life had depended on her and she knew it.

She'd given him water and tried to ease his pain, and then flagged down a passing teamster. Hastily she'd gathered the few scattered belongings left to them and bundled them into her blanket. The teamster had given them a ride back to the town they'd just left. An innkeeper had given them a room and called the town guard, who had decided that it was a matter for the King's Patrol. The Patrol arrived two days after her father had died. They'd given her sympathy and money for a gravedigger, promised to keep an eye out for her team and wagon, noted her name, and then left her to her own devices. The innkeeper had let her work off her debt, and offered to keep her on as a tavern girl. His daughter Gissel had shown her great kindness and likewise begged her to stay on, but Timbal could not bear to stay in the tiny room where she had watched her father die. The same day that her debt was settled, she'd bundled her few possessions into her blanket and set off, following the river road upstream.

She'd regretted that decision more than once before she found the kindly cook at Timberrock Keep. The hardships of the road and the dangers of being female and traveling alone had convinced her that any job that offered her shelter was better than venturing out again. So she'd become a kitchen girl.

She'd never imagined that one day she would live in a keep. Lord Just was well thought of, and a good steward of his lands and people. Lady Lucent was lovely and gracious, as a lady should be. Minstrels played for them every night, and Lady Lucent loved to entertain visiting nobility. She was a decade younger than her lord, and as able as he was crippled. Despite his misfortune, her lord was a kindly man who seemed pleased to see her dancing with other partners and eating heartily while he himself picked at his food. All the servants spoke well of Lord Just, and mourned the fall that had crippled him. They said less of Lady Lucent, but none of it was ill. Timbal decided it was probably because Lord Just had been their lord and master since he was a young man, and so their fondness for him was deeper than what they felt for the woman he had married.

As days turned to weeks, she found she shared the local sentiment. The lord was a kindly man, and even if he never noticed her personally, his easygoing and generous nature meant that his servants lived better than most servants did. As witness her two days off every month! And her being welcome to come into the hall every evening and listen to the minstrels perform. It was a good life for a girl who had been homeless and alone but a few weeks before, and she did not forget to thank the goddess for providing it. She lacked for nothing.

Usually on her days off, she chose to walk into the nearby town, sometimes to treat herself to a meal not of her own cooking at the tavern. But on the day that Azen knocked not just on her soles but her soul, she decided that she would, perhaps, return early to the keep for his evening performance.

Azen was not the only minstrel at Timberrock, but he was obviously the lady's favorite. Timbal had heard the tale of his life, for Gretcha, one of the housemaids, was fond of bragging of all she knew of the great folk and their affairs. She did not deign to speak to lowly kitchen help such as Timbal, but if Timbal were near, Gretcha seemed to take every opportunity to air loudly her special knowledge. Gretcha had come with Lady Lucent from her family home, and had served as a maid in the lady's household since she was a child. And thus Timbal knew that Azen had grown up near Lady Lucent's family home and had been her playmate in her childhood. He was himself the third son of a minor noble. There had been no inheritance share for him, but he had not minded. Instead, he had taken up the minstrel way and spent most of his winters at Timberrock Keep, playing for his old friend and her husband.

The other two minstrels were less impressive to Timbal. The apprentice, Saria, did little more than tune instruments, sing choruses, and flirt wildly. Chrissock, Lord Just's resident minstrel, was an older man with a deep bass voice. He performed with a variety of drums, and specialized in the oldest tales, recited exactly as they had been handed down through the years. Some evenings, Timbal could barely stay awake through his long recitals of ancient battles and who had died and how. He twisted his pronunciation and used words that she didn't understand and sometimes she wondered why any of it mattered anymore. But sometimes he told tales of brave warriors that were as stirring as any romance that Azen had ever sung. And for those, she sat as close to his dais as she could get, hugging her knees and watching him perform with awe.

It was while she was enraptured one evening that she chanced to glance over at Azen. The minstrel was behind Chrissock and to one side. He had been supplementing Chrissock's percussion with his harp, but had broken a string and stepped away from the music to make his repair. He was finished now and was waiting easily to take his own turn performing. And while he was waiting, he was watching Timbal.

At first, she thought it was only chance that their eyes had met. She put her gaze back on Chrissock. The toes of her blue boots tapped in time with his telling. A sideways glance at Azen found him still watching her, a half smile on his face. Her toes lost the time and she glanced down at her feet, confused. Half a chorus later, she dared to look up at Azen again. This time he nodded to her and smiled. A blush flamed her face; she could not say why. He had done no more than smile at her. She put her eyes back on Chrissock and kept them there, desperately willing her heart to stop pounding and hoping her scarlet cheeks would cool.

When the song finally ended and she dared to glance in his direction, he was gone. She plummeted abruptly into disappointment, though she could not have said what she had anticipated. When she looked over her shoulder, she found him. He was standing before Lady Lucent's chair, his head inclined to hear her whispered request. An instant later, she dismissed him with a conspiratorial smile and he returned to his place on the minstrel's dais. Chrissock played another song, this one obviously for the children of the keep. It was the tale of an old man who lived up a steep flight of stairs and had a succession of late-night visitors. It required the children to stamp and clap the rhythm back to him, and Chrissock gradually increased the tempo of the old man running up and hopping down the steps until it all dissolved into an impossible cacophony of stamping and shouting children. He bowed off the stage, surrendering it to Azen.

Timbal lowered her eyes and watched her boots as he sang. His first song was a melancholy tale of love gone awry, with the maiden choosing wealth over fondness and regretting it evermore. His second song was the old one about the miller's daughter floating notes down the river to her true love. His third song was one he had sung before. The refrain mentioned his true love's raven hair, tiny hands, and deep blue eyes. She closed her eyes to listen to it, but was jolted out of her reverie. For in the last stanza, he sang not of her blue eyes, but of her blue boots. She lifted her gaze, shocked, but his face was calm, his eyes on his patron as he sang. If anyone else had noticed the change in lyrics, they did not react. She wondered if she had imagined it.

Azen sang two more songs before a signal from Lady Lucent declared the evening's entertainment over. The minstrel rose from his seat and stepped away from his harp, lightly leaping down to advance on his patron and bid her good night. Timbal rose with the other maids and servants of the keep and followed them out of the hall into the warm evening. Light still lingered though it was fading fast. Tomorrow's work meant another early morning for her. She went up to her room to get her ewer, and then strolled down to the well to fill it. She hummed as she went, the refrain of Azen's last song still ringing in her head.

Gretcha was at the well before her, filling her own ewer. Timbal waited while she scooped handfuls of water to splash her face and finally to drink before eventually handing the bucket over to Timbal. The housemaid silently watched her lowering the bucket into the well. Timbal did not know her well, and was shocked by the note of resentment in her voice when the older girl spoke to her.

"Don't let him make a fool of you, missy."

"I'm sorry. What did you say?" The bucket plashed into the water.

"You heard me." Gretcha was already turning away from her. "Don't pretend to be stupid. The minstrel Azen. Yesterday, he asked me if I knew your name. I told him yes, that you were named 'Trouble.' And his name is the same for you. He's toying with you. Don't take him seriously.

Surely your mother taught you that minstrels are never to be trusted? He'll flirt with anyone, of course, and sleep with any girl who opens her legs to him after a few sweet words from that golden tongue. Enjoy it, if that's the sort of girl you are. But don't expect it to come to more than that. He's Lady Lucent's minstrel, and everyone who's worked here more than a season knows that. But you're new. So I thought I'd warn you. Just to be kind."

"Thank you," Timbal faltered, though the girl's tone had been anything but kind. Gretcha made no response but turned and sauntered away, her filled ewer in hand.

As Timbal hauled the bucket up, to drink, and wash her face and then fill her own ewer, she wondered. Did Gretcha think that what she had said was a kind warning? Timbal doubted it. There had been jealousy in her voice, or something like it. Something nasty and vengeful. She wondered if somehow she'd made an enemy at Timberrock, but could think of nothing she'd done to Gretcha.

Nothing save draw Azen's attention.

He'd asked Gretcha what her name was. That meant he'd noticed her as more than a face in the crowd. She smiled to herself. He might be Trouble, but she doubted he was trouble she couldn't handle. She wondered if he'd been 'Trouble' to other serving girls and then nodded to herself.

Was that it? Had the minstrel once been attentive to the housemaid? Or was he truly, as Gretcha had accused him, a pastime for Lady Lucent? Lord Just's legs were withered. Timbal wondered if that meant his other lower parts were useless. She had heard of highborn ladies and lords that did not keep their marriage vows but dabbled where they would. She thought again of how the lady summoned and then dismissed the minstrel, and wondered if she summoned and dismissed him for other duties as well. Were they secretly lovers, joined at the heart? She imagined the minstrel clasping the lady to his breast and kissing her. A strange thrill shot through her, one tinged with envy. Oh, she was being stupid! To have thought for one instant that she could have caught the eye, let alone the heart, of a handsome young minstrel like Azen! Of course he would be at his patron's beck and call, performing whatever services she wished of him. Everyone knew that minstrels never truly gave their hearts. What had she been thinking? She filled her ewer and carried it back to her room.

Yet that night, despite her best efforts to clear her thoughts of him, she fell asleep still humming the refrain, with "blue boots" where "blue eyes" should have been. And the dream she had of him awoke her long before dawn, and did not allow her to easily fall asleep again.

Her love for him was like poison ivy, she thought. She rose early and went to her work, resolved not to allow her thoughts to touch on him. But they did. And with every touch of her mind, her infatuation spread and enflamed her. Infatuation, she told herself sternly. A silly little girl's wild dream of a handsome and popular older man. What was wrong with her? He was the least eligible of the men in the keep. All he could do for her was break her heart, or get her pregnant if she were foolish enough to dally with him. Set him out of your thoughts and get about your work, girl!

So she told herself sternly and to absolutely no avail. Useless to recall that she knew next to nothing about him, and that what she did know indicated than any sensible girl would avoid him. He was a minstrel, and possibly the Lady Lucent's lover. He had no fixed home, no income other than the largesse of his listeners, and probably few possessions other than the clothes on his back and his harp. The only thing she could share with him was trouble.

She was scrubbing the big iron stew pot when he came into the kitchen yard. It was the biggest pot the keep owned, and it was seldom empty. Once she was finished with it, it would be filled with water, onions, turnips, carrots, and a tough haunch from an old milk cow. It would cook for a day, and for the next week or so, more vegetables and pieces of meat would be tossed in to replace most of what was ladled out to the serving folk. Sometimes the soup kettle would go a month without a scrubbing out. And when it was finally time for a cleaning, it had to be rolled out of the kitchen onto the flagged court, where the lucky cleaner of the pot might spend half the morning scraping and scouring to get all the scorched scraps out of it.

Timbal had tied back her hair and covered her head with a rag. She'd turned the pot on its side and was on her hands and knees, with her head and shoulders inside the kettle, scraping away. Two small dogs had appeared from somewhere. Tails wagging, they awaited every handful of scraped-off debris, cheerfully snapping and snarling at each other to see who would claim it. In the midst of one of their yap fests, she heard her name in a questioning tone. "Yes?" she replied as she backed hastily out of the pot.

"Excellent," Azen replied merrily. "I'll see you then." The minstrel swept her a theatrical bow that fluttered his blue summer cloak, and turned away from her.

"I don't know what you asked me . . ." she called after him.

He turned around, walking backward away from her. He was smiling. "And yet you agreed? I call that a good sign for me!"

"Agreed to what?" She could not keep the smile from her face, even as she touched the greasy cloth that covered her hair, and wondered suddenly how foolish she had appeared to him, with her rear end sticking out of a soup pot.

"You agreed to walk out with me this evening, after your chores are done. I'll meet you at the bottom of your stair." He had not paused in moving away from her. Now he turned and walked rapidly away.

"Don't you have to sing tonight?" she called after him.

He spun around once, laughing. "Only if you want me to!" he replied. "It's my night to do as I please," he added, and then he turned a corner and disappeared behind the milk shed. She stared after him. Her heart was hammering, the kettle scraper in her hand forgotten. What did it mean? For a time she remained crouched on her haunches, staring after him, her task forgotten. Should she go? She had said she would. But she had said "yes" before she knew what he was asking, or even who was speaking to her. She hadn't really said "yes" at all! Would she have, if she had emerged from the pot and heard what he was asking her? Of course not! She had decided he was not for her. An instant later, she admitted the truth to herself. Yes. She would have.

And she had.

It seemed Cook gave her every dirty and disgusting task the kitchen offered for the rest of that day. When finally the day's work was done, she was greasy and sooty and bone weary from scrubbing. Any other night, she would probably have gone straight to her bed. Instead, she hurried down to the women's bathhouse. She scrubbed herself there and washed tangles and grease from her hair. She wrung out her hair and knotted it up on the back on her head, and hurried back to her room. Unfortunately, Azen was already waiting at the foot of the stairs. He arched his brows in surprise at her dripping hair. "Just a moment!" she assured him, flustered beyond words, and fled up the rickety steps.

She changed hastily out of her servant's dress and into the only "good" clothes she owned. Her skirt was green with white trim, and her blouse was pale yellow. As she fastened the simple silver hoop earrings that her father had given her on her sixteenth birthday, he was very much on her mind. What would he have thought of what she was doing now? Would he have approved of her walking out with a minstrel? For an instant, sadness washed over her that she could not ask his permission or opinion. She wondered what had become of their old cart and team, and if the men who had killed her father had profited from his death. Then she shook her head clear of such thoughts. They had never helped her, not in the days right after his death and certainly not now. She would have to make her own way in the world, and live with her own decisions.

She tore a comb through her dark hair, braided it, and pinned it up, hoping the wet would not be so noticeable. She pulled on her blue boots, took a breath, and left her small room to descend the stairs. Thoughts of her father had driven some of the giddiness from her. If she made any mistake with this man, she reminded herself, she'd have no one to rely on except herself.

She cautioned herself to wariness, but as she came down the steps, Azen was looking up and smiling at her. His dark eyes seemed suddenly a pool that she might drown in. "There you are!" he exclaimed, as if completely surprised by her presence. He lifted a small covered basket from the ground and hung it on one arm while offering her his free one. It seemed only natural to take it, and once she had, she could think of no polite way to let go of it. "I know a place where the night birds sing," he told her, and off they went.

She did not have to talk much at first, for which she was grateful. He entertained her with an accounting of his day, turning his simple tasks to a tale full of humor and mischief. She could not help but laugh, and for a time, he seemed to expect no more from her save that she listen and smile at his nonsense.

The place where the night birds sang proved to be a sandy river beach backed by trees, downstream from the footbridge to town. Where the forest met the shore, he found a bleached-out log for them to sit on. The sun was making its lazy journey toward the horizon, sending the forest shadows reaching toward them. His little basket held a large honey cake for them to share and a bottle of wine. He used his sheath knife to pull the cork, doing it badly. "It will never go back in," he told her gravely. "We'll have to drink it all here, or waste it."

"No more than a glass for me," she demurred, only to discover that he had forgotten to bring any sort of cups for them. He offered her first drink from the bottle, which she shyly accepted, and then made her blush when he smiled slyly before he drank, saying it would be his first taste of her lips. She knew he was altogether too glib and that she should take warning from his clever way with words rather than be charmed by it.

But she was seventeen.

When the bottle of wine was half-gone in shared sips, he began to draw her out with questions, and though she tried valiantly to tell the tale of how she had come to be alone in the world in a calm manner, her throat closed and her eyes filled with tears when she spoke of her father. She looked down at her blue boots, and then reached down to touch them as if by doing so she could remember the touch of his hands when he'd given them to her. That was when Azen put his arm around her. He said nothing, but simply held her for a moment. And when her tears broke forth, he gathered her into his arms and let her cry.

She could not have said how or when she ended up in his lap, leaning her head on his shoulder. Nor did she really know when drying her tears changed to kissing her mouth. His lips held her as firmly as his arms. Perhaps she was not as alone in the world as she had thought. Evening and the forest shadow cloaked them from all eyes. She let him kiss her, and listened only to his sweet murmurs and the language of his knowing hands.

He never asked her if she would and so she never told him no or yes. She did not tell him it was her first time, but he knew, for he spun her a golden string of words and glistening kisses, telling her that opening a woman for the first time was like opening a wonderful bottle of wine, and that the first sip was to be savored slowly. His words formalized his touches, banishing any thoughts of resistance or reluctance. He promised her delight and he delivered it. She did not wonder then if his words were too practiced and his touches too deft. She did not wonder then how many other women he had opened.

In the depths of the night, they walked slowly back to the keep. There was enough moon to silver the road before their feet. He hooked her hand through the crook of his arm and she trusted him to guide her home. They were more than halfway there when she began to wonder what the morrow would bring. She tried to frame a question around her sudden uncertainty.

"What does it mean, to you?" she asked him.

"What does what mean?"

"Tonight, and what we did." She wished she had his gift for words. She spoke so bluntly, she felt as if she threw rocks of question at him.

He was silent for a time. "Something like that means more than can be put into words," he said at last. She tried to take comfort in that answer, but suddenly she wished he would try to put it into words.

"What do I mean to you, I mean? What do we mean to each other?"

"I think that, as time goes by, that is something we will discover," he said easily. "I do not think we should worry about it on a night like this. This is a time to savor the moment, blue boots, not map out all of our lives."

"Spoken like someone who cannot get pregnant," she said, and then wished with all her heart that she could call those words back. Like a hammer, they broke the fragile bubble that had contained the moment.

He was quiet for a time and then said stiffly, "I have heard that women seldom conceive on their first time."

"Except when they do," she replied morosely. She had shattered whatever magic they had made. Now she was suddenly aware that she ached in new places, and that until she bled again, she must fret and fear. The possible consequences that might befall her from this one night loomed large, as did all the consequences of what might not befall her. What had she ever imagined it might mean? That the minstrel loved her, that he would marry her and share his life with her, take care of her if she were ill, help to raise their children?

"Let's not worry about that right now," he suggested, and she wondered what worry he referred to. She did not let go of his arm. It suddenly seemed to her that it might be as much of him as she would ever hold. The road was uneven and she tried not to lurch against him as they walked. The inference that Gretcha had made days ago came back to haunt her suddenly. Was he the lady's plaything? She suddenly longed to ask him if he loved another, if he was bound in some way to the lady.

She bit back that question and instead asked him, "If I asked you something important, would you feel bound to speak the truth to me?"

He laughed, and she was shocked.

"Why do you laugh?" She tried to keep the hurt from her voice.

"Because, without intending, you have nearly spoken the words of the old curse that used to be hurled by one minstrel at another. 'May your tongue be tied to the truth!' they used to curse, and a fearsome curse it was."

"And why was that?"

"Because while we are the keepers of record, and must be meticulously honest and correct about what land was ceded or sold, or the year a couple was wed, or what agreement was made between two nobles, we are also the keepers of dreams. There are times when we must flatter and lie, in order to earn our bread. Heroes become stronger, queens more beautiful, and quests more dangerous when we sing them. So, to curse a fellow minstrel to have his tongue tied to the truth was to condemn him to live a life of frugality, depending only on what he could earn as a record keeper rather than what he might spin for himself by singing dreams to others."

Perhaps she heard in his words more than he meant to tell her. For it seemed to Timbal that he had spun a dream for her that night, a tale that perhaps she was not so alone, and in return she had paid him with the coin that a woman can only spend once. Her virginity was gone, and she knew that to some men, that would matter a great deal when it came time to broker a marriage. She suddenly saw that of the small store of things she possessed, first knowledge of her body had been a good she hadn't counted. Now she had given it to him, and though they had both enjoyed the experience, he was not bound to her by it. She would never be able to look her husband in the face and say, "Never have I known any man but you." That was gone, carried off by the golden tongue of a minstrel.

It seemed useless to rebuke him with that. Doubtless he thought it no more than she owed him for a honey cake, some wine, and some sympathy. He would not understand what he had taken from her. She sighed and he told her, "Cheer up. We are not so far from the keep and your bed."

At the foot of the stair he paused, holding on to her hand. The few torches that still burned outside the keep were but nubs in their sconces. She could scarcely see his face.

"You know, Blue Boots, I don't know your proper name, even."

Shame rose in her. She'd given him her maidenhead, and he hadn't even known her name.

"Timbal," she said quietly. "I am Timbal."

"Ah, a little drum, and one that sets a lively beat. It suits you. And yet I prefer Blue Boots."

Those were his last words as he left her at the foot of the servants' stair. Although he drew her close and kissed her a gentle good night, it did not thrill her as his first kiss had. She stepped back from him, groped for the railing in the dark, and began to climb the stair, treading close to the edge to keep the risers from creaking. She was halfway up when she halted, hearing angry whispers from below.

"There you are! I was sent to find you two hours ago! Where have you been? Did not you give your word you would be standing by, ever ready to serve the need of the Lady Lucent? A fine friend you are to her!"

Even hissing, there was no mistaking Gretcha's voice. Cold washed through Timbal. What was this about? A tryst he had failed to meet? She crouched low, pressing her body against the wall, hoping the darkness shielded her from view. Azen's voice was low, both apologetic and indignant. "Well, how was I to know it was to be tonight? I was told I could have the evening to myself, for once! I cannot recall the last time I was given that freedom."

"And I can guess how you used it, minstrel! Hurry. Don't waste your time in trying to justify it. You may have put all the plans awry. Go to her now, quickly and as quietly as you can. All else has been made ready. You are the only fault in this scheme."

"How much do you know, housemaid?" Azen's voice had dropped. It was bitter with resentment.

"Enough to know that without you no heir can be made! And that, I think, is something you must have known as well, and yet your precious night of 'freedom' was worth more to you than that. All her girlhood she loved you, and counted on you! She would have married you, if only you'd asked her! But no. And now that she needs you, see how well you repay Lady Lucent for her years of favor!"

Gretcha had pushed Azen too far. "Go yap elsewhere, bitch! You know nothing."

She heard his boots as he strode away across the cobbled yard in the darkness. Had Gretcha followed him? Her lighter slippers would make no sound. Timbal was frozen, her heart thumping so loud that her ears rang. What did it mean? And what would become of her if Gretcha came up the steps now and discovered her? She would know she had overheard. Was the secret worth her life? She lost track of how long she crouched there. Her left foot began to buzz with numbness before she dared rise and continue her climb up the stair.

She groped her way to her room, letting her garments fall as they would, and crawled into her bed. And there she lay, sleepless, and wondering exactly how Azen served Lady Lucent. She could think of only one way to interpret Gretcha's words. Azen would get the lady with child, that the lord might claim an heir. And if that were so, if that were his "duty" that kept him at the lady's beck and call, what then could a kitchen maid possibly mean to him? Nothing. A pastime, a way to spend his "freedom." She'd been a fool. When morning came, she rose and went, sandy-eyed, to face yet another day of toil. She felt both changed and unchanged by the events of the night before, and could not say which was more terrible.

She went about her work that day as if nothing had happened. Her premonition that she had been a fool only deepened as the day went on. She tried to find satisfaction in the simple tasks that had occupied her hours, and could not. Her mind wandered, she felt impatient with chopping the onions, annoyed with searching the kitchen gardens for turnips that had not gone wormy. She did not, as a rule, see the minstrel during her workday, so she told herself she should not wonder at his absence. She tried to ignore the hard-eyed look that Gretcha gave her each time they passed, but could not. "I wish I could just die," she said to herself, and then was shocked at her own whisper. She saw Gretcha muttering to two of the upstairs maids at lunch, and then all three of them turned to stare at her. Gretcha's plump little lips writhed back at her in a snide smile. Timbal looked away, pretending she had not seen her smirk. How had she known? Had Azen gossiped of his conquest? Was she a joke among all the house servants now? Her heart sank and her spirits grayed. What a silly strumpet she had been, so easily seduced by the first man who ever kissed her or offered her a bit of sympathy. She spoke to no one that afternoon, but chopped the vegetables with a vengeance and scrubbed the big griddle as if she could scour Azen from her memory.

By evening, she was resigned to knowing she'd been used. Neither Lady Lucent nor Azen appeared for the evening's pastimes. Timbal sat a little apart from the other servants, picking over gooseberries for pies, and listened to Chrissock without watching him. The night seemed overly long, and her task with the berries endless. She stole glances at Lord Just, but without lifting her head. She was not surprised that he looked lonely and preoccupied. He had to know what was going on. Chrissock sang sonorously of battles and warriors long dead, but they were sorrowful songs of old defeats and heroes dying in vain. Lord Just stared through him, his face still and his eyes distant.

The evening ended early. Lord Just summoned Chrissock to come forward for a purse and then apologized for ending his performance early. "I have no heart for music with my lady gone from the keep. When she returns, then we will rejoice. Eda willing, she will bear back to us that which we all most devoutly desire."

Chrissock bowed deeply. "I am sure the goddess will be willing, Lord. You have done all possible to smooth the way for her to favor us."

Timbal glanced around at the other servants, only to find them exchanging equally puzzled looks. It was seldom that any event in the keep was not presaged with days of gossip, and she had heard no rumor of Lady Lucent going on a journey. As the workers of the Timberrock Keep rose to leave the hall, the buzz of gossip increased in volume. But for the most part, all Timbal heard were questions until Gretcha and her two cronies happened to pass near her.

"Oh, yes, they had me packing all yesterday for the trip," Gretcha was assuring her friends. "It's not officially said yet, but the mistress has me doing more and more tasks for her. Soon enough I'll be sleeping upstairs near her room, I expect. Lady Lucent likes to keep all her personal maids close, you know. And she has come to trust me so much, I can't help but think that she'll soon make me her personal maid. I've known about the plans for this journey for days, but of course, intimate servants cannot gossip about the keep like ordinary housemaids."

Gretcha's friends looked both impressed and annoyed to be dismissed as "ordinary housemaids." Timbal desperately wanted to be disinterested. She kept her face impassive as she drifted closer, the basin of picked-over gooseberries on her hip. Gretcha shot a glance back at her. Were her next words intended for Timbal's ears?

"And, of course, Azen the Minstrel must go with our mistress, or what would be the point of the journey? What? You haven't heard?" Gretcha leaned closer to her friends, but her voice carried as clearly as ever. "Well, I suppose I should say nothing . . . but it does no harm to remind you what you already know. Lord Just has no heir and, of course, his health grows no better, and with his, er, difficulties, he is unlikely to get his wife with child. But a baby there must be, if he does not want Timberrock Keep to fall into his cousin's hands when he dies. You've heard of Lord Spindrift? Even his own servants call him Lord Spendthrift. He's gone through all of his inheritance already and rumor is that he's been able to borrow more funds only because he can assure the lenders that when Lord Just dies, Timberrock Keep will be his. And all have heard that he is a cruel man to dogs and horses as well as to women and servants. Lord Just has not allowed him to even visit here since that horrible incident with the hound puppy six years ago! So there's no chance at all that he will let the lack of an heir make Timber-rock Keep fall into his hands! So, there I will leave you all to think what you will! Lady Lucent goes off on a visit to her sister and her husband. She takes with her a very handsome minstrel to keep her company. My guess is that when she returns, the imminent birth of Lord Just's heir will be announced . . . No, no, I won't tell you a word more than that! Not a word! A lady's maid is supposed to be the soul of discretion!" She tittered as she said this, fluttering her hands before her face as if to forbid her friends to ask her any more questions. They looked suitably scandal-ized by what she had implied, but neither ventured a query.

Timbal put her eyes on her gooseberries and increased her pace to pass the threesome. She resisted the impulse to give a bit more swing to her hip as she passed Gretcha. She knew she had the muscle to send the housemaid flying. But then people would wonder why and the truth was too painful to admit. She hated Gretcha because the housemaid knew that Timbal had made a fool of herself over the minstrel. Hated her even more because Gretcha had warned her and she'd ignored the warning. The woman must think her an idiotic slut. Her cheeks burned as she hurried into the clamor and crowding of the kitchen. Everyone was rush-ing to put their chores to bed. As Timbal covered the basin of berries and disposed of the stems and rotten ones, she forced herself to consider the obvious. Gretcha had known of the journey. That meant that Azen must also have known. Yet he hadn't admitted it last night, or even hinted at it. No. He'd simply taken advantage of her, knowing well that he'd soon be on his way and gone for months. Why would he be so heartless?

The reason for that dropped on her like a gush of cold water: If she turned up pregnant, no one would believe the minstrel had lain with her. He'd had her virginity; perhaps the novelty of that was all that had drawn him to her. As she tottered up the stairs to her room, a new fear battered her. He was gone, and if she found herself expecting a child, she couldn't even plead with him to help her. "Sweet Eda, let that not be," she prayed to the goddess. "I'd rather be dead than a mother with no husbandman!"

She spent another near-sleepless night. She berated herself for being a fool to have given in to him, and for being a bigger fool for longing to feel his touch again. She finally fell asleep clutching the dream that he swiftly returned to the keep with some reason for his cruelty. It did not help that she herself could imagine no explanation for how he had treated her.

Instead, she dreamed that she disgraced herself by running out to him as soon as he returned. In her dream, she was heavily pregnant, and he denied and mocked her, and Gretcha led all the servants in first laughing at her, and then driving her away from the keep for her terrible lies about the minstrel. In the dream, she had to flee barefoot, wearing only her servant clothes, and she wept because she had lost her blue boots, the last vestige of her father's love for her.

She awoke late, her tears still wet on her cheeks. She had to rush to dress, and when she hurried down the stairs, she heard Cook calling her name in frustration. She rushed into the kitchen, was scolded harshly for being late, and put to washing up all the dishes by herself.

That night, Lord Just seemed pensive and weary. Chrissock chanted long historical lays about ancient battles. They were boring and depressing. Lord Just drank too much and was carried off to his bed early. Everyone in the keep seemed out of sorts as they drifted away early from their master's hall and off to their own rooms. Gretcha was wearing a new cap and apron, so perhaps she had been elevated to a lady's maid. She stood gossiping with her cronies in the kitchen yard. As Timbal passed them, one whispered something to Gretcha, and then they all burst out laughing. She could not keep herself from glancing toward them, and found them flatly staring at her; she was the object of their mirth and they didn't care if she knew it. She forced herself not to hurry, but knew all the same that she fled as she retreated up the stairs to her room.

There she let her foolish hopes shatter. He'd had all he wanted of her, and now Azen was gone. Was his mission truly to get Lady Lucent with child so that the baby could be passed off as Lord Just's and the line would have an heir? It seemed wildly unlikely, and yet there were songs about such things happening. Both Lord Just and the minstrel had the same dark eyes and curly black hair, but that was true of three-fourths of Buck. And if Azen had been chosen as a stud, why send them off for the deed to be accomplished? Surely it would be more believable if the lady never left her home? But perhaps the process was too humiliating for Lord Just to tolerate under his roof. Or—and like a cold finger down her back, she recognized the truth—was it a woman's decision, one that Lady Lucent had made out of her husband's need for an heir and her need for a bed partner livelier than a crippled old man? But how could she hope to deceive her husband if he were unable to impregnate her? Unless he believed her already pregnant from some effort of his own?

Timbal felt suddenly shamed to be dwelling on the intimate affairs of the nobility. Did not the folk who had taken her in and given her work and a place to live deserve a bit of respect from her? She thought of Azen and resolved to harden her heart. Whatever had happened between her and the minstrel had been her doing as much as his. She'd gone with him, she hadn't resisted him, and if he had no more interest in her than what he'd had, well, she had only herself to blame. Put it aside and go on with her life.

And so she did. For a week or so, Gretcha continued to laugh mockingly whenever she saw her, but Timbal ignored her, and hoped that her shame did not show. The keep was a quieter, drabber place without its mistress. The rains began and did not let up. The kitchen yard became a sodden mucky wreck, and Timbal walked barefoot across it rather than ruin the leather of her blue boots. She did her work by day and went to bed at night. It was her life. It had not seemed intolerable before Azen had stepped into it, and logic told her that it was not intolerable now. She tried to remember how pleased she had been with it when her tasks were new, how happy she had been to settle in at Timberrock Keep. Now it seemed tedious and pointless. She would spend the rest of her life preparing food for other people. That was all. It was life, it was what one did. One worked, and ate, and slept. With time, she'd remember how to do that without it feeling like each breath did no more than carry her one step closer to death.

On her next day off, Timbal resisted the urge to visit the river beach and moon over what had befallen her there. Instead, under lowering clouds, she walked into the village and treated herself to a mug of cider at the tavern and listened to a white-haired old minstrel who specialized in silly drinking songs and humorous tales. She even managed to smile a time or two. At the end of his performance, he announced that he would soon move on to the next town, and asked if there were news he could share with friends and relatives there. Half a dozen people sent greetings to extended family, one man announced the birth of a son, and another issued a warning about an upriver bridge that he proclaimed was so dangerous that carts should avoid it. The minstrel nodded to each message, repeating it back word for word. It was a common way for messages to be sent, especially those intended for the public or for folk who could not read and write.

Next, with a salacious grin, he asked for rumors and gossip worthy of being spread. A minstrel, he told them, could make more from a rumor than most men could from a pot of gold. So he begged them for whatever they had heard, no matter how unfounded. Much of what was offered had to do with the best whores in town, men bragging of their endowments, a warning to "whoever" had stolen six sheep from a high pasture, and a great deal of bawdy innuendo. The minstrel took note of it all with great good cheer, repeating the missives back so dramatically that even Timbal laughed until her belly hurt. Then a field hand from Timberrock Keep, somewhat the worse for drink, stood up to announce that "soon enough there will be an heir at Timberrock Keep. And Lord Just will be just as delighted as if the babe were his!"

"Eda's tits, Lowl, you loud-mouthed drunk!" someone else at the table rebuked him, and gave him a friendly punch in the arm that sent him sprawling to the floor.

Another man at the same table shouted out, "He's drunk! Pay him no mind!"

Even the minstrel seemed to sense that the man had crossed a boundary, for he parroted back, "The field hands from Timberrock Keep are loud-mouthed drunks. Pay them no mind," and received a roar of approval for his amendment. But Timbal sat, suddenly silent, the grin faded from her face and the laughter dried up in her mouth. She put down her coppers for her cider and left, to walk back to the keep alone.

It was pouring rain when she left the tavern. Timbal had not even worn a cloak; there was nothing to do except get soaked by the chilling downpour. For the first half of her walk, she allowed herself to think about Azen as she had known him. She thought of the songs he'd sung, and how it had always seemed he was singing for her, even when his eyes sought out Lady Lucent's. She thought of his softly curling black hair and how it had smelled when it had danced across her face as they made love. She let herself think of his lips, not just his kisses, but his kind words, and how gently he had held her and let her weep out her sorrow for her father. She had one night of him. Could she truly say she knew him, let alone loved him?

Love wasn't based on knowing someone. Love, it seemed to her, simply was. It shamed her that he had treated her so badly and still she was mooning after him, recalling every whispered word and every touch. It was bad enough to be stupid once; did she have to recall her stupidity with such longing? For the first time, she let herself think the thought. Timbal wished she had the courage to kill herself. Wished she were dead and no longer feeling this pain for which she had no remedy.

"But I don't have the courage. El should kill me for a coward, for lacking the spine to do the job myself."

She came to the footbridge she had crossed earlier that evening. The river was up. All the debris that had littered its banks all summer had been lifted and floated down to catch against the footbridge. The water pressed it against the bridge's wooden supports, flowing through the debris and in several places across the top of the bridge. She hesitated, and set a foot out onto the wooden planks. They trembled with the push of the waters, but the bridge seemed sound enough. She glanced back toward the village to see if anyone was coming, wishing she could ask someone's opinion on the safety. But the falling rain obscured her vision, and she doubted the others from the keep would start for home before nightfall. It would be fine, she decided.

In the pouring rain, she stooped down and pulled her boots off. Her bare feet would give her a better grip, and she had no desire for the water to pour inside her boots and ruin them. She clutched them to her chest and walked out onto the bridge. The wooden planks muttered and shuddered under her step. The water was cold as it rushed past her bare feet. Then suddenly it skipped up over the top of her foot, and on her next step, she found herself ankle deep. The water tugged at her and with one hand she snatched her skirts up out of its reach. She glanced back, but she was already in the middle of the bridge. As well go on as back.

Timbal took two more steps before the world bucked and lurched. For a moment, nothing made any sense. Then she realized that she was clinging to the bridge railing with one hand while clutching her precious boots to her chest with the other. The bridge was still there, under her bare feet, but she had lost her grip on her skirts. They tugged at her wetly as the water that was now knee-deep rushed past her. Her mind made sense of the tangle of lumber that loomed over her, pressed hard against the footbridge. The cart bridge upstream had given way, just as the fellow in the tavern had predicted. It had washed downstream, slammed into this bridge, and now other debris and the press of the flood waters was threatening to rip her bridge free of its supports and send it hurtling downstream. With her on it.

Or most likely, not on it, she realized, as timbers groaned and the bridge gave a lurch under her. She could not separate the thundering of her heart from the vibration of the bridge, nor the ringing in her ears from the roar of the water. "I cannot be this afraid," she told herself sternly. "Not if I want to live." And in that instant, she realized that she very much did want to live, Azen or none. The realization that she had asked dark El for death and the god had abruptly granted it to her shook her to her core. "NO!" she shouted above the harsh roar of the furious water. "I don't want to die! I won't die here!"

She flung her precious boots as hard as she could. The pouring rain obscured her vision but she thought they landed on the bank. Then, with both hands free to grip the shuddering railing, she began to lurch and sidle across the bridge toward the shore. She was a body's length from the jutting stone support for the bridge when the wooden part tore free. She knew three seconds of a wild ride on a lurching raft of wood before it became merely a jumble of timber. It parted beneath her and she fell through it, into water thickened with forest debris and the broken jumble of planks and timbers the river had made of two bridges. She caught wildly at chunks of wood that turned under her, dousing her yet again. Her skirts caught on a tumbling snag. The roots bore her under, then up, then under as she frantically tried to breathe, scream, and tear her skirts from her body. Before Timbal could get her skirts free, the snag suddenly discarded her as abruptly as it had snatched at her. A floating plank slapped her, then spun away before she could catch at it. Flotsam that was close enough to bruise her floated tauntingly out of reach when she tried to cling to it.

The choking clog of debris that had smashed the bridge slowly dispersed. In the torrential downpour, she finally caught hold of a splintered section of bridge planks. When she tried to climb up on them, they shifted, dunking her again. She found a new grip and held on, her head barely above the water. Her existence narrowed to a single task. When there was air on her face, she took a breath. When there was not, she held it. When her chilled hands wearied, she clamped them more tightly, willing the pain to keep them awake enough to grip.

Darkness soon cloaked the river, but the rain and the push of the water did not ease. She shifted her grip, was dunked, nearly lost her plank, and then found a new hold with her elbow wedged between two of the boards. She had no breath to weep or cry for help. All she could do was cling and pray to Eda, mother Eda, that she would be carried to shore out of cruel El's reach.

In the dark of night, her raft fetched up against something and stopped. She held to it in the darkness, glad to be still even as she dreaded that some larger snag might come with the current to slam into her. Once, she tried to drag herself up out of the water, but when she did so, the wood she clung to came loose and turned for a moment before once more halting. The rush of water against it now sheared up in a spray. Timbal averted her face from it and stayed as she was. She would wait for morning and light before she tried to move to a safer place. She pressed her elbow down into the crack between the planks and tried to stay conscious.

She did not think she slept, but there came a moment when she suddenly knew that dawn had come and passed before she was aware of it. The rain had lessened but not stopped, and the river still raged past her. But by the gray light of the overcast day, she could see that she and a great amount of branches, planks, and one dead sheep were all tangled into one large mass braced against a fallen tree that jutted out into the river. She did not shout for help. There was nothing but forested riverbank as far as she could see.

The arm Timbal had used as a brace was numb, and her other hand so cold it scarcely worked. Her legs dangled and tugged in the water that swirled past her. It took half a lifetime for her to work her numbed arm free. Slowly, she dragged her body up onto the tangle of timbers and wreckage. She lay there for a time, trying to decide if she was colder now that she was out of the water. She worked her ankles, trying to feel her feet, and moved her arm. When finally it tingled, she shrieked breathlessly at how much it hurt, until she remembered to give thanks to Eda for being able to free it at all.

Perhaps her prayer to the more kindly goddess of the fields angered sour El. She had lifted her head to try to decide her best path back to the riverbank over the packed debris when she saw what she had feared. A large chunk of the cart bridge had decided to join the rest of itself. It was moving down the river in a majestic chaos, rolling in slow splashing turns that sent gushes of white water shooting up. It was coming straight at her. It was unavoidable.

She scrambled up on the debris raft, slipped, fell between pieces of wreckage, and for one nightmare instant was trapped beneath it. Then she saw a slice of daylight and frantically clawed her way up into it. She got her head above water, hooked an arm over a tree trunk, and then just had time to see the bridge bearing down on her. "Damn you El!" she shrieked to the merciless sky. He'd taken everything from her, father—lover, even her precious blue boots. Taking her life would probably be the only act of mercy he ever committed.

Much later, she would wonder if she said those words aloud, or if a

god did not need the words spoken to respond to them. The last thing
El would do was to give mercy to anyone. By a superhuman effort, she
pulled herself up on the floating junk just as the bridge hit it. Timbal
saw it turn as it came, saw it crashing toward her, and then saw a blast
of white light.

A DRENCHED WOMAN awoke on the bank of a river. Her wet hair was
strewn across her face. Her clothes were waterlogged, her skirts tattered.
She was barefoot. Blood was thick on her hands. It took her a little while
to understand that a cut on her head was still seeping blood. And she
could not recall who she was or how she had come to be there.

The sun had come out and a thin light warmed the air. She managed
to stand, and then to limp. She followed the river downstream until she
saw a bridge, then climbed up the bank, through a shallow edging of
forest, and found a road. She followed it, staggering gamely along until
a woman driving a donkey cart came by and gave her a ride.

She awoke later in a room at an inn. She gazed around her groggily,
then lifted her hands to look at the heavy bandaging that wrapped one
of her forearms. Her head was bound also, her hair cut away from one
side of her skull. She could not remember who she was or how she had
come to the inn. A girl came to her room, bringing her a simple meal
on a tray. "You're Timbal," the girl told her. "You used to work here,
but you left here months ago. Looks like you fell in the river, or maybe
got beat up and left to die in the storm. But don't you worry. You're safe
here, and with friends. The King's Patrol has been looking for you for
quite a while. They found your father's wagon and team, and the men
who killed him. They had to sell off the team and wagon when they
couldn't find you, but the money they got for them has been waiting for
you for a while now. So don't you worry. We'll take good care of you."

It was all too much to take in. It took several long days for her to
accept the past the innkeeper and his employees assigned to her. It took
longer than that before she could cross the room without staggering
sideways. Gissel, the pleasant girl who had been tending her, assured
her that she had plenty of money to pay for her care, but Timbal soon
insisted on coming down and resuming her tasks at the inn. The work
seemed familiar and pleasant enough. Bits of her old life came back to
her, and she fit them together as best she could. No one could tell her
where she had gone after she left the inn's employ, or how she had come

back, and eventually she let that year of her life go. The money from her father's team and wagon gave her a nice little nest egg, and she was able to add to it with her wages from the inn.

She cut the long hair on one side of her head to match the short curly crop that was rapidly covering the scar where the healer had stitched her scalp closed. Soon she could serve in the tavern again as well as cook in the kitchen. She made friends easily with the regulars and was a favorite with the King's Patrol when they were in town. Her life, she decided, was good. The only time she became melancholy was when minstrels came to the inn to entertain, and even then, it was only certain old songs that brought tears to her eyes.

Three months after her accident, she was waiting tables on the evening that the good news arrived from upriver at Timberrock Keep. "Lord Just has an heir!" a young teamster announced loudly as he entered. Timbal was shocked at the roar of approval that went up. That night it seemed that everyone in the little town and surrounding farmsteads flocked into the inn to raise a mug to the wonderful tidings. Timbal was kept busy trotting back and forth from the kitchen to the hearth tables, and only learned in snatches of gossip from Gissel why the rejoicing was so raucous. It was no newborn child they celebrated; the people of Lord Just's holdings had reluctantly given up the hope that their beloved but crippled lord could sire a child. Instead, they had lived in fear that his lands and holdings must be inherited by his cousin Lord Spindrift. All knew how he had already plunged his own inheritance into ruin and taken all his folk with it, enacting taxes no one could possibly pay and running up debts that would never be settled. The prospect of the reckless young noble becoming their lord was now at an end.

Lady Lucent had traveled to her home, taking with her a minstrel loyal to her and her husband, so that her adoption of her sister's son might be witnessed and made legal before Lord Spindrift could mount an objection. To hear the teamster tell the tale, it had been a plot long in the making, with the minstrel sworn to secrecy and the lady herself begging on her knees that her sister would give up her youngest son to them. By all accounts, he was a good and likely lad, open-faced, friendly, and an excellent horseman. All the folk at Timberrock Keep were rejoicing, and all who lived in Lord Just's holdings could now know and share the good tidings.

Timbal rejoiced in the lively trade and good spirits that provoked such excellent tips that night. The names rang familiar in her ears, but of course they would; had not she worked at this very inn since before her accident? She was accustomed to names and bits of old news that jangled oddly in her mind and almost stirred a memory to the top.

So there was no reason for her melancholy to deepen over the days that followed. Yet it did. She awoke weeping in the dark of the night, felt a weariness that had no reason, and could not find a smile for anyone's jest. She knew her life was good and nightly thanked Eda for blessing her. But, as she explained it to Gissel, "I cannot find my heart. I feel I have lost something, that I am missing something very important, and can know no peace until I find it."

"You lost your father not that long ago," Gissel ventured, but Timbal shook her head.

"I grieve him. I recall him, in flashes. His face seen by firelight, and how his hands clasped my shoulders, and even that he taught me to thank the goddess for every good fortune. No, Gissel. I recall enough of him to miss and mourn him. But there is something else. Something I had and I lost."

"Tomorrow," Gissel announced firmly, "we will tell my father we need a day off and we will walk up to Smithfield. It's the next village on the river. We'll visit my cousins, for I want you to meet Seck. I believe you'll like each other, and he may be exactly the cure for whatever you've lost."

Timbal was reluctant, but Gissel pestered her until she agreed. Her father agreed to give them both the day off, for trade was slower in winter. But he frowned at Gissel's plan to visit her cousins, reminding her, "Seck has been seeing the farrier's daughter. I heard he was quite taken with her."

Gissel shrugged that off. "Perhaps he is, but I am not. And once he meets Timbal, he will likely forget all about scrawny Missa and her shrew's tongue."

They set out the next morning, catching a ride with a carter that Gissel knew. He was taking a load of late cabbages to Smithfield and would be happy to give them a ride back as well. Timbal sat on the tail of the cart while Gissel shared the seat with the carter, and soon divined that this was a ride that had been arranged well in advance of any favor that Gissel hoped to do for Timbal. He even kissed her before he set them down at her cousin's house.

Her father's gossip was correct. Seck was not even home that day, having gone to his sweetheart's house to help her father repair a fence.

Timbal found she didn't care. The cousin's house was a noisy place with several small children and an adorable new baby. The women there were as friendly as Gissel, and Seck or no Seck, the visit lifted Timbal's spirits. She was reluctant to bid them farewell and lingered as long as she could. It was evening when they set out for the Smithfield inn where Gissel's carter was going to pick them up for the ride home.

"Oh, and if I'd known, I'd have sent you on your way sooner, so you could have had a bit of music there, too," Gissel's cousin told her. "I've heard rumors of the minstrel playing at the inn. Tall and dark he is, and setting all the girls to swooning over his voice, but not a one of them will he look at! They say he mourns a lost lover, and always plays his last song to her memory."

That was enough to pique the curiosity of both girls, and they hurried, shawls up against the light rain, until they came to the inn. Gissel's carter was late, but they found a table near the back. Gissel's cousin had been right. The inn was crowded with a mostly female population. The minstrel was repairing a harp string when they came in, his head bent over his work. "I'll get us some cider while we wait for your carter," Timbal offered, and Gissel declared, "He's not 'my' carter. Not quite yet!"

"Oh, but he will be," Timbal called over her shoulder and made her way through the throng to reach the tavern keeper.

The minstrel struck up while she was trying to get the man's attention. The chords rang strangely familiar to her ears. She did not recall learning the song, but she knew it. It was about a warrior come home from his wandering too late. His love was lost to him, carried off by death. A strange prickling ran over her skin, lifting the hair on her scalp. Slowly she turned as he sang of his lost love, and her raven hair and her tiny hands. Then he sang of her blue boots.

Cider forgotten, she pushed her way slowly through the crowd, ignoring the unkind comments of those she jostled. She found him by the hearth, seated on a low stool, his harp leaned against his shoulder as he played. His fingers knew his strings, and as he played, his eyes rested only on the chair before him. Enthroned on the chair were a pair of blue boots. They were clean, but water stained. She knew them. Then suddenly she knew herself. She looked at the minstrel. Her eyes devoured him, and at the sight of him, a flood of memories thundered through her blood.

Azen did not see her. Not until she reached the chair and took the blue boots from the seat. Wordless and pale, he said nothing as she sat down and pulled them onto her feet. But when she stood, he was waiting for her. He was shaking as he embraced her. "I thought I had lost you!" he managed to say through the uproar of the crowd's delighted response. "Gretcha told me you were dead. That they'd found your boots on the riverbank, that you'd thrown yourself in!"

"Gretcha lies about many things."

"Yes. She does. Blue boots, you must never go away from me again." He folded her close and held her tight.

"Eda willing, I never shall," she promised him.

Neil Gaiman

As demonstrated by the subtle and melancholy story that follows, memory can be a very unreliable thing, even in matters of the heart. Or perhaps particularly in matters of the heart . . .

One of the hottest stars in science fiction, fantasy, and horror today, Neil Gaiman has won four Hugo Awards, two Nebula Awards, one World Fantasy Award, seven Locus Awards, four Bram Stoker Awards, four Geffen Awards, one Mythopoeic Fantasy Award, and a Newbery Medal. Gaiman first came to wide public attention as the creator of the graphic novel series The Sandman, still one of the most acclaimed graphic novel series of all time. Gaiman remains a superstar in the graphic novel field. His graphic novels include Breakthrough, Death Talks about Life, Legend of the Green Flame, The Last Temptation, Only the End of the World Again, MirrorMask, and a slew of books in collaboration with Dave McKean, including Black Orchid, Violent Cases, Signal to Noise, The Tragical Comedy or Comical Tragedy of Mr. Punch, The Wolves in the Walls, and The Day I Swapped My Dad for Two Goldfish.

In recent years he's enjoyed equal success in the science fiction and fantasy fields with his bestselling novel American Gods winning the 2002 Hugo, Nebula, and Bram Stoker Awards, Coraline winning both Hugo (2003) and Nebula (2004), and his story "A Study in Emerald" winning the Hugo in 2004. His novel The Graveyard Book won the Hugo and the Newbery Medal in 2009. He also won the World Fantasy Award *for his story with Charles Vess, "A Midsummer Night's Dream," and won the International Horror Guild Award for his collection* Angels & Visitations: A Miscellany. *Gaiman's other novels include* Good Omens *(written with Terry Pratchett),* Neverwhere, Stardust, *and, most recently,* Anansi Boys. *In addition to* Angels & Visitations, *his short fiction has been collected in* Smoke and Mirrors: Short Fictions & Illusions, Midnight Days, Warning: Contains Language, Creatures of the Night, Two Plays for Voices, *and* Adventures in the Dream Trade, *and* Fragile Things. *He's also written* Don't Panic: The Official Hitchiker's Guide to the Galaxy Companion, A Walking Tour of the Shambles *(with Gene Wolfe),* Batman *and* Babylon 5 *novelizations, and edited* Ghastly Beyond Belief *(with Kim Newman),* Book of Dreams *(with Edward Kramer), and* Now We Are Sick: An Anthology of Nasty Verse *(with Stephen Jones). His most recent books are* The Graveyard Book, *and two YA novels,* Odd and the Frost Giants, *and, with Gris Grimly,* The Dangerous Alphabet. *A movie based on his novel* Stardust *was in theaters worldwide in 2007, and an animated movie based on* Coraline *was in theaters in 2009.*

The Thing About Cassandra

So there's Scallie and me wearing Starsky-and-Hutch wigs, complete with sideburns, at five o'clock in the morning by the side of a canal in Amsterdam. There had been ten of us that night, including Rob, the groom, last seen handcuffed to a bed in the Red Light District with shaving foam covering his nether regions and his brother-in-law giggling and patting the hooker holding the straight razor on the arse, which was the point I looked at Scallie and he looked at me, and he said, "Maximum deniability?" and I nodded, because there are some questions you don't want to be able to answer when a bride starts asking pointed questions about the stag weekend, so we slipped off for a drink, leaving eight men in Starsky-and-Hutch wigs (one of whom was mostly naked, attached to a bed by fluffy pink handcuffs, and seemed to be starting to think that this adventure wasn't such a good idea after all) behind us, in a room that smelled of disinfectant and cheap incense, and we went and sat by a canal and drank cans of Danish lager and talked about the old days.

Scallie—whose real name is Jeremy Porter, and these days people call him Jeremy, but he had been Scallie when we were eleven—and the groom to be, Rob Cunningham, had been at school with me. We had drifted out of touch, more or less, had found each other the lazy way you do these days, through Friends Reunited and Facebook and such, and now Scallie and I were together for the first time since we were nineteen. The Starsky-and-Hutch wigs, which had been Scallie's idea, made us look like we were playing brothers in some made-for-TV movie—Scallie the short, stocky brother with the thick moustache, me, the tall one.

Given that I've made a significant part of my income since leaving school modeling, I'd add the tall good-looking one, but nobody looks good in a Starsky-and-Hutch wig, complete with sideburns.

Also, the wig itched.

We sat by the canal, and when the lager had all gone we kept talking and we watched the sun come up.

Last time I saw Scallie he was nineteen and filled with big plans. He had just joined the RAF as a cadet. He was going to fly planes, and do double duty using the flights to smuggle drugs, and so get incredibly rich while helping his country. It was the kind of mad idea he used to have all the way through school. Usually the whole thing would fall apart. Sometimes he'd get the rest of us into trouble on the way.

Now, twelve years later, his six months in the RAF ended early because of an unspecified problem with his right knee, he was a senior executive in a firm that manufactured double-glazed windows, he told me, with, since the divorce, a smaller house than he felt that he deserved and only a golden retriever for company.

He was sleeping with a woman in the double-glazing firm, but had no expectations of her leaving her boyfriend for him, seemed to find it easier that way. "Of course, I wake up crying sometimes, since the divorce. Well, you do," he said at one point. I could not imagine him crying, and anyway he said it with a huge Scallie grin.

I told him about me: still modelling, helping out in a friend's antique shop to keep busy, more and more painting. I was lucky; people bought my paintings. Every year I would have a small gallery show at the Little Gallery in Chelsea, and while initially the only people to buy anything had been people I knew—photographers, old girlfriends, and the like— these days I have actual collectors. We talked about the days that only Scallie seemed to remember, when he and Rob and I had been a team of three, inviolable, unbreakable. We talked about teenage heartbreak, about Caroline Minton (who was now Caroline Keen, and married to a vicar), about the first time we brazened our way into an 18 film, although neither of us could remember what the film actually was.

Then Scallie said, "I heard from Cassandra the other day."

"Cassandra?"

"Your old girlfriend. Cassandra. Remember?"

". . . No."

"The one from Reigate. You had her name written on all your books."
I must have looked particularly dense or drunk or sleepy, because he

said, "You met her on a skiing holiday. Oh, for heaven's sake. *Your first shag*. Cassandra."

"Oh," I said, remembering, remembering everything. "Cassandra."

And I did remember.

"Yeah," said Scallie. "She dropped me a line on Facebook. She's running a community theatre in East London. You should talk to her."

"Really?"

"I think, well, I mean, reading between the lines of her message, she may still have a thing for you. She asked after you."

I wondered how drunk he was, how drunk I was, staring at the canal in the early light. I said something, I forget what, then I asked whether Scallie remembered where our hotel was, because I had forgotten, and he said he had forgotten too, and that Rob had all the hotel details and really we should go and find him and rescue him from the clutches of the nice hooker with the handcuffs and the shaving kit, which, we realised, would be easier if we knew how to get back to where we'd left him, and looking for some clue to where we had left Rob, I found a card with the hotel's address on it in my back pocket, so we headed back there and the last thing I did before we walked away from the canal and that whole strange evening was to pull the itchy Starsky-and-Hutch wig off my head and throw it into the canal.

It floated.

Scallie said, "There was a deposit on that, you know. If you didn't want to wear it, I'd've carried it." Then he said, "You should drop Cassandra a line."

I shook my head. I wondered who he had been talking to online, who he had confused for her, knowing it definitely wasn't Cassandra.

The thing about Cassandra is this: I'd made her up.

I WAS FIFTEEN, almost sixteen. I was awkward. I had just experienced my teenage growth spurt and was suddenly taller than most of my friends, self-conscious about my height. My mother owned and ran a small riding stables, and I helped out there, but the girls—competent, horsey, sensible types—intimidated me. At home I wrote bad poetry and painted water colours, mostly of ponies in fields; at school—there were only boys at my school—I played cricket competently, acted a little, hung around with my friends playing records (the CD was around, but they were expensive and rare, and we had all inherited record players and hi-fis from parents or older siblings). When we didn't talk about music, or sports, we talked about girls.

Scallie was older than me. So was Rob. They liked having me as part of their gang, but they liked teasing me, too. They acted like I was a kid, and I wasn't. They had both done it with girls. Actually, that's not entirely true. They had both done it with the same girl, Caroline Minton, famously free with her favours and always up for it once, as long as the person she was with had a moped.

I did not have a moped. I was not old enough to get one, my mother could not afford one (my father had died when I was small, of an accidental overdose of anaesthetic, when he was in hospital to have a minor operation on an infected toe. To this day, I avoid hospitals). I had seen Caroline Minton at parties, but she terrified me and even had I owned a moped, I would not have wanted my first sexual experience to be with her.

Scallie and Rob also had girlfriends. Scallie's girlfriend was taller than he was, had huge breasts, and was interested in football, which meant that Scallie had to feign an interest in football, Crystal Palace, while Rob's girlfriend thought that Rob and she should have things in common, which meant that Rob stopped listening to the mid-80s electropop the rest of us liked and started listening to hippy bands from before we were born, which was bad, and that Rob got to raid her dad's amazing collection of old TV series on video, which was good.

I had no girlfriend.

Even my mother began to comment on it.

There must have been a place where it came from, the name, the idea: I don't remember though. I just remember writing "Cassandra" on my exercise books. Then, carefully, not saying anything.

"Who's Cassandra?" asked Scallie.

"Nobody," I said.

"She must be somebody. You wrote her name on your maths exercise book."

"She's just a girl I met on the skiing holiday." My mother and I had gone skiing, with my aunt and cousins, the month before, in Austria.

"Are we going to meet her?"

"She's from Reigate. I expect so. Eventually."

"Well, I hope so. And you *like* her?"

I paused, for what I hoped was the right amount of time, and said, "She's a really good kisser." Then Scallie laughed and Rob wanted to know if this was French kissing, with tongues and everything, and I said, "What do *you* think," and by the end of the day, they both believed in her.

My mum was pleased to hear I'd met someone. Her questions—what Cassandra's parents did, for example—I simply shrugged away.

I went on three "dates" with Cassandra. On each of our dates, I took the train up to London, and took myself to the cinema. It was exciting, in its own way.

I returned from the first trip with more stories of kissing, and of breast-feeling.

Our second date (in reality, spent watching *Weird Science* on my own in Leicester Square) was, as told to my mum, holding hands together at what she still called "the pictures," but as told to Rob and Scallie (and over that week, to several other school friends who had heard rumours from sworn-to-secrecy Rob and Scallie, and now needed to find out if it was true), the day I lost my virginity, in Cassandra's aunt's flat in London: The aunt was away, Cassandra had a key. I had (for proof) a packet of three condoms missing the one I had thrown away and a strip of four black-and-white photographs I had found on my first trip to London, abandoned in the basket of a photo booth on Victoria Station. The photo strip showed a girl about my age with long straight hair (I could not be certain of the colour. Dark blond? Red? Light brown?) and a friendly, freckly, not unpretty, face. I pocketed it. In art class I did a pencil sketch of the third of the pictures, the one I liked the best, her head half-turned as if calling out to an unseen friend beyond the tiny curtain. She looked sweet, and charming.

I put the drawing up on my bedroom wall, where I could see it from my bed.

After our third date (it was *Who Framed Roger Rabbit*) I came back to school with bad news: Cassandra's family was going to Canada (a place that sounded more convincing to my ears than America), something to do with her father's job, and I would not see her for a long time. We hadn't really broken up, but we were being practical: Those were the days when transatlantic phone calls were too expensive for teenagers. It was over.

I was sad. Everyone noticed how sad I was. They said they would have loved to have met her, and maybe when she comes back at Christmas? I was confident that by Christmas, she would be forgotten.

She was. By Christmas I was going out with Nikki Blevins and the only evidence that Cassandra had ever been a part of my life was her name, written on a couple of my exercise books, and the pencil drawing of her on my bedroom wall, with "Cassandra, February 19, 1985" written underneath it.

When my mother sold the riding stables in 1989, the drawing was lost in the move. I was at art college at the time, considered my old pencil-drawings as embarrassing as the fact that I had once invented a girlfriend, and did not care.

I do not believe I had thought of Cassandra for twenty years.

MY MOTHER SOLD the riding stables, the attached house, and the meadows to a property developer, who built a housing estate where it had once been, and as part of the deal, gave her a small, detached house at the end of Seton Close. I visit her at least once a fortnight, arriving on Friday night, leaving Sunday morning, a routine as regular as the grandmother clock in the hall.

Mother is concerned that I am happy in life. She has started to mention that various of her friends have eligible daughters. This trip we had an extremely embarrassing conversation that began with her asking if I would like to meet the church organist, a very nice young man of about my age.

"Mother. I'm not gay."

"There's nothing wrong with it, dear. All sorts of people do it. They even get married. Well, not proper marriage, but it's the same thing."

"I'm still not gay."

"I just thought, still not married, and the painting, and the modelling."

"I've had girlfriends, Mummy. You've even met some of them."

"Nothing that ever stuck, dear. I just thought there might be something you wanted to tell me."

"I'm not gay, Mother. I would tell you if I was." And then I said, "I snogged Tim Carter at a party when I was at art college, but we were drunk and it never went beyond that."

She pursed her lips. "That's quite enough of that, young man." And then, changing the subject, as if to get rid of an unpleasant taste in her mouth, she said, "You'll never guess who I bumped into in Tesco's last week."

"No, I won't. Who?"

"Your old girlfriend. Your first girlfriend, I should say."

"Nikki Blevins? Hang on, she's married, isn't she? Nikki Woodbridge?"

"The one before her, dear. Cassandra. I was behind her in the line. I would have been ahead of her, but I forgot that I needed cream for the berries today, so I went back to get it, and she was in front of me, and I knew her face was familiar. At first I thought she was Joanie Simmond's youngest, the one with the speech disorder—what we used to call a stammer but apparently you can't say that anymore—but then I thought, *I* know where I know that face. It was over your bed for five years. Of course I said, 'It's not Cassandra, is it?' and she said, 'It is,' and I said, 'You'll laugh when I say this, but I'm Stuart Innes's mum.' She says, 'Stuart Innes?' and her face lit up. Well, she hung around while I was putting my groceries in my shopping bag, and she said she'd already been in touch with your friend Jeremy Porter on Bookface, and they'd been talking about you—"

"You mean Facebook? She was talking to Scallie on Facebook?"

"Yes, dear."

I drank my tea and wondered who my mother had actually been talking to. I said, "You're quite sure this was the Cassandra from over my bed?"

"Oh yes, dear. She told me about how you took her to Leicester Square, and how sad she was when they had to move to Canada. They went to Vancouver. I asked her if she ever met my cousin Leslie—he went to Vancouver after the war—but she said she didn't believe so, and it turns out it's actually a big sort of place. I told her about the pencil drawing you did, and she seemed very up-to-date on your activities. She was thrilled when I told her that you were having a gallery opening this week."

"You *told* her that?"

"Yes, dear. I thought she'd like to know." Then my mother said, almost wistfully, "She's very pretty, dear. I think she's doing something in community theatre." Then the conversation went over to the retirement of Dr. Dunnings, who had been our GP since before I was born, and how he was the only non-Indian doctor left in his practice and how my mother felt about this.

I lay in bed that night in my small bedroom at my mother's house and turned over the conversation in my head. I am no longer on Facebook and thought about rejoining to see who Scullie's friends were, and if this pseudo-Cassandra was one of them, but there were too many people I was happy not to see again, and I let it be, certain that when there was an explanation, it would prove to be a simple one, and I slept.

I HAVE BEEN showing in the Little Gallery in Chelsea for over a decade now. In the old days, I had a quarter of a wall and nothing priced at more than three hundred pounds. Now I get my own show, every October for a month, and it would be fair to say that I have to sell only a dozen paintings to know that my needs, rent, and life are covered for another year. The unsold paintings remain on the gallery walls until they are gone and they are always gone by Christmas.

The couple who own the gallery, Paul and Barry, still call me "the beautiful boy" as they did twelve years ago, when I first exhibited with them, when it might actually have been true. Back then, they wore flowery, open-necked shirts and gold chains; now, in middle age, they wear expensive suits and talk too much for my liking about the stock exchange. Still, I enjoy their company. I see them three times a year; in September, when they come to my studio to see what I've been working on and select the paintings for the show; at the gallery, hanging and opening in October; and in February, when we settle up.

Barry runs the gallery. Paul co-owns it, comes out for the parties, but also works in the wardrobe department of the Royal Opera House. The preview party for this year's show was on a Friday night. I had spent a nervous couple of days hanging the paintings. Now my part was done, and there was nothing to do but wait, and hope people liked my art, and not to make a fool of myself. I did as I had done for the previous twelve years, on Barry's instructions, "Nurse the champagne. Fill up on water. There's nothing worse for the collector than encountering a drunk artist, unless he's a famous drunk, and you are not, dear. Be amiable but enigmatic, and when people ask for the story behind the painting, say 'My lips are sealed.' But for God's sake, imply there *is* one. It's the story they're buying."

I rarely invite people to the preview any longer: Some artists do, regarding it as a social event. I do not. While I take my art seriously, as art, and am proud of my work (the latest exhibition was called "People in Landscapes," which pretty much says it all about my work anyway), I understand that the party exists solely as a commercial event, a come-on for eventual buyers and those who might say the right thing to other eventual buyers. I tell you all this so that you will not be surprised that Barry and Paul manage the guest list to the preview, not I.

The preview begins at 6:30 p.m. I had spent the afternoon hanging paintings, making sure everything looked as good as it could. The only thing that was different about this particular event was how excited Paul looked, like a small boy struggling with the urge to tell you what he had bought you for a birthday present. That, and Barry, who said, while we were hanging, "I think tonight's show will put you on the map."

I said, "I think there's a typo on the Lake District one." An oversized painting of Windemere at sunset, with two children staring lostly at the viewer from the banks. "It should say three thousand pounds. It says three hundred thousand."

"Does it?" said Barry, blandly. "My, my."

It was perplexing, but the first guests had arrived, a little early, and the mystery could wait. A young man invited me to eat a mushroom puff from a silver tray. Then I took my glass of nurse-this-slowly champagne and I prepared to mingle.

All the prices were high, and I doubted that the Little Gallery would be able to sell them at those prices, and I worried about the year ahead.

Barry and Paul took responsibility for moving me around the room, saying, "This is the artist, the beautiful boy who makes all these beautiful things, Stuart Innes," and I would shake hands and smile. By the end of the evening I will have met everyone, and Paul and Barry are very good about saying, "Stuart, you remember David, he writes about art for the *Telegraph* . . ." and I for my part am good about saying, "Of course, how are you? So glad you could come."

The room was at its most crowded when a striking red-haired woman to whom I had not yet been introduced began shouting, "Representational bullshit!"

I was in conversation with *The Daily Telegraph* art critic and we turned. He said, "Friend of yours?" I said, "I don't think so."

She was still shouting, although the sounds of the party had now quieted. She shouted, "Nobody's interested in this shit! Nobody!" Then she reached her hand into her coat pocket and pulled out a bottle of ink, shouted, "Try selling this now!" and threw ink at *Windemere Sunset*. It was blue black ink.

Paul was by her side then, pulling the ink bottle away from her, saying, "That was a three-hundred-thousand-pound painting, young lady." Barry took her arm, said, "I think the police will want a word with you," and walked her back into his office. She shouted at us as she went, "I'm not afraid! I'm proud! Artists like him, just feeding off you gullible art buyers. You're all sheep! Representation crap!"

And then she was gone, and the party people were buzzing, and inspecting the ink-fouled painting and looking at me, and the *Telegraph* man was asking if I would like to comment and how I felt about seeing a three-hundred-thousand-pound painting destroyed, and I mumbled about how I was proud to be a painter, and said something about the transient nature of art, and he said that he supposed that tonight's event was an artistic happening in its own right, and we agreed that, artistic happening or not, the woman was not quite right in the head.

Barry reappeared, moving from group to group, explaining that Paul was dealing with the young lady, and that her eventual disposition would be up to me. The guests were still buzzing excitedly as he was ushering people out of the door, apologising as he did so, agreeing that we lived in exciting times, explaining that he would be open at the regular time tomorrow.

"That went well," he said, when we were alone in the gallery.

"*Well?* That was a disaster!"

"Mm. 'Stuart Innes, the one who had the three-hundred-thousand-pound painting destroyed.' I think you need to be forgiving, don't you? She was a fellow artist, even one with different goals. Sometimes you need a little something to kick you up to the next level."

We went into the back room.

I said, "Whose idea was this?"

"Ours," said Paul. He was drinking white wine in the back room with the red-haired woman. "Well, Barry's mostly. But it needed a good little actress to pull it off, and I found her." She grinned modestly: managed to look both abashed and pleased with herself.

"If this doesn't get you the attention you deserve, beautiful boy," said Barry, smiling at me, "nothing will. *Now* you're important enough to be attacked."

"The Windemere painting's ruined," I pointed out.

Barry glanced at Paul, and they giggled. "It's already sold, ink splatters and all, for seventy-five thousand pounds," he said. "It's like I always say, people think they are buying the art, but really, they're buying the story."

Paul filled our glasses: "And we owe it all to you," he said to the woman. "Stuart, Barry, I'd like to propose a toast. *To Cassandra.*"

"Cassandra," we repeated, and we drank. This time I did not nurse my drink. I needed it.

Then, as the name was still sinking in, Paul said, "Cassandra, this ridiculously attractive and talented young man is, as I am sure you know, Stuart Innes."

"I know," she said. "Actually, we're very old friends."

"Do tell," said Barry.

"Well," said Cassandra, "twenty years ago, Stuart wrote my name on his maths exercise notebook."

She looked like the girl in my drawing, yes. Or like the girl in the photographs, all grown up. Sharp-faced. Intelligent. Assured.

I had never seen her before in my life.

"Hello, Cassandra," I said. I couldn't think of anything else to say.

WE WERE IN the wine bar beneath my flat. They serve food there, too. It's more than just a wine bar.

I found myself talking to her as if she was someone I had known since childhood. And, I reminded myself, she wasn't. I had only met her that evening. She still had ink stains on her hands.

We had glanced at the menu, ordered the same thing—the vegetarian meze—and when it had arrived, both started with the dolmades, then moved on to the hummus.

"I made you up," I told her.

It was not the first thing I had said: First we had talked about her community theatre, how she had become friends with Paul, his offer to her—a thousand pounds for this evening's show—and how she had needed the money, but mostly said yes because it sounded like a fun adventure. Anyway, she said, she couldn't say no when she heard my name mentioned. She thought it was fate.

That was when I said it. I was scared she would think I was mad, but I said it. "I made you up."

"No," she said. "You didn't. I mean, obviously you didn't. I'm really here." Then she said, "Would you like to touch me?"

I looked at her. At her face, and her posture, at her eyes. She was everything I had ever dreamed of in a woman. Everything I had been missing in other women. "Yes," I said. "Very much."

"Let's eat our dinner first," she said. Then she said, "How long has it been since you were with a woman?"

"I'm not gay," I protested. "I have girlfriends."

"I know," she said. "When was the last one?"

I tried to remember. Was it Brigitte? Or the stylist the ad agency had sent me to Iceland with? I was not certain. "Two years," I said. "Perhaps three. I just haven't met the right person yet."

"You did once," she said. She opened her handbag then, a big floppy purple thing, pulled out a cardboard folder, opened it, removed a piece of paper, tape browned at the corners. "See?"

I remembered it. How could I not? It had hung above my bed for years. She was looking around, as if talking to someone beyond the curtain. "Cassandra," it said, "February 19, 1985." And it was signed, "Stuart Innes." There is something at the same time both embarrassing and heartwarming about seeing your handwriting from when you were fifteen.

"I came back from Canada in eighty-nine," she said. "My parents' marriage fell apart, and Mum wanted to come home. I wondered about you, what you were doing, so I went to your old address. The house was empty. Windows were broken. It was obvious nobody lived there anymore. They'd knocked down the riding stables already—that made me so sad. I'd loved horses as a girl, obviously, but I walked through the house until I found your bedroom. It was obviously your bedroom, although all the furniture was gone. It still smelled like you. And this was still pinned to the wall. I didn't think anyone would miss it."

She smiled.

"Who *are* you?"

"Cassandra Carlisle. Aged thirty-four. Former actress. Failed playwright. Now running a community theatre in Norwood. Drama therapy. Hall for rent. Four plays a year, plus workshops, and a local panto. Who are *you*, Stuart?"

"You know who I am." Then, "You know I've never met you before, don't you?"

She nodded. She said, "Poor Stuart. You live just above here, don't you?"

"Yes. It's a bit loud sometimes. But it's handy for the tube. And the rent isn't painful."

"Let's pay, and go upstairs."

I reached out to touch the back of her hand. "Not yet," she said, moving her hand away before I could touch her. "We should talk first."

So we went upstairs.

"I like your flat," she said. "It looks exactly like the kind of place I imagine you being."

"It's probably time to start thinking about getting something a bit bigger," I told her. "But it does me fine. There's good light out the back for my studio—you can't get the effect now, at night. But it's great for painting."

It's strange, bringing someone home. It makes you see the place you live as if you've not been there before. There are two oil paintings of me in the lounge, from my short-lived career as an artists' model (I did not have the patience to stand and wait), blown-up advertising photos of me in the little kitchen and the loo, book covers with me on—romance covers, mostly, over the stairs.

I showed her the studio, and then the bedroom. She examined the Edwardian barber's chair I had rescued from an ancient barbers' that closed down in Shoreditch. She sat down on the chair, pulled off her shoes.

"Who was the first grown-up you liked?" she asked.

"Odd question. My mother, I suspect. Don't know. Why?"

"I was three, perhaps four. He was a postman called Mr. Postie. He'd come in his little post van and bring me lovely things. Not every day. Just sometimes. Brown paper packages with my name on, and inside would be toys or sweets or something. He had a funny, friendly face with a knobby nose."

"And he was real? He sounds like somebody a kid would make up."

"He drove a post van inside the house. It wasn't very big."

She began to unbutton her blouse. It was cream-coloured, still flecked with splatters of ink. "What's the first thing you actually remember? Not something you were told you did. That you really remember?"

"Going to the seaside when I was three, with my mum and my dad."

"Do you remember it? Or do you remember being *told* about it?"

"I don't see what the point of this is . . . ?"

She stood up, wiggled, stepped out of her skirt. She wore a white bra, dark green panties, frayed. Very human: not something you would wear to impress a new lover. I wondered what her breasts would look like, when the bra came off. I wanted to stroke them, to touch them to my lips.

She walked from the chair to the bed, where I was sitting.

"Lie down, now. On that side of the bed. I'll be next to you. Don't touch me."

I lay down, my hands at my sides. She said, "You're so beautiful. I'm not honestly sure whether you're my type. You would have been when I was fifteen, though. Nice and sweet and unthreatening. Artistic. Ponies. A riding stable. And I bet you never make a move on a girl unless you're sure she's ready, do you?"

"No," I said. "I don't suppose that I do."

She lay down beside me.

"You can touch me now," said Cassandra.

I HAD STARTED thinking about Stuart again late last year. Stress, I think. Work was going well, up to a point, but I'd broken up with Pavel, who may or may not have been an actual bad hat although he certainly had his finger in many dodgy East European pies, and I was thinking about Internet dating. I had spent a stupid week joining the kind of Web sites that link you to old friends, and from there it was no distance to Jeremy "Scallie" Porter, and to Stuart Innes.

I don't think I could do it anymore. I lack the single-mindedness. The attention to detail. Something else you lose when you get older.

Mr. Postie used to come in his van when my parents had no time for me. He would smile his big gnomey smile, wink an eye at me, hand me a brown-paper parcel with "Cassandra" written on in big block letters, and inside would be a chocolate, or a doll, or a book. His final present was a pink plastic microphone, and I would walk around the house singing or pretending to be on TV. It was the best present I had ever been given.

My parents did not ask about the gifts. I did not wonder who was actually sending them. They came with Mr. Postie, who drove his little van down the hall and up to my bedroom door, and who always knocked three times. I was a demonstrative girl, and the next time I saw him, after the plastic microphone, I ran to him and threw my arms around his legs.

It's hard to describe what happened then. He fell like snow, or like ash. For a moment I had been holding someone, then there was just powdery white stuff, and nothing.

I used to wish that Mr. Postie would come back after that, but he never did. He was over. After a while, he became embarrassing to remember: I had fallen for *that*.

So strange, this room.

I wonder why I could ever have thought that somebody who made me happy when I was fifteen would make me happy now. But Stuart was perfect: the riding stables (with ponies), and the painting (which showed me he was sensitive), and the inexperience with girls (so I could be his first) and how very, very tall, dark, and handsome he would be. I liked the name, too: it was vaguely Scottish and (to my mind) like the hero of a novel.

I wrote Stuart's name on my exercise books.

I did not tell my friends the most important thing about Stuart: that I had made him up.

And now I'm getting up off the bed and looking down at the outline of a man, a silhouette in flour or ash or dust on the black satin bedspread, and I am getting into my clothes.

The photographs on the wall are fading too. I didn't expect that. I wonder what will be left of his world in a few hours, wonder if I should have left well enough alone, a masturbatory fantasy, something reassuring and comforting. He would have gone through his life without ever really touching anyone, just a picture and a painting and a half memory for a handful of people who barely ever thought of him anymore.

I leave the flat. There are still people at the wine bar downstairs. They are sitting at the table, in the corner, where Stuart and I had been sitting. The candle has burned way down, but I imagine that it could almost be us. A man and a woman, in conversation. And soon enough, they will get up from their table and walk away, and the candle will be snuffed and the lights turned off, and that will be that for another night.

I hail a taxi. Climb in. For a moment—for, I hope, the last time—I find myself missing Stuart Innes.

Then I sit back in the seat of the taxi, and I let him go. I hope I can afford the taxi fare, and find myself wondering whether there will be a cheque in my bag in the morning, or just another blank sheet of paper. Then, more satisfied than not, I close my eyes, and I wait to be home.

Marjorie M. Liu

New York Times *bestseller Marjorie M. Liu is an attorney who has worked and traveled all over Asia. She's best known for the Dirk & Steele series, detailing the otherworldly cases of the Dirk & Steele detective agency, which include* Tiger Eye, Shadow Touch, The Last Twilight, *and* The Wild Road. *She also writes the successful Hunter Kiss series, which includes* The Iron Hunt *and* Darkness Calls. *Her latest books are* In the Dark of Dreams, *the tenth Dirk & Steele novel, and* A Wild Light, *the third in the Hunter Kiss series. She lives in Indiana.*

In the taut and suspenseful story that follows, she takes us to a post-apocalyptic future, one of people just managing to scrape out a meager living from the soil, where every shadow has teeth and very real and deadly Things That Go Bump in the Night lurk in the darkness, kept at bay only by the strangest of alliances—and by the power of the blood.

After the Blood

Lost in the forest, I broke off a dark twig
and lifted its whisper to my thirsty lips . . .
—PABLO NERUDA

I didn't have time to grab my coat. Only shoes and the shotgun. I had gone to sleep with the fanny pack belted to my waist, so the shells were on hand and jangled as I ran. I had forgotten they would make noise. Not that it mattered.

No moon. Slick gravel and cold rain on my face. Neighbor's dogs were barking and I wished they would shut up, but they didn't, and I kept expecting one of them to make that strangled yip sound like Pete-Pete had, out in the woods where I couldn't ever find his body. I missed him bad, nights like these. So did the cats.

The cowbell was still ringing when I reached the gate, and I heard a loud thud: a hoof striking wood. Chains rattled. I raised the shotgun, ready.

"They're coming," whispered a strained voice, murmuring something else in German that I couldn't understand. "Amanda?"

"Here," I muttered. "Hurry."

Hinges creaked, followed by the soft tread of hooves and wheels rolling over gravel. Slow, too slow. I dug in my heels, hearing something else in the darkness: a hacking cough, wet and raw.

"Steven," I warned.

"We're through," he said.

I pulled the trigger, gritting my teeth against the recoil. The muzzle flash generated a brief light—enough to glimpse a hateful set of eyes. And then, almost in the same instant, I heard a muffled scream. I fired again, just for good measure.

Steven slammed into the gate. I ran to help him set the lock—one-handed, shotgun braced against my hip. I heard more coughs—deeper, masculine—and got bathed in the scent of rotten meat and shit. All those unclean mouths, breathing on me from the other side of the fence. A rock whistled past my ear. I threw one back with all my strength. Steven dragged me away.

"Son of a bitch," I muttered, breathless—and gave the boy a hard look; his body faintly visible, even in the darkness. "What the hell are you doing here?"

Steven let go. I couldn't see his face, but I heard him stumble back to the horses. I almost stopped him, needing an answer almost as much as I feared one—but I smelled something else in that moment.

Charred meat.

I stood on my toes and reached inside the wagon. Felt a blanket, and beneath, a leg.

When? I wanted to ask, but my voice wouldn't work. I clung to the edge of the wagon, needing something to lean on, but that lasted only until Steven began leading the horses up the driveway. I followed, uneasy—trying to ignore the sounds of rocks hitting the fence and those raw hacking coughs that quieted into whines. Sounded like dogs crawling on their stomachs, begging not to be beaten. Made me think of Pete-Pete again. My palms were sweaty around the shotgun.

Steven remained silent until we reached the house. Lamplight flickered through the windows, which were crowded with feline faces pressed against the glass. It felt good to see again. Steven dropped the reins and walked to the back of the wagon. He was a couple inches taller than me, and slender in the shoulders. Just a teen, clean-shaven, wearing a dark wide-brimmed hat. His suspenders were loose and his pants ended well above his ankles. A pair of old tennis shoes clung precariously to his feet.

"They hurt him bad," said the boy, unlatching the backboard. "Even though he saved their lives."

"He didn't fight back?" I asked, though I knew the answer.

Steven gave me a bitter look. "They called him a devil."

Called him other things, too, I guessed. But that couldn't be helped. We had all expected this, one way or another. Only so long a man could keep secrets while living under his family's roof.

I tried to hand my gun to the boy. He stared at the weapon as though it were a live snake, and put his hands behind his back.

"Steven," I said sharply, but he ducked his head and edged around me toward the back of the wagon. No words, no argument. He did the job I was going to do, taking hold of those blanketed ankles and pulling hard. The body slid out slowly, but the cooked smell of human flesh curdled through my nostrils, and I had to turn away with my hand over my mouth.

I went into the house. Cats scattered under the sagging couch and quilt, while kittens mewed from the box placed in front of the iron-bellied stove. I left the shotgun on the kitchen table, beside the covered bucket of clean water I had pulled from the hand pump earlier that evening, and grabbed a sheet from the line strung across the living room. I started pulling down panties, too, and anything else embarrassing.

Just in time. Steven trudged inside, breathing hard—dragging that blanket-wrapped body across my floor. He didn't stop for directions. Just moved toward the couch, one slow inch at a time. A cat peered from beneath the quilt and hissed.

I helped sling the body on the couch. A foot slipped free of the blanket, still wearing a shoe. The leather had melted into the blackened skin. Steven and I stared at that foot. I wanted to cry—it was the proper thing to do—but except for a hard, sick lump in my throat, my eyes burned dry.

"What about you?" I asked Steven quietly. "They know you brought him here?"

"I put the fire out," he replied, and pulled off his hat with a shaking hand. "Don't know if I can go home after that."

I rubbed his shoulder. "Put the horses in the barn, then take my bed. This'll be awhile."

"Our dad," he began, and stopped, swallowing hard. Crumpling the hat in his hands. He could not look at me. Just that blackened foot. I stepped between him and the couch, but he did not move until I placed my palm on his chest, pushing him away. He gave me a wild look, haunted. I noticed, for the first time, that he smelled like smoke.

But I didn't have to say a word. He turned and walked out the front door, head down, shoulders pinched and hunched. Some of the cats followed him.

I stayed with the body. Sat down at the bottom of the couch, beside that exposed foot. It took me a long time to peel off the shoe. Longer than it had to. I wanted to vomit every time I touched that warm, burned skin. I peeled and pulled, and finally just cut everything away with a pair of old scissors. Steven passed through only once, from the front door to my bedroom. If he looked, I didn't know. I ignored him.

I unrolled the body from the blanket. Worked on all those clothes—and the other shoe. Stripped off what had been hand-sewn pants made of coarse denim, and a shirt of a softer weave. The beard I knew so well was gone. So was that face, except for blackened skin and exposed bone. His mouth was open, twisted into a scream so visceral his lower jaw had unhinged.

"Stupid," I whispered to him, rubbing my eyes and running nose. "You had nothing to prove."

Same as me. Nothing to prove. Nothing at all.

I had brought in a knife with the scissors—sterilized in boiling water and wrapped in a clean rag covered in some faded drawing of a black mouse in red pants. I did not want to touch the blade, but I did. I did not want to hold my arm over that open mouth, but I did that, too. Sucked down a deep breath. Steeled myself. Cut open my wrist.

Nothing big. I wasn't crazy. But the blood welled up faster than I expected. My vision seemed to fade behind a white cloud, and I almost lay down on that burned body. But I took a couple quick breaths, grit my teeth, and stopped looking at the blood.

Just that mouth. Just that mouth I held my wrist over. Swallowing all those little drops of my life.

It took a while. I didn't want to make a mistake. This was the worst I had ever seen. So bad I began to wonder if this was the end, the last and final straw. Got harder to breathe after that. My throat burned. Cats pawed my legs and took turns in my lap, butting my chin and kneading my thighs with their prickly little claws. One of them licked a charred finger, but didn't try to chew, so I let that go.

My wrist throbbed. So did my head, after a time. I kept at it. Until, finally, I noticed a little color around his lips. A hint of pink beneath the blackened skin. I closed my eyes, counting to one hundred. When I looked again, it wasn't my imagination. Pink skin. Signs of life.

I pressed my wrist against his burned mouth and felt his lips tighten just a hairsbreadth. Good enough for me. I was exhausted. I didn't move my wrist, but stretched out on the couch beside him, ignoring the smell and crunch of cooked skin. A cat walked up the length of my hip, while another perched on the cushion above me, licking my hair. Purrs thundered, everywhere.

And that mouth closed tighter.

I closed my eyes and went to sleep.

I WOKE CHOKING, water trickling down my throat.

But there was also a hand behind my head and something hard on my lips, and both flashed me back to the bad days. I sat up fighting, heart all thunder. My fist slammed into a hard chest.

A naked man squatted in front of me, gripping a cup of water in his hand. Scared me for a moment, terrified me, part of me still asleep—but then I took a breath and my vision cleared, and I saw the man. I saw him.

He was bald, scorched, raw. Not much better than a half-cooked chicken, and certainly uglier. But his eyes were blue and glittering as ice, and I smiled crooked for that cold gaze.

"Henry." I wiped water from my mouth, trying not to tremble. "Aren't you a sight?"

"Amanda," he replied. But that was it. Only my name. That other hand of his still held the back of my head. I looked down. My wrist had been bandaged. I saw other things, too, and dragged the quilt from the couch to toss over his hips. His mouth twitched—from bitterness or humor, I couldn't tell—but he leaned in to kiss me.

Just my cheek. Slow and deliberate, lingering with our faces pressed close. I slid my arms around his neck and held tight.

"Don't make me cry again," I whispered.

Henry dragged in a deep breath. "How did I get here?"

"Steven."

He leaned harder against me. "Did anyone see him?"

"We haven't talked about what happened. But I'd say yes." I pulled away, speaking into his shoulder: a patchwork of pink and blackened flesh. "He said you saved lives."

"I gave in." Henry's fingers tightened in my hair. "I killed."

"Monsters."

"I killed," he said again, shivering. "I violated God's rule."

You did what you had to, I wanted to tell him, but those were cheap words compared to what he needed; and that was more than I could give him.

Bedsprings creaked from the other room. I glanced toward the window. Still dark out, but it had to be close to dawn. I heard birds, and the goats; and farther away, that dog barking. I tried to stand. Henry grabbed my wrist. "You need to rest. What you did last night—"

"I'm fine," I lied, blinking heavily to keep my vision straight. "Stay here."

But he didn't. He wrapped the quilt around his hips and limped outside with me, followed by several cats, bounding, twining, pouncing in the grass. Little guards. Cool air felt good on my face, and though Henry did not take my hand, our arms brushed as we walked.

I had built the rabbit hutch inside the barn. Horses stirred restlessly when we entered, and so did the goats in their dark pen, but the chickens were quiet. I felt all the animals watching as I undid the latch and reached inside for a sleek brown body. The rabbit trembled. So did Henry, when I handed it to him.

"I wish you wouldn't watch," he murmured, but almost in the same breath he bit the rabbit's throat. It screamed. So did he, but it was a muffled, relieved sound. I looked away. All the other rabbits were huddled together, shaking. I could hear Henry feeding, and it was a wet sucking sound that made my skin crawl and my wrist throb.

I counted seconds. Counted until they added up to minutes. Then I took another rabbit from the hutch and held it out, head turned. Henry took it from me and walked away. No longer limping. I heard the rabbit scream before he reached the door.

I did chores. Freshened the water for the goats, brushed the horses down with handfuls of hay and the palms of my hands. Thought, again, about building a pen for some pigs and how much I'd have to trade upriver for several in an upcoming litter I'd heard about in town. I wanted to get set before winter. Trees needed cutting, too, for firewood. I had been putting that off.

When I left the barn, I found Henry near the garden, digging a hole just large enough for two dead rabbits. Soil was wet and smelled good, like the tomatoes ripening on the vines. I saw light on the horizon.

"I'll finish that," I said. "You need to get inside."

"I need a walk," he mumbled. I realized he had been weeping. "I don't want to see Steven."

"Too bad." I crouched, taking his hand. His skin appeared healthier, burn marks, fading. "You may be all he has now. Besides, it's too close to dawn for a walk. Don't be stupid."

"Stupid," he echoed, and pulled his hand away. "You should have seen how my dad—how *they*—looked at me. How they'll look at Steven now. My fault, Amanda. I was too weak to leave."

The rabbits were still warm, but hollow, flattened. Drops of blood coated their throats. I dropped them into the hole Henry had dug and pushed dirt over their bodies.

"Staying was harder than leaving," I said, but that was all. The house door creaked open, somewhere out of sight, then banged shut. Henry tensed. I backed away. I doubt he noticed. Too busy watching his brother, who strode down the path toward us—just a shadow in the predawn light, shoulders hunched, hands shoved deep in his pockets, hat tilted low over his eyes.

I left them alone. Went back to the house for my shotgun and a coat, and then headed down to the fence. Looking for monsters.

Cats followed me.

THE LAND HAD been in the family a long time. Long enough for stories to be passed down, stories that never changed except for the weather, or the animal, or the person: stories involving my kin, who were neighbors and friends to the Plain People. Or the Amish, as my mother had called them, respectfully.

She was dead now, gone a couple years. She and my father had both survived the Big Death, though cancer and infection finally killed them. Mundane, compared to what had destroyed most everyone else: a plague that struck cities, a virus that killed in hours or days. My brother was lost that way—gone to college in Chicago, which didn't exist anymore. It was for him that I didn't like hearing stories about the Big Death, though some refugee survivors seemed to get kicks from the attention they received when telling the tale. Blood in the streets, and riots, and the government quarantining the cities and suburbs with tanks and barricades, and guns. No burials for the millions dead, no burials for the cities.

Just the forests that had grown up around them. An unnatural growth, some said. Cities of the dead, swallowed by trees. And, in the intervening years, other strange things. Unnatural visitations.

But folks didn't like to tell those stories. Plague was easier to swallow than magic.

The fence around my land was made of wood planks instead of strung barbed wire. Maybe my great-grandfather had built the thing, or his father—I didn't know for sure—just that it was older than living memory, and had been tended and mended over the last hundred years by people who knew what they were doing; so many times over, there probably wasn't much original wood left in the damn thing.

It was a good fence. And I'd made my own additions.

Still dark out. Skies clearing, revealing stars. I checked the gate at the end of the driveway. Couldn't see much on the other side, except for a splash of something dark on the gravel. Blood, maybe. No body. Dragged away into the woods with Pete-Pete's bones. I undid the lock, crossed over. Shotgun held carefully. Cats walked with me, but didn't hiss or flatten their ears. Just watched the shadows beyond the road, in the trees. I didn't hear anything except for birds.

"Hiding from the light," said a quiet voice behind me. I didn't flinch. One of the cats had glanced over its shoulder, which was warning enough.

Henry stepped close, still naked except for the quilt. I said, "You should be in the house."

"I have time. Not safe here, all by yourself."

"Got an army." I held up my gun and glanced at the cats. "Steven?"

He said nothing. Just took a few jolting steps toward the woods. I grabbed him, afraid of what he would do. He didn't fight me, but the tension was thick in his arm. I pretended not to see the sharp tips of his teeth as he pulled back his lips to scent the air.

"They're in there," he said, his voice husky. "I tasted their blood last night."

I tightened my grip, both on his arm and the shotgun. Cats twined around our legs. "Did you like it?"

Henry looked at me. "Yes."

"It's not a sin," I said, "to be yourself. *You* told me that."

"Before I was turned into this." He touched his mouth, pressing his thumb against a sharp tooth. "I was called a demon last night. Dad put the torch to me himself, and I didn't stop him. I kept hoping he would stop first."

I squeezed his arm. "Come on. Before the sun rises."

"I have time," he said again, but gently, holding my gaze. "Please, let's walk."

So we did. On the dangerous side of the fence, outside the border of the land; my cornfields, and the potatoes, and the long rows of spinach, green beans, tomatoes, and cucumbers. I didn't have a rabbit problem. Cats strolled along the rails and through the tall grass, which soaked the bottoms of my jeans. Henry did not notice the wet, or chill. He watched the forest, and the sky, and my face.

"Stop," I said, and knelt to examine a weather-beaten post. It was hard to see. I had no batteries for the flashlights stored in the cellar, but I had traded for some butane lighters some years back, and those still worked. I slipped one from my pocket, flipped the switch. A little flame appeared. I needed it for only a moment.

"It looks fine," Henry murmured.

"You always say that," I replied, and held out my finger to him. He hesitated—and then nipped it, ever so carefully, on the sharp point of his tooth. I felt nothing except a nick of pain, and maybe sadness, or comfort, or affection—love—but nothing as storybooks said I should feel; no shiver, no lust, no mind-meld. I had done my research in the library, which still stood in town, governed by three crones who lived there and guarded the books. I had read fiction, and myths, and looked at pictures on the backs of movies that couldn't be played anymore. But in the end, none of it meant much. Problems just had to be lived through.

I smeared a spot of my blood on the fencepost and said a prayer. Nothing big. It was the feeling behind the words that mattered, and I prayed for safety and light, and protection. I prayed to keep the monsters out.

We moved on. A hundred feet later, stopped again. I repeated the ritual. Weak spots. No way to tell just from looking, but I knew, in my blood, in my heart.

"They got through last night," Henry said, watching me carefully. "Past the fence to the front door. That's what started it. I was in the barn, cleaning the stalls. I heard Mom scream."

"I'm sorry." I glanced at the sky—lighter now, dawn chasing stars. Sun would soon be rising. "I'll swing around the farm today and see if I can't shore up the line without your folks seeing me."

"Take Steven with you."

I shook my head, patting the tabby rubbing against my shins. "Won't do that. If they try and hurt him—"

"Then we'll know. It's important, Amanda."

I started walking. "Have *him* talk to me about it. His choice. No pressure from you."

Henry stayed where he was, clutching the quilt in one hand. His broad shoulders were almost free of burned skin; and so were his arms, thick with muscle. He had been teethed on hard labor, and it showed.

But Henry was a good-looking man when he wasn't burned alive; and it hurt to feel him staring at me. Staring at me like I wanted to be stared at—with hunger, and trust, and that old sadness that sometimes I couldn't bear.

I looked away, just for a moment. One of the cats meowed.

When I turned back he was gone.

NO ONE KNEW, of course. About the blood on the fence. Prior to last night, no one had known about Henry's affliction, either. Just Steven and me.

Small town. Caught on the border of a government-registered Enclave, one of hundreds scattered across the former United States. Not many official types ever came around, except a couple times a year with fresh medicines and other odds and ends—military caravans, powered by gas. No one else had fuel. Might be some in the quarantined cities, but I couldn't think of anyone who would go there. The virus might still be active. Waiting in the bones.

Twenty years, waiting. Little or no manufacturing in all that time; no currency, no airplanes, no television or postal service, or ice cream from the freezer; or all the little things I had taken for granted as a kid and could hardly remember. Just stories now. Lives that were and would never be again. The past, gone unmissed.

Maybe it was for the best. Survivors of the Big Death had to make do with leftovers. Farming experience was more valuable than guns. So was living without electricity and plumbing. Which meant—to the dismay of some—that Amish, and folks like them, now held the real power. Government was encouraging them to spread out, establish new agricultural communities—from Atlantic to Pacific. Nothing asked for in return, though it had created an odd dynamic. I'd heard accusations of favoritism in business dealings, complaints about cold shoulders and standoffishness. Other things, too—bitter and sour.

But not all communities were the same, and if you were a good neighbor, the Plain People were good to you. Even if, when you knew them too well, they had their own problems. Religion was no cure for dysfunction.

I rode in the wagon beside Steven. Brought my shotgun—unloaded in case anyone checked. Shells were in my pockets. Knives, hidden inside my boots. We weren't the only ones on the road, which had been one of those two-lane highways back in the old days. Still a highway, just not for cars—which rusted at the side of the road. Relics of another age. None had been dumped in the fields. Plenty of land, maybe, but it all needed to be used to grow food. Vast vegetable gardens and grazing cattle surrounded several battered trailer homes. Little kids playing outside waved to us, and went back to chasing the dog.

Steven and I didn't talk much until we reached the border of his family's farm. I made him stop twice and pricked my finger for blood. Blessed the fence.

"God has a plan," Steven murmured, watching me.

I glanced at him. "I hate it when you and Henry say that."

"Better God than the alternative." He leaned forward, studying his hands—his trembling hands. "I want God to be responsible for what changed us. I want God to have a reason for us being different. We're not demons, Amanda."

"I agree," I replied sharply. "Now let me concentrate."

"You don't even know how you do it," he murmured, still not looking at me. "Or why your blood works against . . . them."

Because I will it to, whispered a small voice inside my mind. But that was nonsense—and even if it wasn't, years of considering the matter had given me nothing worth discussing. The same instincts that had led me to dot fenceposts with my blood seemed just as powerful as the driving urge of birds to fly south for winter, or cats to hunt—or Henry to drink blood.

I worked quickly, and climbed back into the wagon. Steven clucked at the horses. I kept my gaze on the fence, watching for weak spots—listening for them inside my head. But it was near the gate where I saw the breaking point.

"Those boards are new," I said, jumping down and crouching. "Or were, before last night."

"Dad replaced them. No one told Henry or me." Steven's voice was hoarse, his face so pale. He looked ready to vomit. "Found out too late."

"You don't have to do this. We can go back."

He closed his eyes and shook his head. "I need them to understand. None of us could stop what happened."

Not before, I imagined him adding. *But we could stop it this time.*

I stared past Steven at the woods. "It's been hard for you, these past few years. Helping your brother pretend he's human. Keeping up the illusion, every day, in your own home."

A strained smile touched the corner of his mouth. "Lying all the time. Praying for forgiveness. Wears on the soul."

"Cry me a river," I said. "You know you're a good person."

"By your standards, maybe."

"Ah. My weak morals. My violent temper. The jeans I wear." I gave him a sidelong glance. "I thought pride was a sin."

He never replied. I finished blessing the fence and pulled myself back into the wagon. Less than a minute later, we turned up the drive, almost a quarter-mile long, from the fence to the house. It was a sunny day, so bright the white clapboard house near glowed with light. Purple petunias grew in tangled masses near the clothesline; chickens scattered beneath billowing sheets, pecking feed thrown down by a little girl dressed in a simple blue dress. A black cap had been tied over her head, and her curly brown hair hung in braids. She looked up, staring at the wagon. Steven waved.

"Anna is getting big," I said, just as the little girl dropped the bowl of chicken feed and ran toward the house—screaming. I flinched. So did Steven.

He stopped the horses before we were halfway up the drive. I slid out of the wagon, watching as a man strode from the barn. He held an ax. My unloaded shotgun was on the bench. I touched the stock and said, "Samuel, if you're not planning on using that cutter, maybe you should put it down."

Samuel Bontrager did not put down the ax. He was a stocky, bow-legged man; broad shoulders, sinewy forearms, lean legs; and a gut that hung precariously over the waist of his pants. He had a long beard, more silver than blond. Henry might look like him one day. If he aged.

Last time I'd seen the man, he had been admiring a new horse; a delicate high-stepping creature traded as a gift for his eldest daughter. Smiles, then. But now he was pale, tense, staring at me with a gaze so hollow he hardly seemed alive.

"Go," he whispered, as the house door banged open and his wife, Rachel, emerged. "Go on, get out."

"Dad," Steven choked out, but Samuel let out a despairing cry, and staggered forward with that ax shaking in his hands. He did not swing the weapon, but brandished it like a shield. Might as well have been a cross.

I took my hand from the shotgun. "We need to talk."

Rachel walked down the porch stairs, each step stiff, sharp. Her gaze never left Steven's face, but her husband was shaking his head, shaking like that was all he knew how to do, his eyes downcast, when open at all.

"Out," he said hoarsely. "I saw a crime committed last night that was against God, and I will not tolerate any who condone it."

"You saw a young man save his parents from death." I stepped toward him, hands outstretched. "You saw *both* your sons take that burden on their souls." *To keep you safe*, I didn't add. *Making amends for what they couldn't do years ago.*

I might as well have spoken out loud. Rachel made a muffled gasping sound, a sob, touching her mouth with her scarred, tanned hands. I saw those memories in her eyes. Samuel finally looked at his son, his gaze blazing with sorrow.

"You held them down," he whispered. "You held those men down . . . for *him*."

I gave Steven a sharp look, but he was staring at his father. Pale, shaking, with some strange light in his too-bright eyes.

"They were going to kill you," he breathed. "I did nothing wrong. Neither did Henry. We did *not* forsake the Lord."

"You held them down," Samuel hissed again, trembling. "And *he* ripped out their throats. He used nothing but his *mouth* to do this. We *all* saw it. He was not human in that moment. He was not a child of God. He was . . . something else . . . and I will *not* have such a monstrosity in my home. Nor will I bear the sight of any who would take that monster's side."

"Samuel," I said, looking past him as his weeping wife, who swayed closer, clutched her hands over her mouth. "Those were not human men he killed."

"Then what was my son, if those were not men?" Samuel tossed his ax in the dirt and rubbed a hand over his ashen face. "I would rather have died than see my own child murder."

He was telling the truth. I expected nothing less from a man of his faith. Nor could I condemn it. He believed what he believed, and it was the reason so many towns and Enclaves had become safe places to live. It was also why so many local men of the Amish were gone now, in the grave.

And why Anna Bontrager did not look like either of her fair-haired parents.

"Steven," I said quietly. "Get out of the wagon. We're going."

"No," he whispered, flashing me a desperate look. "Tell them, Amanda."

Tell them what happened years ago in the woods.

But I looked at Steven, and then his parents, and could not bring myself to say the words. Not yet. Maybe not ever.

"Steven and Henry's belongings," I said instead. "We'll take them."

"Gone," said Rachel, so softly I could barely hear her. She drew close to her husband's side, and her bloodshot gaze never left Steven's face. "Burned."

Steven sank down on the wagon bench. Breaking, breaking—I could hear his heart breaking. I suddenly hated Henry for not being here. For asking me to do this.

I grabbed my shotgun off the wagon and touched Steven's leg. "Come on. Let's go."

He gave me a dazed look. Samuel, behind me, cleared his throat and whispered, "Take the wagon and horses. I don't want anything he touched."

I ignored him, still holding Steven's gaze. I extended my hand. After a long moment, he took it, and I pulled him off the wagon. He kept his head down and did not look back at his parents. I pushed him ahead of me, very gently, and we walked down the long driveway toward the road.

Samuel called out, "Amanda."

I stopped. Steven did not. I glanced over my shoulder. Samuel and his wife were leaning on each other. I wanted to pick up handfuls of gravel and throw it at their faces. I wanted to ask them to remember the bad days, and that violent afternoon. Maybe the choice *not* to act had always been clear to them, but not to Henry. Not to his brother.

"If you keep the boy with you," Samuel began, but I held up my hand, stopping him.

"Don't," I said. "Don't threaten me."

"No threats," Rachel replied, pulling away from her husband; pushing him, even. "We care about you. Our families have always been . . . close."

More close than she realized. Close enough that she would not want me here, should the truth be known. All those little truths, wrapped up in lies.

All I could do was stare, helpless. "Then don't do this to Steven. No matter what happened last night, you *have* to forgive him. It's your way."

Rachel's face crumpled. Samuel clamped his hand down hard on her shoulder.

"Forgiveness isn't the same as acceptance. Steven *will* be held accountable," he said, with ominous finality.

Rachel shuddered. For a moment I thought she would defy her husband, but she visibly steeled herself and gave me an impossibly sad look that reminded me of my mother when she would dig out old pictures of my brother.

"I know about the violence that was committed against you," she whispered, so softly I could barely hear her voice. "But don't let that be an excuse to harbor violence in your heart."

"Or my home?" I gave her a bitter smile. "There are just as many kinds of violence as there are forgiveness." I looked at Samuel. "You set Henry on fire. You killed your own son. No one's free of sin in this place."

I turned and walked away. Steven waited for me at the end of the driveway. I grabbed his arm and marched up the road, holding him close. Even when the Bontrager farm was out of sight, I didn't let go.

I said, "You told them what happened to me?"

"She just knew," Steven whispered. "It was the same men, and she knew."

I didn't want to think about that. But I did. I had time. It took us more than an hour to walk home. Longer, because I detoured to check other parts of his family's fence; and then mine. No need to bless any other borders in these parts. Folks had their own problems, but not like ours—though this road, between his place and mine, had a reputation amongst locals: few traveled it at night. Years ago, men and women had gone missing; parts of them found at the side of the road, chewed up.

We walked slowly. Met only two other people, the Robersons: a silver-haired woman on a battered bicycle, transporting green onions inside the basket bolted to the handlebars; and her husband, ten years younger, riding another bike and hauling a homemade cart full of caged chicks. On their way to town central. Mr. Roberson wore a gun, but his was just for show. I was the only person in fifty miles who still had bullets. But no one knew that, either, except Henry and Steven.

Steven kept his head down. I forced myself to wave. Mrs. Roberson, still a short distance away, smiled and raised her hand. And then glanced left, to the young man at my side.

Her front tire swerved. She touched her feet to the road to stay upright, but it was rough, and she almost spilled her onions. Her husband caught up, deliberately inserting himself between his wife and us. He touched his gun.

And then they were gone, passing, pedaling down the road. I stopped, turning around to stare. Mr. Roberson looked back. I felt a chill when I met his gaze.

"Amanda," Steven said.

"What?" I replied, distracted, thinking about the farm and the land, and those crops I would need help harvesting. I thought about the pigs I wanted to buy, and all the little things I needed that only town businesses—businesses run by the Amish—could provide.

"I'm sorry," he said, and then, even more quietly: "Everyone is going to know. My parents will have already told the Church about Henry and me. We won't be able to stay here."

"They think Henry is dead."

"Doesn't matter. You won't have it easy, either."

"I don't care," I lied.

We got home. A small part of me was glad to see it still standing. Cats waited at the gate. Several perched on the posts, watching the woods, and one of them—a scarred bull-necked tom—lay a dead mouse on my boot when I stopped to undo the lock and chain. I thanked him with a scratch behind the ears, and then nudged the small corpse into the grass.

Steven did not talk to me. He headed for the barn. I didn't ask why. I went into the house, trying not to trip on cats, and set my shotgun down on the kitchen table. Blinds had been pulled. Henry sat on the couch in the dark room. He still wore the quilt. Kittens squirmed in his lap, chewing the fingers of his right hand. In his left he held a small heart carved from wood.

"I wondered, all these years, where this had gone," he said softly.

"You could have asked."

"Maybe I was afraid of the answer." He tore his gaze from the heart, and looked at me. "You had it hidden under your mattress."

I tilted my head. "Been going through my things?"

"It was an accident," he said, unconvincingly. "Why was it there?"

So I could touch it at night without having to see it, I almost told him. *So I could remember watching your hands as you made it.*

Instead I said, "Today went badly. But we both knew it would."

Henry stared down at the kittens. "I hoped otherwise."

I hesitated, watching him, wondering how so much had changed. Seemed too far in the past—too painful—but I remembered, in clear moments: fishing on Lost River, eating corn fresh from the stalk under the blazing sun; holding hands, in secret, while hiding under the branches of an oak during some spring storm. We had loved being caught in storms.

I walked to the cellar door, grabbed a candle off the shelf, and lit the wick with the butane lighter. Down the stairs, into the cold dark air. Shadows flickered, some cat-shaped; fleeting, agile, skipping across the cellar floor, in and out of the light as they twined around my legs. I passed crates of cabbage and potatoes, and dried beef. Walked to a massive chest set against the wall and knelt in front of the combination lock. A new shiny lock, straight from the plastic; part of a good trade from an elderly junk woman named Trace who rode through a couple times a year.

Cats butted their heads against my hips, rubbing hard, surrounding me with tails and purrs. I opened the chest. Held up the candle so that I could see the boxes of bullets, and guns wrapped in cloth. Two pistols. One rifle. One hundred boxes of ammunition. Twenty alone were for the shotgun, making a total of two hundred shells. My father's stash. He had been a careful man, even before the Big Death.

And now I was a rich woman. But not in any way I wanted to make public.

"Going to battle?" Henry asked, behind me.

"Make love, not war," I quoted my father, and shut the chest, nudging aside paws that got in the way. I locked it one-handed, and turned to face Henry. He still wore nothing but the quilt. Candlelight shimmered across his smooth chest and face. His gaze was cold. Had been for years, since the change.

"Been a while since I saw you without a beard," I said.

"I never could bring myself to shave it," he replied softly. "I didn't want to look unmarried."

I tried to smile. "Too bad. I've heard you're a catch. Aside from an aversion to the sun, and all the blood."

"Aside from that." Henry's own faint smile faded. "About today. Whatever happened, I'm sorry."

"Talk to Steven." I walked to another metal chest, this one unlocked. Inside, clothes. I set down the candle and pulled out my father's jeans and a red flannel shirt. Musty, old, but no mice had been in them. I fought back a sneeze, and held out the clothing to Henry. He did not take them. Just stared.

"You're a dead man," I said bluntly. "To them, you're dead. Would've been that way even if your father hadn't set you on fire. You couldn't pretend forever."

His gaze was so cold. "That doesn't change who I am."

I tossed the clothing at his feet. "You changed years ago, even before what happened in the woods. You've just been slow to admit it."

I picked up the candle, stood—and his fingers slid around my arm. Warm, strong grip. I closed my eyes.

"Wife," he whispered.

I flinched. "Don't call me that."

Henry tried to pull me closer. I wrenched my arm free, spilling hot wax on the stone floor and myself. Cats scattered. Upstairs, a door banged. Footsteps passed overhead. I stopped moving. So did Henry. My eyes burned with tears.

"Amanda?" Steven called out from the cellar door. "Henry?"

"Coming," I croaked, stumbling toward the stairs. Henry grabbed my arm again, and pressed his lips against my ear. He whispered something, but I couldn't hear him over the roar in my ears and my thudding heart.

"Not again," I finally heard, clearly.

"What?" I mumbled.

But Henry did not answer. He let go, and passed me. I heard him say something to Steven, but that was nothing but a buzz, and I pushed him aside, running up the stairs, from the darkness, from him.

Steven stood in the kitchen. He had been crying. His eyes were red, same as his nose and cheeks. He glanced from my face to Henry—who appeared behind me at the top of the stairs—and his expression twisted with grief or anger. I could not tell.

"I made a bed in the barn," he said.

"I'll cook something," I replied, because it was the right thing to say, and I couldn't think. "Then we'll talk about where to put you. The attic will be too cold in winter, but so will the barn."

"Won't be here that long," Steven said. "Not me, not any of us."

I stared at him. Henry said, "Steven."

But the young man gave us a look so hollow it chilled my bones. He backed away, across the living room to the front door, whipping off his hat and crushing it in his hands.

"I see what I see," he said, and then turned, stumbling from the house. Henry started after him. I grabbed his arm, yanking hard.

"Sun," I said.

"I don't care," Henry replied harshly, but stayed where he was, staring at the door. I did not let go. My hand slid down his arm until our fingers entwined. He squeezed, hard.

"What happened?" he whispered. "Out there? What changed us? We were human, Amanda. And then we weren't."

"We're human," I said. "Just different."

"Don't be naïve." He tried to pull away from me, but this time I was the one holding on, stubborn.

"It wasn't our fault," I told him. "Everything was out of our control."

"Not everything," he replied, and grabbed the back of my neck. "I made a bad choice. Crawled on my stomach back to what was familiar and normal. I should have stayed instead. Stayed for good, instead of returning to you only when something was wrong."

"Something was wrong almost once a week," I reminded him. "I pushed you away. We both needed time."

"And now this." Henry's fingers slid into my hair. "What do you want, Amanda?"

"Nothing," I told him. "You're here only because you have to be. You're like a fox smoked out of its den. Secret marriage, secret life. You're good at pretending to be something you're not. Ask yourself what *you* want, Henry. But don't ask me."

I pulled his hand off my neck, and walked toward the front door. He didn't stop me. I escaped into the sunlight.

I WALKED THROUGH the fields and ate a tomato fresh from the vine, biting into the red flesh like it was an apple. I ate a carrot, too, and then some raw ripe corn, but threw down the cob after only a few bites. Restless, aching, heartsick: a man in my house, a boy in my barn, and the world beyond the fence, threatening me now, in more ways than the woods could harm me.

I stood on the border of my land, staring over the fence at the dense shadows beyond the trees. Cats twined around my legs and climbed the boards and posts. Watching the woods.

You're not free, I told myself, holding still, holding my breath. It had always been Henry who was caught—in his own lies, his confusion, his conflict. Before, after. And me, trapped in limbo. Waiting. Not for him, but for myself. Years, waiting, to wake up from the haze and bad dreams. Waiting for a little peace.

I had built my fortress. Guarded it with guns and blood. Told myself it would help. Bit by bit, help. Only nothing had changed. Until now.

What do you want, Amanda?

A cat hissed. I glimpsed movement deep in the woods. A flash of white twisted around two dark spots and a moving hole. I saw it again, never still, but always facing me. Restless and hungry.

I stood for a long time, staring, prickly with heat. Burning up, burning, hardly breathing. *Caught, trapped. Caught, trapped.* Two words that filled my head, droning on and on, until I forced myself to grab the fence, fingers digging into the wood.

What do you want, Amanda?

I climbed the fence. Stopped halfway up, swaying on the rails, and then kept going. Relentless. I jumped down on the other side, the wrong side, tasting blood as I bit my tongue. Cats followed, yowling, ears pressed flat against their skulls. I ignored them and walked across the grass toward the woods. This was my neighbor's land, but his house was far away on the hill. I heard his dog barking. I didn't know if the old man ever entered the woods, but his nights were safe. He had not been marked like me—and Henry, and Steven.

It was late afternoon, sun leaning west, lines of light falling away from the trees. Only a matter of time before the shadows grew thick and long. My feet bumped cats—spitting, hissing, growling cats—but I kept walking. Sweating, heart thudding, stomach hurting so badly I wanted to sit down and vomit.

Instead I stood on the other side of sunlight, a golden barrier bathing the grass between the woods and me. Less than a stone's throw from the dense tangle of branches, vines, knotting together like awful fingers an undergrowth that seemed made to scratch and bind and close around bodies like barbed, clawed nets. Forests had become strange places after the plague—not just here, I had heard, and not just around the dead cities, but everywhere. Made me wonder, sometimes, if there were others out in the world like me and Henry, and Steven. Others, like *them.*

I forced myself to look at the pale monster that waited in the shadows, holding my breath as it licked the edges of its lipless mouth with a long pink tongue. No eyelids. Hardly a nose, just a stub that looked partially melted, as though it had frozen in middrip off that ashen face.

We stared at each other. Years rolled. Memories. I remembered the woods, and the coarse laughter, and the fear. I still felt those hands on my body. I felt naked again, without my shotgun.

"I know you," I breathed, trembling—and then, again, louder. "I know you. Doesn't matter how much you've changed, I still know who you were, before."

I picked up a cat, hugging its quivering body against mine. No purrs. Just a deep-throated growl. I watched that monster in the woods tilt back its head, cutting its cheeks as those long curved nails sank into its thin skin. That pit of a mouth made a rasping sound, like a sob.

"Yeah. You cry," I whispered, scrubbing my wet cheeks with the back of my hand. "Living for night so you can finish what you started. But I'm not going to let you."

Cats pushed hard against my legs, reaching up to claw my thighs. I backed away from the woods, gaze locked on the monster. Branches broke somewhere deeper behind it, and wet coughs hacked the air, followed by a faint whine. Sun was sliding lower. The cat in my arms struggled free, hitting the ground with a hiss. I continued to retreat. Never breaking that gaze, though the terror crept on me, harder and heavier with each slow step, something building in my throat—a scream.

Until, finally, my back hit the fence. I climbed it, flew over it, tumbling over the rails and landing on my ass. I sat there, light-headed, heart pounding. Sweat-soaked. My finger throbbed, and so did my wrist. I looked down. Blood seeped through the white bandage and dotted the end of my index finger, which I had been nicking all day. All my fingers were lightly scarred.

I looked through the rails. The monster was gone, but I heard wet coughs and the struggling movements of slow-waking bodies. Men, rotting, rising from their day-graves; pushing aside leaves and brush; ripping the sod pulled over their bodies. Cats gathered close. I petted heads and tried to stand. Took several attempts. My knees were weak, and my skull throbbed.

But I made it. Sun was sitting pretty on the horizon. I walked, slowly, staring at the land and the fence, and those long rows of crops I had planted with my own hands. For a moment it didn't seem real. I should have been somewhere else. I didn't know where—all I'd had were books and pictures from old magazines, conversations with my parents—but I knew there had been universities and jobs, once—all kinds of work that needed doing, and that had to be easier than growing food to stay alive.

The world had been smaller, before—and brighter. Faraway cities that took only hours to reach. Endless streams of music and art—so much brilliant color—and those never-ending aisles in pharmacies and grocery stores where nothing ever ran out and no one ever went hungry. A world with laws and justice, and safety. Where being . . . a little different . . . was not a black mark on the soul.

The Big Death had stolen away that simpler life.

I saw the house long before I reached it. Small, white, just a box beneath the golden haze of the sky. Red roses grew in massive bushes that surrounded the neat rows of my herb garden.

Henry stood on the porch, dressed in my father's clothes. They looked strange on him—almost as odd as seeing him bald, without a beard. I stopped walking, caught differently than I had been earlier when facing the monster—another kind of heartache.

He saw me standing on the hill, and strode to the edge of the porch. He held a knife and small block of wood, which he pushed into his pocket. Sun was almost down, but not quite; and I was too far away to stop him as he walked down the steps. Smoke rose from his skin. I started running. Henry did not return to the porch shadows. He teetered, but kept moving toward me. Walking, then stumbling. He fell before I reached him, fire racing across his smoking scalp.

I barreled into his body, rolling us both into the grass. Fire went out before we hit the ground—a little patch hidden from the sunlight by a low-rising knoll. I lay on Henry anyway, covering him, pressing my hands against his partially charred face. Blisters formed on his scalp, and his lips were pressed together in a tight white line of pain—but he stared at me, stared as if none of it mattered—just me and him, me and him, like the old days.

"Stupid," I whispered. "Sometimes you make me hate you."

"I hate myself," he said, grimacing as I pulled my hands from his head—taking some of his burned skin with me. It was disgusting. I tried to sit up, but he touched my face, sliding his other arm around me. He was stronger than I remembered, and I closed my eyes, holding my breath as he brushed his lips over mine. Brief, warm. I relaxed, just a little; and the next time he kissed me, I kissed back.

Henry pulled me down beside him. I lay against his chest, listening to his heartbeat. The sky had darkened. I saw the first hint of stars in the purple east. Purrs rumbled as cats pressed near, settling warm against our bodies.

"You were in braids," he murmured. "My first memory of you. Sitting on a white sheet in braids and a dress, playing with a doll. My mother told me to look after you. I remember that."

"I remember other things." I fingered a button on his flannel shirt. "Maybe we didn't have vows ordained by any minister, but we made promises to each other."

"Which I broke," Henry said quietly. "I failed you. Not just that night, or after—but all those years before, when I loved you and never said a word to anyone. You deserved better than that. And now I'm supposed to be *dead*."

I unsnapped a button and slid my hand inside his shirt to press my palm against his bare skin, above his heart. Henry stopped breathing, fumbling for my hand. He held it tightly against his chest.

"You're not dead to me," I said. "But I don't know what to do, Henry."

"If I was a better man, I would take Steven and leave."

Bitter laughter choked me, and my eyes started burning again. "Don't start doing the right thing now. I don't think I could take it."

"Neither could I," he whispered, and reached into his pocket. He pulled out the small block of wood. I thought it must be a scrap from the stove bin. He had started carving into it. I could already see the promise of what it would become.

"It's not much yet," he said, turning it around in his large hands.

"It's going to be a heart." I reached out and touched the edge, lightly.

Henry cleared his throat. "I wanted to make you a new one."

A warm ache filled my chest. I tried to speak, lost my voice, then whispered, "Don't take your time."

Henry exhaled slowly, closing his eyes. I kissed the edge of his jaw—once, twice. When I kissed him again, he turned his head and caught my mouth with his. Gentle at first, then harder. His sharp teeth cut my lip. I tasted blood. He broke away.

I grabbed his jaw. "Don't."

Henry shuddered, twisting out of my grip. "Amanda—"

He stopped, looking sharply to the east. A moment later, I heard the neighbor's dog begin to bark. Distant, urgent. Cats scattered. I sat up, Henry following me—both of us holding still, listening.

"They've left the woods," I said. "Hunting."

Henry made a small, dissatisfied sound. "Hunting just us. I've always wondered why they never actively sought out other families. If all they wanted was to kill—"

I cut him off. "That's all they want."

He frowned, but made no reply. Simply tilted his head, as though listening to something beyond us.

"Where's Steven?" he asked suddenly.

We stared at each other—and I stumbled to my feet, running toward the house. I called Steven's name. He did not respond.

My shotgun was on the table where I had left it. I grabbed the weapon and the fanny pack full of shells. Henry appeared in the doorway. I took one look at his face and knew.

"He's not here," I said breathlessly, belting the ammunition around my waist.

Henry's expression darkened. He turned and disappeared. By the time I reached the porch, he was already at the gate. I followed, running hard down the driveway. Cats bounded alongside me.

Henry glanced over his shoulder, his eyes glinting red in the shadows. I almost slipped, went down—and he was there in a heartbeat, holding me up.

"Steven must have gone home," he hissed.

"Why?" I asked, even as Henry dragged me to the gate. "Why would he do that?"

"To warn our parents, to make certain the fence is locked. Just in case those creatures don't follow us here. On his own, Dad always left the gate open at night. Steven and I were the ones who made certain it was shut."

"You should have told them the truth," I muttered. "*I* should have."

"They wouldn't have listened." Instead of fumbling with the lock and chain, Henry climbed the fence, straddled the top—and reached down to pull me bodily over. I held the shotgun tight across my chest. Cats followed, over and under.

I was ready when I hit the ground, my finger on the trigger. Listening for monsters in the dark. I heard nothing. Not a breath, or cough, or the dragging slough of bellies on the road.

We ran. Henry was faster than me, but I did not tire. Cats raced at my side. I lost count of them. They had never left the land before this night, and I did not know why, now, they came with me. The wind was soft. So was the night, and the light of stars behind thin veils of gathering clouds. Henry was pale and his legs so quick—just a blur.

I heard the screams a long time before we reached the farm. Henry made a strangled sound and burst ahead of me. I lost sight of him in moments. Somewhere distant, that dog was barking. I ran harder. I could hear the roar of my blood, and feel it pulsing like fire beneath my skin. My wrist throbbed. So did my fingers.

I felt more heat when I finally saw the Bontrager farm. Real fire, licking the shadows, climbing wild up the sides of the barn. Horses were screaming, and so were children. I could hear those young, shrill voices, and part of me kept waiting for them to cut out in the same way Pete-Pete had, the same way I kept expecting my neighbor's dog to stop barking, strangled and choking. Caught. Dead.

The gate stood open. Blood pooled beside the road, trailing into a smear that covered the broken concrete toward the woods. I glanced at it but did not slow. Smoke cut across me, burning my eyes and lungs. I rubbed my tearing eyes, coughing, searching out those screaming children.

Something large came at me. All I saw were ragged remnants of clothes and a bloated white belly—but that was enough. I braced myself and fired the shotgun. The boom was thunderous, and I turned my face as hot blood sprayed across my body. Some got on my lips. I scrubbed my mouth with the back of my hand and skirted the writhing mass of white flesh bleeding out on the ground in front of me.

I found the children behind the farmhouse, near the open doors of the storm cellar. Doors, blocked by hulking creatures with curved spines and odd joints that kept them low to the ground, bellies and knuckles dragging. Others drifted near, but these were upright, closer in appearance to the men they had been. Pale, puffy, with holes for eyes. Feces covered their naked bodies. I could smell it, even with the smoke.

Rachel stood with her three little girls—sobbing, all of them—holding that ax in her shaking hands. Samuel lay in the dirt at her feet, bleeding from a head wound. He kept trying to stand, but his legs wouldn't work. He looked dazed, terrified.

But the creatures were not staring at them. Their focus was on Henry.

He stood so still, barefoot in the dirt. Firelight made his face shimmer golden, and the red in his eyes was more animal than man. More demon than animal.

"Come away," he said to them. "Kill me first."

"And me," I whispered, tightening my grip on the shotgun. "Don't lose your chance."

The creatures hesitated, swaying—until one of them, upright and shaped like a man—made a low rasping moan and looked straight at me. I knew that pitted gaze. I had stared into it this afternoon, and years before: that heavy, hungry gaze, and that hungry, searching mouth. I gritted my teeth, gripping the gun so tight my fingers hurt.

Finish what you started, I thought at the creature, and took a deliberate step back. *You know what you want.*

I stepped away again, lowering the shotgun. Playing bait. Cats pressed against my legs, growling. Henry slid toward me, his hands open at his sides. Neither of us looked away from the creatures—monsters, once-men—still men, trapped in those bodies, with those instincts that continued to be murderous and hateful.

But I thought our distraction would work. I was certain of it. Until Rachel moved.

It should have been nothing. She lowered the ax, so slowly; but the blade flashed in the firelight and one of the creatures at the cellar door snapped its jaws at her. She flinched, crying out—and her little girls' sobs broke into startled screams.

Everything shifted, twisted—monsters, turning inward, toward them—all those glittering teeth and long fingernails, those bloated, rippling faces with those tongues that protruded from stinking mouths to lick the rotting edges. I never saw Henry move, but he suddenly stood between his mother and a sharp hand—his teeth even sharper as he leaned in and ripped out the throat of the creature. I ran to help him, cats swarming ahead of me—leaping upon those awful bodies to tear at them with their claws. I heard screams—not human—and jammed my shotgun against a shit-encrusted stomach. I pulled the trigger.

Blood drenched me, and guts. I didn't look. I moved on, reaching into the fanny pack for shells. My hands were hot, slippery.

I loaded the shotgun, glancing up in time to see Henry stand over his wounded father and punch his fist through a distended chest, his hand disappearing through broken ribs and emerging beside a curved spine. The creature screamed, flailing backward as blood poured from the wound. I heard a sucking sound as Henry yanked free. He stood there, so calm—and slowly, deliberately, licked his arm clean. I wondered if he knew what he was doing. His expression was monstrous—totally, utterly, merciless.

And I didn't care. I loved him for it.

I turned, shotgun jammed against my shoulder, ready to fire. But the monsters were retreating, staggering toward the front gate. I ran after them, skidding on gravel, and shot one in the back. I tried to shoot another, but missed.

Henry didn't seem to notice. He knelt beside his father. Samuel could barely hold up his head, and his eyes were dazed, wild. I wondered how he had gone years without acknowledging that anything was wrong beyond the borders of his land, when even others in his community had warned him to be careful at night. His only excuse was those monsters—those changed men—had never been consistent. Weeks could go by without seeing one.

I surveyed the yard. Nothing else seemed a threat. Cats sat in the dirt, fur raised. Growls rumbled from their throats. Corpses everywhere, and the air stank. Rachel dragged her daughters close as she crouched beside Samuel, but she stared at Henry and not her husband.

"You're alive," she whispered to him, and I could not tell if that was fear or wonder in her voice.

He gave her a helpless look, marred by the blood around his mouth, on his clothing and hands. "I'm not . . ." he began, and then stopped, looking past his mother, at me. "I'm sorry if I frightened you."

Rachel looked down. Samuel stirred, pushing weakly at Henry.

"Get away," he mumbled. "Oh my God. Get away."

Henry stared at him and then stood. I moved close, and when his hand sought mine, I gave it to him. Rachel saw, and looked at me, deep and long.

"Steven," I said. "Where is he?"

"Gone," Rachel replied softly, and her face crumpled. "He's gone. They took him first. He tried to fight, and they dragged him away. And then . . . they came for us."

I knew that some of her despair had nothing to do with her missing son. "Rachel. It's not like before. It's over."

"Don't lie to me," she whispered harshly, clutching her belly, finally meeting my gaze. "I recognized *him*. He might have . . . changed . . . but I know *him*."

Him. I leaned back, unable to break her gaze, unable to stop remembering her face, years ago, ravaged with cuts and bruises. Same as mine. Mirrors should have disappeared with the rest of technology. I had buried two of them behind my barn, unable to stand seeing my eyes every time I walked down the hall or entered my bedroom.

"We'll find him," Henry said, tugging on my hand. "We'll bring him—"

He stopped before he said *home*, but Rachel gave him a sharp look. Samuel seemed barely conscious.

"No," said his mother, wrapping an arm around her daughters, all of whom clung to one another, weeping quietly. "No, don't bring him here if you find him."

Henry's jaw tightened. Rachel tore herself from her daughters and stood, staring up at her son, searching his eyes with cold resolve. "It doesn't matter that I love you. It doesn't matter that I would forgive you anything. There's no place for you here. Any of you." Rachel looked at me. "You won't be free if you stay."

I touched my throat. Felt like it was too tight to breathe. I wanted to protest, fight, argue—but I couldn't even speak. Rachel swayed, and turned away. Henry squeezed my hand. Staring at his mother.

We left them. I could hear distant shouts, the sounds of horses. Help, coming. The fire would be visible for miles. Even the nighttime reputation of this stretch of road wouldn't be enough to stop the neighbors.

Henry and I stood at the front gate, staring at the trail of blood that led into the woods.

"He could be dead," Henry said. "You should stay here."

I reloaded the shotgun. It took all my concentration. I wanted to say something brave, but couldn't speak. So I looked at Henry and he looked at me, and when I lifted my face to him, he kissed my cheek and then my mouth. Cats rubbed against our legs.

We entered the woods.

IT HAD BEEN three years. Maybe I expected snakes instead of vines, or razor blades in place of leaves, but everything that touched me was as it should be: a soft tickle of brush, the snag of thorns on my clothing and skin. I was almost blind in the darkness, and I was too loud. I crashed through the woods, crunching leaves and breaking branches, like a wounded creature, breath rasping. Henry moved in perfect silence, and only when he touched me did I know he was close.

"I can smell my brother," he whispered; and then: "I wish I'd had more time to explain."

"You had years." I touched trees to keep from tripping. "Time runs out. When I saw you tonight, I couldn't imagine how you had pretended for so long to be like everyone else. And I don't know how they were so blind not to see that you'd changed."

"Easier to believe," he said quietly. "Easier to pretend than face the truth. Even when I had you and Steven helping me adjust to my new . . .

instincts . . . I kept thinking I could be something else. If I prayed hard enough, if I stayed with the old ways."

My fingernails scraped bark, and I felt heat travel through my skin into my blood, simmering into quiet fire—a sensation similar to knowledge, the same that guided me when blessing fences.

"The world is remaking itself," I found myself saying. "Men die, forests swallow the cities and bones. And what remains . . . changes. Life always changes."

"Not like this," Henry replied. "Not like us."

You're wrong, I wanted to tell him, but heard a low, distant cough. All the calm I had been fighting for disappeared. I reached down, nearly blind, and cats trailed under my shaking hand.

When we found the clearing, it didn't matter that I couldn't see well. I felt the open space, I looked up and saw stars, and my teeth began chattering. I gritted them together, trying to stop, but the chills that racked me were violent, sickening. Henry grabbed me around the waist and pressed his lips into my hair.

"I'm here," he murmured. "Think about what you told my mother. It's different this time."

I squeezed shut my eyes. "I didn't think I'd ever have to come back to this spot."

"It can't be the same one."

I pushed Henry away. "I shouldn't have visited you that night. I should have run and hid when I heard your mother screaming."

He froze. So did I. And then he moved again, reaching out, fingers grazing my arm. I staggered backward, clutching the shotgun to my chest.

"Amanda," he whispered.

"I'm sorry," I breathed, ashamed. "I'm so sorry I said that."

But even as I spoke, my throat burned, aching, and when I opened my mouth to draw in a breath, a sob cut free, soft, broken, cracking me open to the heart. I bent over, in such pain, shuddering so hard I could not breathe. Henry touched me. I squeezed shut my eyes, fighting for control. *Not now. Not now.*

But my mouth opened and words vomited out, whispers, my voice croaking. "When they saw me, when they chased me into the woods, you and Steven shouldn't have followed. You knew . . . you knew you were outnumbered, that they had weapons. If you had just stayed behind—"

"No," he said hoarsely, and then again, stronger: "No."

His hands wrapped around my waist, and then my chest, and he leaned over my body in a warm, unflinching embrace. His mouth pressed against my ear. "I couldn't protect my mother and I couldn't protect you. But I had to try. Nothing else mattered."

I sensed movement on the other side of the clearing. Cats hissed. So did I, struggling to straighten. Henry let go, but stayed close.

Bodies detached from the dense shadows, some on two feet, others crawling over the ground, bellies tearing the undergrowth. I raised the shotgun, but did not fire. One of them separated from the others: tall, bloated head, those black eyes.

I knew him. Rachel had known him. She was right—there was something about the shape of his face, the lean of his body. Still the same. Still *him*. Leader of the pack.

The woods were so quiet around us. A dull silence, like a muted bell. I expected to see a flash of light, or feel that old fire in my veins, but nothing happened. I expected to feel fear, too, but an odd calm stole over me—like magic, all my uncertainty melting into my hands holding the shotgun, down my legs into the soles of my feet. I took a deep breath and tasted clean air.

I heard a muffled groan. Henry flinched. "Steven. Give him to us."

No one moved. I forced myself to take a step and then another, certain I would trip or freeze with fear. But I didn't. I made it across the clearing, Henry and the cats close at my side, those small, sleek bodies that crowded into the clearing, like swift ghosts.

I stopped in front of *him*. Just out of arm's reach. That lipless mouth opened and closed, and his black eyes never blinked. I wasn't certain he had lids. Nor did I question why I could suddenly see him so clearly, as though light shone upon his rotting face.

My finger tightened on the trigger. I let out my breath slowly. My heartbeat was loud. I could feel my pulse, my blood, bones beneath my skin. But I still did not fire, and the creature in front of me stared and stared, motionless. I tried to remember what he had looked like when he was still a man, but that face was a blur. Dead now. All of us had died a little, and become something new.

I heard another groan. Henry strode past me. Bodies stepped in his path. He did not stop. I heard a snarl and a ripping sound, followed by splashing. I smelled blood. The creature in front of me never moved, though the others behind him swayed unsteadily.

"Amanda," Henry called out hoarsely.

I tightened my grip on the shotgun, and sidled sideways, never taking my gaze from the leader, the once-man. A rasping growl rose from his throat, but that was the only threat; and none of the others came near me.

Henry stood beside a massive tree, a giant with a girth that reminded me of a small mountain rising fat and rough from the earth. Roots curled, thick as my forearm—cradling a body.

Steven. He was pale, wasted—and bleeding. So much blood, dripping down his skin into the soil, as though he was feeding the tree. Maybe he was. I heard a sucking sound in the roots, and when Henry bent to pick up his brother, I grabbed his shoulder, stopping him.

"Watch our backs," I murmured, all the hairs on my neck standing up as I knelt beside Steven and set down my shotgun. The boy's chest jerked with shallow rasping breaths, his fingers twitching in a similar rhythm. His wrists had been cut open, as had his chest and inner thigh. Cats sniffed his body, ears pressed flat.

My palms tingled. I almost touched him, but stopped at the last minute and laid my hand against the tree. I didn't know what I was doing, or why, but it felt right.

Or not. A shock cut through me, like static on wool—but with more pain, deep inside my skull. I tried to pull away, but my muscles froze. And when I attempted to call for Henry, my throat locked.

This is what you want, whispered a voice, reverberating from my brain to my bones. *This is what you need.*

A torrent of images flashed through my mind: open human mouths screaming, echoing in the air of stone streets bordered by towers made of steel and glass; men and women staggering, falling, slumped in stiff, decaying piles as blood and rotting juices flowed between cracks in the road, or in grass, upon the roots of trees that grew in shady patches. Bodily fluids, watering the earth.

Heat exploded in my chest. I could move again. I grabbed awkwardly at Steven's clothes, hauling him off those roots. Henry helped. My muscles were weak. So was my stomach. I leaned sideways, gagging. Cats pressed close, dozens, surrounding me.

"Amanda," he said.

I shook my head. "Use your shirt to wrap his wounds. We need to stop the bleeding."

He did as I asked, but glanced over his shoulder at the pale bloated bodies waiting so still in the shadows. "What about them?"

I hardly heard his question. I stared at the spot where Steven had been sprawled—a cradle made of roots—and suffered the weight of all those trees bearing down on me, as though full of watchful eyes, and watchful souls, and mouths that could speak. Steven's blood was invisible against the bark, but I felt its presence.

Something changed us that night, I thought, and those once-men stirred as though they heard, coughs and quiet groans making me cold. They had laughed, before. Laughed and shouted and sung little ditties, and made hissing sounds between their teeth. Horror swelled inside me—mind-numbing, screaming horror that I was here, with them, again—but I fought it down, struggling to regain that spectral calm that had stolen over me.

Henry touched my shoulder. "We can go."

Steven hung over his shoulder like a dirty rag doll. I picked up the shotgun but did not stand. I held up my finger. "Give me blood."

He hesitated, glancing wildly at the monsters surrounding us. I knew what he was thinking. Any minute now they would attack. Any minute, they would try to rip us to pieces and feed on our bodies; as in life, so now in this twilight death. I didn't understand why they waited—though I had a feeling.

"Please," I whispered.

Henry's jaw tightened, his gaze cold, hard—but he leaned forward and bit my finger. Blood welled. I touched the tree.

And went blind. Lost in total darkness. I could feel the sharp tangle of vines beneath me, and hear Henry breathing—listened, with a sharp chill, to wet, rasping coughs—but those sounds, sensations, might as well have been part of another world.

Another world, whispered a voice. *We are more than we were.*

My finger throbbed. I bowed my head. Pressure built in my stomach, rising into my throat—nausea, but worse, like my guts were going to void through my mouth.

Instead of vomit, my vision returned. I saw those dead bodies again, endless mountains of corpses sprawled on stone streets, and the sun—the sun rising between towers, glowing with crisp golden light. Beautiful morning, with clouds of flies buzzing over blood that was still not dry.

We were born from this, said the voice, which I felt now in my teeth, in my spine and ribs. *Blood that killed made us live.*

Time shifted. Again, I witnessed blood, and the fluids from those decaying bodies flow and settle, feeding the roots of grass and weeds, and the trees that grew from stone inside the dead city. I felt a pulse sink beneath the streets into soil and spread. I felt heat.

A rushing sensation surrounded me—as though I was being thrust forward, like a giant fist was grinding itself between my shoulder blades. Faster, faster, and all around me, inside me, I felt a surge of growth—my veins, bursting beyond my skin, branching like roots, bleeding blood into the darkness.

Blood, that became a forest.

A forest that swallowed a city.

Many forests, I thought. *Every city swallowed.*

And the blood spread, whispered the voice. *The blood changed us all. As it changed you.*

I slammed down on my hands and knees, as though dropped from a great distance. Fire throbbed beneath my skin, a white light burning behind my eyes. I remembered that night, naked and bleeding, on the ground—Henry screaming my name, Steven sobbing, both of them beaten bloody—and I remembered, I remembered a terrible heat. I remembered thinking the men had set me on fire, that I would look down and find my skin burning with flames.

We tasted all your blood, whispered the voice. *We tasted a change that needed waking.*

So wake. And feed us again.

I opened my eyes. I could not see at first, but the shadows coalesced, and became men and trees, and small furred bodies, growling quietly. My hand was still pressed to the blood-slick roots of the tree, and something hummed in my ears. I felt . . . out of body. Drifting. When I looked at Henry, I saw blood—and when I looked at the monsters who had been monsters, too, while they were men, I also saw blood. Blood infected; blood changed by something I still didn't understand.

The trees are alive, I thought, and felt like a fool.

The leader of the pack shuffled forward and dragged his clawed fingers over his face with a gape-mouthed groan. He cut himself, so deeply that blood ran down his skin and dripped from his bloated cheek. I heard it hit the ground with a sound as loud as a bell. And I imagined, beneath my hand, a pleasurable warmth rise from the bark of the tree.

"Henry," I said raggedly, without breaking the gaze of the pack leader, the first and last man who had held me down, so many years ago. "Henry, put Steven down. You're going to need your hands."

"Amanda," he whispered, but I ignored him, and picked up the shotgun. I settled it against my shoulder, my finger caressing the trigger, and looked deep into those black, lidless eyes.

Feed us again, I heard, rising through me as though from the earth itself. *All we want is to be fed again.*

I hated that voice. I hated it so badly, but I could deny it. Like instinct, stronger than knowledge; like my blood on the fence or Henry burned by sunlight. We had been changed in ways I would never understand, but could only follow.

"You know what you're doing," I said to the creature, which stood perfectly still, bleeding, staring, waiting. "You know what you want."

What it had wanted, all these years, I realized. Living half-dead, hungry for peace, listening to voices that wanted to be fed. Like me, but in a different way.

So I pulled the trigger. And finished it.

I NEVER DID buy those pigs.

I found someone outside the Amish who would trade with me, and bargained for horses, good strong Clydesdales, almost seventeen hands high. Four of them. I had to travel a week to reach the man who bred them, and all he wanted was four boxes of bullets.

We left at the end of summer. No one bothered us, but no one talked to us, either. We were alone on the hill, though people watched from a distance as Steven and I took down the fence, board by board, and used each rail to build the walls of two wagons. Real walls, real roofs, windows with solid shutters. I had seen abandoned RVs, and always admired the idea of a movable home. Even if it was something I had never imagined needing. What we built was crude, but it would keep the sunlight out.

We left at the end of summer. I wrote a note and left it on the last post standing. My land, free for the taking.

I drove one wagon, while Steven handled the other. One of them was filled with food—everything we could store and can—and the other held Henry and our few belongings. The goats followed without much prodding. Cats were good at herding. When asked politely, anyway.

Henry rode in my wagon. He had a bed behind the wall at my back, and a hollow pipe he spoke through when he wanted to talk. After a day or two, I tied a long red ribbon around my wrist and trailed it through the pipe. Henry would tug on it when he wanted me to imagine our hands touching.

"Do you dream of them?" he asked one day, his voice muffled as it traveled through sawed-off steel. It was sunny and warm, and birds trilled, voices tangled in sweet wild music. Pasture land surrounded us, but beyond the tall grass I saw the dark edge of a forest. I looked at it as I would a narrowed eye—with caution and an edge of fear.

We had traveled more than a hundred miles, which I knew because we followed old roads on my father's maps, and we calculated distances every evening around the fire.

"I dream," I said. "Tell me you don't."

"I can't," he said quietly. "I still taste their blood, and it makes me afraid because I feel nothing. No regret. No sorrow. I pray all the time to feel sorrow, but I don't. My heart is cold when I remember murdering them. And then I feel . . . hungry."

Sometimes I felt hungry, too, but in a different way. I hungered to be back inside the forest, bleeding for the trees, hoping that they would give me knowledge, again. More answers. Not just why we had been changed, but why we had been changed in so many different ways. I told myself that the virus that had caused the Big Death had affected more than humans. I told myself that maybe we had all been infected, but some had lived—lived, ripe for some new evolution. I told myself I was a fool, that it didn't matter, that I was alive, starting a new life. I told myself, too, that I was a killer.

I tugged on the ribbon and he tugged back. "Do you feel cold when you think of protecting your parents and Steven, or me?"

"No," he said. "Never."

"Then you're fine," I replied. "I love you."

Henry was silent a long time. "Does that mean you forgive me?"

I closed my eyes and pulled the ribbon again. "There was nothing, ever, to forgive."

From the second wagon, behind us, I heard a shout. Steven. I pulled hard on the reins, untied the ribbon from my wrist, and jumped down. The cats that had been riding on the bench beside me followed. I took the shotgun.

Steven stood on the wagon bench, still holding the reins. Fading scars crisscrossed his face and throat, and his bared wrists were finally looking less savaged. Pale, gaunt, but alive. He still wore his plain clothes and straw hat. Unable to let go. If he was anything like his brother, it would be years—or maybe never. His gaze, as he stared over my head, was farseeing.

"Someone will be coming soon," he said. "Someone important."

I stared down the road. All I saw was a black bird, winging overhead. A crow. I watched it, an odd humming sound in my ears. Cats crowded the road, surrounding the bleating goats. I couldn't count all their numbers—twenty or thirty, I thought. We seemed to pick up new ones every couple of days.

One of the windows in my wagon cracked open. Henry said, "Are we in trouble?"

"Not yet," I replied, but tightened my grip on the gun. "Steven?"

"We don't need to hide," Steven murmured, staring up at the crow; staring, though I wasn't entirely certain he saw the bird. "She's coming."

I didn't question him. Steven had become more enigmatic since that night in the woods—that second, bloody, night. Or maybe he had stopped fighting the change that had come over him all those years before.

Clear day, but after a while I heard thunder, a roar. Faint at first, and then stronger, ripping through the air. I couldn't place it at first, though finally I realized that it reminded me of the military caravans. A gas engine.

A black object appeared at the end of the road, narrow and compact. Sunlight glittered on chrome. It took me a moment to recognize the vehicle. I had seen only pictures. I couldn't remember its name, though I knew it had two wheels, like a bicycle. And that it was fast.

None of the cats scattered. I steadied myself as the machine slowed, stopped. Dug in my heels. Didn't matter that Steven seemed unafraid. I had no trust in the unknown.

A woman straddled the thing. Dark hair, wild eyes. Her jeans and shirt looked new, which was almost as odd as her gas-powered machine. I saw no weapons, though—and was comforted by the sharp look she gave me. As though she, too, had no trust.

"Your name is Amanda," she said.

I held steady. Made no reply. Watched, waited. The woman frowned, but only with her eyes; a faint smile quirked the corner of her mouth.

"I'm Maggie," she added, and tapped her forehead. "I saw you coming."

Steven jumped down from the wagon. I stepped in front of him, but he tried to push past me and choked out, "Are you like us?"

High in the sky, the crow cawed. Maggie glanced up at the bird, and her smile softened before she returned her gaze to me and the boy.

"No," she said. "You're new blood. I'm from something . . . older."

"I don't understand what that means," I told her.

She shook her head, rubbing her jaw. "It'll take time to explain, but there are others like you. Changed people. I've seen them in my dreams. I'm trying to find as many as I can, to bring them someplace safe."

"Safe," echoed Henry, from behind the wagon door. Maggie glanced sideways, but didn't seem surprised to hear someone speaking. The crow swooped close and landed on her shoulder. Cats made broken chattering sounds. Golden eyes locked on the bird.

"Something is coming," said Maggie, reaching around to place a cautious hand on the crow's sleek back. "I don't know what. But we need to be together. As many of us as possible."

I stared, feeling the cut of her words. Cut, like truth. I knew it in my blood. But I held my ground and said, "You're crazy."

"Amanda," Henry said, and I edged sideways to the back of the wagon. "Wife," he said again, more softly, for my ears only. "What did we run from before, and what are we running toward now?"

"Possibilities," I whispered, pressing my brow against the hammered fence rail, dotted with my blood. I touched the wooden heart hanging from a delicate chain around my neck. "All those frightening possibilities."

"I was never scared of loving you," he murmured. "But I was a coward with the rest. I don't want to be that man again."

And I didn't want to be that woman. I scratched my fingers against the wagon door and turned back to look at Steven, who gave me a slow, solemn nod. I stared past him at the forest—silent and waiting, and full of power. Power it had given us—and maybe others. I leaned against the wagon, feeling Henry on the other side of the wall, strong in the darkness.

My blood hummed.

Jacqueline Carey

Jacqueline Carey is a New York Times *bestselling fantasy/romance novelist best known for her Kushiel's Legacy series. The first novel of this series,* Kushiel's Dart, *won the Locus Award for best first novel in 2001 as well as the 2001 Romantic Times* Reviewers' Choice Award, and was listed by both Amazon and Barnes & Noble as one of the top-ten fantasy novels of the year. Since then, there have five more books in the series, including* Kushiel's Chosen, Kushiel's Avatar, Kushiel's Scion, Kushiel's Justice, Kushiel's Mercy, *and the start of a related series with* Naamah's Kiss. Carey has also written the Sundering books, Banewreaker *and* Godslayer, *a stand-alone novel,* Santa Olivia, *and a nonfiction book,* Angels: Celestial Spirits in Legend & Art. *Her most recent book is* Naamah's Curse, *the second book in the Naamah sequence. She lives in Michigan.*

Here's a compelling and intricate tale that follows the consequences of a promise between star-crossed lovers down through the generations—one with quite a high price in blood.

You, and You Alone

Dying is an ugly business.

I am dying; Anafiel Delaunay, born Anafiel de Montrève. When I am dead, they will call me the Whoremaster of Spies.

This I know.

And I deserve it.

There is blood, too much blood. I cannot count my wounds. I only know it flows without ceasing, and the world grows dark before my eyes. Pain is everywhere. I failed, and we have been betrayed, attacked in my own home. Gods, there were so *many* of them! While I honored my oath, honored the request the Dauphine Ysandre made of me and turned my attention to intrigue beyond the shores of Terre d'Ange so that she might wed her beloved Alban prince, I missed a dire threat closer to home.

My beautiful boy Alcuin is dead or dying; I cannot tell. My vision is fading, and I cannot hear him. I told myself I was honoring my oath when I raised him and made him a member of my own household, but I lied to myself. I trained him and used him for my own ends, he and Phèdre both. Like a fool, I failed to see that the work didn't suit him as it did her, that Alcuin took no pleasure in Naamah's Service, in being an object of desire for the nobles of Terre d'Ange.

And yet he forgave me and loved me anyway—a love far greater than I deserved. I had forgotten that life could hold such sweetness.

Even so, I will fail him one last time here at the end. As the darkness

grows thicker, there is only one man toward whom my thoughts turn—
one man loved, lost, and eternally mourned.

My lips shape his name, and a faint whisper escapes me. "Rolande."

I remember.

A DAY BEFORE I was to depart to begin my studies at the University of
Tiberium, my foster-sister Edmée was nowhere to be found in the manor
of Rocaille, but I knew her habits well enough to guess where she had
gone, and I rode out in search of her.

Sure enough, a half hour's ride from the manor, I spotted her mare
tethered outside a lavender field, idly cropping grass. I tethered my own
mount nearby and plunged into the field on foot.

The sun was high overhead, hot enough that sweat began to trickle
down the back of my neck. I plaited my hair into a braid and persevered,
trudging past fragrant rows of lavender humming with honeybees until
I came upon Edmée lying on her back in the dusty soil, arms folded
behind her head, eyes closed, her face turned to the sun.

"Good day, near-brother," she murmured without opening her eyes.

I sat beside her. "How did you know it was me?"

She shaded her brow with one hand and peered at me. "No one else
would have thought to look for me here. You pay attention to things no
one else does."

I studied her lovely face, trying to gauge her mood. "Are you angry
with me?"

"For leaving me here?" she inquired. "Or for agreeing to serve as my
panderer to Prince Rolande?"

A sharp comment from Edmée was a rarity, and I felt myself flush
with anger. "If you don't want—"

"No, no!" She sat up with alacrity, reaching out to take my hand.
"I'm sorry, Anafiel. You're doing a service to the family, and I'm grateful
for it. It's just . . . I don't know how I feel about being used to advance
my father's ambition." She squeezed my hand, searching my eyes. "I
need you to be *my* advocate, too. I trust you. If you think Rolande de la
Courcel is someone I could come to love, I will believe you. But if you
don't . . ." She shook her head. "I cannot wed a man I could never love,
heir to the throne or no."

"Never," I assured her, all traces of resentment fled. I had known
Edmée de Rocaille since we were children. Even as a girl, she had a

sweetness of spirit I had quickly learned to cherish, and she was truly as dear as a sister to me; dearer, mayhap, since I had no blood siblings of my own. "I promise, if I don't find the Dauphin to be kind, generous, wise, warm-hearted, and perfect in every way, not a word of pandering shall escape my lips."

Edmée laughed. "Well. You might allow him a minor flaw or two. He *is* allowed to be human."

"Oh, no," I said seriously. "Perfect in every way. For you, I insist on it."

She eyed me fondly. "I'll miss you."

I leaned over to kiss her cheek. "I'll miss you, too."

Edmée tugged my hand. "Lie with me here a moment and look at the sky. When we're apart and missing one another, we can look at the sky and remember that the same sun shines on us both."

I obeyed.

The sky was an intense, vivid blue. The scent of lavender hung all around us, so strong it was almost intoxicating, mingling with the scent of sun-warmed earth. The buzzing of the industrious honeybees was hypnotic, making me drowsy. Closing my eyes, I reveled in the feel of the sun on my skin, thinking how much I would miss Terre d'Ange. Between my childhood at Montrève and the seven years I'd been fostered at Rocaille, I'd lived all my life here in Siovale province. I couldn't imagine calling anyplace else home.

The beginnings of a poem, a classic Siovalese ode to the landscape, teased at my thoughts.

"Do you think you'll like him?" Edmée murmured. "Prince Rolande?"

"I don't know," I said. "They say he's high-spirited." I cracked open one eye and peered at her. "And handsome."

Edmée smiled. "I hope he likes poetry."

"I hope so, too."

Was I truly that innocent and carefree in those days?

Yes, I suppose I was.

Remembering hurts.

Prince Rolande de la Courcel, the Dauphin of Terre d'Ange, did not like poetry.

I discovered this in a Tiberian bathhouse, approximately one hour before the recital that was meant to be my introduction to the Dauphin.

My journey to the city of Tiberium in the allied nation-states of Caerdicca Unitas had been long, but uneventful. I was accompanied by my tutor, Leon Degrasse, a gifted poet in his own right and a skilled diplomat who had long served the Comte de Rocaille. Once we arrived in Tiberium, he quickly secured appropriate lodgings, hired a small staff to see to our needs, enrolled me in the University's curriculum, and arranged the aforementioned recital, down to choosing the verses I was to recite and the elegant poet's robe I was to wear.

I'd developed an affinity for poetry early, and was reckoned something of a prodigy, even by D'Angeline standards. My youthful body of work spanned a dozen styles, many in the classic Siovalese mode, many others aping the work of poets before me, and a few seeking to find my own voice. Messire Degrasse gauged it best if I stuck to the classical forms, and so it was that an hour before the event, I luxuriated in the ministrations of the most skilled barber in Tiberium's most prestigious bathhouse, a warm, damp linen towel draped over my face, running through verses in my mind while the barber combed and trimmed my hair, oiled my skin, and buffed my nails with a pumice-stone.

There I heard them enter, but I paid no heed until one spoke. Folk were always coming and going in the bathhouse.

"Oh, damn my luck!" a man's voice said in Caerdicci, then switched to D'Angeline. "Can't you pull rank for once, Rolande? I'd my heart set on a rubdown and a trim before this damned recital."

Beneath the towel, I startled.

"Isn't the point of this whole Tiberian experience to teach me to understand the common man's concerns?" a good-natured voice replied in D'Angeline. "Behold, the suffering of an ordinary citizen, forced to wait his turn!"

Others laughed. The first man grumbled. "There's no time to wait, your highness. Are you quite sure we must attend?"

"Sadly, yes." The prince's good-natured voice turned dry.

"Politics," someone else said.

"Politics," the prince agreed. "Tonight's prodigy is a foster-son of House Rocaille, hand-picked by the Comte, father of the allegedly fair Edmée, possessor of strong ties to the royal line of Aragonia. And if I must suffer through this tedium, so must my loyal companions."

"You *know* what it's going to be!" the other complained. "Elua have mercy, how often have you suffered through the like at Court, Rolande? Some calf-eyed Siovalese lordling swanning around in fine silk robes, his hair strewn about his shoulders, droning on about spring-fed mountain lakes, dreaming of meadows and tall, nodding flowers, oh yes, fulsome heads bent tenderly on their slender stalks . . .”

Laughter rang in the bathhouse.

I gritted my teeth, fighting a rising tide of humiliation and anger.

“I know, I know.” The prince’s voice was sympathetic, and there was the sound of a hand clapping on a shoulder. “Courage, Gaspar! We shall endure.”

As soon as their footsteps receded, I sat upright, flinging the damp towel away from me and scrambling for my clothes. “For your trouble,” I said to the barber, fumbling for my purse and pressing coins into his hand. He stared after me as I fled the bathhouse, pelting through the streets of Tiberium and arriving at our rented villa, sweating and furious.

“Messire de Montrève!” Leon stared at me wide-eyed as I tore through my clothes press, ignoring the fine robe of green silk laid out on my bed. “What in the world is wrong?”

“A change of plans,” I said grimly, hauling out a plain cambric shirt and my hunting leathers. They would have to do. I donned them in haste, leaving the laces of the vest undone, yanking at the fine fabric of the shirt to rend it. I slung my sword belt with its gentleman’s blade around my hips, fastening the buckle.

“Anafiel, no!” My tutor sounded horrified. “The Senator—”

“May be appalled,” I finished, twining my long hair into a plait and knotting it at the nape of my neck in a rough soldier’s club. “But he is merely our host, Messire Degrasse. It is the Dauphin I seek to impress . . . or at the least, not to bore senseless.” I glanced in the mirror. “Trust me?”

After a reluctant moment, he nodded.

“Good.”

Ah, gods!

You were so ready to dismiss me out of hand, Rolande. And I was so unwilling to be dismissed. Mayhap it would have been better if I’d let it happen, if I hadn’t been so fierce and stubborn and insistent.

Better for you, better for me. Better for Edmée, to be sure. I loved her as a sister, and I will never cease to regret what befell her.

And yet . . .

I loved you. I loved you so very, very much. And does not Blessed Elua himself bid us, "Love as thou wilt?"

I did. Gods help me, I did.

IN THE STUDY next to the dining salon, I paced and ran through lines of the piece I'd chosen in lieu of Messire Degrasse's selections, aware of the murmur of voices exchanging pleasantries in the background, of the sound of wine being poured as the prince and his guests fortified themselves against the tedium to come.

The thought fed my righteous indignation, and I channeled my ire into the performance. When Senator Vitulus introduced me, I stepped forth to a polite smattering of applause.

It died quickly as they took in my unlikely appearance.

I identified Prince Rolande by the choice couch accorded to him and the description I'd been given. His black hair hung loose save for two slender braids at either side caught back in a silver clasp. Strong brows were arched over dark blue eyes. He had a generous mouth made for smiling, but at the moment his well-shaped lips were parted in surprise.

I locked gazes with him.

"Shame, my lord!" I uttered the opening words of the poem in a low, agonized tone. The Dauphin's high cheekbones flushed with unexpected anger, and a shocked whisper ran around the room. "Oh, shame, shame, a thousandfold shame that you should dishonor your father's name thusly!"

One of the prince's companions half rose from his couch; the prince stilled him with a gesture, his gaze not shifting from mine. His mouth had closed and the line of his jaw was taut. Out of the corner of my eye, I saw Messire Degrasse wince.

Ignoring everyone but the prince, I took a deep breath and continued. "Ah, my lord! Will you dishonor even my death? For I say to you, there is no honor in this vengeance you have taken this day, in the battered and torn flesh of one who was a Prince of Troy; bold and shining Hector slain and dragged behind your victorious chariot, rendered fodder for scavengers by your ignoble deed—"

The hard line of the prince's jaw eased. On his couch, he leaned forward, his eyes lit with interest and curiosity.

I recited the piece in its entirety without ever breaking our locked gazes. The others took it for a conceit, a part of the performance; a story out of an ancient Hellene tale, the ghost of Patroclus rebuking his beloved Achilles, with me casting the Dauphin in the latter role. Indeed, I'd meant it to be nothing more.

And yet it was.

I'd had my work admired and praised, but I had never known the sheer exhilaration of captivating a reluctant listener. I'd chosen this piece for Prince Rolande, and Prince Rolande alone. I was reciting it to him, and him alone. It forged a bond between us. As his face broke into a delighted grin, my heart soared. I let my voice take on a fiercer edge, and I reveled in the sparkling approval I saw in his eyes.

When I finished, the prince was the first to applaud, taking to his feet. His companions followed, shouting praise. I bowed deeply, feeling as though I'd run a long race.

Prince Rolande came toward me. "Well done, Anafiel de Montrève. I'd no idea poetry could be so stirring."

I bowed again. "My thanks, your highness."

"Call me Rolande." His mouth quirked. "I am meant to be but a humble student here."

I gazed at his face, the proud, high-boned features. "Call me Anafiel. And at the risk of seeming importunate, I daresay *humble* is a word seldom applied to you, my lord Rolande."

He laughed, extending one hand. "Ah, mayhap! Any mind, well done and well met."

I clasped his hand, and felt his grip harden in the subtle way that men do when taking one another's measure. His hand was firm and callused, clearly more familiar with a sword hilt than a scholar's stylus. I narrowed my eyes at him ever so slightly, and tightened my own grip, shifting my feet unobtrusively to settle into a Siovalese wrestling stance.

Rolande felt it and gave me a bright, hard smile, happy to find me equal to his implicit challenge. "Will you share my couch for dinner this evening? I suspect we have much to discuss."

I smiled back at him. "With pleasure."

OH, EDMÉE! I'M sorry, so sorry.

Dying, I find there are so many people, living and dead, to whom I owe apologies. Edmée, Alcuin, mayhap even that bitch Isabel L'Envers. All the gentry whose trust I have betrayed these long years while I have played the role of the Whoremaster of Spies. Phèdre, my last pupil; my *anguissette* all unwitting of the stakes of the game we play, Kushiel's Chosen, on whom my dying hope rests. I can only thank the gods that she was not here today, and pray that she survives.

And yet would I have done anything differently?

No.

Mayhap.

I don't know.

What did I know of love? I was eighteen, and I knew nothing. I was D'Angeline, I'd been instructed in the arts of pleasure. I'd had casual dalliances here and there like any young nobleman.

I knew nothing.

But then, neither did Rolande.

There are those who think Blessed Elua is a gentle god, but love is not a gentle thing. It is urgent and insistent, and it will not be denied. It will level cities to attain its goal.

Or destroy lives.

THAT NIGHT, THE first night at the Senator's villa, Rolande and I shared a couch and spoke of desultory things: poetry, academics, gossip from home. We did not address my true purpose in coming to Tiberium.

I was glad.

I didn't want to speak of Edmée to him, not yet. Selfishly, I wanted to keep this moment to myself. When Leon Degrasse glowered at me, I ignored him.

All the while, two unspoken things lay between us. The first, of course, was Edmée and the Comte de Rocaille's ambitions. The second was the spark of undeniable attraction that had ignited between us, casting a vast shadow over the other matter.

Rolande did not flaunt his interest, but neither did he try to hide it even though Tiberian culture was more rigid than ours and did not look kindly on dalliances between men. The desire in his gaze was frank and open, firing my blood, making the torches brighter and the wine sweeter.

Never before had I thought to wonder why poets speak of *falling* in love. That night, I began to understand. I felt as though I'd stepped off a high precipice the moment that I locked gazes with Rolande de la Courcel, and I was sinking steady toward unknown depths. The very ground beneath me felt unsteady.

I wanted . . . gods! Wanted to kiss his generous mouth, the line of his jaw. Wanted to slide my hands up his strong arms, to feel the muscles working in his broad shoulders. I wanted to take him up on that subtle challenge, to pit my strength against his, our naked bodies straining and wrestling together until one of us surrendered, and the other claimed a sweet victory . . .

Instead, we made polite conversation until it was time to leave, bidding our host a gracious farewell. Outside the villa, the prince's companions called to him, badgering him to honor a pledge he'd made.

"Will you renege on your word, your highness?" one of them asked smoothly; the fair-haired Barquiel L'Envers, heir to a powerful Namarrese duchy, brother to Isabel L'Envers, another contender for the prince's hand in marriage. I did not care for the dismissive way his gaze skated over me. "There's a first time for everything, I suppose."

"No!" Rolande retorted, stung. "Of course not." He gave me an apologetic glance. "I promised them a visit to Tiberium's finest brothel, such as it is, in exchange for . . ." His voice trailed away.

I raised my brows. "Enduring an evening of tedium?"

He grinned. "Well, yes. You exceeded expectations. Nonetheless, I do keep my word. Come with us?"

I wanted to say no. I'd no desire to visit some Tiberian brothel where the art of pleasure was treated as mere commerce, not a sacred calling.

I opened my mouth and said, "Of course."

Would I have done anything differently?
No.
I couldn't have.

The brothel could have been worse; but it could have been better, too. It catered to a D'Angeline clientele within the city. I endured an endless parade of dancing girls and tittering catamites with kohl-lined eyes.

Many found patrons among the prince's companions, starved for a taste of the luxury and licentiousness of home.

Rolande nudged me with his hip, bumping against the scabbard of my gentleman's sword. "You look disapproving, young Siovalese country lordling."

I shook my head. "Not disapproving, no. It's just . . ." I shrugged. "There is nothing sacred in their calling, nothing sacred here."

"No?" His dark blue eyes met mine. *"Nothing?"*

I swallowed hard, my throat suddenly thick. "Ah, well, as to that, my lord . . ." I didn't know what to say. If he had been anyone else, I would have laughed and clasped the back of his neck, yanking him down for a hard kiss, honoring Naamah's gift of desire. Country-bred or no, I'd lived a life of privilege.

But he was the Dauphin of Terre d'Ange, and he outranked me by many, many degrees. I should not do this, should not even think it.

He laughed softly, deep in his chest, then leaned over, his lips close to my ear, his breath warm. "I've kept my word. Let's go."

Knowing I should say no, knowing I should refuse, I went with him nonetheless. Outside, the night air was crisp and fresh. I breathed deeply, feeling the effects of wine and desire. Six guards in the livery of House Courcel flanked us discreetly, escorting us to the prince's rented villa. Later, I came to know the villa well. That night I paid scant heed to it, following Rolande as he led me to its innermost chamber, where the household staff had hastily lit many tapers.

There, his callused hands cupped my face. "Anafiel de Montrève."

I grasped his taut, sinewy wrists, holding him at bay even though the time to refuse was long past. "Rolande de la Courcel."

His teeth gleamed in the candlelight, shadows pooling in his eyes. "Are we making love or war, my warrior-poet?"

I tightened my grip on his wrists, brushing his lips with a kiss. "Both."

With a swift, decisive move, Rolande hooked one foot behind my right leg, tugging me off balance and tumbling me toward the bed; but I had anticipated it, and I twisted my body sideways, landing atop him and pinning his arms.

"Point to me," I informed him, taking advantage of the situation to kiss him again, harder this time. His full, firm lips parted beneath mine. I eased my grip on his wrists, exploring his mouth with my tongue; tentatively at first, then with increasing hunger. He tasted like wine, sweet and heady.

Strong and sure, Rolande flipped me over, reversing our positions, his legs trapping mine in a scissor-lock. "Point to me. Is this how Siovalese country boys make love, then?" he asked me, his black hair hanging around his face.

I could feel the weight of his body holding me in place, the hard length of his erect phallus pressing against mine beneath his breeches. It was unbearably arousing. "Sometimes."

He grinned and kissed me. "I like it."

We were well matched, Rolande and I. He was taller and stronger, but not by much; I was quicker and more agile, but not by much. We played at wrestling, stealing points and kisses, until it was no longer a game, until there were no victors or losers, only the urgent drive to remove clothing, to feel skin sliding against skin slick with sweat. I kissed his bare chest, bit and sucked his small, hard nipples, reveling in his groan of pleasure, in the feel of his hands hard on the back of my head, freeing my hair from its soldier's club.

"I want you." His voice was harsh and ragged, his phallus throbbing in my fist. There was no trace of humor in his words, only raw demand, and his eyes had gone deadly serious. "*All* of you."

A flare of gilded brightness and surety filled me, so vivid I imagined I could see it reflected in Rolande's pupils. "I am yours," I heard myself say.

The unknown depths claimed me.

I WOULD THAT dying brought clarity.

Did Blessed Elua have some purpose in joining our hearts together in one swift lightning bolt of a night?

I want to believe it; I have always wanted to believe it. Even after Rolande's death, even after I embarked on a path I half despised, I believed it.

It is hard to believe now.

Still, I try.

IN THE AFTERMATH of love, I was self-conscious. My body was ringing like a well-tuned bell, shivering with pleasure, and I wanted nothing more than to sink into sleep, tangled in linens beside the prince in his warm bed; but he was the Dauphin of Terre d'Ange, and I did not know the protocol for this situation.

I'd been sent to woo him on Edmée's behalf, not bed him on my own. A canker of guilt gnawed at me.

"Stay." Gazing at me with half-lidded eyes, Rolande saw my uncertainty. He ran a few strands of my hair through his fingers. "Russet." He yawned. "Like a fox's pelt. You put me in mind of autumn. Stay."

I drew a line down his sculpted torso, his fair skin the color of marble warmed by candlelight. Truly, I'd cast him well as Achilles. "Rolande . . . you felt it, too?"

He didn't ask what I meant. "I felt it the moment you stormed into the salon and charmed me into enjoying poetry. Elua's hand is in this."

"You know why I'm here." It wasn't a question; I'd heard him say as much in the bathhouse.

"Sleep." He rolled over and kissed me. "We'll talk on the morrow."

I slept.

In the morning, everything was different. The world was different, *I* was different. A spark of the brightness I'd felt the night before lingered within me, tinting everything with a golden glow.

Gods help me, I was in love.

Everything about Rolande delighted me: the way he smiled sleepily at me upon waking, his face creased with pillow marks. The breadth of his shoulders, the shape of his hands, his long legs and the muscles of his flanks. The obvious affection he had for his household staff, and the equally obvious way in which it was reciprocated. He had an open, easygoing manner about him which nonetheless managed to retain an element of royal dignity.

"So," he said at the table where we broke our fast with crusty bread drizzled with honey. "Tell me, Anafiel de Montrève. Why should I wed Edmée de Rocaille?"

Coached by my ambitious foster-father, I had a considerable array of compelling arguments at my disposal. I abandoned them all. "Frankly, I'm not sure I can answer."

It surprised him. "Why?"

I shrugged. "You know the advantages as well as anyone, your highness."

His mouth quirked. "Rolande."

I flushed. "Rolande. Marriage to Edmée brings an alliance with the House of Aragon, and the promise of a strong ally on our southern border. But . . . I am here on *her* behalf, too. I promised her I would not press House Rocaille's suit unless I thought you were a man she could love."

He was silent a long moment. "You find me unworthy?"

"*Too* worthy," I said softly. "How can I advocate for Edmée, feeling what I feel today? I have compromised myself." I paused. "Or do I attach too much significance to the matter?"

"*No.*" Rolande's reply was swift and firm. "No. But . . ." He leaned back in his chair, gazing at the ceiling. "I don't have the luxury of choosing, Anafiel. I am my father's only child, his sole heir. No matter what I will, I must wed, and carry on my bloodline."

"Blessed Elua says otherwise," I murmured.

"Blessed Elua was a god, not a king's son," he said dryly. "He had no concern for mortal politics."

"I would not have you break Edmée's heart." I swallowed. "*I would not break her heart.*"

Rolande studied me. "Are you in love with her?"

I shook my head. "I love her like a sister. I, too, am an only child; Edmée is the nearest thing to a sibling I have, she and her young brother David."

"Is *she* worthy of *me*?"

Stung, I shot him a fierce glance. "Of you or any man, your highness! I would not be here if she were not."

"Peace, my warrior-poet!" Rolande said in a mild tone, raising his hands. "I suggest you counsel her honestly." His broad shoulders rose and fell in a helpless shrug. "It may not be the course diplomacy recommends, but I think it is the best one nonetheless."

You were right, Rolande; but you were wrong, too.

If the world had been a different place, a kinder, gentler place in which all of us obeyed Elua's precept, everything might have been different.

It wasn't.

You were too good for this world, you and Edmée alike.

I wrote honestly to Edmée.

She wrote honestly in reply, her letters tinged with affectionate dismay. *My father sent you to court a royal bridegroom for me, and you seduce him instead? Either you found him so lacking you seek to protect me, or so perfect you must keep him for yourself. Which is it, Anafiel?*

Meet him and decide for yourself, I wrote to her.

So I shall, in time, she wrote in reply. *How can I not be intrigued by a man bold enough to capture your heart? If there is room for both of us in his, I can imagine far worse fates, near-brother.*

Those words freed me from the shackles of guilt that weighed at me,

freed me to enjoy my time in Tiberium with Rolande. The weeks that
followed the arrival of Edmée's second letter were some of the happiest
I had known. Days were consumed with study; nights were filled with
revelry and love. With the exception of barb-tongued Barquiel L'Envers,
Rolande's companions regarded our relationship well enough, and I
formed friendships with several of the others. Even the Tiberians and
the university Masters were reasonably tolerant, won over by Rolande's good nature. It was Maestro Gonzago de Escabares, an Aragonian
historian, who began calling me Antinous after the name of a young
man who was once the beloved of a Tiberian Imperator. The nickname
spread, and was meant more affectionately than not.

And then things changed again.

In the late days of autumn, the great rhetorician Master Strozzi made
me a most unusual offer.

"Young Antinous," he said to me in his private study, stroking his
beard. "You are in a position to provide a service of untold value for
your Prince Rolande. There is but one price. You can never, ever speak
of it to him."

I stared at him in outright astonishment. "What in the world do you
mean?"

Master Strozzi lifted one hand in a portentous gesture. "I can speak no
more unless you swear on Rolande's life that it will never leave these walls."

I shook my head, rejecting the offer without a thought. "No. We keep
no secrets from one another, he and I."

He shrugged and lowered his hand. "As you wish. Be advised that
you speak of this meeting at your peril; and his."

That night, I told Rolande of the extraordinary conversation. He
heard me out patiently, and when I had finished, he said, "I think you
ought to take him up on it."

I stared at him, too. "Are you mad?"

"Think on it," Rolande said. "He takes a conspirator's tone. If there
are those who seek to use you to get at me, best to learn it now. Easier
to avoid the serpent in the path before you than the asp at your heel."

The following day, I begged another audience with Master Strozzi
and told him I'd had a change of heart.

He listened impassively to me, his hands folded on his desk. "You
are here at the prince's bidding." I opened my mouth to deny it, and he
forestalled me with one lifted finger, his gaze flinty. "Did you imagine

for one instant I did not know exactly what you would do when I made the offer? We've had our eye on you ever since Prince Rolande left the brothel with you." At my startled reaction, a hint of a smile curled his lip. "Ah yes, it was noted. Whores make some of the best spies."

My skin prickled. "Who is *we*, Master?"

Master Strozzi rose from his desk and paced, hands clasped behind his back. "Who indeed? We are everyone and no one; we are everywhere and unseen. Did you think my warning in jest? It is a simple matter to slip poison in someone's food. How well do you know Prince Rolande's household staff?"

I didn't answer, my thoughts racing.

"Oh, of course you could dismiss them all," he said, following my unspoken thoughts. "Even the cook who's known him since he was a babe. But who would you hire to replace them? Who can you trust?"

"You are threatening the Dauphin of Terre d'Ange," I whispered in shock. "It is a dire business. I will go to the ambassador."

His smile widened. "I am a respected scholar. Who would believe such a thing? No one in a position to help you." He waved one hand. "Any mind, I am not threatening the prince. Now that you understand what is at stake, I am restating my offer to you." He leaned over me. "You're a quick-thinking young man. Observant, too. We can teach you to hone those skills, the better to serve the prince. Would you like to be able to anticipate a man's actions as surely as I anticipated yours?" He paused to let the words sink in, pricking my curiosity. "To read a man's thoughts on his face? To catch a lie before it's spoken?"

"At what price?" I asked.

Master Strozzi gave an eloquent shrug. "Only your silence. You will return to Prince Rolande and tell him that I offered to counsel you in the art of selling access to royalty, bending a sympathetic ear to select causes for coins. Then you will begin your true lessons in the arts of covertcy."

Easier to avoid the serpent in the path before you than the asp at your heel . . .

I made my choice. "I will do it."

WAS IT THE right choice or the wrong one?

I think it was the right choice.

The choice I made afterward . . . that, I will never know.

. . . .

I LIED TO Rolande, who believed me without a second thought, having no cause to do otherwise. I kept my silence to protect him, and began my lessons, thinking to divine the nature of this omnipresent, invisible menace.

I studied the arts of covertcy.

To my surprise, my instructor was not Master Strozzi, but Maestro Gonzago, the Aragonian historian who had dubbed me Antinous. He had a keen mind, and I admired him. When he asked me to aid him in compiling research for a treatise on the history of relations between Aragonia and Terre d'Ange, I was flattered.

Less so, when I learned the truth.

"Why, Maestro?" I asked him. "Why this . . ." I gestured vaguely, having no idea what *this* meant. "This . . . vast scheme?"

"The currents of history may turn on a single branch," he said in a pragmatic tone. "Many branches together may form a dam. The patterns of influence interest me. Do they not interest you?"

I wasn't entirely sure what he meant. "I think so, yes."

Maestro Gonzago gave me a shrewd glance. "I am a mere scholar, but you are a well-positioned branch. I will teach you to leverage your placement wisely. What you do with this knowledge is your choice."

All my life, I'd been reckoned clever and observant; but I never learned to *see* the world as I did until Gonzago de Escabares taught me to do so. He taught me to look and to listen, to distinguish a man's trade by his clothing, his success at it by the set of his shoulders, his origin and history by layers of accent and dialect. To gauge a man's state of mind by his gait; to gauge a woman's happiness by the tone of her voice, the tilt of her head. He taught me to study faces, to watch for the myriad minute expressions that we make unawares, and the meanings thereof.

He taught me the nine telltales of a lie.

He quizzed me mercilessly about what I had seen throughout the day until observing and memorizing became a force of habit. He sent me on errands with my ears filled with wax plugs, forcing me to rely on my eyes; and when I had mastered that skill, he sent me out with drops of belladonna in my eyes, rendering the world over-bright and my vision blurred, painful and useless, forcing me to rely on my ears as I blundered my way across the city.

Later, both. I had to trust my nose.

And I learned; day by day, week by week, month by month. All the while lying to Rolande and feeling sick in my belly about it; but I learned.

Come spring, Maestro Gonzago revealed the scope of the puzzle and the final price to me.

The Unseen Guild.

How much of what I was told was truth, and how much lies? That is another thing I will never know.

All these long years, I saw no evidence of the Unseen Guild's hand in Terre d'Ange, no sign that their reach extended as far as they claimed, was as dire as they claimed.

But *someone* is behind the plot that took my life.

I may have made a terrible mistake.

If Rolande had not been recalled to Terre d'Ange, things might have fallen out differently. I was there when he received the official missive from a royal courier clad in the dark blue livery of House Courcel, a silver swan on the insignia on his breast. I watched Rolande read the letter, his face turning pale.

He raised his head and met my eyes. "Father orders me to return forthwith. The Skaldi are raiding along the border of Camlach, and the realm takes it amiss that the Dauphin gallivants in Tiberium while D'Angelines die. I'm to take command of the border patrol."

"Then you must go," I said promptly, knowing his sense of honor would permit nothing less. "And I with you."

Rolande hesitated. "You would be safer—"

"Don't even suggest it!" My voice was fierce. "Would you dishonor me? I'm a lord's son, trained to the sword. My place is at your side."

He looked relieved. "I'll have word sent to the University."

Guilt pricked me. "I'll tell Maestro Gonzago myself. I owe him that much."

"Ah, your research project." Rolande gave me a curt nod. "Go, but be swift about it, Anafiel. We're meant to leave in a day's time."

Maestro Gonzago winced at the news. "So soon!" he said in dismay. "I knew it was a possibility, but I prayed we'd have more time." With unwonted urgency, he clutched my hands. "You've a choice facing you, young Antinous. All that I've taught you is in the service of an organization committed to gathering and sharing information that might alter the paths of history. Do you swear loyalty to the Unseen Guild, its resources will be at your disposal."

"And if I don't?" I asked softly.

"You *can* walk away from this. As ever, silence is the price." His grip tightened. "If you break it, death."

I'd come to love the lessons, to love the insight into human nature I'd gained; but I hated living a lie. Hated lying to Rolande.

With sorrow, I withdrew my hands from his grasp. "I'm sorry, Maestro. I did not mean to waste your time. But I think . . . I think if I swear this oath, I will come to regret it one day. One day, it will pit my oath against my love for Rolande, and there will be no winners in that battle. So . . . I choose silence."

There are a multitude of fleeting expressions that cross our faces unaware, manifesting in the eye blink between reaction and thought; I knew, because Maestro Gonzago had taught me to see them. And in that instance, I saw the faintest hint of relief flit across his features.

"So be it," he said with apparent regret. "I will report your decision. For my part, my door will never be closed to you, my dear Antinous. I hope you will remain in contact with me."

I bent my head and kissed his cheek. "I shall."

YOU KEPT YOUR word, Maestro; better than I did.

You were a good teacher, and a good friend, too. I have valued our enduring relationship. You tried to warn me.

The Skaldi have found a leader who thinks.

Mayhap that is why I am dying.

The memories come faster now. Faster and faster. I am awash in their current. I cannot stop them.

DURING THE YEAR I spent patrolling the Camaeline border with Rolande, the Skaldi had not yet found a leader who thought, but they were tenacious and doughty warriors, pouring through the high mountain passes to stage raids on vulnerable villages, looting them and taking female captives.

Rolande was a natural leader skilled at commanding men, always willing to hurl himself into the forefront of a battle. Where he went, we followed. Not a man who fought under him begrudged him his status.

As good-natured as he was, he kept strict discipline. When word reached him that one of his men had gotten a young widow with child and abandoned her, he dismissed the fellow in disgrace and took personal responsibility for the woman and her infant son, promising they would never again lack for aught. As ever, his sense of honor demanded nothing less.

It was a difficult time, but it was an exhilarating time, too. After my first battle, I felt sick and strange to myself. That never changed, although I grew accustomed to the feeling. In a sense, I was glad not to lose it, for it meant I had not become inured to the horrors of warfare.

But the fighting itself . . . there was a certain terrible glory in it. Anyone who has lived on the dagger's edge between life and death will know what I mean; to those who have not, I cannot explain it.

It brought us closer together, all of us; and especially Rolande and I.

Until I confessed the truth to him.

It came after a hard-fought battle in the narrow, winding passes above the village of Liselet, where horses were no use. We'd routed the raiders, and I lost sight of Rolande as he raced after them on foot around a hairpin turn. Ahead, I heard a chorus of defiant roars and the sound of blades clashing.

Three of the Skaldi had made a stand, safeguarding their fellows' retreat, and Rolande was nigh overwhelmed. My heart in my throat, I threw myself at the nearest man, raising my buckler, hacking at his wooden shield, driving him backward. Still, it wasn't enough. For the space of a few heartbeats, our fates hung in the balance . . .

. . . and then more of our own men arrived, turning the tide. We killed two of the Skaldi, and the third fled.

"Shall we go after them, my lord?" Gaspar Trevalion inquired.

"No." Rolande grimaced, one hand pressed to his neck. "We're too close to the border." Blood welled between his fingers. "And I fear I've need of attention."

It scared me.

The wound wasn't serious, requiring only a few stitches to close, but it could have been. An inch or two higher, and it could have severed the big vein in his throat. The thought of coming so close to losing him made me dizzy, and the lingering guilt of my deception was leaden in my belly. I had to disgorge it.

That night, in our shared tent, I told Rolande the truth about Tiberium and the Unseen Guild, speaking in a low whisper.

He rose and walked out into the starlit night without a word. I followed him in anguish past the outskirts of our camp, past the startled sentries, along the verge of a dense pine forest.

Well out of earshot of the camp, he halted. I did, too. He spoke without turning around. "You." His voice was strained. "I don't even know what to say to you, Anafiel. I trusted you with everything I am, and you lied to me." He gave a harsh, ragged laugh. "Is *this* how you honor what we are to one another?"

"*No!*" Beneath the stars, I dropped to my knees. "No!" I struggled to draw breath, feeling as though my chest might crack open. "I thought . . . it doesn't matter. I'm sorry, so very sorry. More than anything, I love you."

He was silent.

"Can you doubt it?" I was desperate and crazed, the words from an ancient oath spilling from my lips, unstoppable. "I swear on the blood of Blessed Elua himself that I love you, and you alone. By the blood that Blessed Elua spilled, for so long as we both shall live, I bind myself to you, and you alone—"

"Anafiel!" Rolande was kneeling before me, his hands hard on my shoulders, eyes wide. "Don't!"

I felt the golden glow of Elua's blessing wash over us both, accepting my oath, banishing my guilt. I smiled wearily at Rolande. "Too late, your highness."

He sighed, leaning his brow against mine. "I have a duty to Terre d'Ange. You know I cannot swear the same."

"I know."

YOU, AND YOU alone, Rolande.

It is why I took no wife, fathered no children. It is why my own father disavowed me, for throwing away my heritage on a romantic whim.

So he said.

My mother understood, and gave me her name. That is when I ceased to be Anafiel de Montrève, and became Anafiel Delaunay.

Edmée understood, too.

"I LIKE HIM, Anafiel." Her fingers curled into mine as we strolled. "I do. I like him very much."

I smiled at her. "I'm glad, near-sister."

We were heroes in those days, in those long winter nights in the City of Elua. The Dauphin and his band of Protectors, guardians of the border. After a year of hard-fought skirmishes, we had pushed the Skaldi back.

Rolande courted Edmée; she accepted his suit. Together, the three of us accepted the arrangement.

A betrothal was announced, a spring marriage planned. Shunned, Barquiel's sister Isabel L'Envers glowered impotently.

I didn't care.

I was happy.

FASTER AND FASTER, memory comes.

Edmée.

SPRING IN TERRE d'Ange, a green haze of leaves on the trees. There was a royal fete; a hunt. A prelude to a wedding.

She rode beautifully, Edmée did. She always had.

I was behind her.

I saw the saddle lurch sideways as her mount leaped the hedgerow; I heard her startled sound of dismay.

I saw her fall.

I do not remember jumping the hedge, I do not remember dismounting. I remember hearing the sound, the *crack* of her slender neck breaking. I remember kneeling beside her, holding her hand and begging her not to die, watching the light fade from Edmée's eyes as she did anyway, sweet and apologetic.

Just like that.

Others had gathered. I looked at their faces; fast, so fast. I saw a mingled expression of guilt and furtive triumph cross Isabel L'Envers', swiftly giving way to solemn grief. Then and there, I knew.

But I could never prove it.

WOULD IT HAVE made a difference if I had been able to prove it, Rolande? Ah, gods! Why couldn't you just *believe* me?

You were angry, I know. Furious with grief at Edmée's death, and beneath it, still angry at me for concealing the truth from you. For lying to you. You didn't want to hear my suspicions.

I was right, though.

. . . .

THE GIRTH ON Edmée's saddle was frayed to the point of snapping. It might have been tampered with, but it might merely have been worn, too. Several stable hands were dismissed for carelessness. When I hunted them down to query them, one had vanished—gone from the City of Elua, gone home to Namarre, according to rumor.

I tried to locate him, and failed.

"Leave it be, Anafiel!" Rolande said in disgust when I returned. "Like as not, the lad's sick at heart over what his carelessness has wrought."

I shook my head. "Someone put him up to it. You didn't see Isabel's face."

"I've known Isabel L'Envers for most of her life, and she's as heart-sick as all of us at Edmée's death," he said in an even tone. "She's been a considerable comfort to me while you've been haring around the countryside, chasing after shadows."

I was unable to keep the bitterness from my voice. "Of that, I haven't the slightest doubt."

Grief-racked and angry, we quarreled; quarreled and hurt one another in intimate ways that only two people who know each other's every weakness and vulnerability can do.

I had a sharp tongue; I should have held it.

I didn't.

Instead, I pushed Rolande away, pushed him into Isabel's consoling arms. I couldn't stop myself from lashing out at him. Amidst our quarrels, we parted. She played him skillfully, while I and my aching heart, my lost heritage, my unproven suspicions, and my forlorn oath were relegated to the outskirts of D'Angeline society.

Come autumn, he wed her.

It was a somber ceremony, overshadowed by the memory of recent tragedy. I was not invited to attend, but I heard about it. By all accounts, it was lovely and appropriately solemn. If I had done nothing, mayhap their poignant tale of romance found in the wreckage of sorrow would have charmed the nation.

But I wrote a poem.

A satire; a tale of a noblewoman who seduced a stable lad and convinced him to do a dire deed with terrible consequences.

. . . .

I HAD TO, Rolande. My voice was all that was left to me. Here at the end, I will admit that I don't believe Isabel intended Edmée's death; that she intended petty vengeance, nothing more.

But Edmée died, and Isabel was responsible for it.

So I had to.

FOLK IN THE City of Elua were delighted by my allegations, ever ready to be appalled and titillated by scandal.

Isabel de la Courcel was furious.

So was Rolande, so was his father the king, Ganelon de la Courcel. But they could no more disprove the rumor that the Dauphin's new bride was a murderess than I could prove it.

I was summoned to Court.

I denied authorship of the poem, but I was not believed. I was declared anathema, and all existing copies of my known poetry were destroyed. With banked fury in her gaze, Isabel argued for banishment.

Not looking at me, Rolande spoke against it. His father concurred, content with the punishment.

I was not banished, only made miserable.

There are always those who relish beating against the currents, and so I was able to eke out an existence in the City of Elua as a former prodigy, once beloved of the Dauphin and sure to be named the King's Poet, now living in disgrace, reduced to writing bawdy poems and satires on commission.

It was a bad year—a very, very bad year.

It changed when Ysandre was born.

Rolande's daughter.

How IS IT that love always catches us unaware?

I see a lot of *you* in her, Rolande. The relentless nobility, the determination, the firm sense of obligation. Although Ysandre looks a great deal like Isabel, I do not see her mother in her.

Only you.

. . . .

STANDING ON MY doorstep, surrounded by guards, Rolande swallowed hard, the knot of his throat rising and falling. "You heard?"

I stared at him, wondering why in the world he was here. "Yes, of course. Congratulations."

"Anafiel . . ." He caught my hand, and I let him. "I have no right to ask you anything, but I am asking nonetheless. My daughter, Ysandre . . ." The knot of his throat rose, fell. "I begin to fear that you may have been right about certain matters. I begin to fear that a good deal of intrigue may surround her."

I was silent.

Rolande's eyes were so blue, so earnest. "I have no right—"

"You have every right," I said softly. "What's changed?"

He smiled a little, sadly. "Mayhap you've heard, my uncle Benedicte is planning a visit. He has grown children he wishes to introduce to the court. Isabel grows fearful and speaks of intrigues against me, against our daughter. There is a dark, suspicious edge to her I've never known before. I need to know Ysandre has people who will protect her, who will have *her* interests at heart. Like you did with Edmée. Remember?"

My heart ached. "I remember."

Rolande squeezed my hand. "Will you?"

I lifted his hand to my lips, pressed them against the signet ring he wore with the crest of House Courcel emblazoned on it. "Of course. On the blood of Blessed Elua, I swear it."

He sighed.

My throat was tight, too. "Will you come in?" I asked, hoping against hope.

He didn't look away, and there was hunger in his gaze. "Yes."

It was good and glorious and terrible all at once, a tempest and a homecoming, an apology and a benediction. Afterward, Rolande wept. I stroked his hair, dry-eyed. Although my love for him was undiminished, I wasn't the innocent young Siovalese country lordling he'd fallen in love with anymore.

Presently, he whispered a question. "Has there been . . . is there anyone else, Anafiel?"

I gazed at his beautiful face, his eyelashes spiky with tears, and pitied us both. "No, Rolande," I murmured. "I swore an oath. For so long as we both live, I am bound to you, and you alone."

He bowed his head. "I would release you from it if I could." His voice was low and uncertain. "Would you want that?"

"No." I lifted his chin with one hand, the memory of the golden warmth of Elua's blessing spilling over me. "Only don't shut me out again."

Rolande smiled with relief. "Never."

You kept that promise, Rolande. And yet you left me anyway.

It hurts.

I don't want to relive it, but I am dying, and I cannot stop the memories from coming.

The City of Elua buzzed with the news of our reunion. Isabel gnashed her teeth in fury. What passed between them in private, I didn't know, but in public, Rolande held his head high and acknowledged me with quiet dignity.

I was not wholly absolved, the ban on my poetry remaining, but I was once again welcome at Court—or at least tolerated.

Even so, I avoided it for the most part. I had few friends there. Rolande and I spoke of those we trusted the most, men we had ridden and fought with. Gaspar Trevalion. Quintilius Rousse, who had accepted a naval commission. Percy, Comte de Somerville, kinsman to Rolande's mother the queen and a Prince of the Blood in his own right.

Based on what I'd learned in Tiberium of the Unseen Guild, a plan began to form in the back of my mind.

This time, I was wise enough to keep my mouth shut on my thoughts.

And all too soon, concrete concerns in the world displaced vague and nebulous ones. Once more, the Skaldi were raiding in strength, angling for control of one of the major mountain passes. Rolande's uncle Benedicte de la Courcel was bringing a contingent of seasoned warriors from La Serenissima on his impending visit. King Ganelon was minded to use the occasion to mount a large-scale offensive and seize the pass for good.

Once again, I was to fight at Rolande's side.

"Achilles and Patroclus side by side once more," Rolande said lightly, dallying in my bed.

"Hush." I covered his mouth with one hand. "Don't make ill-luck jests. It didn't end so well for *them*." I took my hand away. "Any mind,

I fear I cast you wrong. *You* would never sulk in your tent while your honor was at stake."

"Oh?" He raised his strong brows. "Who, then?"

"Knowing you as I do now?" I smiled wryly. "Noble Hector, mayhap; but I don't like to speak of him, either."

Rolande folded his arms behind his head. "It ended badly for most of them, didn't it?"

"It did," I agreed.

He eyed me complacently. "You'd have gotten away, though. Wily Odysseus, that's who you would have been."

I shuddered. "Let's not speak of it, truly."

A date was chosen, plans were made. It was decided that the command should be shared among three men: Percy de Somerville, Benedicte de la Courcel, and Rolande. Princes of the Blood, all three.

Even before we set out, folk were calling it the Battle of Three Princes. But only two of them came home alive.

WHICH IS WORSE, remembering or dying?

I cannot say.

THE SKALDI MADE their stand in a vast meadow high in the Camaeline Mountains—a green meadow in which thousands upon thousands of starry white flowers blossomed, a meadow dotted with lakes and rocky outcroppings.

Overhead, the sky was a flawless blue, and the white tops of the mountains where the snow never melted glistened.

The Skaldi awaited us at the far end, clad in furs and leather, hair braided, steel weapons and wooden shields in their hands. A handful were mounted on shaggy mountain ponies, but most were on foot.

They outnumbered us by half, but we had steel armor, better weapons, and a sizable cavalry.

The air was thin and clear, very, very clear. It reminded me of my childhood in the mountains of Siovale. I breathed slowly and deeply, stroking my mount's withers. She stood steady as a rock beneath me. She was a good mare, sure-footed and battle-seasoned.

Rolande eyed me sidelong, eyes bright beneath the brim of his helm.

All along the line of the vanguard, leather creaked and metal jingled. "Ready?"

I frowned at the uneven terrain. In private, I'd argued in favor of sending the foot soldiers out first, but the Three Princes, none of whom were mountain-born, had overridden my concerns.

Rolande read my unspoken thoughts and lowered his voice. "Anafiel, I'm not willing to give up one of our greatest advantages. If they don't break and flee by the third charge, we'll fall back and let the infantry engage them while we regroup. Well enough?"

I knew my duty. "Well enough, my liege and my love," I murmured. Saluting him with my sword, I added in a ringing tone, "Ready!"

He grinned.

His standard-bearer raised his staff, flying the silver swan pennant of House Courcel. Some fifty yards to the right, a second standard was hoisted, flying the pennant of House Courcel and the insignia of La Serenissima on his uncle Benedicte's behalf. To the left, Percy de Somerville's standard-bearer raised the apple tree of House Somerville.

Rolande lifted his sword and nodded at his trumpeter.

One trumpet blew; two, three, ringing clear and brazen beneath the clear blue skies. At the far end of the valley, the Skaldi roared and beat their blades against their wooden shields.

We charged; charged, hewed down men where they stood, wheeled and retreated, dodging ponds, boulders and crevasses.

Once . . .

Twice . . .

I was hot beneath my armor, sweating through my padded under-tunic and breathing hard, my sword streaked with gore and my sword arm growing tired. The ranks of Skaldi were growing ragged, wavering. A young lad with tawny-brown hair, long-limbed and tall for his years, rallied them, urged them to hold fast. At his tenacious insistence, they did.

"Third time's the charm!" Rolande cried.

Cries of agreement echoed across the meadow.

One again, the trumpeters gave their brazen call; once again, we clapped heels to our mounts' sides and sprang forward.

I know which is worse.

Remembering; oh, gods, by far. Dying is easier.

. . . .

I WAS A Siovalese country lordling, and I knew mountains. I rode a sure-footed horse for a reason.

I'd made sure Rolande did, too.

Not his standard-bearer. When the lad's mount caught a hoof in a crevice and went down with a terrible scream, left foreleg broken, there was nothing I could do but check my mare.

Uncertainty rippled down the line.

While Rolande raced to engage the Skaldi, men and horses in the center of the vanguard hesitated.

Those on the flanks, men under command of Percy de Somerville and Benedicte de la Courcel, had farther to travel.

Rolande plunged alone into the ranks of unmounted Skaldi, his sword rising and falling.

His standard-bearer's mount rolled and squealed in agony, crushing her rider, sowing chaos. Cursing and sweating, I yanked my mare's head with uncustomary viciousness and rode around them, putting my heels to her.

Too late.

I saw Rolande surrounded, dragged from the saddle. I saw the crude blades rise and fall, streaked with blood. *His* blood.

I fought.

Others came and fought, too. Too few; too late. Oh, it was enough to seize the pass, enough to guarantee a victory in the Battle of Three Princes. Still, it came too late.

As soon as the line had pressed past us, a handful of soldiers and I wrestled Rolande's ruined body across my pommel, retreating with him. My good mare bore the burden without complaint.

Behind the lines of skirmish, I wept with fury, unbuckling his armor, trying in vain to staunch the bleeding of a dozen wounds. "Damn you, Rolande! You promised! Don't leave me!"

Beneath the blue sky, his blood soaked the green grass, drenched the starry white blossoms. A faint sigh escaped him, bringing a froth of crimson to his lips. "I'm sorry," he whispered in a hoarse voice. One gauntleted hand rose a few inches, then fell back to the ground, limp. "Anafiel. I'm sorry."

And then the light went out of his blue, blue eyes, just as it had faded from Edmée's.

He was gone.

. . . .

Why couldn't you have waited, Rolande? You always had to be first into the fray.

Why?

It was a bitter, bitter victory won at the Battle of Three Princes.

For a long time afterward, I wished I had died with Rolande. Once the initial crushing weight of grief had faded, I flung myself into excesses of debauchery, making a circuit of the Thirteen Houses of the Night Court, sampling the highs and lows of all that carnal pleasure had to offer as though to mock the vow I'd never wished to be free of, now broken with Rolande's death.

It was the other vow I'd sworn that kept me alive; the vow to protect his daughter, Ysandre, now the infant Dauphine of Terre d'Ange.

For Rolande was right, intrigue surrounded her; from the moment of his death, a dozen challengers set their sights on the throne. Slowly, slowly, I gathered my grief-addled wits and began to assemble a net of spies, informants, and a few trusted allies. I remembered words spoken to me long ago by Master Strozzi in Tiberium.

Whores make some of the best spies.

I set out to cultivate them, aided by goodwill generated during my period of debauchery.

I kept my finger on the pulse of the world, learning that a well-placed word at the right time could thwart the most ambitious plot. The only one I failed to foil, I did not regret. In a fitting twist of irony, Isabel died by poison at the hand of one of Prince Benedicte's scheming offspring; but her daughter lived, which was all that mattered to me.

Here and there, I had dalliances—always with women, for no man could compare in my eyes to Rolande.

None were serious, except mayhap for Melisande Shahrizai. Beautiful, calculating Melisande, with a hunger for life's sharper pleasures, the only person clever enough to guess what I was about with my intrigues. In a moment of weakness, when the black grief was upon me, I told her of the Unseen Guild and how I regretted betraying Rolande's trust to this day.

She understood. We were ill suited in many ways, but Melisande understood me.

. . . .

TOO WELL, MAYHAP.

Even now, I cannot believe Melisande would have wished me dead . . . but I have been wrong before.

The Skaldi have found a leader who thinks.

And Melisande knew his name.

THE WHOREMASTER OF Spies.

Even as I wove my net among the pleasure-houses of the Night Court, I never set out to become such a thing; and yet it happened. It began with the best of intentions.

There were six years of peace along the Skaldic border after the Battle of Three Princes. When reports of renewed raiding came, I did not volunteer. Instead, mindful of a promise Rolande had made, I journeyed to the Camaeline village of Trefail, where I found the widow's son Rolande had promised to care for. His mother was dead, and his half-Skaldi nurse was preparing to desert him.

I took him home, the Skaldi sacking his village in our wake. In the City of Elua, I adopted him into my household and gave him my name— or at least my mother's name, if not the one I was born with.

Alcuin; Alcuin nó Delaunay.

When I began training him in the arts of covertcy, I'd not thought to employ him to serve my ends. It was merely a set of skills to teach him. But ah, gods! He was so bright, so eager to learn, so grateful to have been rescued. From the beginning, Alcuin simply assumed he would aid me in my work in whatever manner possible when he was grown.

Somewhere along the path, I began to assume it, too. I hardened my heart against any remorse.

Phèdre was another matter. From the beginning, I knew what she was and why I chose her.

WHERE ARE YOU, my *anguissette*? Kushiel's Chosen, marked by the scarlet mote in your eye, bound by fate to experience pain as pleasure. No wonder Melisande delighted in you so.

I am grateful you were not here today.

Anafiel Delaunay's last pupil.

I pray I taught you well; and that I was meant to do so.

MAYHAP I SEALED my fate when I paid the price of Phèdre's marque and took her into my household. It can be unwise for mortals to meddle in the affairs of the gods; but I was the only one who recognized her for what she was.

What else was I to have done?

Alcuin and Phèdre, my beautiful boy and my god-touched girl. I did not mean to use them; and yet I did.

I should not have used them so, especially Alcuin. I should have seen that the work did not suit him, that he merely wished to please me. When all is said and done, Naamah's Service is a sacred calling. But the goddess absolved him of any transgression, and still, and still, Alcuin found it in his heart to love me in a manner I never expected nor deserved; one desperate mouthful of sweetness at the bottom of a bitter cup. I owed him a better life than I gave him.

So many strands, so many threads unraveling!

It is all falling apart. A sharp sword can cut through the most intricately woven of webs. I will die without knowing who plotted my death, without knowing what it means that the Skaldi have found a leader who thinks, without knowing if Ysandre found a way to cross the deadly Straits and wed the Alban prince to whom she was betrothed.

But I kept her safe, Rolande. Your daughter, Ysandre. She is a grown woman now. I kept my oath. When she came to me for aid, I gave it to her; and yet there is something I missed. But I can do no more. Now it is in the hands of the gods, and their chosen.

Did I cross the will of the gods? Here at the end, I pray I have not offended mighty Kushiel, punisher of the damned, in taking his chosen as my pupil; I pray he will use Phèdre to administer his cruel mercy and bring justice to those who have murdered me; to continue the task of keeping Ysandre safe.

I obeyed Blessed Elua's precept, of that I am sure. I loved you, Rolande. While you lived, I loved you with all my heart; you, and you alone.

Even dying, it is true.

All I can do is pray into the falling darkness, hoping to find you on the other side . . .

And die.

Lisa Tuttle

"'Till Death We Do Part" says the familiar vow—but what about after *that? Once your lover is gone, might your love be strong enough to draw them* back? *And would you want it to?*

Lisa Tuttle made her first fiction sale in 1972 to the Clarion II *anthology, after having attended the Clarion workshop, and by 1974 had won the John W. Campbell Award for best new writer of the year. She has gone on to become one of the most respected writers of her generation, winning the Nebula Award in 1981 for her story "The Bone Flute"—which, in a still controversial move, she refused to accept—and the Arthur C. Clarke Award in 1993 for her novel* Lost Futures. *Her other books include a novel in collaboration with George R. R. Martin,* Windhaven; *the solo novels* Familiar Spirit, Gabriel, The Pillow Friend, The Mysteries, *and* The Silver Bough; *as well as several books for children; the non-fiction works* Heroines *and* Encyclopaedia of Feminism; *and, as editor,* Skin of the Soul. *Her copious short work has been collected in* A Nest of Nightmares, Spaceship Built of Stone and Other Stories, Memories of the Body: Tales of Desire and Transformation, Ghosts and Other Lovers, *and* My Pathology. *Born in Texas, she moved to Great Britain in 1980, and now lives with her family in Scotland.*

His Wolf

The wolf was standing on the grass behind the library. It wasn't one of those big, powerful, northern timber wolves you see in the movies, but the much smaller, leaner, actually kind of scrawny-looking gray wolf that was long ago native to Texas.

At least, I'd *thought* they were extinct . . . but then I remembered stories the students told about panthers, bears, and other dangerous animals that had survived in patches of woodland they called the Big Thicket, and the hairs on the back of my neck prickled. I just *knew* this was a wild animal, nobody's pet.

And yet I wasn't afraid. Instinct might have made my heart beat faster and charged my muscles, but I didn't want to flee *or* fight: I was purely thrilled by this strange meeting, feeling as if I'd been allowed to walk into a different world.

I took a step.

"Lobo! Here!" A man's voice rang out, sharp as a whip crack, and the animal turned away. My heart dropped, and then I was annoyed. *Of course* somebody owned this animal. Some stupid, posturing fool.

Hitching my heavy book bag up my shoulder, I folded my arms across my chest and checked him out.

I've heard it said that people resemble their pets, and there *was* something a little lupine about him—maybe it was his lean, rangy body, or the way he stood, as if ready to take off running, or leap to the attack. He wore a plain gray T-shirt, shorts, and running shoes, but nothing else about him looked either casual or modern. His dark face had a keen, hungry edge, emphasized by the narrow blade of his nose. His age I guessed to be near my own, in that shadow line between youth and age. He certainly wasn't a student, and I didn't recognize him as a member of the faculty or the support staff. I'd never seen him before, and he didn't look like he belonged. He was as out of place here as the wolf.

Speaking quietly, he said, "He won't hurt you."

"Do I look scared?" I snapped. "And what do you mean by calling a Mexican wolf 'Lobo'? Doesn't he deserve his own name?"

He smiled without showing his teeth. "What makes you think he's a Mexican wolf?"

"Because there haven't been wolves in Texas for a long time—unless they wandered across the border."

"We're a long way from the border here, ma'am."

Of course we were. And the wolf hadn't exactly walked here by himself. I realized that I was still clinging to my fantasy of a wild creature, and embarrassment made me lash out.

"Yes, of course, you could have bought him anywhere—Houston, New Orleans? These hybrids are popular because *some* people think they're too special to just buy a dog. Gotta take a walk on the wild side. What'd they tell you, he's ninety-eight percent purebred *canis lupus*? So you call him 'wolf,' like that'll make it true."

"I didn't buy him. I don't know *what* anybody says he is, and I don't care. Why shouldn't I call him Lobo?"

"It's . . . insulting. Imagine if people called you *hombre*."

The tight smile again. "They call me wolf-man."

I'd heard that name before, from snatches of overheard student conversation, but didn't know its significance, so I shrugged. "Maybe, but you have your own name. Doesn't Lobo deserve as much?"

The wolf gave a small groan, and I saw that he was quivering as if longing to break free.

The man laughed, a short bark, and gave me a measuring look. "What've you got in that bag, barbecue?"

I frowned. "Books. Why?"

"I'm trying to figure what's the big attraction."

"Maybe he senses that I care. Why don't you let him come?"

For a second, I thought that he would refuse, but he snapped, "Go free."

Immediately, the wolf sprang at me. I kept still, not from fear, but simply careful, as I would be with any strange dog, not to alarm him with any sudden moves. And he was equally careful, sniffing at me gently, almost daintily, before moving closer, inviting me to stroke his head.

"He's very friendly," I said.

"No he's not." At my look, he went on. "I don't mean he's aggressive—he'd *never* attack a human being, and only fights dogs if he's forced to defend himself. But he's always kept his distance, from everyone—everyone but me."

Lobo had relaxed. Now he was leaning into me as I scratched behind his ears; he was loving it. I laughed. "You're kidding. Look at this big baby! He's starving for attention."

"He gets plenty. I know you think I'm some kind of stupid bad-ass hick, but I *do* look after him."

The real hurt in his words took me aback. "Of course! It's obvious you care about each other." As I spoke, I looked up, straight into the man's eyes. They were brown, mostly dark, but flecked with a lighter color: the flashing gold of the wolf's eye, and I was suddenly breathless in the unexpected intimacy of his gaze. I didn't even know his name. Gathering my wits, remembering my manners, I put out my hand. "How do you do? I'm Katherine Hills."

The barest flicker of hesitation, then he gripped my hand. "Cody. Cody Vela. Listen, I can't hang around. I—Lobo's waiting for his afternoon run."

The wolf's ears pricked.

"Oh, well, sure. It was nice meeting you," I said, feeling flat.

"Want to come along?"

My heart leaped like a crazy thing, but I grimaced and gestured at my long cotton skirt and sandals. "I'm hardly dressed for running, even supposing I could keep up with you two."

"Come along for the ride. I'm going into the Thicket. Ever been there? No? Really?" He sounded astonished. "Then you have to."

I rarely acted on impulse, and hadn't gone off with anyone "for the ride" since I was fifteen, but I agreed, and followed after the lean, dark man and the lightly stepping wolf as if it were a perfectly natural thing to do.

His car, a big, black, new-looking SUV, was parked a short distance away, on the street. It wasn't a spot convenient to anywhere, hidden away behind the blank, limestone back wall of the library, and since the visitor parking lot was never crowded on a weekday afternoon, I wondered what had brought him here.

"Do you work on campus?" I asked as I buckled up.

"What do you mean?"

"Are you employed by the college?"

He laughed sharply. "Oh, definitely not!"

"Related to one of the students?"

Shaking his head, he started the engine and pulled away from the curb. "Are you saying you've never heard of the wolf-man?"

"I only moved here in August. So I haven't had time to learn about all the local characters, or go into the woods."

"*Tsk-tsk*. What *have* you been doing with your time?"

"Planning my classes, teaching . . ."

"What department?"

"English."

"You like books."

There was an understatement! Literature was the great passion of my life. I murmured a restrained agreement, and gazed out the window as we left the quiet, shady college grounds, expecting he'd change the subject.

"What's your favorite book?"

"Oh, I couldn't possibly name just one."

"Favorite author?"

That was easier. "Virginia Woolf."

"Of course." He turned his head, and I met his gaze quickly, nervously, before he returned to watching where he was going, smiling to himself.

"What do you mean, 'of course'?"

"I knew you reminded me of somebody. That long, graceful neck, beautiful, deep eyes, full lips . . ."

I felt a warm flush of pleasure at his admiring words.

"People must have told you that before? Don't they call you the Woolf-woman?" He grinned. "That should be your nickname on campus, around the English department, at least."

"I don't have a nickname. Not that I've ever heard." Nobody here was interested enough to give me a special name, but I wasn't going to tell him that. That he knew something about Virginia Woolf intrigued me. "So who's *your* favorite author?"

"Dostoyevsky. Although I like Stephen King a lot. And James Lee Burke. There, I've surprised you. You probably thought I dropped out of high school—well, I did, but that doesn't mean I don't read. I like read-ing. *Good* books, that is."

We passed the city limits sign, and he picked up speed.

"City limits"—it struck me as a sick joke to apply the name of city to a town with a population that only brushed six thousand when college was in session. Almost every day I asked myself what I was doing here.

"So what brought you to this neck of the woods?"

"I needed a job; the college needed an English teacher. It was all kind of last-minute; we'd both been let down." I didn't feel like going into detail.

"You're not from the South."

"Chicago."

"Wow. I've never been there. It must be different." He went on to ask questions that were easy for me to answer without touching on anything too personal. As I talked about weather and food and Oprah, he took the highway heading south, driving past the turn-off to the poky little trailer I called home. A few minutes later, he turned east, onto a road I'd never taken because it didn't *go* anywhere except deeper into the woods and swamps of rural east Texas.

"Do you drive out to run in the country every day?"

"Pretty much. Sometimes we stick closer to home, but I prefer places where we won't meet anybody. He needs at least two good runs a day. It's not natural for a wolf to be stuck inside a house or a car all day, even if I have to be."

"You take him with you?"

"We go everywhere together," he said. "Wolves are pack animals. That thing people say about a lone wolf, it's just wrong. Maybe, if I had some others, and a big enough yard . . . but I won't make him live like a prisoner."

I'd had a dog when I was a kid, but not since. One thing I'd had in mind when I moved to Texas was to rent a place with a fenced yard and a landlord who wasn't opposed to pets, and it was the detail that my new home had previously been used as a "hunting cabin" and included a sizable kennels, that made me agree to a year's lease, sight unseen. But when I saw the kennels—the concrete floor, the high chain-link fence—they looked like Guantanamo.

"You got a problem with that?" He challenged my silence.

"Not at all. I'd love to have a dog, but I couldn't leave it alone five days a week. I guess it's even more important, if you're going to buy a wolf—"

"I didn't *buy* him."

I gazed ahead at the empty road, dappled with long shadows, and the dark depths of the forest on either side. "You found him?"

He made a noise that might have been agreement, and I said, "A full-grown wolf? He must have belonged to somebody. Couldn't you find his owner?"

His face showed nothing, but his hands tightened on the steering wheel. "If I could find the bastard who had him first, I'd kill him. Slowly. I'd make him die in agony, do to him what he wanted to do to my wolf."

The icy malice in his voice chilled me. "What happened?"

"It was just after I'd gotten back from"—he hesitated—"well, that doesn't matter. I'd been away, and then I came back. About two years ago. I grew up in these parts, and when I was a kid, I used to go hunting and fishing and camping in the Thicket, but not after I grew up. I hadn't set foot in the woods for ten years, at least, until that day I suddenly got this urge. I just wanted to get away from everybody and everything, away from civilization, so I drove east, into the woods, and turned off the highway onto one of the old timber routes, and drove until it was too rough and grown over to drive any farther, and then I left the car.

"I kept to the trail, of course. Everybody who grows up in these parts knows how easy it is to get lost if you don't. There are stories about people getting lost for days within a couple miles of the road, that's how thick and tangled it is. You can be in the middle of a swamp before you know it, with that kind of mud that sucks you down.

"I knew how it was. I'm not stupid. But after I'd been walking for about an hour, I started feeling that this old road wasn't going to take me where I had to go. *Had* to go. I didn't know why, or where it was, but I felt more and more that there was some point to this trip, and if I kept to the trail, I was never going to find out what it was.

"So I left the trail. I used my knife to mark my path, so I could find my way back. I'd done it before, only back then, I'd had a reason—a deer I'd shot but hadn't killed, a duck or a quail I'd brought down into the brush—and this time the only thing I was following was some kind of instinct or intuition."

He shook his head, gazing out at the road ahead but seeing, I was sure, the forests in his mind. "I'm not somebody who gets 'feelings,' you know? I never believed in that woo-woo psychic spirit stuff. I still don't, except . . ." He scowled, gripping the wheel harder, and behind us, Lobo gave a deep sigh.

"I can't explain why I left the trail and slashed my way deeper into the woods, why I went that way and no other. But I did, and I reckon I walked at least a mile, to a place so far off the map you'd swear nobody else had been there in about a century, except that there was this wolf, chained by the neck to a tree, and he damn sure hadn't done that to himself.

"I thought he was dead, at first. I thought I'd come too late. But then as I crouched next to him, I felt his heart still beating. It was a near thing, though. God knows how long he'd been stuck there, with no chance of freeing himself, with nothing to eat or drink."

Angry tears started to my eyes. "Who'd do such a thing?"

"A *person*." He almost spat the word. "In the old days, people told their kids stories about the big, bad wolf, and men who were especially cruel and horrible were said to be like animals, maybe werewolves. But the things ordinary men do every day are a million times worse than anything a wolf would do. A wolf would never torture another animal to death, or lock it up. They kill out of instinct, in order to survive, because they *have* to—not because they just feel like it, not because they're evil. Not like *us*. Man is the scariest animal on the planet, but from the beginning of time, the wolf has gotten the bad rap. We've tried to pretend that evil is out *there*, lurking inside animals beyond the camp-fire, and not where it really is, in here." He tapped his chest.

"You saved his life."

"Yeah. And he changed mine." He shrugged. "Don't they say, if you save a life, you take responsibility for it? I guess I could have taken him to one of those animal-rescue places, but that would have been like leaving him to die in prison, or risk him falling into the hands of some other sadistic bastard. It was up to me to make sure that the life I'd saved was worth living. It's not that hard, you know. Enough food, plenty of exercise outdoors, companionship. Lucky we like the same things."

As he spoke, he took a sudden turn off the road, hardly slowing as we moved onto a heavily rutted, unpaved track. I held on for dear life as we rocked and bounced deeper into the forest.

"I thought this was a state park?" The way the trees loomed over us, old and heavy with moss, so thick they blocked the sun, made me uncomfortable.

"Some of the Thicket's a national preserve, but we tend to steer clear of their trails," he said. "No pets allowed, and if too many people start seeing a wolf, they might come looking for the wolf-man. This old road here, it was used for logging. I think it winds up in some old ghost town. There's all sorts of old forgotten stuff in here."

He parked off-road, in a small clearing. He opened his door, got out, opened the back door and stood looking in at the wolf, who was standing on the backseat, absolutely still, utterly focused. One charged moment passed in silence, then Cody barked, "Go free!" and the wolf leaped out of the car, the most beautiful, graceful thing I'd ever seen. He seemed to fly, and in motion, he was perfect, so beautiful it made my chest ache.

"You okay?"

Cody was staring at me. I had to blink hard, but managed not to sniff as I nodded and said, "He's just so . . . amazing."

He went on looking at me for an uncomfortably long time before he nodded, slowly, and said, "More than you know. Will you be okay here by yourself?"

I nodded, but I really wasn't sure.

He handed me his keys. "If you get too hot, run the air conditioner for a while, listen to some music if you get bored. Does your phone have a camera?"

"Sure. Why?"

"Just, if you see an ivory-billed woodpecker, you want to be sure to get a picture."

It was only when he flashed me a grin that I realized he was teasing, and managed to respond: "Actually, I was hoping to see Bigfoot."

I watched him go, light and strong and quick on his feet as he sprinted away into the deep, shadowy forest, and although his movements didn't have the amazing grace of the fleet, four-legged animal, still he had his own male, human beauty, and when he vanished into the dark, I felt something squeeze my heart.

IT WAS STILL hot and almost unbearably humid, even so late in the day, even though it was already October, but I was afraid of draining the battery if I ran the air-conditioning, so instead of curling up in relative comfort with one of my books, I wandered. I kept to the trail, of course, and peered into the undergrowth in hope of seeing one of the rare orchids or carnivorous plants that flourished in these parts.

I didn't find anything rare, and I got bitten to pieces by mosquitoes before deciding, fairly swiftly, to turn back. I didn't belong here. Once in the clearing again, knowing that I had the option of locking myself inside the SUV, or even driving away, I felt better. There was a sinister atmosphere about this patch of southern woodland, or maybe I just thought so after Cody's story. Everybody knows there are people who delight in cruelty to animals, and if Cody had told me he'd rescued the wolf from starvation in somebody's garage or basement, I would not have been surprised. But why would anyone go so far into a trackless wilderness to chain and abandon, to condemn to a lingering death, such a beautiful, innocent animal?

Something about the mental image struck me as mythic: a wolf-Prometheus bound to a rock? But it had been a tree, and the only classical myth about wolves that came to mind was Romulus and Remus, abandoned babies nursed by a she-wolf.

I was still brooding on the subject when the two of them came back, the wolf panting but still full of energy, bounding across the clearing to do a happy dance around me. Cody, dripping with sweat, his gray T-shirt soaked and clinging to his muscular chest, jogged raggedly after him. He looked exhausted, until he saw me, when his face lit up, and he carried himself differently, with a new spring in his step.

The sight of him, the way his expression changed, the sheer joy in it, as if he'd half expected me to be gone, sent a surge through me, some sort of emotional electricity connecting us. Can these things be explained? Is there any reason in it? Sometimes, once in a lifetime, if you're lucky, you see someone, and you just *know*. I was suddenly, ridiculously, happy.

Neither of us said a word.

There was a cooler full of cold drinks in the back of the car. Cody poured water into a dish and set it down for Lobo, then stripped off his shirt and poured the rest of the bottle over his head, shaking it off as unselfconsciously as if he'd been alone. I pretended not to notice, but my eyes were drawn to his naked chest, and I was standing so near that I could smell his clean, salty sweat and feel the heat that radiated from him. It was all suddenly too much; the surge of pure lust that I felt was so powerful that I couldn't breathe. I had to close my eyes and lean against a tree.

"Want some?"

My eyes flashed open; I saw that he was holding out a can of cold beer. "Thanks," I said, and took a quick gulp.

He looked at me with a sly grin. "Don't know why *you* should feel weak. You been secretly working out with the weights in your bag?"

"No, but the mosquitoes must've got two pints out of me, at least."

He laughed, and I gulped down beer more quickly than usual. But when he offered me a second, I shook my head. "No, I can't—I shouldn't—I—"

"I guess you need to be getting back?"

I nodded.

We were silent in the car, as he drove. There was so much to say, I couldn't think how to begin. He seemed comfortable with the silence. I listened to the steady, regular panting from the backseat, and the hum of the tires on the road, and breathed in the musky scents of man and animal, and as I relaxed into the moment, I felt the hard, tight knot that had been inside me for so long slowly loosen.

Seeing my mailbox coming into view, I remarked, "That's where I live, right there."

And he turned, hard, cutting across the highway into my driveway.

I gave a little yelp of surprise.

"What's wrong? I thought you said . . . ?" We were bouncing and rolling along the badly rutted track when he stepped on the brake.

"I didn't mean you should turn."

"You didn't want me to take you home?"

Yes, and stay with me forever, I thought. "My car's on campus."

"Oh, right. Of course. Well, I'll take you there, no problem," he said. "Do I need to back out?"

"You can turn by the trailer," I said, and a moment later we were in the clearing where my shabby home stood in solitary splendor. He looped smoothly around the clearing in front of it, and in a matter of seconds we were back on the highway.

I felt sorry. Why hadn't I asked him in for a drink? So, I didn't have anything but a box of green tea and a couple of Cherry Cokes; there was beer in his cooler. Then, as I was trying to think how to rescue the situation, he spoke:

"Listen, do you want to go get something to eat?"

I looked at him. He was hunched forward, staring at the road.

"That would be nice."

His shoulders relaxed. "I don't know about *nice*. I'd love to take you to a fancy restaurant, but Lobo wouldn't be welcome."

I laughed. "Are you kidding? You really don't go *anywhere* without him?"

"Did you think I was lying?"

"Whoa, you're sensitive! No, but people exaggerate. I've done it myself. And—well, to change your life that much—"

"Why is that so hard to believe? Haven't you ever changed your life to suit another person? People do it all the time. They do it when they fall in love. You don't live like you're single when you're married. Women do it when they have kids, every time. So I've done it for an animal—why not? I like him better than any—well, let's say, better than ninety-nine percent of all the people I've ever met."

We went to Whattaburger. It felt very retro, having a date at a drive-in, very old-fashioned teenage, and that was pretty appropriate to the hormonal rush his presence caused, a desire so strong it took away my appetite for anything but him.

HE ORDERED THREE hamburgers, and fed one of them to Lobo, bit by bit. When the two of them were finished, my own burger was still nearly untouched. Cody advised me to eat up: "You're driving him crazy."

"He can have it."

"Something wrong with it?"

"No!"

"You're not hungry?"

I shook my head. "The milkshake's enough."

"Go on, then. Cement your friendship with a burger."

"The whole thing? I mean, bun and lettuce and all?"

"Unless you want it."

I enjoyed watching Lobo wolf it down. As I turned away, wiping my fingers on a napkin, I noticed some college kids walking past, heading for either the Taco Bell or the 7-Eleven, on foot because, as freshmen, they were required to live on campus and not allowed cars. One of the girls gave the SUV a sharp look as she walked by, and I recognized her as one of my students. She saw me through the lowered window just as I saw her, and her eyes widened. I couldn't help smiling as I raised my hand in a casual salute: yes, your boring English teacher does have a life outside the classroom! She lowered her gaze without responding, and hurried away.

Cody said, "Let's go. Unless you wanted something else?"

"No, nothing," I said, and while it was true, I had hoped we could sit and talk awhile. I still knew almost nothing about this man, except that he was happy to allow a wolf to set his schedule. "I guess Lobo wouldn't be too happy about sitting in a drive-in after the food's all gone."

"Not when he can smell more burgers being taken to other cars."

"So now what?" I asked, as he started the engine.

"Now I take you to get your car, like you asked."

I didn't want our date to be over, but I reminded myself there could be others, and so, as we headed toward campus, I invited them to dinner at my place the next evening.

I felt Cody's happiness like my own, and I think it was.

I WAS STILL feeling happy the next afternoon, and even more excited as I anticipated the night to come, when I got the message that Nadia Sorenko, head of my department, wanted to see me. I wasn't worried, not even when I saw how serious she looked as she gestured to me to take a seat, and I was totally unprepared for her first question.

"What is the nature of your relationship with Cody Vela?"

I gaped at her stupidly. "What . . . ?"

She leaned forward across her desk. "The kids call him the wolf-man. You know who I mean? There's a disturbing rumor going around that you were seen sitting with him in his SUV yesterday evening."

I bristled. "Well, so what if I was?"

She repeated, "What's the nature of your relationship?"

I was afraid I was blushing. "I only met him yesterday. I'd hardly call that a *relationship*."

She nodded slowly. "Not a *business* relationship?"

"What are you talking about? What business? And isn't it *my* business who I talk to on my own time?"

"Not when he's the local drug dealer." She smiled a bit grimly. "You didn't know? Oh, yes. And it's not a part-time, share the joy, home-grown pot kind of thing. Have no illusions—he might be a local boy, but the man's a criminal, with connections to organized crime."

I tried to swallow. My throat was sore. "I—I had no idea."

"How did you meet him?"

"I saw his wolf. I was curious, I guess."

"His wolf." She shook her head. "Some wolf. Half coyote, half

German shepherd, you ask me. But the kids all believe his stories: It's purely wild; he found the little cub in the woods, the only survivor of a pack butchered by hunters, or it saved his life when he was attacked by a panther—which one did he tell you?"

"He didn't say anything like that."

"Must have guessed you weren't as gullible as your students. They think the Big Thicket is more than a few scattered remnants, that it's primeval, magical, filled with wolf packs, big cats, and extinct birds, not to mention ghost lights and hairy ape men." Her interest in me waning, she stole a glance at her computer screen and sighed. "All right, Katherine. Now you know what he is, you'll steer clear. And if you ever see him on campus, call security."

LEAVING CAMPUS, HALF an hour later, I went to the grocery store and bought three steaks, potatoes, green beans, a bottle of wine, cheese and crackers, grapes, a frozen cheesecake . . . I reasoned that since I didn't have his phone number, I couldn't cancel, and the least I could do was give Cody a chance to defend himself. Maybe he could explain everything: He was working undercover for the DEA, or the victim of identity-theft . . .

I was totally in denial.

When I heard his car, I went outside and stood in front of the trailer, my arms crossed, holding myself. Lobo sensed my mood instantly and hung back by the car, just watching as Cody, less aware, only lost his smile and his jaunty, swinging stride when we were in touching distance.

"What's up?"

I told him what my boss had said.

He didn't prevaricate, bluster, or deny the charge, and he didn't make light of it, either. He sucked in his lips. "You didn't know?"

"Like I'd get in a car and go for a ride with a drug dealer!"

He sighed. "You're a good person. I'm not used to being around good people."

"I can't see you anymore."

"I understand." Yet he didn't move. He stared at the ground. Behind him, Lobo gave a low, sad whine.

"Please go."

He raised his eyes. "I've done bad things. Most people would say that makes me a bad man. But—I could change. If I stopped dealing drugs, broke free of the people I've been working for, promised to go straight—would you give me another chance?"

"What do you mean?" I was hedging, scared.

"You know what I mean. I want to be with you."

"I want to be with you, too," I said in a rush. "But only if—well, it has to happen first. For real. I can't just take your word for it, you know, that you're suddenly all straight and honest. It has to be clear, to everyone, that you're not a criminal anymore, or I lose my job."

"Of course. Just give me a chance. That's all I'm asking. I can't just snap my fingers; there are people I have to deal with. And to get clear, really, I'd probably have to leave the state."

"I'll go with you," I blurted without thinking about it.

Our eyes met. "What about your job?"

"The job's not the most important thing. I'm not asking you to change just so I can keep my job!"

He nodded slowly. "I don't want mine anymore. I didn't used to care. It was easy money, so I did it, thinking it was my choice. But lately, especially since I found Lobo, I've started to change. I'd like to make a clean start. But, well, I'm so involved now, I can't just walk away. I know too much, and there's a history . . . There's people who won't want to cut me loose."

"So what's going to happen?" I asked, my stomach in knots. "Will they let you go?"

He gave a little shrug like it didn't matter, but I saw from his eyes that he was scared as well as strong. "I'll just have to make them. I have to, now—for you."

I thought he would come forward and kiss me—I wanted him to—but he moved back toward the car instead, opening the door and snapping his fingers for Lobo before he looked around at me again.

"I'll come back for you when it's safe," he said. He shut Lobo into the back and opened his door and got into the driver's seat, and then he hesitated again, and gave me a long, burning look.

"I'll come back to you as soon as I can, Katherine. I love you."

I stared back at him through repressed tears, unable to say those words back to him, too choked up to say anything at all, although later my silence would haunt me, and I hoped he read in my eyes what I felt.

A WEEK DRAGGED slowly by. There were classes and meetings and other people to keep me occupied during the days, but in the evenings I was lonely and plagued by fears about what danger Cody was putting himself in for my sake. And I hadn't even told him I loved him! Why hadn't I rushed over and kissed him, at least?

Another, different fear also tormented me: the idea that Cody didn't really love me, that he hadn't meant what he'd said, that he'd just been playing with me, saying what he thought I'd believe, the way he'd told different people different versions of how Lobo had come into his possession. What if none of it was true?

Friday morning, as I stepped outside the trailer, turning toward my car, I found the wolf waiting for me.

He looked thinner and scrawnier than ever, his head hung down. He was visibly trembling, panting hard, seemingly on the point of collapse. Naturally I looked for some sign of Cody or his black SUV, but the shivering animal was my only early-morning visitor.

"Here, Lobo," I said softly, patting my side. He came at once, pressing himself against my legs, sending the vibrations of his fast-beating heart through me.

Somewhere in the trees, a mockingbird sang, and there was the sound of a heavy vehicle grumbling away down the highway. I told myself that Cody could have paused beside my mailbox, just long enough to let Lobo out before making his escape . . . but then, I was sure, even if he'd driven away at top speed, the wolf would have gone chasing after his master's car until his heart burst. And if Cody *were* able to command Lobo to go to me, surely he would have sent a note of explanation.

My hand, digging into the thick ruff of fur at the wolf's neck, discovered no collar. Cody had told me he would never chain him, and the collar was for appearances only, always notched loose enough for him to slip his head through.

I knew then that something terrible had happened; Lobo had escaped, and come to me for help.

Taking him inside with me, I locked the flimsy door and called the police.

I stumbled through a story about finding a "dog" I thought belonged to a man named Cody Vela—at the mention of his name, I was put through to someone else who instructed me to tell him everything I knew about Mr. Vela and his associates.

I told him I didn't know anything, I'd just seen him around, and when the dog turned up this morning, obviously upset, I was concerned . . .

He told me then that Cody had been murdered, but he couldn't give me any details because it was part of an ongoing investigation.

"But you should be aware, that animal's more wolf than dog. I advise you to call the county animal-control office and let them take care of it."

Hearing that Cody was dead was a terrible shock. At least, it should have been, but somehow I couldn't feel it. It didn't seem real.

What was real, what I had to deal with immediately, was the weary, frightened animal that had come to me for help.

Of course I didn't call the animal-control officer. Looking after his wolf was now the only thing I could do for the man I'd so briefly thought of loving and then lost. I made just one more phone call that morning, to the secretary in the English department, to say I was suffering from food poisoning and my classes would have to be canceled. Then I devoted myself to my new responsibility.

We spent the weekend getting to know each other, and learning to trust. I was a bit apprehensive about letting him off the leash, in case he simply ran off and got lost, but he needed exercise, and taking him out to the Thicket where there was no one to stare or get scared, and no other dogs to hassle him, seemed the best option.

I'm a walker, not a jogger, and I knew I could never keep up with him the way that Cody could. Arriving in the same clearing where Cody had parked on the day we met, I let him out of the car and told him, "Go free!" He did. But as soon as he was lost to view in the shadowy depths of the forest, I got scared and shouted for him to come back. He reappeared within seconds, clearly alarmed by *my* alarm, and after that unpromising start, I had a hard time convincing him to leave my side so he could get the exercise he clearly needed.

It turned out that Lobo was even more worried about losing *me* than I was about him. He didn't like to let me out of his sight. If I was in the trailer, he wanted to be there, too; if I was outside, he was happy to stay out, but not on his own. Eventually we reached a compromise: if the door to the trailer was open, he knew he could reach me, and so he became more relaxed about roaming around, exploring the area. At night, he stretched out on the floor of my bedroom, blocking the door with his body: If I decided to go anywhere, he'd know about it.

Just as he had with Cody, he was happy to jump into my car at any time, and willing to wait for me when I ran errands—at least, for a few minutes. I didn't dare test his patience, knowing that if he got anxious or bored he could destroy the interior of the car I was still paying for. That first weekend, I never left him for more than the five minutes it took me to dash into a convenience store to pick up some food for us both.

By the end of the weekend, the wolf was part of my life, and I understood what Cody had felt. There was no hardship in adapting my habits to fit in with his; I wasn't interested in a way of life that had no room for this wolf. I didn't think twice on Monday morning; of course I took him with me.

A ripple of excitement ran around the classroom as we walked in.

"Don't worry," I said calmly. "He's had a good run this morning, so he'll probably just lie on the floor and go to sleep while I talk. Don't any of you guys copy him."

That got a laugh, bigger than it deserved. I was suddenly much more interesting to my students.

"What kind of a dog is that?" one of the girls asked.

"He's a wolf."

"What's his name?"

"Cody." It just came out. All through the weekend I had called him by various terms of endearment, but hadn't thought about changing the name Cody had given him.

But now, quite suddenly, I had done it.

The animal himself raised his head and looked at me when I spoke Cody's name, recognizing it, and it was obvious from the caught breaths and exchange of looks among the students that they had, too. Everybody had heard the news of the death of the local drug dealer, Cody "Wolfman" Vela, most of them in far more lurid, graphic detail than I'd picked up from local radio.

I wondered if I'd just made a huge mistake and put my job on the line. But I couldn't have done anything else.

Luckily, the kids loved him, and weren't going to do or say anything that would get him banned. They were more attentive in class, and although word must have spread fairly quickly around campus, even if it caused Nadia to wonder about my honesty, I didn't get called into her office again. Maybe death had absolved me; anyway, nobody could blame an innocent animal for the sins of his master, and *somebody* had to look after him. I found out that my wolf wasn't the first animal to become an accepted fixture on campus: There was a cat in the science department, some teachers had brought their dogs, and, in one case, a parrot, without causing any trouble.

Over the next few days, I learned more about Cody's death than I really wanted to know. Probably no death by violence is easy, but his had been especially hard; it was referred to as a "punishment killing," with talk of mutilation and torture. Some people wondered if the wolf-man's famous pet had managed to inflict any damage on his killers—it might help the police if anyone was reported with unexplained animal bites. It was widely assumed that Cody's wolf must now be dead, too. Such is the fearsome reputation of the wolf; few would believe that he would sooner hide, or run away, than attack armed men. I knew better, knew it was foolish to judge an animal by human values, yet even I couldn't help feeling that Lobo had let Cody down. His response seemed shameful and cowardly. The man who had saved his life was dead, and the wolf hadn't done a thing to stop his murder, hadn't tried to rip his killer's throat out.

And yet, if he had attacked armed men, he'd be dead too, and I couldn't bear that.

Although I mourned the loss of the man I could have loved, the truth was that I'd never really known him. The wolf to whom I'd given his name was more real, and now even more important to me. Maybe it was because I now had the responsibility for another life, so I couldn't afford to indulge in feeling sorry for myself, but the two weeks that followed Cody's death were rich and interesting, full of life, hardly a sorrowful time at all.

At the end of October, a norther blew in, and as I felt the cold for the first time since leaving Chicago, I put on my favorite sweater and rust-colored corduroy pants, and felt my spirits rise.

Cody's mood changed, too, that day, but not, like mine, for the better. He seemed restless, distracted, and somehow aloof from me, not his usual self at all. Despite a good, long run, he didn't snooze through class but sat with his ears pricked, glancing at the door every now and then as if waiting for someone who never came. When a couple of students tried to pet him, he retreated under my desk. After we got home, it was worse. He didn't want to stay in the trailer with me, but every time I let him out, I had to get up again a few minutes later to answer his anxious scratching at the door.

"Cody, make up your mind!" I told him. "It's too cold to leave the damn door open tonight!"

A minute later, he went out again. I settled down to mark some essays, and this time I wasn't disturbed for almost an hour, when I heard a low but terrible sound outside, a deep groan that sounded almost human.

I jumped up and flung the door open, calling his name. It was dark outside, the profound darkness of night in the country, but even deeper than usual because there was no moon. A single, low-energy bulb fixed to the right of the doorframe cast a little murky light in a small semi-circle around the steps, but beyond that I was blind.

"Cody?" I called again, my voice strained and cracking with worry. "Cody, sweetheart, where are you? Come here, Cody!" I hurried down the steps.

"Katherine?" The voice came out of the darkness, a voice I'd never expected to hear again.

Then a man walked out of the darkness, and it was Cody Vela, alive, stark naked, and staring at me with a look that mingled confusion and longing. He came closer still, close enough to smell, and the scent of sweat and musk took me back to the day we'd met, and stirred the same desire.

"I thought you were dead!" I cried.

"Me, too." He shivered convulsively, and he reached for me at the same moment I reached for him, and then we were hugging each other, and it was crazy, but I'd never wanted anyone so much in my life, and nothing else mattered. I could feel that he felt the same way, and when he started to nuzzle my neck, and his hands moved down to squeeze and caress my bottom, I almost fell onto the ground with him. But even though he was naked, I wasn't, and the awkwardness of trying to get undressed was just enough to give me pause, and so I managed to pull him inside, where it was warm, and we could make love in the comfort of my bed.

The first time was hungry and desperate, but after that we were able to take things more slowly, indulging in sensuality and exploration, teasing and playing, until, finally, resting, we talked.

I expected an explanation, a movie-worthy plot involving doubles and disinformation, or lies and kidnapping, but there was nothing like that. He had no idea how he'd turned up naked and disoriented in the woods outside my trailer.

His last memory before that was of intense, agonizing pain. He'd been on the edge of death, horribly tortured by three men, one of whom he knew, two he'd never seen before: "But I'd know them again," he said darkly.

The traumatic memories made him break out in a cold sweat; although he spared me the gory details, his hands went convulsively to his genitals, ears, mouth, knees, chest, seeking the remembered damage.

But he was whole, there were no wounds, not a trace of any injury, as I had already so pleasurably discovered. He'd switched on the small, pink-shaded light on the night table as we talked, and it was clear to us both that his lean, muscular body was unmarked except for the pale, curved line of a very old scar on the side of his neck, and a screaming face tattooed on his left bicep.

I thought about drugs, hypnotism, false memories, but before I could say anything he continued. "I wanted to die. After what they'd done to me, I knew I couldn't live, but dying was so hellishly slow. But then I knew it was happening, because the pain wasn't so bad, and I couldn't see, or hear those bastards taunting me anymore—I realized they must have taken me somewhere, and left me, because I wasn't in my house anymore. I wasn't tied to a chair. I was curled up on my side, on the ground, outside—hard earth—sticky with blood, but not really hurting, and Lobo was licking my face."

He reared up in bed, alarmed. "Lobo! I yelled at him to run when those guys grabbed me—but he must have come back. If those bastards got him—"

"He's fine," I said, putting my arms around him and hugging him tight. "He came here to me the morning that . . . that they said you were dead. I've been looking after him. He's outside—do you want me to—?"

I started to get up, but he pulled me back until we were both lying down again. "Later. Long as I know he's okay."

"So Lobo found you," I said. "And then what, the police arrived? They took you to the hospital?" I was struggling to make sense of it.

He made a small, negative movement with his head on the pillow. "No cops, no doctors, no hospital. Just Lobo. But that wasn't right, because he was *huge*—or I was really little—and he put his head down and picked me up, very gently, in his mouth.

"I wasn't scared. I was glad. I relaxed, and knew he was going to take care of me. I thought I'd died and been born again as a wolf cub—as one of Lobo's pups. I thought, I get to have another chance at life, this time as a wolf, and I thought maybe that would be better than what I was the first time around."

I said, "So you died and turned into a wolf?"

He laughed, and rolled on top of me. "Does this feel like wolf to you? Is this fur? Are these claws? Is my nose cold?" He licked my face, then kissed me and laughed again. "I'm not dead, and I am definitely still a man!"

"I don't understand."

"Neither do I, my love. I'm just telling you the last thing I remember, I guess it was a dream, and I was asleep until I woke up in the dark out there and heard you call my name." His face wrinkled in puzzlement. "How did you know I was there?"

"I didn't. I thought you were dead, I told you." I closed my eyes and held on to him as tightly as I could, feeling the unmistakable warmth and weight of him pressing me against the bed, inhaling his scent, yet even still fighting the fear that I'd lost my mind. "Oh, this must be a dream," I said sadly.

"Does this feel like a dream?" he asked. "How about this? Hmmm?"

Surely no dream could ever be so real, so physical.

We made love until sleep overwhelmed us both.

When I woke, the little room was full of daylight, and I was alone in a bed with tumbled sheets and the heavy, cloying odor of sex. He must have just gotten up to go to the bathroom, I told myself, but anxiety made me sit bolt upright, and I couldn't keep it out of my voice as I called, "Cody?"

There, blocking the doorway, in his customary sleeping spot, was the wolf. He lifted his head in response to his name and sleepily blinked his amber eyes. I recognized the animal I loved, but this time I also saw a second awareness, a different intelligence, looking back at me, and I knew.

I can't say that I understand, even now, but there's no doubt that the wolf Cody rescued was no ordinary animal. Once upon a time, a man called Cody saved a wolf. Later, when the man was about to die, that wolf saved him, taking his soul inside himself. I called the wolf Cody before I knew how true that was.

He comes out at the dark of the moon. For me, it's wonderful. Life has been good to me. I have my work, the company of my wolf, and four nights a month, the undivided attention of my lover. For him, he's told me, the wolf-time passes like sleep. He's conscious, he can think like the man he was only during the moon-dark days, and although he loves me dearly, there's more to life than love. I'm not afraid of him, but there are some bad men out there who should be.

When you really think about it, which is more frightening: a man who turns into a wolf, or a wolf who becomes a man?

Linnea Sinclair

A former news reporter and retired private detective, hot new author Linnea Sinclair is the author of eight butt-kicking action-adventure science fiction romance novels, including Finders Keepers, An Accidental Goddess, Games of Command, The Down Home Zombie Blues, *and her Dock Five Universe series:* Gabriel's Ghost *(RITA Award winner),* Shades of Dark, *and* Hope's Folly. *Her most recent novel is* Rebels and Lovers, *the fourth book in the Dock Five Universe.*

In the fast-paced, action-packed story that follows, she proves once again that trust between lovers, once lost, is a very hard thing to regain. In fact, attempting to regain it might just cost you your life . . .

Courting Trouble

"Apparently there is nothing that cannot happen today."
—MARK TWAIN

C aptain Serenity Beck knew the very moment things went horribly wrong. It happened right between the words "confiscate" and "impound," which—thanks to the translator encircling her left ear—she heard twice: first in Nalshinian and the second time in Trade-Standard.

"We repeat. Refusal to pay grants us license to confiscate your cargo." The bulbous orange triped that bore the title of Esteemed Dockmaster of Jabo Station reached forward to stroke the blue-tinged holoscreen hovering over his desk. An image of the *Star of Pandea* appeared in the lower left. "And, if necessary, place your ship under impound."

"It's not a matter of refusal." Serri spoke slowly, hearing the echo of her cadence through the dockmaster's lang-trans, which—since Nalshinian ears were under the jaw—dangled around his blubbery neck. "We're a Dalvarr-licensed hauler under contract to Widestar. You have no authority to impose a tariff."

"We have your ship in our bay." Filar jabbed one stubby digit at the *Pandea*'s image, setting the metal rings on his billowing sleeves clanking. "Possession, Captain Beck. It is eleven points of all law. Therefore, we shall present ourselves at your airlock in thirty minutes to collect the cargo."

Thirty minutes wasn't even enough time to alert the Dalvarr Trade Collective or Widestar corporate legal division, and Filar knew that.

Just as he knew there was no way the *Pandea* had the ability to pay a three-hundred-thousand credit "tariff." This wasn't lawful possession. This was thinly disguised piracy. Extortion.

Serri was out of options. All she had left was her anger—and nothing to lose by unleashing it. She fisted her hands at her sides. "You motherless son of a Garpion whore! It'll be a cold day in hell before I'll allow you or your people access to my ship!"

Too late she realized the translator's vocabulary was limited to trade, technical, and legal terms. His Esteemedness looked genuinely puzzled. "We do not see what climactic conditions have to do with the fact that we have in our possession an order of procurement authorized by the Council of Jabo Station United." He wheezed loudly. "And by the way, we have three maternal parents, none of whom reside in the Garpion Sector." His four tiny eyes blinked rapidly. "Thirty minutes, Captain Beck."

Serri strode from the office, hands still fisted. She had thirty minutes to collect her business partner, Quin, and try to figure out why Gop Filar so desperately wanted the forty-seven containers from Widestar that Rez Jonas assigned to them three shipdays ago. She should never have trusted Rez, but one of Quin's favorite lectures was that personal grudges had no place at the trading table—especially grudges with ex-lovers and ex-employers. Rez and Widestar fit both categories. Quin's Skoggi senses had picked up nothing duplicitous during the transaction, though admittedly Rez made only a brief appearance, his assistant handling the details.

Unless Quin lied about what he sensed.

No, she couldn't believe that. Quintrek James of Daq'kyree's detractors had many unkind names for the former High Council administrator, but liar wasn't one of them. If anything, Quin could be brutally honest, and his empathic ability tended to keep others honest as well. The fact that Quin could read her emotions never bothered her—and had proved handy in more than one sticky trade negotiation. Business was growing, enough that after six years as the *Pandea*'s pilot, she'd been able to buy a thirty-percent share of Quin's transport business two months ago. The *Star of Pandea* was now her ship too.

So were the *Pandea*'s troubles.

She spotted Quin's felinoid form in a booth at the Wretched Beast, one of Jabo Station's more popular multispecies bars. He was large even for a Skoggi, his head and shoulders clearly visible above the glossy blue tabletop. Black fur covered his pointed ears, wide side ruff, and back, all the way to his plumy tail, but he had a triangle of white over his eyes and muzzle that extended down his chest. In almost direct contrast to his fur and his bulk was the wraithlike silver-skinned Kor in bright yellow robes sitting across from him.

Damn. She didn't need an audience to their troubles. Worse, the Kor were chronic meddlers and Thuk-Zik was no exception. If she even hinted something was wrong, the yellow-robed male would latch on to her like a high-security docking clamp.

But Thuk-Zik was rising even as she approached. "I must be on my way. Good trading, Nom Quintrek. Nomma Captain Beck." He moved away, the hem of his robe fluttering as his clawed feet tapped against the metal decking.

"Good trading, Nom," Serri called after him, keeping relief at his departure out of her voice. *Thank you, saints and blessed Vakare.* She slid into the booth.

Quin was nudging his bowl of meat tea with one wide furry paw, causing the gelatinous liquid to shimmer. "You should have been here five minutes ago," he said, with that lilt his voice held when he spoke Trade-Standard. "We had quite a chin wag about who's brassed off at whom at Widestar Trading."

She glanced over her shoulder to make sure no one—especially another Kor—was within earshot, then lowered her voice. "Widestar is going to be brassed off at us. Filar has a grab order with our names on it—unless you have a spare three hundred thousand to make him go away. He knows damned well we don't. He'll be at our airlock in twenty minutes."

The white muzzle raised out of the bowl. Golden eyes narrowed. "Tailless bastard!"

"Pay your tab. We need to get there before he does."

THE VOICES IN Nicandro Talligar's head were talking to him again. It came with the job.

"Status?" asked a familiar gravelly male voice.

Nic tucked himself into the recesses of a maintenance alcove in the corridor outside the Wretched Beast and flexed his left wrist, activating the tympanic implant's transmitter. "Filar took the bait."

"Any reason to believe he suspects?"

I'm not Brackton, he almost told Leonoso, but held back. His case agent didn't need to be reminded of the mission failure at Able-Trade. But Nic *wasn't* Depvar Brackton. He'd never blown his cover, not in five years, not even when threatened with death. After what happened at Widestar, the job was everything to him. The agency knew that and—he suspected—used that.

"Everything's clean."

"Keep it that way. Next contact in thirty-eight." The transmission cut off with the usual sharp click.

He was about to move out of the alcove when a woman in a dark green flightsuit jogged by, her long dark braid swinging across her back. The ship's patch on her left sleeve was emblazoned with a silver star. A very large black-and-white Skoggi in a matching dark green CI—command-interface—vest bounded on all fours by her side. The patch on his vest showed an identical silver star.

Nic's chest suddenly went tight. He recognized and expected to see the Skoggi. Quintrek James—a familiar name in political circles—was owner of record of the *Star of Pandea*, a jump-rated short-hauler working the ass end of the Dalvarr System along with the usual assortment of pirates, mercenaries, and con artists. Which was the reason Nic Talligar was here—tracking cargo that the Dalvarr Intelligence Agency had, three days ago, deliberately placed on board Quintrek James's ship.

But what in hell was Serenity Beck doing here? The answer was in her green uniform with its silver star emblem on the sleeve. She was ship's crew, very likely ship's pilot.

Death threats he could handle. But Serri Beck was trouble—a seriously unexpected complication. And one that made his chest go tight and his breath hitch.

If Nic thought Serri disliked him six years ago, there was no doubt in his mind that she was really going to hate him now! Damned shame he couldn't return the favor. But six seconds of watching her sprint past him just destroyed six years of his hard-won sanity. And might well destroy his career.

He almost flexed his wrist to contact Leonoso. But he couldn't—not for thirty-eight hours. Mission rules. Cursing himself silently, he waited for a boxy anti-grav cargo auto-pallet to whirr by before slipping out of the shadows to follow her. Some rules were about to be broken.

. . . .

SERRI QUICKLY TAPPED in the codes to open the freighter bay's air-lock. Quin bounded through ahead of her, tail flicking as if to propel him forward. The Skoggi raced across the metal decking for the hulking deltoid-shaped ship that nearly filled the bay. Rampway lights, triggered by the thought-receptors in Quin's vest, winked on as he approached.

"Try scrambling the airlock codes to give us time," he called out. "I'll bring main systems online."

"They'll fire the ion cannons at us before we even hit the lanes," she called back as the airlock door wheezed closed. Not many stations packed a full complement of ion cannons. But Jabo had a reputation for using them to prevent captains skipping out on dockage fees.

Quin hesitated in the ship's hatchway. "I'm not looking to escape but to obfuscate. If they can't get in our cargo holds, they can't rob us of our cargo."

There was that. Serri programmed in a second override to the cor-ridor airlock pad, then bolted for the rampway. If the manifests were accurate, Filar's interest in their cargo made no sense: forty-seven con-tainers of Tillithian fermentation essence. A small winery operating out of a hydroponics outpost was the documented recipient. Partial payment was in account on Jabo. It wasn't the usual setup, but they needed to stop for fuel and water anyway. Even full payment wouldn't cover Filar's bogus importation tariff.

"Anything?" she asked Quinn as she jogged onto the bridge.

The Skoggi was hunkered down in the command sling, lights on his CI vest blinking in syncopation with lights on the ship's consoles as the vest translated his thoughts into actions on a ship made for humanoid hands, not Skoggi paws. "I've jammed the access doors to bays two and three. One and four, however, are being enthusiastically uncooperative."

"And Filar won't find it unusual that we can't get into our own cargo holds?" Her partner's perfect plan suddenly held huge flaws.

"Not when we tell him the winery has the only unlock codes. To pre-vent us from selling the essence elsewhere, of course. Considering that we took prepayment."

Yeah, with an invoice for unpaid tariffs served on her as soon as she left the bank. Serri hated coincidence. She just wished coincidence didn't like her so much.

She leaned her arms on the back of the command sling. "Let me take a look." Quin knew his ship, but Serri had learned a few tricks from a—onetime—friend who'd worked security at Widestar and had a talent for things less than legal. But if it kept the *Pandea*'s cargo in her holds, it was worth the heartache of resurrecting Nic Talligar's memory. She still didn't know what hurt more: the fact that Rez Jonas—her almost-husband—was having an affair with his sultry-but-stupid administrative assistant at Widestar, or that her closest friend since her university days provided excuses for her almost-husband and Sultry-but-Stupid.

She'd been in love with Rez for over two years. But she'd been friends with Nic for seven. All Rez gave her was heartache and shame. At least from Nic, she'd learned something useful.

Like whom she could trust. And whom she couldn't.

With a frustrated sigh, she brought up ship's schematics. Losing cargo would not only hamper their ability to get future hauling contracts, but it would damage the reputation that Quin had worked so hard to rebuild the past ten years. If Serri could have, she'd make Quin dump the containers on Jabo's decking and bolt. But Jabo Station packed ion cannons. And she had no reason to believe leaving their cargo behind would ensure their safety.

She had Cargo One jammed when the ramp alarms beeped. "Shit! The motherless son of a Garpion whore is early."

"Not Filar or his guards," Quin told her as she tapped on the ship's exterior vidcams. "Human male. No intention of violence."

She glanced at Quin. He was using his Skoggi senses to take a reading. Their visitor might not intend violence, but . . . "I double-locked the corridor hatchway. How in hell—?"

She swung back to the monitors. It was as if her illegal tinkering resurrected a ghost. The scars on her heart suddenly felt fresh and raw. Her onetime close friend hadn't changed much in six years, though his short dark hair looked a bit shaggier and he was definitely in need of a shave. But instead of a light green Widestar security uniform, he was in a black spacer jacket and dark pants. She'd bet, however, that his infamous charm hadn't changed one bit. His lock-picking skills certainly hadn't lapsed.

"You know him?"

She could tell by Quin's concerned tone that he'd felt her surge of emotions. "He was friends with Rez Jonas when we all worked for Widestar."

"Perhaps Rez sent him. Or he needs a job. Let him in."

She hesitated, her mind seizing on something so bizarre she couldn't discount it. She couldn't believe—well, yeah, she could—that six years after she walked out on Rez, he'd still hold a grudge.

But if Rez Jonas wanted to get revenge, using his new position as Widestar's director of Sector Three exports was a terrific way to do it. Sector Three—the Outrim region of the Dalvarr System—was the *Pandea*'s main territory. "Quin, has it occurred to you that Rez might have set us up?"

"All the more reason I wish to speak with this friend of yours."

She shoved herself out of the command sling. If Quin was hurt because of some juvenile plan of Rez's to get back at her, she swore she'd hunt the man down and pummel him out of existence.

"We have only ten minutes. See if you can't jam Cargo Four." She grabbed her Z9 laser rifle from the bridge's weapons locker, then headed quickly down the corridor to find out just what Nic Talligar was doing on her rampway—and back in her life.

"IF YOU'RE HERE for a job, we're not hiring."

Nic studied Captain Serri Beck, standing in the *Pandea*'s airlock, and knew without a doubt that he was courting trouble. It wasn't just her tone. It was the lethal Z9 in her hands. Best to get right to the point.

"Filar's Bruisers are on the way here," he told her as she stared at him, her dark eyes hard and cold. He remembered lights dancing in those same eyes, her demeanor playful, impish. That playfulness was gone, but her ability to spark his emotions wasn't. He forced his focus from her to the shadowy airlock. "We don't have much time. You can shoot me when this is finished."

"Ammo's pricey these days. Spacing you would be cheaper." But she motioned him through the airlock with a hard jerk of the rifle's tip.

He hesitated, a thousand things he wanted to say dying on his tongue. Things he should have said six years ago. Things he still couldn't find a way to say now. He stepped past her into the freighter's interior—the usual gray serviceable bulkheads with yellow-striped conduit crisscrossing overhead. His bootsteps clanked in time to hers on the decking gridwork. Something trilled and beeped farther down the corridor.

"I can help, but you need to trust me." He knew that was asking a lot.

"That's up to Quin, not me."

He nodded, and moved on with the feeling that if it had been up to her, she would have shot him on the rampway.

It didn't surprise him that Serenity Beck had hooked up with Quintrek James of Daq'kyree. Nic knew Quintrek's history, and the rumors surrounding the former royal adviser's resignation a decade ago. He couldn't bring the details of the scandal to mind, only that Quintrek had walked away from a powerful and prestigious position on the Skoggi High Council.

Serri, like Quintrek, had a strong sense of justice. But, unlike Quintrek, she hadn't waited to review all the evidence. If she had, her life might well have been different. *Nic's* life . . . He pushed the thought away. He couldn't change the past. The only thing he could do was to help her and Quintrek now—and try not to blow the mission in the process.

"Quin, this is Nicandro Talligar," Serri said as they stepped over the hatch tread and onto the bridge.

Nic inclined his head in respect to the Skoggi perched in the command sling. "An honor, Esteemed of Pride Daq'kyree."

A wide paw resplendent with furry white tufts waved dismissively. "Piffle. Little honor in being caught in Filar's claws. Tell me what Rez Jonas should have, but didn't." Quin turned toward Serri. "Cargo Four won't lock."

"On it." She swung away, pushing the rifle to one side as she dropped into a chair in front of a console.

"Wait. You have to let Filar take the cargo," Nic said, as Serri angled back toward him. "I know that's not what you want to hear. Think of it as a temporary inconvenience on the way to solving a larger problem."

Dark narrowed eyes peered up at him. "The larger problem is Filar's threatening to impound this ship, Talligar."

"He won't go that far. Trust me."

"He will, and I don't trust you. Neither does Quin."

"Dumping cargo doesn't engender client loyalty," Quin intoned.

"There won't be clients shipping anywhere in Sector Three if we don't find out what Filar's up to," Nic countered. "You're not the first to get hit with this scheme. But we tagged your cargo and can track it to whoever Filar sends it to—which is who we suspect is behind this."

Quin's whiskers twitched, but he was nodding. "I take it 'we' is more than you and Rez Jonas."

Nic had briefly considered using that as cover, and probably could have convinced the empathic Skoggi that it was the truth. That was, after all, part of his job. But Nic's lies to Serri—and the way Rez Jonas used her—always haunted him. She deserved honesty this time.

"Jonas has no idea I'm here. I'm a special agent with the DIA's organized crime squad." Cover blown. He could almost hear his boss roaring in anger from her plush offices at HQ, more than halfway across the Dalvarr System, adding his name next to Brackton's on her list of incompetents.

He heard Serri's snort of disbelief instead. "That's a great pickup line, but we don't have time for—"

"Trouble," Quin said harshly, pointing to one of the screens on an opposite console where a line of hulking red-suited Breffans shoved through the freighter bay's hatchlock, ram-cannons in hands. "Filar's Bruisers have arrived."

SERRI LISTENED AS Quin—being typically Quin—peppered the orange-freckled Bruiser chief with questions. But whether Quin was playing the part that Nic had asked him to, or whether he discounted Nic's story and was actually trying to save their asses—and their cargo—Serri couldn't tell.

Serri, being typically Serri, vacillated between righteous anger and an unexpected—and ridiculous—feeling of relief at Nic's presence by her side. She didn't know what to make of Nic's story. But the fact that she didn't trust him didn't blind her to other facts: He was intelligent, resourceful, and had a definite talent for unorthodox solutions. They needed one of those—desperately—right now.

Quin's arguments were changing nothing. The Breffans didn't care about the legitimacy of the order they served. Not surprising, considering that the broad-bodied, leathery-skinned, freckled Breffans weren't used in security for their empathy, but for their multilimbed dexterity. The purple-freckled female guard holding a rifle on Serri and Nic also held a pistol and a transcomm in two of her other three hands—if Serri as much as made a twitch for the rifle slung across her back, the guard could shoot her dead with two different weapons. The guard's fourth hand scratched lazily at her left thigh.

The Breffan chief finally stalked away, clomping noisily up the *Pandea*'s rampway in counterpoint to the *Pandea*'s cargo flowing out of her holds.

With a shake of his head, Quin padded back over to where she and Nic stood, then sat on his haunches. Serri knew that he wouldn't discuss anything in front of the guard. She glanced down at him. He mirrored her frown with a slight narrowing of his eyes. One ear twitched, flattening.

Quin was not happy.

Neither was Serri. For all the things she didn't know, there was one thing she did: Nic Talligar knew more than he was saying about Filar and Rez Jonas.

Minutes later, noise from the *Pandea*'s airlock drew her attention. The orange-freckled Breffan chief clomped back down the rampway, cannon in one hand, datapad in another, his remaining two arms stiffly at his side.

With an annoyed grunt, he went down on one knee so that his face and Quin's were almost level. "Paw print here." He held out the datapad.

"I shall read it first." Quin's voice held a haughty tone that Serri knew went back to his council days. "If you'd like to sit—"

"I'll wait," the chief said. "It's only the basic one-page transfer of ownership."

Transfer of ownership? Not transfer. Impound. Shock roiled through her. They'd already given up the cargo as Nic told them to. And now . . . this. Serri felt sick. She'd trusted Nic again. And been betrayed. Again.

Quin's whiskers quivered as his paw hovered over the screen. "This is beastly. We shall be filing a criminal complaint against this station."

The chief shrugged. "Boss says since we got the cargo, he can be generous. For a mere hundred fifty thousand, he'll drop impound charges and you can keep the ship."

Quin's paw jerked. "Bugger!"

Nic stepped forward. "Deal."

"Deal?" Serri's voice rasped as she swung toward him. What kind of game was this now? Or maybe not a game at all, but the truth coming out. Nic wasn't trying to help them, he wasn't a DIA agent trying to stop Filar. He was working for Filar, extorting as much as he could out of Quin.

"But we need time," Nic was saying, "to transfer the funds."

The Breffan tapped his datapad. "Fifteen minutes."

"Two hours."

"Thirty minutes."

"Hour and a half."

"Hour."

"Deal."

More taps on the datapad. "Paw print here confirming payment at the dockmaster's office in one hour," the chief said to Quin.

Quin glanced at Nic, then, with the slightest of nods, slapped his paw down.

"Don't even think about trying to leave without paying," the chief said, shoving the datapad back into his utility belt. "Cannons'll pick you off before you're even halfway to the outer beacon."

"Understood," Quinn said.

The chief nodded and, with purple-freckles in tow and the rest of his team filing out behind them, headed for the corridor.

Serri waited until the airlock door groaned closed. "What in hell's going on? We don't have a hundred fifty thousand credits!" She glanced from Nic to Quinn then back to Nic again. "They took the cargo. Deed done. Now go arrest them or whatever it is you do. And get us our ship back."

Discomfort colored Nic's features, his brows angling down. "I can't do that. I'll catch hell as it is because you know who I am. But it would jeopardize the entire mission if station admin finds out."

"I take it that means the DIA isn't giving us a loan."

"I don't have the authority—"

"Then what in hell are Quin and I supposed to do? Rob a bank?" She didn't try to keep the sarcasm out of her words.

"Don't have to," Nic said. "Filar can't extort money from you if you're not on station."

Abandon the Pandea? "You're asking us to walk away—"

"Not walk. Climb. Six levels up to the auxiliary maintenance grid so I can disable the station's weapons' system."

This was beyond unorthodox. The man was insane. "You're going to dismantle an entire bank of ion cannons?"

"Nope." He pulled out a thin microcomp from an inside pocket of his jacket. "I just have to shut down the station's ability to fire them."

Serri's mind whirled. "Not you." She pointed to herself then to Nic. "Us."

"I can't. You're not trained—"

"Weapons systems, computers? Sure as hell am, Talligar. Or are you forgetting who was your study and sim partner in the university?"

"Serri, this is dangerous."

"And this is my ship, and Quin's my partner. I'm not stupid enough to let you stroll out of here with only your word as guarantee. I had a taste of your trustworthiness six years ago, thank you very much." She tugged her rifle forward. "I'm going with you or you're going nowhere."

He looked hurt. "Quin trusts me."

"I feel your plan has merit," Quin admitted. "And empathically I sense no duplicity from you. But I agree with Captain Beck. We have far more to lose than you do." He nodded. "I trust you will do all you can to keep her safe. And I trust she will do all she can to keep you honest."

Serri raised her chin and looked at Nic in triumph. It meant something that Quin believed him. She wasn't ready yet to grant him that luxury though.

"FILAR MAY HAVE watchers out," Nic told Serri as they strode for the stairwell. He kept his voice low and even. Which was more than he could do for his emotions. He was annoyed. He was angry. His own career be damned, the one thing he did not want to do was put Serri in further danger, and now he had. It didn't make him feel any better that he was armed and so was she—though she'd left the larger rifle with Quin, opting for a more easily concealable pistol. "We need to let them see us enter the bank as if we're securing a loan. Then we slip out the side door and use the maintenance core catwalks from there."

"Just like Scout-and-Snipe."

He huffed out a hard laugh at her comment. "A bit more dangerous, but yeah." He'd met Serri playing the holosim game while at the university. Impressed with her skills, he recruited her to his team—the best decision he ever made. A year later, he recruited Rez Jonas. The worst decision he ever made.

"Why does the DIA care about Filar? Okay, he's dirty, but Jabo Station's had that reputation for decades. What are you really doing here?"

Definitely not what he'd been sent to do—including blowing his cover. He waited until two human dockworkers and a Kortish male in garish yellow robes clambered down the stairs and out of earshot. "It's one thing when pirates get into pissing contests with rival factions. It's another when legit haulers get hit with an extortion scam. And yes, I really do work for the DIA. They recruited me a few months after you left." Serri never even said good-bye, never gave him a chance to explain why he'd kept her busy and away from Jonas all those months.

He glanced over at her as they climbed, chancing a bit of honesty, as painful as he knew it was going to be. "There was no reason for me to stay at Widestar. You were gone."

Something flashed in her eyes. "I'm sure Rez had other infidelities you could have helped him cover up."

They'd reached the next level—one more and they'd exit into the corridor then head for the bank. Nic kept his senses tuned to anyone coming up behind them. It was in Filar's best interest to let them retrieve the supposed funds, but this was Jabo Station. Filar wasn't the only thug. Just one of the bigger ones.

Given that, he'd picked one hell of a time to initiate this discussion. "I never meant to hurt you."

"Well, you did." She pushed ahead of him.

He kept to the right side of the heavily trafficked passageway, tucking them as much as possible between larger groups as they headed for the bank's main entrance off Corridor Supreme. If Filar had his Bruisers following them, Nic didn't see any.

That Filar could be following them on security vidcams was a definite possibility. It was the reason Nic chose Sector United. The vidcams in Corridor Supreme were the least effective and not just because of the crowds, but because two popular pleasure houses there paid good money not to be recorded.

Sector United was crowded—it was the only bank on-station that was multi-species-friendly, including a private office for methane breathers and decking-level teller terminals for four-legged patrons like Skoggi. He guided Serri past the currency-exchange kiosk, then spotted a vacant space along a side wall. He nudged her quickly in that direction. They needed to look as if they waited for a loan officer.

"Serri, I'm sorry," he said as she wedged herself between a fake redsprout tree on her right and a tall blinking advert pillar on her left.

She brushed a synth-frond off her head. "I'm okay."

"No. About Rez and his affair with Janna. It was Rez I wanted to hurt. Not you. Never you." He didn't know why it was so important to tell her that now, but it was. He suddenly had a bad feeling about this mission, and about what exactly he'd have to do to make sure Serri and Quin got off station alive and in possession of their ship.

Emotions played over her face, her eyes darkening, her mouth parting slightly. He had to force himself to look away from all that, from what it made him want to do, because they now had forty-three minutes to get up four more levels, pull the plug on station defenses, and get back down to the *Pandea* before alarms started wailing. And before Filar's Breffan Bruisers figured out just what he'd wanted that extra hour for.

Suddenly, she grasped his forearms, pulling him closer. Nic was very aware that he had three minutes to spare, and that three minutes wasn't nearly time enough to kiss Serri like he wanted to. People in hell want ice water, his grandfather always used to say. He'd take what he could get.

But her face didn't hold a look of passion but concern. "A pair of Bruisers just came in."

Nic shot a quick glance over his shoulder. Time to disappear. "Side exit. Go."

She threaded her way through the crowd of bank patrons. He took one last look at guards—the Breffans hadn't seen them, he was sure—and then followed on her heels, cursing silently. He should have demanded more time.

There was a maintenance storage room about fifty feet to the left of the bank. At least, there had been two years ago, which was the last time Nic was on Jabo Station. But when they came around the curve in the corridor, something else had been added: two more red-uniformed Bruisers. One leaned against the bulkhead, checking something on a transcomm in his upper left hand; the other watched the crowd through narrowed eyes.

He pulled Serri behind a pylon.

"They're looking for us," she said. It wasn't a question.

"They're also blocking access to the maintenance core." Where they would have been able to continue with much less chance of being seen.

"There must be others."

"That's the closest workable one on this level that I have the code for."

"Since when do you need a code for a lock?"

"Since we only have forty minutes to do what we have to and get back."

One of the Breffan guards raised his face, peering over the crowd of stationers. Spotting them? Nic couldn't take the chance. The guard was already heading toward them. Nic put his arm around her shoulders, aware now of movement to their left. A deep voice, shouting. Then a sharp trill of high laughter.

"Looks like someone's on his way to a party," he told her, turning her quickly toward the group of drunken revelers. "Let's go crash it."

. . . .

THEY STANK. SOMEONE—more than one someone, Serri guessed with fair accuracy, wrinkling her nose—had spilled sour ale on his clothes, and another someone standing far too close to her and Nic had pissed on himself. Or herself. Crammed into the small lift as they were—a nonstop to Level Ten—there was nowhere to get away from the stench and the harsh laughter and—

Vakare-be-damned, if that bastard behind her patted her ass one more time she was going to ignore Nic's admonition to "blend in," and clock the drunk right across his drooling face.

She inched closer to Nic, regretting that too because he smelled clean like soap and leather and, well, like the Nic Talligar she remembered.

It was Rez I wanted to hurt. Not you.

She played his words over in her mind as she listened to Nic ramble on in an unintelligible conversation with several of the drunks, his new-found friends. There was no escape, not from the drunken dockworkers headed for the Crimson Flask on Level Ten, and not from Nic Talligar who never wanted to hurt her.

So he said.

He never hurt you before. He was your best friend.

But how in hell was helping Rez cover his affair with Janna hurting Rez? If she lived through this, she was going to sit Nic down and demand an answer. And have Quin there to make sure Nic didn't lie.

Though she might suffocate from the noxious fumes before that happened. She gave up and leaned her face against Nic's jacket. And was surprised when his arms came tightly around her. And even more surprised to feel his mouth brush the side of her forehead.

He's playacting. We're just another pair of drunks headed for some-one's party.

But being held by Nic felt good. And it wasn't just because he smelled good. It was because . . . he was Nic. Her onetime closest friend she never wanted to see again. Ever.

This was definitely not good.

The lift shimmied to a stop, doors opening. The whooping and laugh-ing increased, along with general mayhem as the partygoers stumbled toward the bar's entrance.

She and Nic stumbled along with them. Suddenly he yanked her sideways.

"Hey, party's this way!" someone called out.

"Be righ' there," Nic called back, words slurred as he swayed against her. "Gotta puke."

That elicited a chorus of groans and epithets as Nic bent over, one hand braced against the wall.

"Arm around my shoulder. Block their view." His voice was low, urgent.

She steadied him and realized he didn't want his new friends to see the tiny decoder in his hand. He was picking the lock on a door clearly marked "No Admittance."

"I really don't think they care," she said quietly, meaning that he was accessing the door, not that he was pretending to be sick.

"Anyone watching?"

She turned slightly. The line of dockworkers in the corridor had dwindled. "Nope."

He shoved the door open and pulled her inside. "They care," he said, closing the door, extinguishing all light. Then light flared. Nic, with a small handbeam. They were in a storage closet.

"They care," he repeated. "You ever know a Jabo dockworker who could afford drinks on the house for fifty people at the first bar, and now a second party here?"

"Someone's rich relative died?"

He shook his head and played the beam around the room. "The woman with the long white braids on the lift with us is our hostess. Got paid good money for doing something interestingly illegal. And it involves filched cargo and bogus tariffs."

"She works for Filar."

"No. Rez Jonas." He focused the beam on another door on the left wall. "This way."

Her mind frantically processed the information and refused to let her feet move. "But why would he risk his own cargo? He's working with you, isn't he?"

He grabbed her wrist and pulled her forward. "I don't know, and no, he's not," he said, putting the decoder against the door. "Jonas had no idea we're tracking his cargo. Yours is one of several shipments the DIA tagged at the source. Some ended up at Able-Trade, some went to Fortune Exports, and some to Widestar." The door unlocked with a low pinging sound. "We didn't know where the problem was. Now I think we do."

"But why would he want his own cargo stolen?"

He ushered her through the door into a dimly lit room that wasn't a room at all, but an open, hangarlike area crisscrossed with catwalks, ladders, maintenance tunnels, and accessways that comprised the station's core.

"I can think of a dozen reasons ranging from kickbacks to idiotic corporate backstabbing," Nic said, shoving his handbeam and decoder back onto his utility belt. "But what worries me more is whether Jonas knew you were piloting the *Pandea*."

She followed him toward a descending catwalk that she hoped was sturdier than it looked. "He was at the depot when we took consignment. But he didn't stay long. I thought he was still uncomfortable around me."

"My guess is he was uncomfortable with your Skoggi partner, who might sense something was wrong. Like the fact Jonas was targeting you."

Targeting? She grasped the handrail on the catwalk to steady herself. "Why would he target us?"

"We need to keep moving." He touched her shoulder gently. "Again, I don't know. It could be he's still pissed because you walked out in the middle of his fancy engagement party."

After she'd tossed photos around the party of Rez and Janna writhing on top of a Widestar boardroom conference table. She'd heard later he almost lost his job. And she never did figure out who to thank for sending her the damning images.

"And yours is the only ship under threat of impound," Nic was saying.

"That could be Filar's doing."

"All our intelligence to date shows that Filar is just the front end. Rez wanted you and Quin to do the Jabo run. He wanted you here today."

Serri saw that so clearly. "Filar had the seizure papers waiting for me."

"My point. Rez knows you'd fight forfeiting your ship, and also knows you don't have the money to pay Filar's ransom. The banks were probably told to deny you a loan. Our mistake—and it was a big one—was that we didn't even try to get the funds. Filar now knows you have no intention of paying. So he's wondering if you're going to break dock and take a chance the ion cannons just might miss." He hesitated, then: "Or maybe that's exactly what Jonas wants you to do."

"Rez wants me dead?" Her voice sounded suddenly hollow

He turned and looked back at her, his eyes dark. "I have no intention of letting that happen."

She realized that she'd stopped again. She quickened her steps to catch up to him, her boots clanging dully on the metal gridwork. Saints help them. Quin. What if Filar or whoever Rez had here on station made a move against the *Pandea*? But Quin could sense anyone entering the bay, sense their intentions. Granted, only in a general capacity: He was Skoggi, not some magical, mystical creature. But Serri had to believe that someone intent on killing would be broadcasting very intense emotions. Still . . . "I need to warn Quin."

"If they're monitoring transmissions you might be endangering—"

A sudden clanking sounded above them. Serri's heart rate spiked. Nic shoved her to her knees, then dropped down beside her, pistol out. She drew hers and stared up toward the sound, peripherally aware of Nic checking all around them.

He was right. This was far more dangerous than Scout-and-Snipe. And immeasurably more important. The security training Widestar put all their pilots through seemed woefully insufficient.

A few more clanks and pings, punctuated by bootsteps. Through the uneven lighting dotting the stairlike catwalks, Serri could discern a form moving on a platform about two levels above. She didn't know whether to hunker down and make herself appear smaller, or tense her body and get ready to run.

After another series of pings, Nic leaned toward her, mouth against her ear, "Repair worker. Should leave—"

A loud clang.

"Now." He rose, one hand on her arm, bringing her with him. "If you're going to contact Quin, make it quick."

She pulled out her transcomm as Nick trotted carefully back down the catwalk. She moved as he did, and kept her voice low. "Quintrek, Captain Beck here. Ran into Thuk-zik. I think you've locked up the market on gossip. You were dead-on right about those rumors." She cut the transmission, praying Quin would pick out the keywords in her unlikely and uncharacteristic message.

Praying he was still alive and on board to even receive it.

THREE MINUTES. WELL, maybe five, but no more than that. Nic had five minutes to open the auxiliary maintenance compartment without setting off any alarms. He went down on one knee, running the small decoder over the door's locking mechanism, which was housed about six inches below the palm pad and ident reader.

"Anything?" Serri asked softly behind him.

"It's a Drammond Six-K-One." He swept the decoder in an arc. "Good antipick deterrents, double-back code verifier. Nice."

"Nic, we've got twenty minutes."

"We have four. If I can't get this open in four, the rest of those minutes won't matter." He brought up a sequence but the 6K-1 wasn't interested. Damn it. He tried a second, then a third. He could feel Serri's concern and impatience. She was worried about Quin.

He was worried because he was working blind, and not just because he couldn't get a damned code fix on the damned 6K-1. It was because he had no clear concept of what Rez Jonas was up to. Only that it wasn't what either he or his boss had expected. But without filing a sitrep, he couldn't get answers from agency intel.

Of course, filing a sitrep now would set off more alarms than sloppily picking the damned lock would.

Pay attention, Nicandro.

"Reverse those two parameters."

He glanced to his right and almost bumped noses with Serri. "What—"

"Those two." She pointed to the small screen. "Have you forgotten what you taught me back at Widestar? That's a loop created by an inaccessible exit command."

He wasted another second to stare at her in amazement—and admiration—then reversed the two parameters and got to work.

"We're in." The *snick-click* of a well-picked lock never sounded so good. He would have kissed her, but there was no time. Plus, she was angry enough at him as it was. "Ten minutes, max."

The room was little more than a dimly lit narrow closet, about twelve feet wide. It wasn't the usual auxiliary control system, but an unmanned maintenance substation that serviced nonenvironmental systems. Newer stations no longer used them because of their potential overall vulnerability, but Jabo had been here for more than a half a century, and Filar and his predecessors were kept busy with rival pirate factions zapping each other in the corridors. The fact that someone might be able to compromise a few of the station's nonenvironmental systems was farther down on the list of concerns.

Nic hoped.

Serri had already angled a console screen around that displayed system status. "Three intruder traps."

"I see them. Can you—"

"First one's already diverted."

He realized then that she had a slim strafer pen in her fingers. Later, he'd ask her just what a nice girl like Serenity Beck was doing with such a delightfully illegal device. He prayed they had a "later." For now, he let her work. Her record for unraveling code traps in Scout-and-Snipe had been damned near flawless.

"Shit!" She pulled the pen back abruptly, angling it away from the screen.

A searcher worm. Someone had upgraded the station's security programs recently.

"I can create a subprogram to distract it," she said, "if we have enough time."

They didn't. Frustration flooded him. "Options, Serri. Let the ship go. I'll do everything I can to get you and Quin safely back in-system."

Her lips thinned. "That's no option. I could get another job, but Quin put everything he had into the *Pandea*." She hesitated. "The bad guys must have the cargo by now. Case solved. Just go tell station admin who you are, make them give me my ship back."

It sounded so easy. It *would* be so easy. There was a DIA stealth ship full of enforcement agents two hours out that could definitely provide the muscle, but that was something else he wasn't permitted to reveal for at least another thirty-five hours. "Serri, if I could, I would. I can't."

"Please."

The desperation in her voice tore at him. He wiped one hand over his face. "The best I could do is release some data so that you can prove a case against Jonas. You could get an attorney to file a civil case for damages—"

"When? A year? Two? Three? Didn't you hear me? Quin has no resources left, financially and emotionally. I've worked with him for six years. He's the kindest, most honorable, most decent being I've ever met. But since those death threats—"

"Death threats?" He knew the entire file on the Skoggi. It didn't contain any threats, or the agency would have pulled the tagged cargo off the *Pandea*, knowing a secondary problem would muddy the investigation. "Because of—"

"Old news: his resignation from the council. He said it was probably just a sick joke, especially after all this time."

"Damn it." Nic spun for the door, angry at HQ for sloppy research, angry at Serri for not telling him sooner, and angry at himself for not asking all the questions he knew that he should have but didn't. Finding Serri again restarted his heart but shut down his brain. "This could be the real reason Jonas assigned the cargo to your ship."

"But why would Rez care about Skoggi politics?"

"Because Rez Jonas's maternal grandfather was Manton Suthis." The details on Quintrek James that eluded him earlier came back now with blinding clarity. "Suthis was the attorney for a Dalvarrian mining cooperative that allegedly funneled illegal political contributions to key Skoggi administrators ten years ago, in exchange for government contracts."

She stared at him. "Quin never mentioned names. Just that he had proof, but the court refused to investigate."

"That didn't stop Suthis from committing suicide." And Rez, Nic remembered, had always been devoted to his grandparents. His devotion might now have taken a deadly twist.

Serri stepped toward him. "Quin—"

"I'll take care of Quin. I need you to skew that weapons program. When you're on your way down to the ship, comm me. If I don't give you the all-clear"—and he hesitated, then pulled out his transcomm, knowing that she wasn't going to like this option, knowing that his boss would like it even less—"contact Director Jessamyn Emory at DIA headquarters." He rattled off a private comm number, sending it to Serri's transcomm at the same time. "She'll get you off-station."

Her lips parted, fear and something else flickering across her features. A concern, a compassion that reminded him of the old Serri, his closest friend, the woman he'd loved in secret for years. "Nic . . ."

His chest tightened. *You're still my best friend* would make him deliriously happy. Maybe then he'd have a chance. But he'd settle for *I don't hate you as much as I used to.*

"I . . . be careful."

"Comm me. And keep the safety off your pistol." He slipped out the door, then bolted for the catwalks.

SERRI HATED SEARCHER worm code. More than that, she hated that she'd left Quin alone and vulnerable. And that Nic might even now be too late.

She could lose them both. The thought came and went because she didn't have time for pity, though her heart ached and her throat felt tight. She had a searcher worm to choke. And a weapons guidance program to screw up.

It took ten minutes before the worm choked, the program freezing up long enough for her to launch a worm of her own into the ion cannons' guidance system. It wasn't her best work; it would unravel in about an hour, leaving station techs swearing at yet another inexplicable program malfunction that suddenly restored itself. But it bought her, Quin, and Nic time.

She slipped out of the maintenance compartment into the shadowy cavernous core of catwalks and access tunnels. Twenty minutes had passed since Nic left. She sent Nic a brief "on my way," then moved as quickly as she could down the rickety catwalk stairs, transcomm still in hand as she listened for a confirmation back from him. She needed to know that Quin was safe. And Nic . . . his reappearance after all this time set off emotions in her she wasn't sure what to do with. Maybe he hadn't been trying to hurt her when he'd covered up Rez's infidelity. Maybe he was simply caught between two people he cared about, and didn't know what to do. Or maybe—

Her transcomm pinged. Nic. But no, it showed Quin's ident. Then the signal disconnected. If it was an error, he'd call back, but she didn't for a moment think that's what it was. She quickened her pace, abandoning her intention of using the main corridors. She'd stay in the relative safety of the maintenance rampways and tunnels until she was sure what was going on.

Why hadn't Nic confirmed back to her?

Another ping. Quin again. This time the screen stayed lit. There were the low sounds of someone talking, many of the words distorted. Quin must have activated his transcomm through his CI vest, and was letting her know what was going on in the *Pandea*'s bay without others in the bay realizing that he'd done so.

Still moving quickly, she strained to catch snippets of conversation—no, threats—between Quin and Gop Filar. Then, heart pounding, she broke into a run.

Because there was one thing she didn't hear along with the threats: Nic's voice.

He should have reached Quin by now, and she didn't know if she was more worried that he hadn't—or that he had. Because Filar's "You are out of options" went right to the pit of her stomach.

It sounded as if someone had tried and failed.

Nic couldn't fail. He was a DIA agent. He was trained. He was some-one she cared oh-so-deeply about—even if she didn't want to admit that to herself.

She reached the first level of freighter bays. If she exited through the yellow-ringed maintenance panel on her right, she'd be about thirty feet from the *Pandea*'s airlock. Though the only voices she could hear through Quin's open transcomm were his and Filar's, Filar could have the bay full of his Bruisers. Barging in was a move she wouldn't even do in Scout-and-Snipe, let alone in real life.

But she could take advantage of the way the freighter levels were structured, with maintenance pits underneath each bay. She bolted down half a level. Quin was still arguing. That gave her hope.

She found the pit for the *Pandea*'s bay, checked it for alarms and, finding none, pocketed her transcomm, then turned the manual lock. The panel was heavy, but she only needed it open far enough to slip through. She went into Scout-and-Snipe mode: listening, sensing. Nothing but the creak, groan, and whoosh of the station, and the lingering scent of grease. She stepped into the shadowed pit, her eyes picking out pinpoints of light from the various control consoles on the far bulkhead.

A slight exhalation of breath whispered behind her. She flinched, fear spiking, her fingers fumbling for her pistol just as a hand covered her mouth. An arm wrapped hard around her midsection, pinning her arms. Heart pounding, she twisted, trying to free one arm so she could—

"Serri." Her name, hushed, in her ear.

Nic's voice.

Nic?

The arm loosened, the hand pulled away. She spun, right hand fisted, her breath coming in hard gasps as she stared at the familiar lines of Nic's face in the dim lighting. Relief poured through her. "Why didn't you answer my message?"

"Your transcomm's off line." He kept his voice low.

Not off line. She yanked it out. "Quin," she whispered, handing it to him.

He listened for a moment, nodding, then tugged her forward, his free hand on her wrist. "All right. We'll come up underneath the ship. Use the rampway as partial cover. Did you get the targeting programs skewed?"

"We have about forty-five minutes before they'll reset. What happened with Quin?"

"Filar and three guards were in the *Pandea*'s airlock when I got there," he explained as they trotted toward the far side of the bay. "Quin refused to leave the ship until about five minutes ago."

"That's when he called me."

"He should have stayed onboard."

She heard worry and frustration in the tight tone of his voice. "He's Skoggi. He can sense you. He doesn't want us locked out of our own ship. If he's on the ramp, then he's telling us it's time to break dock and leave."

"I have every intention of granting his wish. He'd just better not mind an extra passenger."

She didn't want to know why his words made her heart beat faster. "I assumed you were coming."

"Not just me. Filar." He slowed as they neared a set of tall servo-stairs, then motioned her behind him. "I'm on point. Set your pistol to stun only. I want that bastard alive and spilling everything he knows about Rez Jonas."

They were going to kidnap the Jabo Station dockmaster? "You can't possibly be—"

"The Crystal Flame scenario, Scout-and-Snipe."

She remembered. "Nic, we never got past level seven in that one."

"This time, though, we're going all the way." His wry grin was confident even in the low lighting. "Trust me."

She had to. They were out of options and almost out of time. The ion cannons would come back online in forty minutes.

THE SERVOSTAIRS WERE rickety and, once Nic reached the halfway point, no longer lit by the dim illumination of the pit's emergency lights. Overhead a series of movable hatchways were crisscrossed by cables and pulleys and dangling things that—in spite of the narrow light offered by his handbeam—managed to gouge his shoulders and his back. Serri didn't fare much better. More than once he heard her sharp intake of breath.

He was leading a civilian into a potential firefight, violating a half-dozen DIA regs he could quote from memory, but his distinct uneasiness had nothing to do with those regs. It wasn't that he doubted Serri. Serenity Beck could be tough when tough was needed. It was that she was Serri, and he would do everything he could to protect her.

Even if it meant his own life.

There was a reason the Crystal Flame scenario was so difficult to complete. It was because level eight set up a do-or-die situation: sacrifice a team member or go back to level one.

The top of the servostairs widened into a platform. He clambered up, then guided Serri next to him. She had the transcomm to her ear.

"Status?"

"Quin's switching between Trade and Skoge. It's making Filar's trans-lang crazy. But it sounds like Quin's trying to bribe him."

"Keep listening. Some of what he's saying is likely aimed at us." He ran his fingers over the gritty, pitted metal panels inches over his head, feeling for a manual release. He found it, pulled, and was rewarded by a soft double click. It was open. His heart hammered. He took a deep breath. He had to forget for now that Serri was Serri. This was the mission; he was a professional. Personalities—hell, his heart's desire—could not come into play.

"Quin's telling Filar that he has a collection of Nonga vases he can show him onboard."

Nic glanced at her. It was exactly where he wanted the Nalshinian dockmaster: locked in the *Pandea*'s brig. "You sure Quin's not telepathic?"

"You know as much about the Skoggi as I do."

"Is Filar going?"

She was silent. Then: "Sounds like it."

"Here's what we do. Crystal Flame, level seven. We stun whatever Bruisers are outside the ship. Then you watch in case backup arrives. I'll take care of Filar and his escort."

"Wrong, Talligar. It's my ship. We take out the guards, then *I'm* on point. I think I know where Quin's leading Filar so we can trap him."

"You could tell me—"

"We're wasting time. Thirty-five minutes before those cannons come back on line."

Shit. He'd forgotten about that. He pointed to her transcomm. "Anything more?"

She was frowning. "Signal's disconnected. I don't like it."

Neither did he, but rushing into this could be fatal. He carefully slid the portal panel to the left, pinpointing the locations of at least two guards by their noises. "Now," he whispered, and shoved himself through.

The freighter bay seemed almost dirtside-daylight bright to his eyes, even with the large ship hulking above him. He assessed his position immediately, spotting the two guards about twenty-five feet from the end of the rampway, just inside the bay's safe zone. Good. They'd be locked behind a blast wall when the ship powered up. He crouched quickly next to a landing strut, feeling Serri behind him. He motioned for her to take out the one on the left. A quick glance showed her pistol raised. He took aim. They had to fire at the same time or risk retaliation.

"Now," he whispered again.

He fired, aware of the low hum from her pistol in tandem with his. He hit the guard on the right center mass, but Serri's guard turned and her stun charge hit him in the shoulder. His guard dropped like a crate of unsecured cargo, but hers twisted, falling to one knee as one hand raised a pistol and another punched something on his transcomm.

Serri fired again, taking the guard center mass this time. The big Breffan landed on his back, pistol and transcomm clattering beside him.

Nic lunged to his feet, swearing silently. "We have to assume he set off an emergency signal," he said as Serri appeared next to him. "Tell me where Quin—"

"No time." She pushed ahead of him and ran up the rampway.

He caught up with her at the airlock.

"Stand clear." Her fingers tapped a pattern into the lockpad's small screen.

"Filar's got a Bruiser with him."

"Then he's coming for a ride too."

The airlock doors groaned shut behind him. He grabbed her arm. "We could end up with a hostage standoff." Just like Scout-and-Snipe. "They've got Quin." And the Nalshinian and the Breffan were both much larger than the Skoggi—probably the sole reason, other than greed, that they'd agreed to come onboard. "I know how to handle this," he continued tersely. "You don't. Where are they?"

She hesitated for half a breath. "Either his quarters—lower deck, starboard forward—or Cargo Two, starboard aft. I vote for the latter. It has a null-field generator for hazardous cargo. Kills transcomm signals so Filar can't call for help."

Quin's signal had ended abruptly. He hoped that it was because of the null-field. He moved past her for the ladderway. Then she was right beside him, damn it, reaching the small compartment at the base of the ladderway before he did. She poked at a control panel set into the bulkhead and motioned him forward. She kept her voice low. "Cargo holds have a refrigeration option."

And freezing temperatures put Breffans into hibernation mode. "How long until—"

"Five minutes on temperature, thirty on cannons."

He could hear tension in her whispered words; saw anxiety in the thin line of her lips. He held up one hand. "We go barreling down that corridor, we could both get killed. Wait." He crouched down and edged around the corner. The corridor ran most of the length of the ship, with access to Cargo Four the closest to their location. He damned the fact that he hadn't brought a thermal sensor or miniature spybots. But this was just supposed to be a preliminary mission to make sure the tagged cargo left the station. Amazing how many things could go wrong in so short a span of time.

And so right. He glanced back over his shoulder. Serri. He drew a quick breath. "Any noise, hit the deck. Understand?"

She nodded, though he doubted she'd comply. He soft-footed across the corridor, Serri at his back. He hesitated in the hatchway for Cargo Four, then, with a sharp wave of his hand to Serri, moved again. Ten, fifteen strides, watching back and front. Closer now, he heard sounds. Hard sounds but definitely voices.

Which meant the hatchway to Cargo Two was open.

Which meant Serri's hibernation ploy wouldn't work. Oh, the cold would slow the Breffan down. But he wouldn't be woozy on his feet and Nic wanted him woozy. Multilimbed Breffans had an obvious advantage in a firefight.

A sharp clank, like the top of a metal container slamming down, echoed. Nic hesitated.

"No more time," a voice boomed. Filar's. "We have not seen anything of value. Your ship—"

"A few more moments, Your Esteemedness." That was Quin, definitely. "If I can't find the matched set of thirty-ninth century Nonga vases—which I swear are in here somewhere—then I know I can find . . . Yes, here they are! Look!"

"Now," Serri whispered urgently, but Nic was already moving forward. Quin was Skoggi so Quin knew they were there. And if he had Filar peering inside a cargo container, this was going to be the best— and possibly only—chance they'd get to make a surprise entrance.

Nic charged through the open hatchway, adrenaline spiking, pistol primed and ready as he took in the location of everyone and everything in the hold. Quin—hunkered down on a low set of servostairs to the right of a very large open cargo container. The orange-freckled Breffan guard on the left, on tiptoe, half leaning over the edge. In the middle were enormous buttocks draped in purple diaphanous trousers that ended in three booted feet firmly planted on the top of a second set of servostairs.

The Breffan jerked back from the edge of the container, eyes wide, one arm rising, but the rapidly chilling air made his movements sluggish.

"Freeze!" Nic bellowed, wishing it actually was freezing in the hold. "Or your boss won't be sitting anytime soon."

"It's not like you could miss," Serri intoned on his left.

A loud wheeze vibrated in the container as the purple trousers wriggled and Filar struggled to right himself. "We demand to know—"

Filar's words ended in a shout of surprise as the servostairs under his feet collapsed. Nic caught lights flashings on Quin's CI vest and a quick twitch of whiskers as Filar, legs flailing, pitched headfirst into the container.

"Your Esteemedness!" The Breffan angled one arm over the edge.

"Don't move." Serri took a few steps closer, pistol grasped securely in both hands.

"If he's hurt—"

"Piffle. It's mostly quilts and draperies in there," Quin said. "A short kip would do him good."

A roar of unintelligible Nalshinian served as Filar's contribution to the conversation.

Quin clambered down the stairs, tail flicking.

"On your knees." Nic aimed his pistol at the guard's head. "Then on your stomach, arms out."

"You're crazy," the Breffan said, switching a threatening look between Nic and Serri.

"And you and your boss are in a shitload of trouble," Nic continued. "Down. Now."

The Breffan charged, a hulking multiarmed form, one hand snagging Serri's arm. She stumbled but there was no clear shot—and no choice. Nic fired his stunner. The guard fell, taking Serri with him, arms and legs tangled, thrashing.

"Serri!" Nic's heart felt as if it were in his throat. He grabbed a handful of red fabric and yanked the Breffan backward. The guard rolled on the decking with a soft gurgle and flailing of limp arms.

"Shit." Serri angled up on one elbow, coughing, as Nic holstered his pistol. He dropped to his knees by her side. "Guess he played Scout-and-Snipe too. 'Guard takes agent as hostage' is level seven, Crystal Flame."

And in level seven, the hostage often died. But Nic didn't give a damn about sim-games right now. "You all right?"

"I'll have some interesting bruises tomorrow." She swung her legs around, but Nic had her arms, lifting her easily. He wanted to hold her tightly against him so that he could feel her heartbeat.

"Nic, eighteen minutes."

He released her with undisguised reluctance. "Bridge. Get moving. Quin and I will be right behind you."

She holstered her pistol and darted out into the corridor. As her boot-steps faded, Nic pulled handcuffs from his belt and secured the Breffan's upper arms. Quin trotted over with a packing strap to bind the lower ones. Nic pulled two pistols and a laserblade from the guard's weapons belt, stuffing them into his own.

Thumping, thudding, and wheezing noises sounded from inside the large container. Filar, jumping, but unable to reach the top.

"A cargo net should keep him secure." A small light flashed on Quin's vest. A grinding noise from above heralded a suspended sheet of metallic mesh dropping over the container.

And the chill temperatures would keep the cuffed Breffan from waking too soon.

The ship rumbled under Nic's boots. Serri, bringing the engines online. Quin bounded for the corridor. Nic followed, keeping pace.

"So. You intend to tell her?" Quin asked as they neared the ladder-way to the bridge deck.

Nic slowed. "Tell . . . ?"

"A heartfelt, Talligar. She needs to know. Unless you want to wait another six years."

He shot a suspicious glance at Quin. Mind reader? Maybe Nic wasn't the only one with voices in his head. "I don't think she wants to know."

"Piffle." Quin leaped up the stairs two at a time, leaving Nic wondering—and running to keep up.

Quin was already at communications when Nic slipped into the seat at the nav console. The Skoggi's CI vest blinked rapidly, sending and receiving commands. Noisy chatter sounded in spurts from the speakers, mostly perfunctory warnings from station traffic control. Then Quin pulled on a headset and the voices quieted.

"Strap in," Serri called out over her shoulder. "This is going to be rough."

Through the forward viewports, lights flashed. The bay doors parted, revealing blackness dotted with lights from other ships. Somewhere out there was the agency's stealth ship. It would be so easy to contact it for assistance.

And he'd spend the rest of his career chained to a desk—in the remotest sector in the Dalvarr System, where no sane sentient would ever want to be.

"Quin, broadcast an emergency get-clear on the freighter channels," Serri was saying without turning from her console. "We need to get as far away as we can in ten minutes. I don't want to plow through anyone in the process."

"Sending," Quin said.

Nic did a quick mental calculation as Quin's vest flickered. "Will we be out of range of the cannons in ten minutes?"

"It'll be close." Serri fired the lifting thrusters. The ship vibrated. Plumes of dust and debris swirled past the viewscreens.

Close could be fatal, and Nic again damned the fact that his hands were tied by his undercover status. It looked as if this plan could fail as miserably as the one six years ago that was meant to keep Serri in his life.

"We could always tell the chuffers that Filar's onboard. Without mentioning you, of course," Quin added, with a quick nod to Nic.

"Then we'd be dealing with pursuit craft," Serri pointed out. "I'd rather take my chance dodging the cannons. They have a finite range."

Serri redirected the thrusters, easing the freighter out of the bay. Nic silently lauded Serri's skill as she wove her way around bulky tankers that didn't have the *Pandea*'s maneuverability.

Then three shrill bleats erupted from her console.

"Short range. Incoming." Her voice was tense. "Not cannons. Security drones. Could be standard procedure," she continued. "Or they're realizing that the cannons don't work and this is their second-best."

Nic hoped that was it. Unmanned security drones weren't difficult to evade with someone of Serri's expertise at the controls. Plus, drone's lasers had limited range.

"Increasing aft shields to counter," Serri said.

"Those chuffers at traffic control are getting quite vitriolic." Quin sounded amused.

The *Pandea* shuddered. Another alarm trilled. Serri slapped the disconnect as she checked ship's status. "Drone just bit us in the ass. Shields are holding."

She had the ship dodging and darting, trying to avoid any more hits from the drones, but they were persistent.

"Shield down to seventy-two percent. Three minutes to outer beacon."

Suddenly the bridge filled with a rapid high-pitched series of tones. "Shit!" Serri's fingers moved with new intensity over her console. "Targeting sensor warning. They've got a lock on us. It's the cannons."

Nic's heart hammered against his ribs. They'd misjudged or someone had overridden Serri's program. Why and how no longer mattered. Staying alive did.

"Hang on." Serri dropped the freighter into a roll and, after that, into a curving dive. Nic could feel artificial gravity straining to maintain stability; little pockets of weightlessness making his ass rise off the seat as the shields' power draw drained ship's systems.

Serri's screens—and the wailing of alarms—confirmed two near-misses but the second was close enough to damage the shields. "Shields down to sixty-one percent."

"Quin, patch me in to the comm," Nic said suddenly, angling the console's mic toward him.

Serri shot him a quick glance. "You tell them Filar's onboard, they're going to send pursuit ships. I can't outrun those and avoid the cannons."

"They won't send ships when I tell them he's in DIA custody."

"But you said your mission—"

"Screw the mission." He meant that. This was about choices—and not just life-and-death ones. He made his. "Quin, patch me in."

"Mic and speakers are live," Quin said.

"Jabo Station, hold fire. This is Special Agent Nicandro Talligar, Dalvarr Intelligence Agency, onboard the *Star of Pandea*. Cease fire or we'll put your station under full lockdown."

"Talligar, this is Jabo. We have no proof—"

Nic was already working the console. "Transmitting identification now."

His console clicked and beeped. His heart pounded. He could hear Quin breathing heavily, and though she tried to hide it by dropping her hand into her lap, he could see Serri's fist clench.

"Talligar, this is Jabo. Ident confirmed. We're holding fire. However, we should have been informed of your presence and any investigation."

"You can take it up with the agency. In the meantime, be advised that I have your stationmaster, Gop Filar, onboard and under arrest. A DIA enforcement ship is at your outer beacon and will counter any moves against this ship. Talligar out."

The alarms cut off in mid-wail. Jabo had stopped firing. Nic leaned back in his seat and scrubbed at his face with his hands. When he opened his eyes, Serri had swiveled her seat partway around and was looking at him.

"You're going to be in real trouble over this, aren't you?"

"Yeah," he said, and flexed his left wrist. Time to talk to those voices in his head again. They were not going to be happy.

SERRI SWIVELED THE high-backed chair around in the ready room, very glad that the room was now empty. She hadn't been through a debriefing since she left Widestar, but that had been the corporate version. The DIA version was frightening—almost as frightening as their shadowy stealth ship.

She swiveled back. The room's viewports were small. She couldn't tell where she was—disconcerting for a pilot. But she knew they were headed back to Jabo Station with the *Pandea* in tow. She and Quin had permission to retrieve their cargo—minus whatever tracking gizmos the DIA had added—and deliver the forty-seven cartons to the winery. And get the rest of their payment.

She should be overjoyed. She wasn't. Nic was in trouble. More than trouble—he'd sacrificed his career for them. For *her*.

A soft chime signaled the door behind her opening. She swiveled again, expecting Quin, who'd gone in search of some meat tea for himself and coffee for her.

She saw Nic instead, hands shoved in pants pockets, mouth grim.

Her heart sank. But at least they hadn't locked him in the brig. Yet. She rose. "I told them you saved our lives. But they"—she waved her hand toward the empty chairs as if the DIA officers were still there—"didn't seem to care. There must be someone else I can talk to. Someone higher up. I'll do anything I can, Nic. Just tell me what you need me to do. I'll do it."

He stepped up to her as the door closed behind him. "I need your ship. And I need you to lose your cargo again."

"You what?"

"Jonas had Filar pulling cargo forfeitures so that when he hired Quin and sent him to Jabo, the *Pandea*'s 'accident' wouldn't stand out. But Filar had no idea that Jonas's plans involved murder. That's why he's cooperating so willingly with DIA interrogators right now."

"But the station's cannons—"

"Have never destroyed a ship. They're set to disable, and the drones tow you back in."

"Then how was Rez going to kill Quin?"

"There was a bomb in one of the containers Filar was supposed to leave onboard, but, Filar being Filar and being greedy, took them all. Jabo Station just informed us that one of the Bruisers found it while taking inventory. The bomb was set to detonate while you were trying to get a loan. Evidently Jonas never meant to kill you."

Serri collapsed back into the chair. She realized her mouth was hanging open. She closed it. "But why do you need the *Pandea*?" They had Filar and his confession. They'd probably have Rez Jonas in custody very soon. The DIA was not something you could easily run from.

"Because someone's still pulling cargo thefts on other stations and in some dirtside ports. We thought that Jabo Station was part of that larger crime ring. It's not. So we need to do this all over again, but *this* time"—he eased down into the chair next to her and clasped his hands together, on his knees—"we don't want to lie to the ship or her captain. It's not worth the risk."

"Quin—"

"Is calling it a 'grand adventure.' The director hasn't been able to get more than a few words in edgewise."

"So you're not in trouble?"

Nic sighed. "Oh, I'm in deep trouble." He splayed his hands. "The director, though, is willing to—eventually—forgive me. But you're the one I'm really worried about. You're the one who really matters."

"Nic, I—"

"Serri." He folded her hands in his, and she was surprised by how badly she needed his touch right now. "I made a huge mistake six years ago. I kept silent when I shouldn't have, believing it was the right thing to do. And I almost made that same mistake again." He shook his head. "I knew Jonas was cheating on you. But I was afraid that if I told you what was going on, you'd reconcile, because Jonas could always talk his way out of anything before. I needed for it to get to the point where you wouldn't take him back. Ever. I just waited too long. Because by the time that happened, you hated me as much as you hated him. And I'd lost the chance to tell you how much you mean to me, how much I love you."

Shock, confusion—and hope—swirled through Serri. "You . . . were in love with me?"

A wistful smile played over his mouth. "Still am."

"But . . . we were friends."

"I hope we still are."

"Nic—"

"Tell me it's impossible, that there can never be anything between us, and I'll go away. I'll get the director to assign another agent to the *Pandea*. But if it's not impossible, I'd like that chance I wanted, and lost, six years ago." His fingers tightened on hers.

Shock and confusion dissolved. There was only hope. And there was Nic. Her best friend. A man she could trust. A man she could love.

"Are you applying for the position as the captain's lover, Special Agent Talligar?"

"I am."

She leaned forward until their lips almost touched. "You're hired."

Mary Jo Putney

New York Times *and* Wall Street Journal *bestseller Mary Jo Putney is a graduate of Syracuse University with degrees in eighteenth-century literature and industrial design. She is the author of thirty-six books of historical romance and fantasy romance, including* A Distant Magic, The Spiral Path, Dancing on the Wind, The Rake and the Reformer, Silk and Shadows, Lady of Fortune, *and many others. She has won numerous awards for her writing, including two RITAs for best novel, four consecutive Golden Leaf Awards for best historical romance, and the* Romantic Times Career Achievement Award. *Her most recent books are* Loving a Lost Lord *and* Never Less Than a Lady.

Here she conjures up a deadly confrontation with a creature so seductive that it's almost impossible to resist. But one that you'd better resist, if you want to stay alive!

The Demon Dancer

I studied the homeless man's corpse. He was the fifth I'd seen this day. Ragged clothes so dirty they'd clog a washing machine. A battered and long out-of-date Tennessee driver's license giving the poor sod's name and age. And a great big smile on his lined face.

My partner, Jamal Johnson, shook his head. "I can't believe how all these guys died smiling, Dave. I suppose it's some new street drug."

"Maybe," I said, but I didn't believe it. Besides being a New York City detective, I'm a Guardian, from a family that has the kind of powers that used to be called magic. Witch burnings a few centuries back persuaded Guardians to live under the radar. Most of us lead normal lives, gravitating to work that suited our magical talents.

Me, I'm a Guardian hunter. I'm very, very good at tracking people down, especially criminals. Equally good at dealing with them after I found them. Not surprising that I ended up a cop.

My boss is a hardass New Yorker who would scoff at the very idea of magic, but he's learned to send me out to the weird deaths, like this one. Five smiling corpses. No signs of violence.

It could just be coincidence—street people aren't the healthiest cohort—but my Guardian instincts were screaming. "Have you noticed that they've been getting younger? The first guy must have been in his seventies. Each has been a few years younger than the one before. This poor devil is in his late fifties."

Jamal considered. He's no Guardian, but he's a damned good cop. "Probably coincidence, but if some dealer has been going around handing out high-dose samples, they might be taking out the weak more quickly."

"It will be interesting to see the tox report." I checked my watch. It was midevening, and technically I should have been off duty two hours ago. Maybe after we cleared up this scene, Jamal and I could grab some Tex-Mex at the restaurant down the block.

I was about to get back to work when a very, very bad feeling struck me. The kind where you drop everything and *run*.

I didn't quite do that, but I said, "Jamal, I have to be somewhere else ASAP. Can you wrap up here and get a ride back to the station with one of the uniforms?"

He gave me a quizzical glance, but said only, "Sure. See you tomorrow."

We've been partners a long time. No need to explain things. I pivoted and headed for my car, wondering what could have set off such loud alarm bells.

I PARKED RIGHT in front of my East Side destination—a Guardian talent that's useful in New York is being able to find parking when needed— then took the steps of the neat brownstone three at a time. I felt as antsy as if I were the only one who could save a room full of kindergartners from certain death. Instead, I was responding to the silent distress of Bethany Sterling, one of my favorite people in the world.

Bethany swung the door to her apartment open before I could knock. No surprise there since she's also a Guardian. She looked her normal self—petite and straight-backed despite her years, her silver hair pulled into an elegant twist. But her deep-set blue eyes showed the anxiety that had brought me running.

Giving thanks that she seemed all right, I asked, "Lady Beth, what's wrong?"

She smiled wryly as she stood back and ushered me in. "Apparently I wasn't shielding my worries as well as I thought. You always could read me better than anyone else." She closed the door behind me. "You're worried, too. Tell me about it while I make a nice pot of tea."

Briefly I described the dead street people while Bethany filled her electric kettle. It's one of the British types that serious tea drinkers use because it heats water to boiling in seconds. After pushing the on button, she stood on tiptoe for the tin of my favorite Darjeeling tea. I reached over her head to take it from the shelf.

She isn't a lady in the sense of an English title, but she was named for an ancestor called Lady Bethany Fox, so my brother, Charlie, and I like to call her Lady Beth. Not only was she English born, but the title suited her classy nature.

She warmed the teapot, then added tea leaves and poured boiling water on them. "I suspect our worries are related, David. Early this morning I sensed a strange, menacing energy sweeping into the city, and it's getting stronger. Something is very wrong."

"And I have the corpses to prove it. Any idea what the cause might be?"

She set out two teacups and produced a cookie jar filled with her rich, crumbly scones. As she set them on a dainty china plate, she said, "I think a demon has come to New York."

I experienced a moment of severe cognitive dissonance at the contrast between the sweet silver-haired widow and the words she'd just said. But though Bethany Sterling was indeed sweet, she was a Guardian hunter like me, with special abilities to track the ungodly and enforce justice.

I glanced across the kitchen at the old photo that hung over the neat computer table. It showed a young Bethany dressed in parachute gear early in World War II. She'd trained as a secret agent and parachuted behind Nazi lines in France, single-handedly freed a jail full of Maquis, and done a lot of other heroic things.

But she hadn't managed the rescue that mattered most—her equally young husband had been a Guardian healer, like my brother, Charlie, and he died in a prisoner-of-war camp, treating fellow prisoners right up to the end.

So Bethany Malmain Sterling was one formidable woman even at her present advanced age, though she refused to divulge the actual number of her years. She'd also, in her youth, been one very hot babe, with cool blond hair and dangerous blue eyes. I wish I'd known her then. But I'm damned lucky to know her now.

"A demon," I repeated. "This is new? The city has plenty of them, starting on Wall Street."

"This isn't a joke, David," she said with mild reproof. "The—entity—is no metaphor, but a malicious noncorporeal being. A demon that feeds on human energy. Have all the victims been male?" When I nodded, she said, "So it's a succubus."

"A succubus," I repeated. "Ooooo-kay. At least that would explain why the men were smiling."

She judged that the tea had steeped long enough and poured the steaming liquid into the mugs. Then, knowing me, she added a dollop of rare and expensive Highland single malt to my tea. "There are worse ways to die, but I imagine that most of the creature's victims would prefer to live."

I took a long, appreciative swig of tea and whiskey. "Is there any way to get rid of this demon, or will it keep feeding indefinitely?"

"I don't know. I was about to do a search on magematrix.net when you thundered in here."

"Good idea." I took my mug and the plate of scones and followed her to her desk.

She opened her laptop and used her fingerprint ID to enter magematrix.net. The site is a very, very private database and social network for Guardians, who are spread all over the world these days. I don't think there is a better source of information on magic and impossible events anywhere—though I'm not sure. Any equivalent stash of knowledge would be just as secret.

Lady Beth typed "succubus" into the search engine, then scrolled through the results. "Not a very large entry," she murmured. "Some of this data goes back centuries."

I peered over her shoulder to read. The oldest entries had been translated into modern English, with links to the original text if someone wanted to consult that. "So these demons steal human life force through dream sex until they become powerful enough to acquire physical bodies."

She clicked through to a section of original text. "This seventeenth-century report claims that sex demons are escapees from hell. They long to acquire human bodies because that makes the pleasure of their wickedness so much more powerful."

"How do we get rid of this one?"

"A sufficiently powerful mage might be able to dismiss a sex demon from the body it's taken over, but there are no details." Bethany started clicking links at the bottom of the page to see if they led anywhere interesting.

"So maybe we could do an exorcism, if we knew how. This is beginning to sound like a low-rent horror film."

"Truth is stranger than fiction," she murmured. "The earliest account says that when the demon is dismissed from the body it inhabits, it's sucked down to hell forever."

"No way of checking that part, of course."

Lady Beth leaned back in her computer chair and eyed the computer thoughtfully. "Our ancestors were happy to assume that demons came from hell, but today we want different explanations. These beings are quite rare. Are they space aliens? From another dimension that lies alongside this one? Or have we been watching too much *Star Trek*?"

"Probably," I said pragmatically. "A parallel dimension is just as much jargon as saying that these critters are from hell. Let's bag this one before we worry about tagging it."

Her silver brows arched. "Time to scout out the demon?"

"The sooner the better," I agreed.

Bethany nodded and swiveled her chair to face me so we could hold hands. We always did this for particularly difficult cases. As I touched her thin, slightly arthritic fingers with mine, I felt energy spark between us. It's been amazing to work with Lady Beth. Certain Guardian talents follow gender, and most hunters are male. But Bethany could hunt with the best of us.

I closed my eyes and visualized a map of the city. The mental image was like an aerial photo, enhanced by my own experience of many of those streets. When I had visited the scenes of the suspicious deaths, I'd picked up traces of disturbing energy, and with Bethany's help, that came sharply into focus. "There's a nasty, twisted red energy spike not far away. Can you feel it?"

"That's our demon," Lady Beth said, all cool, focused hunter. "And she's become very powerful. Let me see if I can learn more . . ."

I felt my partner's energy stretch out as delicately as a budding flower—and faster than thought, her probe was seized like a swimmer chomped by a killer crocodile. Lady Beth tried to yank free, but the scarlet energy roared hungrily along the trail and stabbed into us like a lightning bolt. Bethany screamed and I blacked out, every cell in my body shocked, as if I were being electrocuted.

I regained awareness to find that we'd both been blasted to the floor. Bethany lay beside me, her face paper white and blood splashed around her. "Lady Beth!"

As I scrambled up, I saw that the blood was pouring from a vicious slash in her left arm. I grabbed a tea towel and turned it into an impromptu tourniquet. At the same time, I gave a furious mental shout. *"Charlie!"*

My younger brother, Charlie, is my best friend, except for Lady Beth. He's also the most powerful Guardian healer in New York, and he works as an ER resident in a hospital only a few blocks away.

My mind touched his and I felt his fatigue. He was just leaving work after a twenty-four-hour shift, and more than ready to get home to his apartment and his gorgeous Guardian fiancée. But he came alert when we connected. Sensing his question, I shot back, *"Lady Beth, her place. She's hurt bad!"*

It wasn't really telepathy, and not really words, but we knew each other so well that he understood the gist of it. *"On my way!"* echoed in my mind.

Most Guardians have at least a little healing power, and I'm no exception. I used what talent I had while desperately trying to staunch the flow of blood. Bethany was cold and shocky, and it looked like a sizable chunk of flesh had been torn out of her arm. Was the demon an eater of human flesh?

Her lashes fluttered up. She looked so damnably frail. "Don't worry, David," she whispered, her voice scarcely audible. "I've had a good life." It sounded perilously like dying words. "We've made a good team."

"Damn it, you can't die on me, Bethany Sterling," I swore. "Don't you *dare* die!"

Luckily, Charlie arrived then. Like me, he had a key to Bethany's house since we're the closest thing she has to family in New York. He'd brought a backpack of first aid supplies with him, but his first move was to drop to his knees by Lady Beth and put one hand on her wounded arm and the other on her forehead.

I could feel the healing energy like a tidal wave of white light. At first it was a struggle, light against dark. I sensed the moment when his healing drove off the shadow of death. He gave a ragged sigh and sat back on his heels as he reached for his backpack. "What happened?"

I gave him a quick rundown of the situation while he cleaned and bandaged the wound. "Nasty," he said. "We're lucky Lady Beth is still with us. I want to check her into the hospital overnight at least. At her age, this is a dangerous injury."

"Nonsense, Charles," Bethany said in a surprisingly strong voice. "Hospitals make me ill. I'll stay here, thank you very much. A cup of tea will fix me up quite nicely."

I put an arm around her shoulders to gently help her to a sitting position. Her bones were as delicate as a songbird's. "Maybe we should take you there, just in case."

There was nothing wrong with her willpower. She fixed my brother with a basilisk stare. "I'm in better shape than you, Charles. You saved my life, for which I'm suitably grateful, but you're so tired you're a menace to society until you get at least twelve hours' sleep. Now give me some nice drug to dull the pain and go home."

Unlike me, Charlie knows when argument is pointless. "Yes, ma'am," he said meekly. "But I want you to stay with her tonight, Dave. Just in case."

"Will do." Not that he needed to ask. No way would I leave Bethany alone after an attack by a demon.

Charlie zipped up his first aid gear. His scrubs were bloody, and not just from Lady Beth's injury. Wearily he got to his feet, almost falling. I caught his arm. "I'll call you a cab." He didn't argue about that, either.

I helped Bethany onto the sofa and refilled the electric teakettle. Since Charlie was gray with fatigue, I carried his backpack outside. "Thanks for coming," I said as we reached the sidewalk. "I've never been so scared in my life."

"Lady Beth won't be with us forever, Dave," my brother said quietly. "She's very old. If you hadn't bandaged her up and called me, we could have lost her tonight."

"I know," I said brusquely, not wanting to think of a world where there wasn't a Bethany Sterling to laugh with. I'd had my share of age-appropriate girlfriends, but none were as easy to be with as Lady Beth. Or as much fun. "But this wasn't her time."

"For which I'm glad. But her time can't be too far off."

I knew that, just as I knew that her inevitable death would devastate me. But pain was better than not caring.

A cab turned down the quiet residential street, and I raised an arm to flag it down. My Guardian abilities included summoning taxis as well as finding parking spots. When I need a cab, the nearest available cab will suddenly decide to turn my way. Clearly, I was born to be a New Yorker.

After sending Charlie home, I climbed the steps back to the brownstone. I'd make Bethany her tea, then roll out a sleeping bag in her bedroom so I'd know if she took a turn for the worse. It wouldn't be the first time I'd stayed here.

Lady Beth had not only recovered enough to make a pot of tea, but she'd also changed into a fancy black sweat suit with sequins scattered around the shoulders and long sleeves that covered her injured arm. It was a dressy version of the sweats she wore when we exercised together. A couple of times a week, we'd go to Battery Park at dawn, summer or winter. She'd walk along briskly while I ran, circling back regularly to catch up with her again. When we'd both had our fill of exercise, we'd grab bagels or croissants or a hot breakfast. Good times.

I frowned. "What are you up to, Bethany?"

I can make hardened drug dealers tremble with that frown, but she just said calmly, "We have to go after the demon tonight, David. The assault created a link between her and me. She is preparing to go out and feast on as many lives as she can claim before she's stopped."

"She almost killed you!" I exclaimed. "You're in no shape to go after a demon. Get some rest. I can find her without your help."

"You can find her, but I don't think you have the power to take her down on your own. Neither do I, but together—we have a chance." Bethany poured tea, this time without adding any single malt. "We must act quickly. If the entry on magematrix.net is correct, there will be many more deaths by morning, because killing is ecstasy for a sex demon who has taken on flesh."

I felt a cold chill, the kind that says something really bad was about to go down. "Do you think that stealing high-octane Guardian energy from us gave her what she needed to get a body?"

"I believe that's exactly what happened," Bethany said soberly. "Now she can cause tremendous carnage, and we're the only people who might be able to stop her."

In other words, duty called. Lady Beth was a fragile, precious old lady, and every instinct I have screamed to protect her. But she was as much a hunter as I am, and we were both sworn to stop evil whenever possible.

"Okay, we'll go get her." I pulled my gun from the shoulder holster and did a ritual check to be sure it was in firing condition. It always was. "Will regular bullets stop her? Silver bullets? Something else?"

"Her body is human and vulnerable. It's her mental power that is dangerous." Bethany bit her lip. "She will have acquired the body of a beautiful, desirable woman. You might have trouble bringing yourself to attack her."

My mouth hardened. I take no pleasure in the prospect of killing people, especially not a woman, but I'd do what was necessary. "Is there any way to drive her out of the body she's taken over so the original owner can regain possession?"

Bethany sighed, her years showing in the near translucence of her pale skin. "I simply don't know, David. All we can do is try."

I nodded. Regular criminals might be scumbags, but they were scummy in human ways. Metaphysical threats like succubi were largely unknown quantities. If either of us survived tonight, we'd have new information for the database on magematrix.net. The deep sense of dread I was feeling suggested that survival was a very open question.

I escorted Lady Beth outside to my car. As we belted ourselves in, I studied my companion's profile. She looked calm, relaxed.

She looked like a woman who was prepared to die.

Once again, I fought down the impulse to protect her. We were equals, and she had as much right to face danger as I did. The excitement of the hunt was beginning to rise in me, and from the brightness of her eyes, the same was true for my companion. We hunt because warrior skills are always needed, and we're careful how we use them. But there's nothing wrong with enjoying ourselves in the process.

I started the car, then closed my eyes to tune into the demon's exact location. "Brooklyn, right?"

"Right. Near the waterfront."

It was late, after midnight, and the streets were mostly empty. But the city pulsed with life still, crazy and exciting and unmistakably New York. My town, and I was sworn to protect the people in it.

We sped over the Brooklyn Bridge, city lights sparkling ahead and behind. I turned north when we reached Brooklyn and headed into a rundown waterfront area of old industry and warehouses. By the time we reached a looming warehouse that backed right up to the water, I knew our destination was a huge and infamous after-hours club. The place had been shut down repeatedly, only to reopen with a new name and what was officially new ownership.

The club's current incarnation was called Bizarro. At this hour on a weekend night, it would be packed with dancers, most of them young and high on drugs, alcohol, dancing, or all three. A fertile field for a monster who craved human life force.

My parking magic held. The streets around the warehouse were lined with the cars of clubbers, but one pulled away in front of the building just as I arrived. I glided to the curb.

The name Bizarro was a scrawl of red neon over a plain door flanked by two bouncers. The demon was inside—I could feel her. I glanced at Bethany, and she nodded confirmation.

Hoping it would all be over in a few minutes, I climbed from the car. After I helped Bethany out, I locked the doors and we headed to Bizarro's entrance. Bethany gestured with her right hand, and one bouncer took out a pack of cigarettes, while the other's bored gaze slid over us. Though magic couldn't make Guardians invisible, a good don't-look spell means that people tend not to notice us.

The pounding bass beat was audible even on the sidewalk, and when I opened the door, music exploded into a paralyzing bludgeon of sound. Even more overwhelming than the music was the fierce, sexually charged energy radiated by hundreds of intoxicated, gyrating young bodies. Instantly my mental shields clamped down to protect me from the intensity.

The black-painted entryway led into the vast, high-ceilinged club. As the floorboards vibrated underfoot, we moved to the edge of the dance area to study the crowd. The writhing mass of humanity looked surreal under coruscating lights of crimson, violet, and electric blue. Smoke of the illegal variety drifted toward the ceiling of the warehouse.

The don't-look spell was still in effect, and no one took any notice of us as we scanned the crowd. Somewhere in that bubbling stew of lust and feral hunger was the demon. It was hard to pin down her location in such psychic chaos.

Warily, I opened my senses to search. Even without Bethany's mental link, I could sense the demon growing ever more exhilarated as she fed off the massed energy of the other dancers. She was taking her time, savoring the slow buildup of lust, but soon she'd move on to the ultimate kick—consuming death energy. She would become a ravenous killing machine, sucking down young lives until we stopped her.

Where, *where* . . . ?

Bethany squeezed my hand and nodded to the left. *There.*

She was too short to see over the crowd, so she must have used her psychic link to the demon. I followed her gaze and spotted our quarry.

The creature was turned away from us, but that was enough to confirm that she'd acquired the body of a highly-desirable young woman. Waves of pale blond hair cascaded down her back, swaying to the beat of the music as she ground her pelvis against her partner. Her skimpy black dress looked sprayed on, and the skirt barely covered her lovely ass.

Her sensual gyrations were enough to arouse any straight man who saw her. I was no exception—but hunters are trained to control lust, at least until after the mission is accomplished.

I clamped down on my lower nature and studied the demon's dancing partner, a tall young man with dark floppy hair. Since I was running hot psychically, I had a swift flash of knowledge: he was Midwestern, a student in New York to interview at a grad school, and having the time of his life in the wicked big city. A lamb for the slaughter.

The succubus whispered something in her victim's ear. He nodded with dazed enthusiasm and wrapped an arm around her shoulders as they pivoted and headed toward an exit at the back of the ballroom. She was taking him outside for sex and death.

I beckoned for Bethany to follow me as I forced my way through the buffeting crowd of dancers. There were advantages to having played football in college. I moved fast, Bethany in my wake as I cleared a path. But the demon had a head start, and she vanished outside with her prey before I could catch up.

I reached the exit door maybe fifteen seconds after the happy couple. "Stay inside!" I ordered Bethany, knowing she'd be safer here.

She took my hand. I felt the surge of her power flowing between us, blending with my magical talent to create a force that was more than the sum of our individual abilities. "Don't touch the demon," she warned. "Her sexuality is a powerful weapon."

Touch always intensifies the transmission of power, as Lady Beth was proving now. Being male, I'd be particularly vulnerable to a succubus. "I'll be careful."

I strengthened my shields and opened the door. It led directly onto a cracked slab of concrete that covered the strip between the warehouse and a battered wharf that pointed across the East River to Manhattan. That opposite shore blazed with lights, the Big Apple in all her beckoning glamour.

In this shabby backwater, the only illumination came from a lamp behind an adjoining warehouse. Just enough light to reveal that the demon and her victim were locked in a feverish embrace, her hips grinding and one raised leg wrapped around his. His life force was surging into her like orange flame. Soon that flow of vital force would end, and the poor sod would be dead. With a smile on his face.

They were so engrossed that neither of them noticed me. I mentally reviewed what needed to be done, touching my pistol in its holster in case I had to draw quickly. I hoped a weapon wouldn't be needed, but it's always best to be prepared.

I took a deep breath, then stepped forward and grabbed the boy's shoulders to wrench him out of the demon's embrace. Though I didn't dare touch her skin to skin, I planted one booted foot against her shapely hip and shoved hard.

She lost her balance and pitched sideways, so I was able to separate the demon from her victim. Bethany was right, it was hard to strike a woman, even a demon.

The kid made a choked sound, then collapsed on the filthy concrete. His aura was weak but steady. Though he'd be dead tired for a few days from having so much vital force stolen, at least he wouldn't be dead.

But I had no time for a closer examination. The demon shrieked with fury at being deprived of her victim and swirled around, her glorious blond hair obscuring her face. As soon as she saw me, she hurled an energy blow that was the magical equivalent of a tactical nuke, arrowing the destructive power dead center at my heart. It almost flattened me.

Heart pounding and gasping for breath, I backpedaled fast, glad that Bethany's strength was combined with mine. Otherwise I'd have been a goner.

Wondering if I could drive the succubus away without killing the host body, I pulled out my Beretta and aimed it at her heart. "One step toward me and I shoot. I'd rather save your body so the original owner can regain possession. You've had your fun, and now it's time to go. Since you can't win, why not just depart quietly?"

The demon looked startled that I was still standing. Then she laughed with rich, sexy pleasure. "A tall, dark, and dangerous Guardian hunter! You're going to taste delicious, my lad! I'll have you for dinner, then your ancient friend for dessert. Usually I prefer young males, but Guardian energy is too rare to waste. When I have absorbed the life force of two hunters, I'll be unstoppable!"

Still laughing, she raised her hand and a sphere of mage light glowed in her palm, illuminating her with soft golden rays. I froze in my tracks.

I was aiming my gun at Bethany.

Not my beloved, silver-haired Lady Beth, who was safely inside the building, but a young, vibrant Bethany. She looked like her World War II photo, with cool blond hair and hot blue eyes, now updated to full color and twenty-first-century club clothes. She wasn't *my* Bethany, but she was still Bethany, despite her glittering destructive power.

Or was this an illusion spell? Could a succubus pluck an image from my mind and take on the form of my deepest, most secret fantasy?

She tossed her long blond hair back over her shoulders, then began strolling languidly toward me. Every curvy ounce of her was undulating in ways that stabbed directly into my lizard brain. It's a scientific fact that men lose intelligence when talking to attractive women, and a succubus is *designed* to drive men wild. No wonder they're so damned dangerous!

Lady Beth's sharp voice interrupted my near-trance. "David! Shoot her! She's not me; she's the demon we came to destroy!"

I should have known that no hunter would stay inside where it was safe when there was danger afoot. I struggled to pull the trigger. Yet, though I knew Lady Beth was right and I could feel her power enhancing mine, I could not make myself shoot, not even to save my life. Not even to save *her* life.

I felt the demon gathering power into a killing stroke, drawing magic to her like a tsunami. Waves of energy rippled through the darkness, most of it drawn from the people inside Bizarro.

She stretched a graceful hand toward me. My pistol fell from my numb fingers and clattered on the concrete. Despite my furious attempts to counter her power, I could no longer control my own body. My hand was lifting, reaching out toward my doom . . .

Lady Beth smashed my arm down and stepped between me and the demon. Catching the succubus's hand, she cried, "No!"

The fiercest magic I'd ever experienced exploded as Lady Beth slammed the torrent of demonic energy back at the succubus, adding the full force of her own vast and highly trained magical power. I was knocked backward, falling onto the cold concrete.

Horrified, I saw Lady Beth vanish in a blaze of annihilating power. One instant she was there, a silver-haired warrior of light. Then she was gone. *Gone!*

"Bethany!" I cried in anguish. I knew Charlie was right in saying she wouldn't be here forever, but I hadn't really expected to lose her *tonight.* I had thought that I would be able to save her at least, if not myself.

I had failed, and now she was utterly gone.

I wanted to howl to the heavens, but that was for later. Now I had a mission to complete. I collected my gun from where it had fallen and lurched to my feet.

The demon lay collapsed on the cracked concrete. Bitterly, I hoped she was dead, but the false Bethany's perfect breasts still rose and fell with her ragged breathing. It was damnably unfair that this creature still lived while my Lady Beth was gone!

I could remedy that. Not caring if I destroyed my career as a cop or was jailed for murder, I raised my gun.

Her eyes flickered and she whispered in a dazed voice, "What . . . what happened?'

It added to my anguish that her voice was a rich, youthful version of Lady Beth's crisp British accent. I said grimly, "You killed Lady Bethany, and I am about to send you back to hell."

Her disorientation cleared and she gasped, "David, don't shoot! The succubus is gone. I'm Bethany. The one you know."

I hesitated, wondering if the demon was enchanting me. The creature looked just like Bethany had when she was young, and the force of her sexuality was plenty strong enough to scramble my remaining wits.

"It's really me, David," she said with a shaky laugh. Cautiously the—woman? demon?—pushed herself to a sitting position. "Look at me with your inner vision."

Doing my damnedest to block my attraction, I scanned her. No sign of demonic energy, but maybe the succubus had the power to baffle even an experienced hunter. "How did you find a body that looks just like a young version of Lady Bethany?" I asked harshly, still unable to trust my senses.

"I . . . I'm not sure." She ran her hands over herself experimentally. "This doesn't seem like a strange body. It feels like me."

Watching her run her hands over her breasts and hips made my mouth go dry. "How do I know you aren't faking me out with an illusion spell?"

Her brows arched. "For heaven's sake, David, you're a hunter! Have I ever been able to fool you with an illusion?"

Her tartness was exactly like the Bethany I knew. Realizing that I was still clutching my pistol, I lowered it to point at the ground, but I didn't put the safety back on. "Lady Bethany couldn't fool me—but maybe a succubus could."

She gave a wry smile. "Perhaps, but with the demon gone, I'm sure the ability to scramble your wits with a glance is gone, too."

Unfortunately, it wasn't. Not wanting to admit how vulnerable I was to her, I sought an explanation. "The succubus attacked and ripped away a piece of Lady Beth's arm. Could this body be cloned from the DNA and matured in a such a brief time?"

She frowned. "That seems impossible, but I can't think of any more plausible explanation. I don't feel any lingering traces of a different human soul here. Or demonic energy, either. There's just . . . me. Feeling much as I did in my youth." Her gaze moved to my gun. "Are you going to let me stand without shooting me?"

"Go ahead." I stepped back. Though still doubtful, no way could I shoot if there was a chance this was the real Bethany.

She got unsteadily to her feet. "Did I imagine it, or was my old body consumed by the power involved in dismissing the demon?"

My lips tightened. "You didn't imagine it."

"It's . . . strange to think that the body I occupied for so many years is gone." She stared at the faint scorch mark where Lady Beth had been standing. "It was a good body."

"For a hunter to die fighting is a good death." But I still hadn't decided whether I was facing the real Bethany, or a very, very clever succubus who wasn't wearing anywhere near enough clothing.

"I wonder . . . am I actually dead and my spirit is just hanging out here for a bit before moving on?" She was shivering hard, no surprise given the cool night and her minimalist dress. Her fishnet stockings were torn and goose pimples showed on her arms and legs. "Or am I really me and properly installed in a healthy young body?"

"I have no idea." I pulled off my black trench coat and tossed it to her, careful to stay out of touching distance. "I'm better at field work than theory."

"Thank you." She pulled on the coat, which fell almost to the ground and could have wrapped twice around her. "How is the demon's victim doing?"

I drew a deep breath, relieved that most of her was covered. Made it a little easier to think. "I think he's okay, but I'll check."

Keeping a wary eye on her, I knelt by the college kid and spread my hand out on his chest. After a moment, I said, "No permanent harm done. He probably won't remember what happened when he wakes up, which is just as well."

"So we succeeded in tonight's mission, though the price was high." Her vivid blue eyes caught my gaze. "What will it take to convince you that I'm really Bethany, not a demon?"

"I don't know," I said bluntly. "When the big battle went down, I sensed the powers of the demon and Lady Bethany, but there was also an intense, alien energy I didn't recognize. What the hell was going on?"

She tied the belt of the trench coat around her slim waist with shaking fingers. "As I blocked the succubus's death magic and turned it back on her, I used a soul-transfer spell to exchange our spirits."

I thought back, trying to analyze the hurricane of power that had blasted us all. "So the unfamiliar magic was that spell?"

She nodded. "Very unusual energy, wasn't it?"

I frowned. "Where the hell did you find a soul-transfer spell?"

She bit her lower lip. Her full, lush lower lip. She'd have to drop a bag over her head not to be alluring, and maybe not even then. "While you were taking Charles downstairs for a taxi, I followed more links on the succubus page. One of them led to a very ancient spell that supposedly would switch souls between two different people."

I swore. "You tested an unknown spell in combat conditions? That's crazy dangerous!"

"I didn't have a lot of choice," she said mildly. "I was going to die anyhow. This way I had a chance of surviving."

Souls are eternal—every Guardian knows that. "I had the impression that Lady Beth had no fear of death."

"I didn't." Her gaze caught mine. "I had other reasons for wanting to live longer in a young body."

My heart began beating faster. "Why?"

"You know why, David," she said softly.

The allure she radiated was a fire in my blood despite her being covered with a trench coat from her chin to her ankles. Demon magic, or was it pure Bethany? "You need to be . . . more specific."

She drew a deep breath. "Ever since I met you ten years ago, when you were just out of the SEALs and paying a courtesy call on an old Guardian lady because your mother told you to, I've wished that I were a few decades younger."

"You never said or did anything to suggest that you felt that way." My throat was tight as my desire to believe warred with the fear that she was still a succubus and wickedly adept at convincing a man to believe in what he wanted to hear.

She smiled wryly. "It's . . . unseemly to be a lecherous old woman yearning for a man young enough to be my grandson. I was grateful that we became good friends. How could we possibly be anything more? Then this demon showed up wearing my body." Her voice hardened. "I thought she owed me something for that. Certainly she could not be allowed to stay in possession of it and use it to kill innocent young men."

If she was acting, it was a brilliant show that she was putting on. Knowing that I needed the courage to risk my emotions as she was doing, I said haltingly, "It's also unseemly for a man to be lusting after a sweet little old lady. So I didn't. But I've never met a woman whose mind and spirit fit mine as well as yours. If you're really Bethany, and not the cleverest damned demon in the universe!"

She'd been tense as the brick wall, but she eased into a smile. "I don't think that succubi are particularly clever. This one was all selfish hunger."

"Maybe she's clever enough to know what I haven't wanted to admit even to myself," I said slowly.

"If you can't be sure what I am by reading my energy, there's only one solution, David." She reached out a hand. "Touch me."

If she was still the succubus, one touch would probably turn me into mental mush, and her next meal. But there was no other way to find out.

I'd always been a risk taker. I took her hand, and energy flared between us like wildfire. Not succubus steal-my-soul-and-consume-my-life energy, though. This was ten years of caring and affection transmuting into fierce, true love. The woman I pulled into my arms was *my* Bethany, no doubts and questions, forever and ever, amen.

Our kiss wasn't the affectionate peck on the check that is exchanged between friends, but a hot, needy lover's kiss. "Bethany," I whispered when I could breathe again. "I never thought we could be together. Not this way."

"Nor did I." She laughed a little. "It's such a cliché to fall in love with a man who's tall, dark, and handsome. But as soon as you showed up on my doorstep, I was head over heels. Proof that age doesn't bring wisdom."

I smoothed back her silky hair, touching her as I'd never touched her before. "It's also a cliché to fall in love with a hot blond babe. The hard part was knowing that that babe was seventy years in the past."

"Not anymore." She rested her forehead against my cheek, her soft breath warming my throat. "I've always dreamed of a Guardian alchemical marriage. Two souls blended as one. I loved my first husband, but we didn't have that. I thought I'd missed my chance."

"Yet here we are." I kissed her forehead. Her vibrant young body was a little taller than her old one had been. "I think we were meant to be together, but we got the timing wrong."

"Time kept us apart—but the demon inadvertently gave us a chance to reset that timing." She slid an arm around my waist and gave me a shining smile. "Let's go home, David. I'm in a hurry for us to have some privacy."

So was I.

Tanith Lee

Tanith Lee is one of the best-known and most prolific of modern fanta-sists, with more than a hundred books to her credit, including (among many others) The Birthgrave, Drinking Sapphire Wine, Don't Bite the Sun, Night's Master, The Storm Lord, Sung in Shadow, Volkhavaar, Anackire, Night's Sorceries, Black Unicorn, Days of Grass, The Blood of Roses, Vivia, Reigning Cats and Dogs, When the Lights Go Out, Elephantasm, The Gods Are Thirsty, Cast a Bright Shadow, Here In Cold Hell, Faces Under Water, White as Snow, Mortal Suns, Death of the Day, Metallic Love, No Flame but Mine, Piratica: Being a Daring Tale of a Singular Girl's Adventure Upon the High Seas, *and a sequel to* Piratica, *called* Piratica II: Return to Parrot Island. *Her numerous short stories have been collected in* Red as Blood, Tamastara, The Gorgon and Other Beastly Tales, Dreams of Dark and Light, Nightshades, *and* Forests of the Night. *Her short story "The Gorgon" won her a World Fantasy Award in 1983, and her short story "Elle Est Trois (La Mort)" won her another World Fantasy Award in 1984. Her most recent books are the collected reprint of* The Secret Books of Paradys *and two new collections,* Tempting the Gods *and* Hunting the Shadows. *She lives with her husband in the south of England.*

It's said that each of us have one special person in the world that we are destined to love, and that to miss meeting that special person, to go through life without them, is perhaps the worst tragedy that can befall you. In the intricate, opulent, and lyrical story that follows, Lee shows us that if you miss your destined lover in one lifetime, it may just be possible to find them in another . . .

Under/Above the Water

1

GOING TO THE lake. Either in her head, or in the soft, hovering drone of the flybus, she heard this refrain, repeating over and over. *Going to the lake*—was someone singing it?

Zaeli refused to look around. All these people smiling at or talking to each other, or reading guide books, or gazing earnestly, hungrily, from the windows at the exquisite ghosts of ruins littered all over the tawny folds and featherings of landscape.

But all I can see—

All she can see behind her eyes, whether closed or open, is Angelo. All she can hear, apart from the tinnitus of the *Going to the lake* refrain, is his voice, dark and beautiful; what it said that evening four years ago, when they were, both of them, twenty-three years old. There in that far distant, ultramodern city that lay along the shores of that other lake. And then, of course, in sequence, she will see the other lake too, the first lake, glimmering in the darkness, and all the spiteful lights of the people hurriedly gathered there. How can it still stab into her like this? She must have reseen it, reheard it all so many times now, hundreds, thousands. Sometimes she also dreams it. The pain never ceases. It never can.

No one can help her. She is a fool to have listened to the relentlessly caring advice which, eventually, has brought her here, into such a different environment, across so many miles and through so much time. And tomorrow it will bring her to shores of the second lake, that lies waiting in those palace-scattered, ancient hills the colors of tobacco, sand, and turquoise.

THERE WAS A halt around midday at a picturesque roadhouse, a copy of palatial architecture done small, and perched on a high terrace. The view was spectacular.

Below lay forests now. The vastly tall and slender trees, with their smoky foliage, were alight with the fiery flickerings of indigenous parrots and *fonds-oiseaux*. At the horizon, the mountains had appeared, melting out of the blue-green sky.

Everyone kept saying how sensational it all was. And it was. There was a lot of discussion of legends, and questioning of the guides. That far-off peak, shaped rather like an uprisen serpent, was that Mt. Sirrimir, where the mythic Prince Naran had shot his arrows up into the third moon, killed it, and brought it crashing down—dead—onto the land?

And how long before they reached the lake to which they were going? Would they be there by sunset?

Naturally. Of course.

The Lake of Loss, that was its name.

Zaeli felt a sudden hot rage, perhaps fresh camouflage for the never-ending pain.

But she gave no outward sign. She leaned on the railing and gazed miles away over the trees. An intermittent upland wind lifted strands of her hair and blew it across her green eyes. The hair was coppery red. She brushed it away with her hand and the hair seemed alien to her, and then the hand did too, and when she rested it again on the rail it lay there, her hand, pale and slim, like a separate object she had set down, which could now scurry off on its own.

Going to the lake. It would not matter. It, like her hair and her hand, and herself, and everything, could mean nothing. She would simply have visited and seen a bit of water, and listened obediently to the local legends. And then she could catch the returning flybus and go back. Back to the place called home. Home, where the heart was not.

You see, I did what you suggested. Another lake. I tried my best.

"It will have done you good."

Yes, thank you, she would answer, politely.

Someone really was speaking to her now, and Zaeli glanced at them distractedly. It was time to move on. To the Lake of Loss.

THE BUS GLIDED smoothly out between the hills just as a crimson solar disc dropped among the mountains. The upper air turned purple, and beneath it, as if held in an enormous bowl, a purple mirror copied every shade and aspect of the sky. It showed how darkness came, too, with the rising on it of a pair of lavender moons, and the tidal star Sunev, pinned in the east like a boiling diamond.

Every person on the bus stared downward now into the mirror of the lake, as they crossed above it, and saw the spangle of their own lighted passing.

But that was all. Reflections, and night: surface. The depths were not revealed.

Staring also, Zaeli told herself that the lake was made only of solid glass. Nothing was below the surface. Nothing was in it. Neither living, nor dead.

WHEN THE GOLDEN bug cruised by above, heading toward the farther shore, the fisherman looked up at it a moment. Such vehicles made very little noise, and sometimes their lights enticed the fish to rise.

He doubted, this fisherman, that the passengers would notice him, or his little wooden insect of a boat, tucked in as they still were against the eastern beach. But soon the sail was up. Propelled by a night wind, the boat ghosted off through the water, breaking the mirrored star and moons with her silver net.

2

FROM THE HOTELS by the lakeshore came a loud and mingled noise. Many diverse musics played and many unmatched voices, human and mechanical, were raised. The multitude of windows and entrances glowed, sending twisted corkscrews of brightness down into the water, trailing away like glowworms into the hills. The largest remaining area of the ruined city stood up there. But it had left its markers too all down the shore, and all about the groups of elegant contemporary hotels, thousand-year-old columns rose, as well as broken stairs or walls or lattices. No hotel garden did not possess at least one fragment of the ruins.

Adjacently, ancient trees lifted. Lit lanterns delicately swayed in the low wind from the lake.

Zaeli had walked down to and then about a mile along the pebble-cluttered beach. At this time of year, the lake was tidal. Its ripples had lapped up as far as they would climb tonight. In an hour, perhaps, it would begin a melodious retreat.

Though lights still glinted at the water's edge, the hotel complex seemed a long way off. The omnipresence of the ruins had grown dominant.

Inevitably so. For once the greater part of the city had been here—*there*, down *there*, beneath the lake itself.

She had stayed in the hotel for dinner, and then a lecture on the legends of the city. The guides gave this, with the assistance of a recreationist docudrama shown on two wide screens.

Then the rest of the party, and the guides, went smugly off to the bar. *I don't belong with these others*, she had thought, *I never have or will*—Zaeli had found a door and stepped out into the night.

For a while, she stood at the water's brink. Overhead, all the stars had burst their shells. Blazing Sunev was now halfway over to the west, pulling at the lake as it went. One moon had hidden behind the other.

Something was moving, out on the water.

Zaeli looked to see what it was. A fishing boat, its sail now furled, a man rowing strongly in to shore. He was a local, obviously, and would not be like the efficient, and probably falsely friendly, staff who worked in the hotels. An indigenous man, oldish, yet toughened, wound in a tight-belted robe, his lower face swathed in the masking scarf that men affected here more often than women.

Zaeli decided that she had better leave the beach, go back to the hotel—her proper place, a sort of zoo built to contain the foreigners, where the local people could be amused by them but not have to put up with them too much.

Abruptly, she felt sullen. She had begun to feel a little better. Not happy, not secure, but less stifled out here, alone, listening to the pulse of the water. But now her mood had darkened again. She should go back—

But just then the boat, surprising her slightly with its abrupt fleetness, nosed in on the shingle. The man stood up and raised one hand in a traditionally courteous greeting. "Good evening," he said. He spoke Ameren, but almost everybody did, and it would be a facet of his courtesy to extend the foreign woman's language to her.

"Hello," she said. "Did you catch many fish?"

"None," he answered gravely. He had a deep and musical voice, well-pitched and calm.

"I'm sorry."

"Ah no," he said. And oddly, from the creasing movement of the scarf, she saw that he smiled. "I never even try now."

Zaeli said nothing. He was an eccentric, or he did not speak Ameren as well as he thought. Or she had misheard him.

But then, he drew up one end of the net his boat had trailed. It was empty. He told her, "I fish for other things. What the lake may give up from the world beneath."

He must mean the drowned city.

"Is it really there?" she asked. "The city?" How childish I sound. Presumably it was, or *something* was. And did everyone here believe the legend? How, when Prince Naran had cloven and brought down the third moon, waters under the earth had erupted to meet it, and, falling back, covered the metropolis, leaving only its outer suburbs along the hills above the water.

But the fisherman simply looked at her. He had dark eyes, blacker than the sky, they seemed. And she thought of Angelo. His face, his body, his life were entirely there before her, standing between her and the fisherman, and between her and all things. It was always worse when it came like this, the memory, the despair, after some brief and so very hard-won interval of respite.

The fisherman was watching her. He would not be blind to the alteration of her face. He might think she was ill, consigned to die in a few months, or that she had recently lost a child, or a parent, or a lover. That something loved beyond reason had, without reason, been wrenched away from her.

She said, "Well, I must go—"

And he spoke over her immediately. "Let me take you across the lake in my boat. There is a special spot where you can see down into the water, all the way to the city. I have seen it very often, and in the past I have sometimes shown others, visitors like yourself."

"No, thank you," she said. "I must—"

"That is up to you." And he made again a most respectful, almost a courtly, gesture, one now that indicated his departure, and turned to leave.

She thought. *He might take me out on the lake and drown me. Is that what I'm scared of? Or rape and drown me? What do I care? What does anything matter? Angelo won't come back out of the water, not this water, not the way he came back then. Not like that—*

"Wait!" she called.

The fisherman paused.

"How much should I pay you?" she said.

Then he turned again and the scarf creased again for his smile.

"No payment. I am rich. Please, the boat is ready. Let us go."

"BECAUSE OF THE star, do you see," he said, as they drifted over the water. "Sunev-la, who draws the tide. The star is only present for a month twice a year, but at those seasons the tide may flow strangely, near the center of the lake. Have they told you of this?"

"They told me the legend," she answered. She did not watch him, but gazed down into the black glass of the lake. She resisted the urge to trail her hand in the water. He did not row now, nor had he reset the sail. Somehow the water itself—or the tide, or the star—drew the boat forward. And therefore helped to retain for Zaeli the illusion that the fluid of the lake was solid glass—or polished obsidian—the ripples a fake. Impenetrable. She could swim, of course. But she had not done so since that evening long ago and far away.

He said, "One region of the city rises from the lake, that is the legend. Not all of the city, by no means. It is the palace of the king, they say, that rises. Did they tell you his name? He was called Zehrendir, and Naran was his brother. But there was no longer a bond between them, for they had quarreled over a woman. She was betrothed to Zehrendir but, or so the legend says, Naran stole her."

"Oh, yes," said Zaeli, absently.

She could see nothing in the water but darkness. And a faint reflection of her own paleness, and the pallor of the fisherman's clothing: two ghosts.

"When the moon fell, the waters covered the city, and Amba—this was her name, the woman both Naran and Zehrendir had wanted—knowing her deserted betrothed had drowned, concealed herself in a high cave of the mountains. There she stayed, and although a streamlet ran through the cave, she would drink none of it. She died of thirst, because the king had died of too much water. So they say."

Zaeli raised her eyes after all and stared at him. What was it in his voice? But the laval silver star was now behind his head, and she found it difficult to make out his already mostly hidden face.

For a bitter moment, tears pushed at her eyes, wanting to pour into them and through. But she had not been able to cry during the past four years, and could not now. Another kind of thirst, maybe.

Instead, words flowed out of her mouth and she listened in astonished shock as she told him, the unknown fisherman: "I was in love once, when I was young. He was . . . he used to be unhappy. I didn't—I never got to know him well—he scarcely saw me—I didn't know him well enough to know why he was so unhappy. He never allowed me near enough. But I think it was—as much in his mind as in his life. And one afternoon I met him in the dreary place where we both worked, and he started to talk to me, only I could barely hear him, and I had to keep asking him what he had said, and then he said 'I *hate them.*' And I said who—was it the people he worked with? And he said 'I hate my *friends.* I hate them. I hate my friends.' And then he walked away."

Her voice was low and intense. "They say you can't love someone you don't know. But you can. Oh, you can. I wondered if I was included in his hatred, but then, we had never even been friends. That evening I went to the lake—there was a lake there, too. I went because I had to go somewhere. I couldn't stop thinking of him or what he'd said—the sort of thing a child says, but he was twenty-three. And when I got to the beach it was getting dark and there were a lot of extra lights, and a medical vehicle. And he—his name was Angelo—was lying on the ground and they were trying to revive him. He had swum out and then—no, not suicide. He had a heart attack, they said, even though he was so young. Someone had seen and got him in to shore. But he died. He died on the beach in front of me. I saw him, just before they put him into the medicare. His eyes were open. They were dark as this lake, *this* one, not the one where he died. His eyes were darker—or less dark—than yours. I can't decide. Isn't that odd?"

Zaeli stopped talking, and after all lowered her hand into the water, which was wet and cold, and curiously electric.

She said quietly to the water, "My life was so restricted and dull. Only love made it worth anything, even though he never loved *me*, only *I* loved *him*. But it's no good, is it, to go on loving somebody dead? Not this way. Being *in* love with the dead. But it doesn't end. Love, I mean. Life . . . ends."

And then the fisherman said, as quietly as she, "Look now, just there. Look. And you'll see the palace shining under the lake."

3

LIKE A CLIFF of apricot marble, the great city stood on the plain.

On all sides, hills rose away from it, and to the west, the mountains towered into a sky that was, by day, the color of the iris of the eye in the fan of a peacock, and, by night, the color of that eye's purple pupil.

The hills, save where palaces and temples occupied them—the over-spill of the city with its gardens and planted forests—were bare. The mountains were arid. But the valley plain was rich with trees and shrubs, grasses and grains, fruits and flowers. Water courses coiled through the valley. They formed pools and tiny pleasure lakes, and fountains in glades.

To this idyllic spot, he had brought his bride-to-be.

He gave her a suite of rooms that ran the entire length of his palace, a complex and miniature palace itself, three floors in height and having, it was said, two hundred and seventy windows, each like a long dagger of purest glass. In the topmost floor of the suite was a private garden open to the sky. Vines, and the slenderest and lightest trees, that bore blue blossoms and golden fruits, surrounded an oval pool where swam blue and silver fish. Here in the evenings the king would visit his betrothed among her maidens, who were all deliriously charmed by him, for he was dark and handsome and gracious. The young woman who was to be his queen, how-ever, came from the paler races beyond the mountains. Her skin was light in tone, and her hair like the gem-resin for which they named her: amber.

Zehrendir the king was very fine, and so was she. They seemed made for each other by higher powers. And certainly, he found himself in love with her from the moment he saw her. But, naturally, Amba was already much included in the life of Zehrendir's court, and in that way she met often too with his half-brother, Naran. Naran was soon smit-ten by Amba. While she, who had looked at her intended husband with admiration and liking, but no particular passion, gradually became infatuated by Naran instead.

One night, all caution abandoned, these two, with a small company of Naran's followers, slipped out in disguise from the palace and the valley, and rode their chariots away across the hills toward the western mountain-wall.

Here then, Amba—who Naran had not stolen at all, or at least only her heart—lived as Naran's lover under the shelter of the serpent peak Sirrimir, which then had another appearance.

The story that Naran next shot down the third moon by means of arrows and sorcery and vast rage was quite untrue. He had no need to rage, only perhaps to feel guilt. And maybe he had never felt that either. Some alien unknown element caused the moon to crash on the world. Conceivably it was not a moon at all, but some awful voyager off its course, a meteorite or a comet or a piece of other debris from space. Yet strike it did. And then the waters upsurged, as do the waters of a pond when a stone is thrown into it, and drowned the city. But Amba never heard of this, nor Naran. For the mountains too were riven, and in the tumult, both he and she died.

BETWEEN THE LOSS of Amba and the deluge, there had been a space of time, quite long—or not long at all, perhaps merely seeming so to Zehrendir the king. During this intermission the city continued to bloom and prosper, and he himself went about his duties with faultless attention. He regularized laws, performed every ritual, he visited among his people and listened patiently to any who required either his help or his council, doing always his best. And the best of this king was, they said, much better than that of any other man. This was natural to him. He could not lose the knack, though he had lost everything else.

But not even the city, or its people, could comfort him, or make him happy.

Nothing could. One song which later passed into legends about him told how one day he had stood alone in some private room and said aloud to its walls: "My friends are gone." Amba had offered a sweet friendliness at least instead of her love, and until the day Naran met Amba, Naran also had been a true friend to Zehrendir—they were, in fact, his only real friends. It was not that Zehrendir had come to hate either of them, let alone the city he had created and which, till that time had been like his friend too, thrilling and heartening him with its loveliness. But all these friends were lost to him forever, Amba, Naran, the city also, because it had ceased to mean anything beyond sheer duty. It was as if all of them had died in a single night.

Was the flood then—the drowner, the toppler, the destroyer—to be his friend?

4

ONE DAY WAS left before the moonstrike would throw itself into the earth like a fist, sending up a column of blackness and fire. On this penultimate day, an old woman was brought into the court of Zehrendir.

About the fabulous audience chamber, where the king sat in a white chair, people were going up and down. Late sunlight sprinkled in jewelry clusters, and splashing the coats of six tame tigrelouves, it changed them to the color of Amba's hair . . .

The day's business for now was over. Zehrendir sat, apparently serene, as if deep in thought. *But all I hear—*

All he can hear is the echo of far-off hoofs and wheels retreating, and the single word "loss," whispered again and again. No one can soothe him. Nothing will ever alter his sadness. This appalling moment, which has already stretched into an eternity, will continue forever unabated.

One of the palace aides approached. Zehrendir dutifully raised his eyes. The man informed his king that a crone had wandered down into the valley. She had said she was gifted with certain magical abilities, and had a message for the king. Now Zehrendir turned his head, and saw an old woman who was as thin as a stick, and muffled from the crown of her head to her skinny feet in veils and scarves. Her eyes could not be seen at all. She looked like a corpse wrapped in garments for its burial or cremation.

Zehrendir had no wish to let her near him, but he felt compassion, for her feet, which, like her hands, were the only things visible of her. They were so old and filthy, and scarred all over, as if, all her days, she had walked barefoot on them across burning rocks, being struck by scorpions that had never quite killed her.

So he beckoned to her. "Good evening, Mother," said the king to her.

And then, even through the windings of her scarf, he thought he could see a pair of eyes that, despite her evident age, were bright and piercingly green, just as those of Amba had been. It shocked him, this. And he briefly believed that he had now lost his mind, in addition to all else. But of course, green eyes were not unknown, in the west. Had she walked here all that way?

The old woman nodded; perhaps she read his thoughts. After that, she spoke to him in the most inaudible of voices, which only he, he supposed, could hear.

"*Attend,*" was all she said. The aide had drawn aside, but Zehrendir was well aware that all the court were now always praying anxiously that some supernatural assistance would be sent to heal the king's dishonor and grief. And that too wounded him, since he wanted happiness for others. Even for Amba and Naran. And this perverse kindness, which he could not help any more than another man could have helped his fury and thirst for revenge, wore him out almost to the same degree as his pain.

The king said to the crone, "Let me ask them to bring you a chair. And some food and drink."

"My feet are my chairs," she answered crankily. "I feed on the air. I have nothing; therefore, I have everything. But you," she said, "have too much, and so are among the poorest in the world."

"No doubt you're quite right," said Zehrendir equably. And he smiled at her, as if she really were his old granny, the one that he had always liked best of his relatives.

When he did this, needless to say, the charm and innocence of his smile showed up, like a lightning flash, every gash that sorrow had carved into his young face. The crone studied this with vast concentration. It transpired that she could see him as no other could. Compared to his hurts, her blighted feet were nothing; they did not trouble themselves, or her. But he was in ribbons and could never mend.

"Attend," she said again.

Obediently, he waited.

"Lift your head, lord king, and see up there, in the roof above you, how that round mirror is positioned? Yes, exactly there."

She is insane, poor thing, he thought. *There's no mirror of any sort hung in the ceiling.*

But when he looked, he saw there was. It hung directly above him, like a huge drop of water in a bowl, but an upended bowl that did not spill. And as he gazed into it, noting that it seemed to reflect nothing, not even the westering light, it curiously grew quite black, like the blackest glass. Two or three ripples passed across its face.

And then its face held another face, a long distance away, not the king's face, nor the crone's—but still, it was one he knew very well.

"Mistakes are made," said the powdery voice of the crone. "Men and women intuitively look for those they expect to meet on the paths of existence. Sometimes there is no meeting at all. Or worse, *much* worse, a *mistaken* meeting. What can be done about these errors? Look up into the water. Look, and you will see your wife, gazing back at you from above the lake, which is yet to come."

5

As ZAELI DID as the man told her, as she gazed down into the water, she did not for an instant credit what he had said. Vaguely, it occurred to her that now was the preordained time when he would bash her over the head and then spring on her, or else simply sling her straight over the boat's side. He might have a lunatic theory that she would be a sacrifice to some lake demon. Or to the ghosts of the drowned king and his people.

But she did not really believe in his violence either. He seemed, rather, mystical, a mage from some uphill village. And he had said he was rich, said it with such modest proud indifference.

The tidal star Sunev, or Sunev-la as he had named it, was now descending between two mountains. Its sidelong light lingered in a vivid mercury trail, interrupted only by the boat's shadow.

Zaeli thought that the light of the star had dazzled her. Then she saw that the round mirror of gold that had appeared just beyond the vessel, there on the water's surface, was neither a reflection nor an afterimage. It was really there. It shone up into her face. And staring, suddenly she saw right through it, as if through a lamp-hung tunnel and a medley of luminous lattices and iridescent pillars and lacy, gilded branches, into a golden room.

In the room, which resembled a large golden cave, sat a man who had raised his face to look up at her. His head and shoulders were hooded about by a wave of blue-black hair. He was a man of incredible good-looks, but with strain and torment in his face. It seemed as if he had undergone some recent and unspeakable torture, soon to be repeated.

His image—so familiar and yet so utterly unlike anyone she had ever known—filled Zaeli with a sense of anguish, and of falling. Although she no longer feared being thrown out of the boat, she was sure that to fall down toward him would be both the most fearful depth and the most sublime apex of all chance.

He appeared, very definitely, to see her in turn. Could he see too that *she* saw *him*?

His eyes were darker than any night.

A whistling note, hardly audible, wavered through the silence. Perhaps it was only in her head. Or perhaps it was a song that tidal eruptive Sunev sang, as it vanished between the mountain peaks.

Zaeli was half aware she had risen to her feet. As she sprang weightlessly forward, kissed the water with her entire body, passed through its upper skin, paraphrasing the motion of the sinking star, she knew only that she was about to die. She was equally glad and mournful at such a mandatory solution.

PART TWO—HISTORY AS WATER

6

SHE WAS BORN again old, and lying on her back in a toffee-brown country under a peacock sky. The sun was just beyond its highest station. A black snake was coiled around her right ankle.

Some faint disturbance in the air gave her the peculiar idea that the life force of the body she now occupied had departed only seconds before her own arrival. The driver had left the driving seat. Now she, Zaeli, was in it.

She sat up cautiously. This body, not formerly her own, was an antique, stiff as warped wood.

None of that, not even the snake, upset her. She was not even surprised. A flood of memories also not her own quivered over the old mind's sky, like a flight of birds. Though she acknowledged them, she did not really need them, Zaeli thought. It was like glancing hurriedly at a map and list of directions that already she had been briefed on.

She got to her feet. At this, the limber snake uncoiled from her. It slid out of sight into a narrow seam in the ground, and Zaeli wondered if the animal was where the former driver of this human vehicle had taken herself. *The soul must be*, she perhaps foolishly thought, *delighted at such new, flexible freedom*. For with every step the thin and elderly human body took, it creaked and ached.

On these wrecked feet, she must walk down through the hills toward the city in the valley, and there address a king, showing to him some sorcerous mystery. She would know what to say only when she came into his presence. What must be revealed—and also what must be hidden.

The body of the old woman, dead of ordinary old age for a handful of minutes, then reanimated by Zaeli's consciousness, started gamely out upon this trek. Zaeli, it was already unfussily absorbing. Gentle as sleep, it soon tidied away her personality behind its own. It would tell her how to place the crablike feet for safety and speed, how to search recesses of the barren land for little wisps of sustenance or water. It would find her shade in which to rest. It knew the route and the rules, and all about the king. And, indeed, it knew the real story of Amba and Naran too, for one dusk many days before, *it* had watched them fly by in a blaze of chariots, cloaks, and amber-copper hair.

Nothing pursues or hunts the crone as she journeys, always descending, with the mountains at her back. Once a wild tigrelouve pads out on to the track. Then the crone, a talented magician in life, speaks to it a soft mantra. And, of course, speaks it in her own language, so in a way, Zaeli speaks it too. The tigrelouve responds by purring and rolling in the dust like a house cat.

If any of Zaeli's personal awareness remains—and surely there must be some atom left, however repressed—it, like the tigress, is subsumed. She is hypnotized.

So they walk as one to the city, drink from a well and pluck a fruit from a tree to refresh themselves, and go through gates of marble and bronze, and up an avenue paved with flat stones of thirty colors and guarded either side by rearing mythic beasts sculpted from basalt-souci. In a porch of the palace, the old woman confronts a guard, a servant, a steward. But the king's people have always had, at the king's behest, a liberal admittance policy. Without undue delay, an aide leads her through the late-afternoon halls, and so to the audience chamber. Here the tame tigresses pay her no attention. But the king says to her, in his dark and musical voice, "Good evening, Mother."

"Attend," she tells him. "I have nothing, therefore everything. You are among the poorest in the world."

"No doubt, quite right," he answers.

She sees his beauty with her own compassion, as an undead dead wisewoman will, she being already beyond life. And deep within, Zaeli stirs for an agitated instant, a butterfly in the web of her cocoon which will not, quite yet, release her.

But then the crone forms her magic mirror in the ceiling, up there amid the jewels.

And even the trapped butterfly of Zaeli notices her own previous young woman's face, that ten minutes—or ten months before, or a thousand years in the future—leaned or will lean down, to gaze into the waters of the Lake of Loss.

"It is Amba," says the king.

That is all he says.

The crone sighs. The body and memory and magical power, which are now are all she humanly is, have noted something else. A terrible catastrophe hangs above the city. And her sorcery knows that it is already too late to warn of it. There is no time left—she has been too long upon her journey. To empty the huge metropolis would be impossible; the panic and clamor would themselves slaughter in droves. And still the moon—or the meteorite or the comet or the piece of space debris—will crash down and the flood rise up. She does not even think they would believe her.

Only he is capable of believing her, the king, Zehrendir, and only in one way, since he has seen Amba's face looking in at him from the mirror.

How still Zehrendir sits in the white chair! He seems less outwardly collected now than static. His head stays tilted up, his eyes wide to meet the eyes of the one he had loved, and whom he had mistaken for one who would love him. It had not occurred to him she was no longer Amba and had never been, but instead was a woman from a future a hundred decades off in the history of the world, when he and his love and the falling moon and the flood are only dim, muddled legends.

The body of the crone steps jerkily forward. It is more of an automaton now, because the consciousness of Zaeli is returning quickly, beating and beating its wings to get through.

Like a sort of wooden puppet badly moved, the crone goes to the king and stares into the night of his eyes. Though young and strong, he is quite dead. She, of all things, can recognize the state.

She sadly speaks a single phrase. "My love," she says, still in the language of the city, "my Angelo."

Then the outer shell of her, physical flesh and bone, drops to the floor and lies there, still at last. Not for her the unstoppable cataclysm to come, nor for him. And for the doomed city, there will be one last night of peace—but even this is to be marred. For in another hour, they will learn that their king is dead.

THE FISHERMAN HAD watched the flying bug of the bus cruise by high overhead. Such transports did not make enough noise to disturb the fish. Their lights might even entice a catch to the surface.

He had doubted, this man, that the bus passengers would take any note of him. Soon after, he raised the sail, and the boat, propelled by the vital night breeze, ran along the water, trailing the silver net.

He was very old, the fisherman. Tough still, and never sick, but he had seen so much of life and time, and how they came and went away.

He could remember back before the foreigners first traveled here in any numbers, with their sugar-cake hotels and airborne buses. He did not mind them, but sometimes the thought of them tired him. He felt that tiredness tonight. It was not unpleasant. For a while he sat quietly, thinking of his wife, who had been dead now seven years. He missed her, and the son they had lost. But he had never supposed they would not, all three, meet again.

Above, the stars burned fierce as foreign neons, Sunev-la most of all. The moons were pale by comparison. He checked for fish, none had been tempted. His thoughts strayed to the legend of the shattered moon and the realm beneath the lake. He drifted asleep as he mulled the legends over, and in his sleep, without shock or pain, he died.

But his body lay there lifeless for only a few moments before a blade of phosphorescence seemed to sheer up out of the water. It flowed across the idle net. It sank into the body of the fisherman.

In that way, Zehrendir too was born again old, but he was born so under the peacock-purple of the night.

Like Zaeli, he found that to have an elderly body was a startling handicap. But Zehrendir was both a romantic and a pragmatist. He knew that he must utilize what lay to hand. Nor did he lose himself in the fisherman. The fisherman had not been any sort of mage, had not had that special talent and inclination. To inhabit his brain and absorb its memories and contents was an education rather than an obscuration of self.

Nevertheless, Zehrendir proceeded without haste. He tried out the new-old body for its fitness and acumen, and found how well it could reef the sail and employ the oars of the boat. Unlike the fisherman however, Zehrendir cut a hole in the net. He had accepted that he had been transferred into a place which, from the knowledge left behind in the fisherman's brain, he knew to be centuries into the future.

At some stage of rowing toward the western shore, Zehrendir also accepted the legendary remnants, which were all the fisherman had known, of the cataclysm. Then he ceased to row. It was both too dark on the lake, and too idiosyncratically lit by moons and tidal star, to see if he wept. But the boat meandered some while, and the fish swam in and out of the broken net, like blue and silver tears.

Eventually, hours on, with Zehrendir its motive force, the old man's body rowed in to the shore, where glints and splinters of hotel lights zigzagged on the star-pulled tide.

He had known where she would be, the woman whose face he had seen. He had known she would be here beside the lake. He knew she was not Amba—and knew that she was. She was the one that he had mistaken Amba for. Zehrendir, yet a king and a young man inside the swathing of the fisherman's flesh, felt a surge of ecstatic laughter at this divine and cosmic jest. There was no trepidation in him. It was rather as if a strangler's cord had been cut from his throat. He had rowed the last of the distance very fast, and the old arms ached and gnawed, but what did he care?

He let go the oars, and stood up, raising his hand in a traditional greeting which had stayed current through time. He spoke in Ameren, since the fisherman had had a good command of it. It was *her* language. "Good evening," he said.

"Hello," she said, like a sleepwalker. "Did you catch many fish?"

He knew that she had not yet seen him within the lake. Time had been bent to another's will, to the will of something frightening in its power—and yet benign.

"None," he replied, with the gravity of a riotous joy concealed.

"I'm sorry," she said.

Oh, my beloved, thought Zehrendir the king, *be sorry for nothing. For here you are before me, your hair like crimson copper and scarlet amber, your skin like ivory, your eyes the color of a leaf in rain. And somehow now—now you will be mine and I yours. Though I have no knowledge how, or why.*

Even her strange foreign dress did not concern him, let alone her youth contrasted to his present old age.

Even the gulf of history and deluge between them.

He showed her the empty net. For Zehrendir, it was all at once the symbol of an endless possibility. "I fish," he said, "for what the lake may give up from the world beneath." He did not understand quite what he meant by that. Or he did. For what the lake gave up was himself, and her too. And here the opened net of destiny had captured them both.

Not long after this, he sees her recognize him. Her face fills with such despair and hurt he knows it is her loss of him which has torn her to pieces, and now stands between them.

"Let me take you across the lake. . . . There is a spot where you can see all the way down to the city. I have seen it very often," he adds, glorying in the cunning of a lie which is also a truth, for truly he *has* seen the city, in his past.

Then she denies him. He respectfully turns away. This is flirtatious etiquette, like that of a dance. He is aware that she will instantly call him back, and she does.

"How much should I pay you?"

"I am rich," he tells her. He is. He has nothing now, and so has everything.

She enters the boat and he takes them out on to the mirror of the lake, the black-and-silver coffin-lid drawn over his world and under hers, and which must mean everything—and therefore, is nothing at all.

They are both by now distracted, abstracted, but they talk about the legend, and then she talks of the trauma in her own past, the past of this present time. As he attends to her, Zehrendir realizes very well what she has confessed to him. She, as he had done, had mistaken another for the one who would love her, the expected one: himself. But the mistake is over, and here and now are only they.

When the golden round of mirror evolves from the water, Zehrendir watches as she gazes into it. It corresponds to the moment, so long ago, when he had looked up and seen her looking back. When their eyes had met.

He does not attempt to bar her flight into the lake. They have already passed each other, in his time, now again in hers, she sinking like the star, he rising like the star, passing *through* each other, crossing between past and future, then and now, life and death, nullity and love.

As soon as she vanishes, which really does coincide exactly with the vanishing of Sunev between the mountains, the old man's body lapses back in the casket of the boat. Just as it had those hours earlier.

The vessel swings about mildly again for a while, then, guided by a wind visible only in its firm effect, skims off toward the eastern shore.

7

IN FACT, THE water felt only cool to her.

Which was lucky, as she had discovered herself far out in the lake and swimming strongly, if without any particular urgency. And all this in a sort of half darkness, even though dotted by indefinite lights.

Zaeli stopped swimming. She trod water, and looked around. She could not see the strident glare of the hotels. Above, only one moon loitered, low in the sky. The tidal star had also set; it had been setting, she recalled, when she dropped into the lake.

The currents of the water swirled and furled about her, not causing her any difficulty, more as if trying to persuade her to something . . .

What had she *meant* to do? To drown herself? Had she really meant to do that? But they said that, for a good swimmer, it was usually very difficult to drown. It took a lot of self-discipline, and exhaustion.

Zaeli did not feel even slightly tired. In fact, the lake seemed to refresh her.

Then she remembered the boat and the gracious old man, his mostly swathed face and extraordinary eyes. She was certain that he had not pushed or thrown her overboard. Yet he, and the boat, were gone. There was no trace of him.

Had she dreamed him, in some kind of trance, when first she began to swim out from land? Surely not. In her prison of despair, she had never dreamed such things, only of Angelo, his words, his death on the beach.

Very curiously too, Zaeli thought, she did *not* feel despair, not now. Despair had been her constant and only companion—where was it? It was almost annoying that it was gone.

The last moon turned to a dense purple and seemed to dissolve into the night.

Zaeli's memory flipped like a leaping fish. She saw the country below the lake: the brown hills, the tigress purring in the dust at her old and distorted feet; the groves and gardens, and the high gates of the palace. She saw herself as then she had been, clothed in the carapace of the old woman. And then the form of her lover, face and body, hair and eyes, a young king in that country, and she heard his voice, known to her, dark and beautiful—

A hill seemed to have risen, just then when she was not looking, over there across the lake. It was blacker than the sky and had blotted up the stars. But in a few moments, every star in the galaxies instead flamed out all through it.

Stupefied, she asked herself if this were the western shoreline, the neon lights of the hotels. But such ignorance passed.

He RECOGNIZED THE night.

In itself, this was a bizarre realization, for, after all, why *should* the night, which he had known since infancy, be *un*recognizable in the first place?

Yet it was as if he had come a vast way through alien landscapes and unaccustomed scenes, where the moons and stars, even the darkness itself, had other shapes and natures . . .

And now he knew at last where he was, and the sky and the dark were his familiar associates. Which too was quite at odds with the fact he still did not grasp what place it was where now he found himself.

The darkness grew, for the second moon was setting. The other two must already be down.

By starlight, then, he went on walking—it seemed he must—along the slope of a great hill, and glanced sometimes to his right at the huge, inchoately flickering body of water that lay below, and unfolded itself to the western horizon. He could just make out the mountains beyond. One of them was not as he remembered. It now resembled a serpent risen on its coils.

8Probably Zehrendir had walked for a couple of miles before he began to sense that the appalling pain of loss no longer dragged on him. Once a weight of lead, his heart was nearly weightless. And so he paused, and cast about in his thoughts after Amba, actually searching for the misery and hurt which were all she had left him of herself. They had become his familiars too, his constant companions. Where had they taken themselves? Then he saw again, in retrospect, an old woman who had said to him, "Attend." And a mirror floating through shadow to night, to show him the face of Amba. And after this, he beheld *himself* as a fisherman, clad in the body of the dead. And he played over in his mind the music of his meeting with the other woman, there on the farther shore. The woman who was not Amba, but *was* Amba. She for whom Amba had been, by him, mistaken.

Memory showed how she had slid into the lake and disappeared like the setting star. In his former time, that star had never existed, but here he had known and named it, just as he had come to know, and might have named, everything. He considered again the deluge, and the city. But he did not weep, not now.

Just then, from the hilltop, light blazed out like a funeral pyre, brighter than a sun.

Part-blinded, he stared at it. So many miracles had happened, one more was only a commonplace. In any event, the fire dimmed, and then faded altogether. Following which, there was left only the night to walk through, toward the summit of the hill.

ABOVE THE WATER, the night was hot. Zaeli shook her hair and kicked off her soaking shoes. Her clothes were torn, and clung to her.

The landmass was dark again now. It was not the mainland shore. Some island perhaps?

Something had risen in the east. It cast her shadow in front of her. At first, she took the glowing round for a belated flybus, but it was not moving. Its light guided her up the slope, and began to chalk in a phantom architecture above her. It was a ruin, large and complex, strung over with what must be a tangle of vines.

She thought, *He said, one region of the city rises from the lake—*

They were not vines but water weeds that roped through the colonnades, twisted in the lattices. A soft-water shell shone like a pearl in the corner of a glassless window slender as a dagger. A tall man stood on the other side.

FOR A WHILE, having reached the ruined building, Zehrendir paced about in it. A quiet, almost reverential tinkling and dripping of spent waters filled it. In spots, he identified features, still recognizable, that he had seen often: a statue of a maiden with an urn, an arch of elephs, an avenue where gold studs, green now as limes, had been set into the stone.

This palace was, or had been, his—long, long before.

When the third moon, tiny as the tidal star, had flown high in the east, he saw through a narrow window the figure of a woman, standing out on the hill.

8

SPENT WATERS TRICKLING and tinkling, and vines that are water weeds, and green gold, and substance passed into ruin, and a risen moon, lighting the way like a lamp.

Both of them, standing in the echoing hall, speak at once.

"You," she says.

"You," he says.

They hesitate. And attempt a second introduction.

"I—" she says.

"I—" he says.

Then they become silent again, and wait there with some yards of stone and iridescent shade between them.

Each knows the other completely. Returned into their own young bodies, the stress and marvel of this is terrifying. And since she has learned to speak his language, and he hers, he is speaking her language and she is speaking his language, even inside their heads.

Then he speaks to her in his own tongue, which she understands. She will answer him in hers, and he will understand that.

"You are not Amba. I know this."

"I'm not Amba. And you—are not Angelo."

"My name is Zehrendir."

"Zaeli," she says, "my name is Zaeli."

They look at each other, have never looked anywhere else.

The water trickles like silver, like history or time, trickles away through the stone fingers of the columns. The little moon burns like a gold mirror through the broken roof.

In its spotlight, he laughs suddenly. She knows his laugh, although never until now has she heard it. Which makes her laugh in turn. Her laugh is Amba's, it is the laugh Amba never gave him, and which now Zaeli does.

It is simple to cross the space. The moon is already doing it—*Look— it's easy—do you see?* They cross the space. Their hands touch. They swim together as if beneath deep water, until every surface of their flesh and hair, their lips, is magnetized to contact. They breathe each other like oxygen. They are each other's air and earth, water and fire. And some other element too, which is profoundly nameless. They are each other's world.

Endless slips of time and place. Their bodies lie together on carved beds clouded by silk, or on mattresses lying bare as a bone on a concrete floor. Or on velvet grasses, or on tussocky sands weaponed with shingle. In baths of marble and blue cascade, and shower cubicles in rented rooms with geometric signs on the sensible plastic curtaining.

The feast of this single lovemaking takes in all the uncountable meetings they have missed, been cheated of. Flesh to flesh, whirling through diamonds and thunders, like the leap and fall of suns, the traveling of planets. The true world goes out in the explosive flame, and the little last moon dissolves like an ember.

Then they are lying in the foundation of the dead palace, in utter blackness, and total peace.

But where now? Where next can they go? His world is ended, hers has never begun. They are together, yes. Yet—

For how long?

9

A couple of hours before morning, some of the tourists who came to the lake on the flybus were still wide-awake. Four of them were wandering along the shore, from which by then the tide had drawn the water off to almost a quarter of a mile. Another, staving off an impending hangover, leaned at an open window high in his lake-facing hotel room, drinking an iced mineral water and stuffing himself with deep breaths. Various others were due to be awakened. Certain of the hotel staff too had stayed deliberately unsleeping and watchful. There were always a few who kept this vigil, either inadvertently or with forethought. Frequently, nothing happened.

Tonight, it did.

To start with, the effect was subtle. A dilute sheen appeared far out, as if another moon were up, or some premature prelude to the dawn. It was not in the sky, however. And as the radiance gradually intensified, morphing from platinum to ormolu and so to a nearly radioactive gold, no one could mistake that the sun, if such it was, was rising deep down inside the vast body of the lake.

The light then sped up, and soon reached a savage climax. This maintained itself. Everything else caught and flared up in its gleam, the shores, the hills, the scattered ruins. Even the distant mountains took on a metallic blush, as they did at sunrise. Only the hotels dulled to insignificance.

The lake was itself by then a composite incandescent marigold, and from it, though the dazzle made them rather hard to define, outcrops of brilliance had seemed to rise up from the water. They resembled buildings of ancient design, sumptuous, with windows that flashed off their own daggered highlights.

Down on the lake-emptied shore, the four astounded tourists heard faint sounds of voices, perhaps of singing and music, a rolling noise of wheels, and once, a catlike purring, too large and close to be possible. The older woman in the party was afterward always sure she had seen a chariot from legend dart through just under the water. The two younger men found a fishing boat that was lying on the pebbles, and tried to row it out over the effulgent firefly soup of the lake. But the light confused them completely. They rowed in a circle and careered, defeated but giggling, back to the beach.

Up in his window, the drunken man was cured by astonishment, and a slight worry that he had gone mad. *Not* had a glimpse into another dimension, where the deluge had never occurred, and the city lived forever—*decidedly* not.

As for those who had watched on purpose, they too were thrilled by fear and amazement. But they did not think that they had lost their minds.

. . . .

THE SHOW, AS some of the visitors later referred to it, lasted about twenty minutes by the clocks of the hotels. About thirteen by any accurate and consulted wristwatch.

When finally the light went away, which it did very quickly, merely fluttering and going out like an ordinary candle, or—as someone said—as if an electric connection had fused, there was only absolute blackness briefly muddled with afterimages. And then the east began to kindle legitimately for morning.

By the breakfast hour, almost everybody, apart from the specific watchers, had become or been convinced that the glow in the lake was all a clever trick, put on by the area sponsors. They joked about it all day, and for days and months and years after. They told people back home that they too really should go to see the lake below Sirrimir, the lake with the legend, and look out for this fantastic performance that was laid on for your last night.

But the guides, they professed to have slept all through the event. They always did. They always would.

Meanwhile, the body of the young, red-haired woman was not discovered until it washed up on the noon tide. It seemed that she had gone for a swim, and though so young, her heart had stopped. She had not drowned.

10

"PERHAPS YOU MIGHT care for some *kvah*, madame, sir?"

"Oh yes, thank you," he replied, before he knew quite what he said, or where he was. "For both of us, please."

The attentive voice that had called through the door acquiesced and went away.

Then he turned and looked at her, his new wife, just waking from slumbering beside him in the overland sleeper, as the pullcar rattled gruntingly southward.

Outside, the woods were thinning to wide blue fields, while overhead, the blue-pink sky was prettily decorated by birds.

He knew now where he was, just as he knew the language. For a moment he studied her, too, making certain that she, as he, was not entirely bemused.

But she only kneeled up by the window and said, "The sky is always that color. Am I right, Zeh?"

"Yes, Zaeli."

"How do we know?" she inquired, but then she looked at him, and they moved into each other's arms, and were, to each other, the flawless completion of all known havens, lands, and states. One exquisite constant in an ever-dismantling chaos.

Over there, some clothes of an inventive cut awaited them. And some luggage lay in its cubby that he, and she too, instinctively recognized. Just as they did the quaint trees and the blue-blossoming fields and the sky like a painting on china. But only as if they had been briefed on such things a few minutes before arrival.

None of this would matter anyway. They knew *each other*.

"We speak *this* language now, it seems," he said, smiling.

"I suppose it will seem less odd quite soon," she sagely assured him.

"Or more so?"

"Zeh, is *kvah* coffee? I think it is."

"Or milk. Or beer . . ."

They ceased to talk about the *kvah*.

They had met only recently, and were soon married, in some city to the north.

The train rattled on the hard rails, real as all reality.

It was carrying them home, to her tall old house by the blue and ever-tidal lake. With every second, they remembered more—and forgot more, too. Already they had almost forgotten their former lives, those other things they had lost, since both heart and mind had been refilled to the brim. They were changing smoothly into those people that now they were. This now was the reality, and everything else, any other lives, quite likely some sort of dream. *This* was real: two lovers going homeward to a lakeshore, while behind the painted china sky, the stars crossed unseen.

Peter S. Beagle

Learning to operate a computer can be difficult for the uninitiated. Some computers, however, may be trickier to run than others . . .

Peter S. Beagle was born in New York City in 1939. Although not prolific by genre standards, he has published a number of well-received fantasy novels, at least two of which, A Fine and Private Place *and* The Last Unicorn, *were widely influential and are now considered to be classics of the genre. In fact, Beagle may be the most successful writer of lyrical and evocative modern fantasy since Bradbury, and is the winner of two Mythopoeic Fantasy Awards and the Locus Award, as well as having often been a finalist for the* World Fantasy Award.

Beagle's other books include the novels The Folk of the Air, The Innkeeper's Song, *and* Tamsin. *His short fiction has appeared in places as varied as* The Magazine of Fantasy & Science Fiction, The Atlantic Monthly, Seventeen, *and* Ladies' Home Journal, *and has been collected in* The Rhinoceros Who Quoted Nietzsche and Other Odd Acquaintances, Giant Bones, The Line Between, *and* We Never Talk About My Brother. *He won the Hugo Award in 2006 and the Nebula Award in 2007 for his story, "Two Hearts." He has written the screenplays for several movies, including the animated adaptations of* The Lord of the Rings *and* The Last Unicorn; *the libretto of an opera,* The Midnight

Angel; *the fan-favorite* Star Trek: The Next Generation *episode "Sarek"*; *and a popular autobiographical travel book*, I See By My Outfit. *His most recent book is the new collection*, Mirror Kingdoms: The Best of Peter S. Beagle.

Kaskia

Even afterward, Martin never could bring himself to blame the laptop. Rather, he blamed his foolishness in buying a computer at once so far beyond his means, his needs, and his abilities. "Goddamn bells and whistles," Lorraine told him scornfully at the time. "LEDs, apps, plug-ins, backup gadgets—you've always been a fool for unnecessary extras. You think people will look at that thing and think you're a real computer geek, an *expert*." She gave that little sneeze-laugh he'd once found endearing, and went off to call her buddy Roz and relate his latest idiocy in detail. Sucking a forefinger, cut while he was struggling to open the box, he heard Lorraine saying on the phone, "And on top of that, he bought the thing from his cousin Barry! *That* asshole. You remember—right, right, anything that falls off a truck is legally Barry's. I am *telling* you, Roz . . ."

The trouble was, of course, that she'd been right. Martin was fond of Barry—if he thought about it, he'd have to say that Barry had been his closest friend since childhood, given a very limited experience with close friends. But he had few illusions about his cousin's probity or loyalty: even in the first flush of his infatuation with the new computer, he'd known that nothing Barry told him about it was likely to be true. The brand was completely unfamiliar, the keyboard had too many function keys beyond the usual twelve, and there were other keys and markings with strange symbols that Barry never even tried to explain to him. "It's one of a kind, absolutely unique, same as you. I feel like I'm in Shakespeare, bringing two great lovers together."

Directions had not been included, but Jaroslav, the amiable graduate student two doors down the hall, who actually *did* know quite a lot about computers, came over to set up Martin's laptop for him. It took considerably longer than expected, due in part to Jaroslav's unfamiliarity with the operating system, and in equal measure to his fascination with the computer's programs and connections. "No, that cannot be it, that makes no *sense*. Well, I suppose that would work, it *seems* to work, but I cannot understand . . . yes, *that* works, but *why* . . . ?" He made no more sense out of the keyboard than Barry had, and was clearly only half-joking when he muttered, "With this thing, I am lucky to know to set the clock, where to plug in the mouse." By the time he was done his Iron Man T-shirt was sweated through, and he was talking to himself in Serb. Afterward, Martin noticed—on the occasional times they passed in the lobby or hall, or outside the building's laundry room—that Jaroslav avoided meeting his eyes.

Despite Martin's vast ignorance of the workings of his new computer, however, it functioned better than any machine he had ever owned since a beloved bathtub motorboat that ran up a flag and fired pellets at his rubber ducks. Lorraine had once commented that electronic devices seemed to commit suicide in Martin's presence, and it was a hard point to argue. Yet the strange laptop never misbehaved: never froze, never crashed, never devoured work he had forgotten to back up—never, in short, treated him with the kind of spitefulness that had always been his lot from anything involving electrons and wires. He realized that he was actually grateful, and from time to time found himself thinking of it not as a machine, but as a quiet and singular friend.

Often now, when he came home in the evening from the large chain grocery where he was the produce manager, he would sit at his worktable (dinner having long since evolved into a solitary pursuit for both Lorraine and himself), and let the computer talk to him, either on-screen or through the excellent earphones that Barry had grandly thrown into the deal. The computer had a sound system, with built-in speakers, but Lorraine complained about the noise, and Martin liked the earphones better anyway. They gave him a curious private peacefulness that made him feel as though he were at the bottom of the ocean in an old-fashioned diving suit, talking with a companion he could not see. Not that he had ever worn any sort of diving suit, or actually been in water deeper than his high school swimming pool. Martin had not been to very many places in his life.

He did no store work on the new computer; there was an intimidating, unforgiving desktop model in his backroom cubicle for that. The laptop was for telling him stories at the swirl of a mouse: it was for bringing him news, delivering such e-mail as he ever received—while most considerately eliminating all junk and spam—and for showing him not only the old *films noir* and television episodes of his youth, but a wider, richer world, a world he had resigned himself early in life to seeing in snippets at best, but never to know in all its sprawling, vulgar magnificence. The laptop seemed genuinely to care for him: *him*, Martin Gelber, forty-one years old, balding and lonely, spending his days with fruits and vegetables, and his nights with a wife long since a stranger. Absurdly—and he knew bitterly well just how absurd it was—Martin began to feel cherished.

He was also aware that he had no more than scratched the surface of the laptop's talents and capacities. There were keys he carefully avoided touching, software settings he never once changed from how Jaroslav had left them, areas of the screen where he never let the mouse wander. Now and then he was tempted to click on some mysterious button—just to *see*—but Martin had the sad virtue of understanding his own capacity for disaster, and the allure of adventure always faded quickly. He was more than happy with the computer the way it was, and the way they were together.

Except for the One Key.

Martin called it that, having seen *The Lord of the Rings*, and read Tolkien's books as well. The One Key lived alone on the upper right corner of the keyboard, well past Print Screen and Scroll Lock and Pause/Break . . . past the tiny blue lights indicating that Num Lock or Caps Lock or Scroll Lock again were engaged . . . an ordinary key, no different from any other, except for being without a letter, a number, or—as far as Martin could discern—any obvious purpose. It was simply the One Key: it was just *there*, like a wisdom tooth, and it drew him from the first as the little closet had drawn Bluebeard's seventh wife, or the chest full of plagues had enticed Pandora. Martin, being Martin, and *aware* that he was Martin, left it strictly alone.

And left it alone.

And went on leaving it alone, until the afternoon of his day off, when there was nothing on TV—not that he ever watched television much anymore—and Lorraine was away with this or that shopping friend—and the One Key was now somehow looking as big as the lordly Backspace or Enter. Martin stared at it for quite a while, and then said, suddenly, loudly, and defiantly, "What the *hell*!" and pushed it.

Nothing happened.

Martin had, of course, no idea what he had *expected* to happen. He had a reasonable assumption that there wouldn't be an explosion—that the computer wouldn't either levitate or fall completely to pieces—and that a cuckoo wouldn't pop out of the screen with a message from something eternal in its beak. But he had rather anticipated that a deep-toned bell would ring somewhere, surely, and that it would be answered. Every key has a function, he told himself, a programmed reason for existing: there *would* be a response. Martin waited.

A green spark appeared in the center of the computer screen, slowly swelling and swirling, taking on the aspect of a sparkling pinwheel galaxy as it filled the screen. Martin clapped the earphones on his head, hearing a staticky crackle that was not at all like static, but fell into rhythmic, distinctly repetitive patterns that seemed to be trying to form words. The green galaxy revolved dizzyingly before his eyes.

"I don't understand," Martin said aloud, startled to hear himself speak. Suddenly frightened, he considered turning off the laptop. But he didn't, and the vision continued to dazzle his eyes and sizzle in his ears. On an impulse, he moved to the keyboard and typed the same words: *I don't understand.*

This time, the response was immediate. The sparkling scene vanished, to be replaced by the image of a face. It was not a human face. Martin knew that immediately, for while it provided the usual allotment of features, they were arranged in a configuration that could only be described as shockingly, impossibly beautiful—Martin actually lurched back, as though hit in the stomach, and made a softer version of the sound that one makes on such occasions.

Words formed under the face. Martin recognized them as words: they were the equivalent in pixels of the sputtering that had been shaping itself into language in his earphones. To him, dazed as he certainly was, it seemed the speech of space, the common dialect of planets and comets alike. All he could think to do was to type his own words over once again, staring at the lovely, terrifying, utterly perfect alien face as he did so. *I don't understand.*

Nothing changed on the screen for some time. Martin occupied himself primarily in praying that Lorraine would not return just then; but also in marveling that a face so beautiful could simultaneously reveal itself as obviously unhuman, yet lose none of its appeal. Nor could he pinpoint the exact reason he knew what he knew—but he *knew*, and he went on waiting for an answer.

The laptop screen changed again. The face vanished—Martin found himself reaching helplessly toward where it had been—and the screen filled once more with the characters of that otherworldly language. Martin groaned . . . but in almost the same moment, the words dissolved and reformed themselves into something approximating English. He leaned close to the computer, squinting to read them.

Me what
You
Hel who lolo
Me me

First Contact! Martin had seen enough science-fiction movies to know about first contact. The ludicrousness of a computer—a laptop, at that—connecting a suburban produce manager with another world and another life form was not lost on him, as stunned and overwhelmed as he was. "Why *me*?" he demanded aloud. "Why not a scientist, an astronomer, whatever? Come *on*, for goodness' sake!" But all the same, he typed into the screen *Where are you? What is your name?*

There was no response for what seemed a very long while, as excited and impatient as he was. He tried to calm himself, thinking that he and the alien—*his* alien, if he was the first to discover her, like an island or a mountain—might likely be communicating over light-years, not mere miles. This was hardly Instant Messaging, after all. Even so, he was fidgeting like a child, unable to sit still, by the time the reply came back.

You what
Talk
Who no gone gone
Me

The next word, which Martin thought must have been an attempt at a name, dissolved back into a flurry of words—or sounds? or mathematical symbols? or plain lunatic gibberish?—in the original possibly cosmic tongue. In turn he went back to his own first contact cry: *I don't understand.*

"Story of your life, Gelber," he said aloud to the computer. "Find a girl to go to the prom with, she lives too far away for a cab ride and she doesn't speak English. Your life in one line, I swear."

The computer said back to him in what was still a braver try at his language than any attempt he had yet made at hers:

Me belong Kaskia
Belong who you

Kaskia. Her name was Kaskia, or else she—belonged? a slave?—to someone of that name. Martin refused to believe that anyone who looked like that could be anyone's servant, let alone a slave. He took a long breath and typed back *Martin. My name is Martin.*

He heard nothing back for the rest of the day, even though he forlornly pressed the One Key again and again. Lorraine came home in a good mood, the one benign side effect of her shopping expeditions, and they enjoyed a relatively placid evening, practically together. Martin yearned to get back to the laptop, and Lorraine clearly had phone calls to make—Martin knew the look—but instead they watched a public-television documentary on the history of the Empire State Building, even sitting still through the semi-annual fundraising supplications. *Maybe having a special secret makes you nicer,* Martin thought. *Easier to get along with.* He wondered what Lorraine's secret might be.

When Lorraine went to bed, he booted up the laptop and tried, cautiously and apprehensively, to contact the being who called herself—itself?—Kaskia, but to no avail. Applying the One Key repeatedly summoned no starry crackle to his screen, nor did appealing directly to the computer's elaborate message-tracing systems produce any unearthly footprints at all. The entire contact—the entire vision—might never have occurred.

Martin mourned it all through the next day's work at the supermarket. Unlike the protagonists of any number of films and stories, he never for a moment took his encounter with the unearthly for a hallucination or a dream. There had been a connection, however fragmented, with a creature from another place or reality; and the idea of such a wonder never occurring again for the rest of his life made that life seem to him even duller and more pointless than he already knew it to be. "I won't stand for it," he said aloud to himself, while showing Jamil the proper way to stack the red cabbages. "I won't." Jamil took it as a slight to his cabbage-stacking technique, and was deeply wounded.

Three further days passed, during which Martin spoke less and less, both at home and at work, and spent more and more time trying to coax the strange laptop to find Kaskia's world for him again. The computer remained not so much mutinous as regretfully firm, almost parental, as though it had decided that passing the borders of his own understanding was simply bad for him. The One Key remained so unresponsive that he came to fear that he might have damaged it by punching it in frustration when he lost contact with Kaskia. During that time, he could hardly endure to look at the laptop, which Lorraine noticed, teasing him about it. "What happened? Novelty wear off? Barry'll sell you a new toy any-time, if you can find him." Martin hardly heard her.

On the fourth night, sleepless, he finally wandered to his worktable, sat down at the laptop, and played several games of solitaire, as he could have done at any of the store computers. Then he reread his e-mail, browsed a favored newsletter, played a round of Battleship against himself, and tapped the One Key, almost diffidently, with his head turned away from the screen. He had not even put his earphones on.

When he heard the static of the spheres, he did not turn immediately, but moved very slowly, as though that other place were a wild bird he was trying not to startle away. The screen was, as before, aswarm with wheeling green sparks, and though Martin waited patiently, neither words nor the image of the wondrously alien beauty appeared. Finally he was unable to resist typing once again *My name is Martin*, and then, after some thought, adding boldly, *Your name is Kaskia*.

The reply was long in coming, leaving him to fear that he really had frightened her off; and then to speculate on whether an astronomer or mathematician could work out, just from the time it took his electronic missive to receive an answer, how distant Kaskia's world actually might be. He vaguely recalled Barry as having been good with algebra and trig-onometry in high school, and thought about setting him the problem.

Words shivered into place on the screen.

Kaskia. You Martin. Where you.

Martin slapped his palms exultantly on the table, and then quickly deadened the vibrations, for fear of waking Lorraine. "It's real!" he whispered, raising his head to look toward the ceiling, and far past it. "Oh, sonofabitch, it's real!" And either her English or the transmission was clearly improving, along with her comprehension. She must have one of those universal translators, like on *Star Trek* and those other shows. Or maybe she was just a fast learner.

He was up most of that night, happily reenacting all the first contact scenes and dialogue he remembered from movies and television. He placed himself and his planet in the universe for her, as best he could (though she seemed, to his chagrin, to have little knowledge of her own world's relation to any other); and even told her, out of his own small store, something of the Earth's history and geography. Kaskia was rather less informative, which he put down to her continuing difficulties with the language and her consequently understandable reticence. He did learn that she lived in some sort of grandly sprawling extended-family setting, that she was a singer and musician—apparently quite well-known, as far as he could make out—and that she felt happy and fortunate (if that was what the word she used meant) to find him a second time. The galaxy was very big.

The contact began to break up toward morning, presumably due to the rotation of both worlds and the slow, endless drift of the entire cosmos. But he understood by now when it would be possible for them to speak again; and when he asked her shyly if he might see her image once more—it took her some little time to grasp the meaning of the request—the face that had so literally made him forget how to breathe reappeared for a moment, sparkling against the stars. Then it was gone, and the screen of the laptop went blank.

Sleep was neither an issue nor an option. He lay down on the living-room couch—not for the first time—and stared at the ceiling, consumed by a need to tell *someone* about his discovery, whether or not he was believed. Lorraine was out of the question, for a good many reasons, while Jaroslav was still avoiding him in the hall, and shopping elsewhere. As for his fellow workers, matters of authority forbade his taking any of them into his confidence . . . except perhaps for Ivan, the black security guard. Ivan read on the job, whenever he could get away with it—he had often been seen reading as he walked through the parking lot—and Martin, as management, should not have sympathized with him, or protected him, for a moment. But he did. Most of the books Ivan read were science fiction; and Martin had a growing feeling that, out of all the people he knew, Ivan might very well be the only one who might sympathize with *him*, for a change.

Ivan did. Ivan said, "Wow, man, that is a *good* story." He slapped Martin's shoulder enthusiastically. "That's like Niven writing Bradbury. I didn't know you were into that stuff. You got any others?"

Martin did not waste time protesting the complete truthfulness of his account. He said, "Well, I'm not a writer, you know that—I'm just fooling around. You think I ought to change anything? I mean, if *you* were writing it?"

Ivan considered. "One thing, I'd find a way for them to meet up. Not rocket ships, no Buck Rogers shit like that, I'm thinking transporters or some such. I mean, that's exciting, man—that's *risky*. Yeah, he's seen her picture, he's seen *somebody's* picture, but what if she turns out to have a tail and horns and six-inch teeth? Mail-order brides, you know?"

"Well, I don't think the guy's thinking about getting together with her. I mean, she's sort of famous on her world, and he's married, and he could be a lot older—"

"Or *she* could. He don't know how long it takes her planet to get around the sun, or anything about the biology. She could be seven hundred or something, you never know." Ivan patted Martin's shoulder again. "Tell you one thing, *I'd* sure like to have a laptop like the one you thought up. Dell ever makes that puppy, I'm first in line."

Martin spent a good deal of time looking at the computer himself, even when the link to Kaskia was not open. His growing sense of the laptop's true potential had, paradoxically, begun to distance him from the machine that he still believed loved and cared for him. "You scare me," he said aloud to it more than once. "You're with the wrong guy, we both know that." To his mind, the One Key, employed skillfully by someone who knew what he was doing, could probably open channels quite likely beyond the reach of the Hubble Telescope. "But that's just not me," Martin said sadly. "I wish it were. I really do."

He did finally get in touch with Barry, who, as expected, claimed absolute ignorance of the laptop's provenance, and could offer no clues toward tracing its history. "I told you everything I know the day I put it in your hands, kid." He gave Martin the warm, confiding smile that not only attracted new victims every day, but continued to reseduce the old ones, who knew better. "I told you, you belonged together. Was I wrong? Tell me I was wrong."

Martin sighed. "It's like the time you sold me the motorcycle."

Barry's grin widened. "The Triumph. The Bonneville T100. You looked great on it."

"I almost killed myself on it. It was way too much power for me. I sold it two weeks later and only got half what I paid you for it." Martin rubbed his left shoulder reflectively. "This computer's the same way."

"I can't take it back," Barry said quickly. He looked alarmed, which was exceedingly rare for him, and it was Martin's turn to smile reassuringly.

"I don't want to sell it. I just wish I could live up to it." He sighed again. "I wish we really did belong together."

Lorraine came home from work then, and Barry promptly disappeared without a further word. Martin thought, *Those two understand each other better than I understand either one of them.* He wondered whether Lorraine had heard the last thing he said to his cousin. He wondered whether he cared.

The link, or channel, or the hailing frequency, or whatever it actually was, seemed to be open to wherever Kaskia was every five days, sometimes in the afternoon, like that first time, but most often at one or two in the morning. He often asked Kaskia what time it was there, but she seemed to have no concept of measuring time that Martin could translate into his mind. They usually spoke, through the good offices of the laptop screen, until nearly dawn, when Martin would slip quietly into bed beside Lorraine and try to catch at least two or three hours of sleep before heading off to work. It was a wearying regime, but generally manageable.

Kaskia's English had improved further each time they communicated. When Martin questioned how she could be learning the language so fast, since she had not known of its existence until a few weeks before, she replied lightly, *Must be good teacher you.* Asked whether Martin could possibly learn her language in the same way, her answer was a somewhat puzzled *How could you.* She had not yet mastered question marks, or else there was a translation issue involved that he did not understand.

Which did not mean that she did not ask questions. She asked constantly and charmingly—if sometimes startlingly—about the smallest details of Martin's life, from when and where and how he slept, to the names of every fruit and vegetable he handled in his work, and whether there were *nildrys* on his planet. Martin never found out what *nildrys* were, but retained the distinct impression that a planet—or did she mean a house?—without *nildrys* was beneath contempt.

She herself liked best to talk about her pet, whose name on the computer screen was *Furtigosseachfurt*, and who sounded, in Kaskia's description, like a cross between a largish ferret and a squirrel. He was quick and affectionate, liked to have his back scratched and his belly tickled, and on occasion he hid from her behind a rock or high in a tree, and then she had to find him. Her messages regarding the creature took up so much time that Martin would rather have spent on many other matters, and he even found himself skimming a bit over writing from the stars. But they were also so tender and guilelessly touching that they brought Martin just as often close to tears. Once she wrote *Sometimes he is all I have. Sometimes not. You.* Because of the lack of question marks, you could imagine, if you wanted to, that she might be saying that Martin was at times all she had. Martin wanted to think so.

One day the green sparks on the screen formed one word and nothing more. *Dead.*

Martin never thought for a moment that she was speaking of anything but the ferret-squirrel. She never mentioned family at all, and only rarely spoke of friends or acquaintances. He wrote as earnest a condolence as he knew how, sent it off into space expecting no reply, and got none. He wrote another.

Not being an obsessive person by nature, it never occurred to him that his concern for the sorrow of a person infinitely far away across the galaxy might in any way affect his work, or concern anyone else. But in fact, his increasing distraction had indeed been noticed by his superiors at the market, and by Lorraine as well. This was less of a worry for her than it might have been—Lorraine had survived far worse disasters, and had already chosen her parachute and a cozy landing strip. But she retained a certain rough fondness for Martin, and actually wished him well; so when she confronted him for the last time, it was without much malice that she said, "I have a bet with myself. Twelve to seven that when I walk out of here, you won't notice for three days. Want to cover it?"

Martin's response was as distant as Kaskia's planet, though of course Lorraine couldn't know that. He said quietly, "You left a long time ago. I did notice."

Somewhat off balance, Lorraine snapped, "Well, so did you. I'm not even sure you were ever *here.* Stop playing with that damn computer and look at me—you owe me that much. I'm at least more interesting than a blank screen!" For Martin had the laptop open, and was indeed staring at the empty screen, only now and then cutting a quick peripheral glance at her. Lorraine demanded, "What the hell are you looking at? There's nothing there!"

"No," Martin agreed. "Nothing there at all. Good-bye, Lorraine. My fault, I know it, I'm really sorry." But the last words were entirely by rote, and he was looking at the computer screen again while he was speaking them. Lorraine, who had not planned to leave quite this soon, gave a short sneeze-laugh and went to make a phone call.

She would have collected on her bet, for Martin was too occupied with the One Key to be paying attention when she did leave the next day. They were into the second five-day cycle since his last communication from Kaskia, and he was growing anxious, as well as frustrated. He had reached the point lately of stepping outside when the night was at its darkest, and staring until his eyes blurred and burned up at the black, empty sky, currently just as much help to him as the empty computer screen. He would never have said—and never once did—that nothing else mattered but hearing once again from a nonhuman woman unimaginably far away on the other side of the other side, and he could not make anything else be real. All he could do, at this point, was simply to keep saying her name, as though that would make her appear.

And when he returned to the laptop she was there. Rather, the green sparks were crowding his screen, leaping this way and that, like salmon fighting their way home. And there was that unchanging alien face that chilled and haunted him so . . . and there was a message, as the sparks flew upward into words:

> I miss
> so much so much
> I miss
> help me

It was as though her grief had driven her language back to the basics with which their conversation across the night had begun—how long ago it seemed now to Martin. Nevertheless, the cry for comfort was clear; and he, whom so few had ever truly needed or called on for aid, would respond. He began to type, letting the words come without reading over them:

> Dear lovely Kaskia,
> I too know something about loss.
> I never had such a pet as yours—
> I cannot have pets, because I have
> always been allergic to animals.

Do you know what that means,
allergic?
It means that the skin and the fur
and the hair of most animals
makes you ill,
sometimes very ill indeed.
I think sometimes that I have been
allergic to people,
even to my customers in the produce department,
and to my fellow workers.
I think I would do better with animals than people,
if I were not so allergic.
You have lost a great friend,
but at least you let yourself have him,
you took the risk of having a friend,
and he had you,
so you cannot ever really lose each other.

The words rolled steadily up the screen and disappeared into the night, and the stars beyond. Martin wrote on, haltingly, but never looking back.

I have not been as brave as you,
so I have no friend like that,
except you.
We cannot really know each other,
and I suppose we never will,
but I have come to think of you as a dear friend,
and I cannot bear to think of you so unhappy.

He took a deep breath here, paused just for a moment, and went on.

I am very lonely.
I have always been lonely.
It is my fault.
Do not let your grief shut you off.
It is too easy,
and it lasts too long.
Oh, Kaskia, so far away

The screen, with his last words still on it, went abruptly blank. Martin stared. The laptop was vibrating under his hands, making a sound like an old-fashioned sewing machine, or a car about to throw a rod. It stopped presently, and new words began to appear on the screen. They were like the sparkling pixel words that Kaskia had first tried before she began to absorb English, but the hand—and, somehow, the tone—were definitely not hers. Martin typed, as before, *My name is Martin Gelber*, and added, with a touch of defiance, *I am Kaskia's friend*.

That got somebody's attention immediately. He was answered by what came across the screen as a bellow of fury.

YOU.

Martin repeated, *My name is Martin Gelber. I am a friend of Kaskia's*—

I KNOW YOU.

The laptop seemed to shiver in the face of such outrage, however faraway.

THE ONE TRIES COMMAND MY CHILD.

Martin stared at the screen in bewilderment and horror. He typed back *Child? I'm talking about Kaskia!*

The new voice was slower to reply this time, and not quite as accusatory.

MY CHILD. MY DAUGHTER.

Martin thought of Ivan at the supermarket. Then he typed, *I didn't know.*

The voice on the laptop screen still resolved in capitals, but the tone no longer came across as menacing.

WOULD NOT. KASKIA LIKES TALK. STORIES. LIKES STORIES.

"Yes," Martin said softly, remembering; and then typed, *Yes. So then she is not a famous singer and musician?*

LIKES SINGING.

Of course, he replied. *The sad story about her pet dying?*

DEAD. YES. OLDER SISTER'S.

Martin said, "Oh dear."

GOOD GIRL. GOOD GIRL.

Yes, Martin typed again. *Smart girl. Don't punish, please.*

The voice did not answer. Martin wrote, slowly now, *Your daughter changed me. I don't know how, or in what way. But I am different because of her. Better, perhaps—different, anyway. Tell her so.*

Still no answer. Martin was no longer sure of the voice's presence, but he asked, *One other question. Every time we spoke, Kaskia and I, there was an image of the most beautiful woman I have ever seen. I thought it was a picture of her. Not?*

GOOD-BYE KASKIA FRIEND.

"Good-bye," Martin said softly. "Good-bye, Kaskia."

The laptop went dark and still. Martin touched the One Key, but nothing happened. He had an odd feeling that nothing would again; the computer had served its purpose, at least for him. He shut it off, unplugged it, wrapped the power cord around it, and put it in a drawer.

After two cups of strong percolated coffee, he called Barry. When his cousin—hungover and grumpy, by the sound of him—answered the phone, Martin said, "Barry? Do you remember the old Prince Albert sting?"

"Prince *Albert*?" Barry was definitely hungover. "Say *what*?"

"You remember. Big fun for bored kids on rainy afternoons. Call up a smoke shop, a candy store, ask them if they've got Prince Albert in a can. Remember now?"

A hoarse chuckle. "Right, sure, yeah. They say yes, and we say, 'Well, let him out right now, he can't breathe in there!' Then we giggle like mad, and they call us little motherfuckers and hang up. What the hell put *that* in your head?"

"Just Memory Lane, I guess."

"Hey, I heard about Lorraine. That really sucks. You okay?"

"I guess. Not really sure what okay is right now. I guess so."

"Okay means there's better out there, lots better. Seize the weekend, like they say in Rome—old Cousin Barry's going to hook you up with one of his Midnight Specials. Meanwhile you're crazy free, right?"

"Crazy, anyway." To his own surprise, Martin realized he was smiling. "We'll see about the free part."

There were bathroom-sink noises at the other end. "'Scuse me—trying to make an Alka-Seltzer one-handed. Hey, you still happy with that computer I sold you? I got a buyer, if you're not."

Martin hesitated only briefly. "No, I'm fine with it. Great little machine."

Barry cackled triumphantly. "*Told* you it'd change your life, didn't I?"

"No, you didn't. But thanks anyway."

Martin's smile widened slowly. Standing alone in the kitchen, he closed his eyes and listened to the stars.

Yasmine Galenorn

Harder even than trying to live in two worlds is being trapped between them, like a bug between sheets of glass . . .

New York Times *bestselling author Yasmine Galenorn is a mystery and paranormal romance author perhaps best known for her seven-volume Otherworld series, which details the adventures of the half-human, half-faerie D'Artigo sisters, who work for the Otherworld Intelligence Agency, and which includes* Witchling, Changeling, Darkling, Dragon Wytch, Night Huntress, Demon Mistress, *and* Bone Magic. *Galenorn is also the author of the five-volume Chintz 'n China series, including* Ghost of a Chance *and* Murder Under a Mystic Moon, *which straddles the borderline between mystery and fantasy; and she has also written eight books on modern paganism, the most popular of which is* Embracing the Moon. *She also writes under the pseudonym India Ink. Her most recent book is a new Otherworld novel,* Harvest Hunting.

Man in the Mirror

He'd been rambling around the house for years in a fog so thick that he could no longer count the years that had passed. Chained to the house by a chance meeting in a mirror, he was a shadow of his former self, a whisper on the wind, a glint of light against the glass.

The house had sat empty for ten years, although his mother still came in to clean every now and then, but mostly, there was silence. The only way he kept up with what was happening in the world was to listen to the conversations between May, his mother, and the rare friends she brought with her.

He'd come to believe he'd never have another chance to laugh, to smile, to be grateful for what existence he had. And he'd been lonely. So lonely, wondering if he'd ever have the chance to speak to anyone again. If nothing else, he wanted out—wanted to move on.

But today, something shifted—a breeze echoing through the empty rooms swept with it the hint of perfume—the fragrance of hesitation, of anger—and desire. And the scent touched him, woke him fully. Someone new had arrived. Someone he once hated, but now who promised him the chance of life again. The house would become a home again, and perhaps—perhaps he would have a chance.

SOMETIMES, THE ONLY way to exorcise old ghosts is to pack your bags and move in with them. And so, on one of those rare clear mornings in the Pacific Northwest—before the clouds had a chance to gather—I loaded my Pathfinder and left Seattle for what I hoped would be the last time. For all its beauty, the city was a constant reminder of the nightmare that had haunted me for over a year.

Three hours and two pit stops later, I pulled up in front of the rainbow-arched trellis straddling the drive leading to Breakaway Farm. Wild rose canes wound around the latticework, waiting for spring, sparkling with early dew. The trellis guarded an iron gate barring the road to the house, and in the moments just before sunrise, mist rolled silently along the ground, an ankle-deep shroud obscuring the path.

I let the motor idle as I slipped out of my seat and wandered over to the gate, staring at the lock. The key dangled like a promise from my key chain, a glimmer of hope that maybe, just maybe, I could find some semblance of peace. On the other hand, now that I was actually here, the idea seemed a little crazy. Maybe I was just stirring up trouble for myself.

It was simple, really. All I needed to do was gather my courage, unlock the gate, and drive in. Breakaway Farm was mine now, and nobody but my lawyer knew that I was moving here. There was nothing to stop me. Nothing but my own fear. The question was: Was I ready to face the past and conquer my demons? Or maybe, a little voice in the back of my mind whispered, the question I should be asking myself was really: *Was I ready to face the future?*

Could I accept what I'd done, learn to live with it, and get on with my life? Even harder: Could I accept what had been done *to me*? It's one thing to live with your own sins, quite another to be forced to relive the sins of another every time you looked in a mirror.

I rubbed my throat where the scars lingered. Their crimson brilliance had long faded, but the thin, white lines were still visible, and when I touched them, they burned. I knew it was all in my mind; it had taken only a few weeks for the actual slashes to heal, but every time I thought about them, the images that flashed through my mind were as fiery and painful as they had been that night.

A loud mew from the backseat startled me out of my thoughts. I turned around. Circe wanted out of her carrier.

"You've been such a good girl." I stroked her ears between the bars of the cage. She'd slept for most of the drive over from Seattle. "What a good girl!"

As I stared into her emerald eyes, the calico chirped, her squeaks intermingled with the rumble of a purr. *She* trusted me. Maybe it was time that I learned how to trust myself again.

Taking a deep breath, I looked at the gate. It was now or never. Either go forward and risk the unknown, or admit failure. I couldn't very well return to the dead-end life I'd left behind in Seattle.

My stomach in knots, I fit the key into the lock. The gate creaked open, protesting years of disuse. As it swung wide, I latched it to the post to keep it from crashing shut, and then, with one last look at the highway behind me, climbed back into the SUV and slowly edged along the graveled road bordered by tall cedar and fir trees.

Huckleberries littered the ground, along with fallen trees covered with moss and toadstools. A flicker of movement caught my eye. A fox? A coyote? A neighbor's dog? It had been a long time since I'd set foot in the country. Unnerved, I rounded the curve. The drive opened into a semicircle parking space in front of a footpath leading to a three-story house hidden behind a veil of tree limbs and bushes.

I turned off the ignition and squinted at the tangle of vegetation. It would be nice if my Muse would give me a sign—any sign—that I was doing the right thing. I waited. *Nothing.* Why couldn't she reassure me that I was making the right decision? But no lightbulbs appeared over my head, no sibyl sang her song for me. This was my journey, and my journey alone.

As I climbed out of the car, exhausted by the turmoil of the past few months, all I wanted to do was to sleep. But I hadn't slept through the night since . . . *hasty backpedal.* No, not ready to go there. Not yet. A glance at the eastern sky showed dawn giving way to day. Thin clouds blended into the pale blue that passed for morning.

I poked my head into the backseat. "Hold on for just a few more minutes longer, babe. I've got to check out the house first." Circe stared at me, blinked slowly, sniffed the stirring of fresh air, then promptly curled up and fell asleep.

Slinging my purse over my shoulder, I set out for the house.

The path was crowded on both sides by a thick row of late-blooming herbs. They grew wild and tall, gone to seed, but still their fragrance lingered in the air, musty and old. Dizzy from the scent, I stumbled and almost blundered into a spiderweb that an orange and black striped argiope had spun across the path. It reared, crooking its jointed legs in the air, and I pulled back as it scuttled away into the lilacs. Spiders made me nervous, with their quick, darting movements.

Breathe deep, calm the soul. That's what the doctor had ordered. I inhaled slowly, holding my breath for a count of four, then let it out in a slow stream. As the stirrings of panic subsided, I plunged through the arbor to the end of the drive and out.

And there it was . . . *Breakaway Farm.*

Framed by two spectacular cedars, the house looked part castle, part cottage. Toss in a southern front porch and five acres of thickly wooded land and . . . bingo . . . Breakaway Farm.

I sucked in a deep breath, staring up at the old house. She might be lonely and abandoned, but she still had life to her. That much, I could feel. The morning light reflected off an unusually clean pane of glass on the second story as a gust of wind elicited a ringing peal from a set of wind chimes.

A flash . . . was someone staring at me from behind one of the third-floor windows? I squinted, looking closer, but the image vanished. *If it had ever been there in the first place.*

I made my way around back, wading through the knee-high grass and ferns that blanketed the ground. Another glance at the upper stories told me that there had to be a roof up there somewhere beneath the thick layers of moss and lichen, but the vegetation was so thick, it was hard to see. Ivy wound around the chimney, tendrils waving down at me. I completed the circuit and returned to the porch, staring up at the door, the key clenched in my hand.

It all came down to this. Could I go through with it? Unlock the door, and go in? I glanced back at the driveway where my Pathfinder sat, crammed with everything I possessed. No, there was no going back—but how could I go forward?

I held the house key up to the sky. When the lawyer had given it to me, it had rested in a black velvet box. Large and old-fashioned, an engraved R curled down the shaft, surrounded by delicate roses, and it hung on a black satin ribbon. R for rose . . . R for Jason Rose . . . the man who had almost ended my life.

A WOMAN WAS on the porch.

With difficulty, he pulled himself out of his foggy cocoon, and, by sheer habit, dusted off his jeans. His shirt was a cardigan—too warm for the summer, but he felt neither warmth nor cold. A glance in the mirror told him that he was probably out of style, but with his straight back, slightly gaunt but not unappealing face, wheat-colored shoulder-length hair, he cleaned up pretty good. The pallor in his cheeks would be a giveaway, but only in the brilliant light. If he kept to the shadows, she need not notice at first. And she would be his ticket out. His ticket to freedom.

He had reached the point of no return, and like the others, had been trapped in the house. The mirror had kept his spirit here, chained to the walls in which he'd once lived. The others walking in his world didn't like him, they stayed away, finding him strange and unnatural in their dark and endless night. But he . . . he was just who he'd always been. Except, he was alone. Or had been . . . until his dark twin had returned. Now he had hope, something he'd never thought he'd have again.

He'd spent a lot of time watching the seasons pass as the years went by. When his mother came to clean each week, he'd pray she'd see him. And yet, when it came time to make himself known, he'd hide. She'd try to free him. And to free him, she'd risk her own life. So he watched from a distance and listened. Now and then she'd talk to him like she had before the *accident*, before he'd unleashed the djinn. Once it was unleashed, you could never recork the bottle. That much he'd learned, the hard way.

After a quick calculation, he headed for the mirror. He hated the thing, and yet, from here he could travel to any room with mirrors or windows. He could look out on the world and watch the world pass by, but the living couldn't look *in*, unless they were gifted with the Sight. They could see only the shallow surface, the image reflected in them.

As the tumblers of the lock began to turn, he slipped into the antique mirror that stood against one wall in the bedroom. After all, what better place to first lay eyes on your new bride?

"EXCUSE ME."

Startled, I turned, almost twisting my ankle. I found myself facing an elderly woman who might have been fifty, might have been eighty. Her hair shimmered white under the early streaks of sun, and she wore it in a tight chignon, held by a butterfly barrette. Her dress was a tidy periwinkle, with an apron tied at her waist. She smiled and I caught a glimpse of myself in her brilliant blue eyes.

"I'm sorry, I didn't mean to startle you," she said, her gaze flickering over me again. "But are you Laurel Rose?" She held out her hand, a smile creasing the ancient topography of her face.

Wary, I nodded and glanced around, wondering where she'd come from. I hadn't heard her approach.

As if reading my mind, she said, "Out of the woods. Where else?"

For a moment, I stood disconcerted, uncertain what to say next. I had the feeling that she could see right through me, as if I were made of light, fractured by a prism. I gathered my wits enough to say hello.

"I'm May. May O'Conner." With a gentle bob of her head, she added, "Jason's aunt."

I leaned against the newel post, a stab of pain knifing through my forehead. The headache that had been looming all morning suddenly hit full-force. *Jason's aunt* was not who I needed right now. The man who almost murdered me had never been complimentary when he spoke of his family. But then again, he'd never said a good word about anybody but himself. I searched May's face, scanning for a resemblance, but to my relief found nothing.

"How do you do?" I stammered.

"Oh, fit and tidy, fit and tidy." May winked at me, then pointed to the door. "I've come to welcome you to the neighborhood."

I fingered the key, surprised by her friendliness. I'd expected a stormy confrontation when I finally met her, accusations for defending myself, tearful threats, but not this welcoming matter-of-factness.

She motioned to the door. "Shall we go in? I'll show you around."

This was it, no more room for procrastination. Either I claimed Breakaway Farm or left defeated. And if I left here . . . I held my breath and inserted the key into the lock.

The door, carved with figures too weathered to discern, swung open with a faint creak. I stepped back, allowing May to enter first. Our eyes locked as she drew me in and flipped on the lights. I was relieved to see them flicker to life—the lawyer had said he'd take care of the utilities, but you never knew whether tasks would get done when you delegated them to other people.

"Breakaway Farm is a solid house, and will take you through the years." May's words echoed through the long hall. "She's been empty for around nine years, since . . . since my Galen died. I've kept the house up, hoping that perhaps Jason might change his mind and want to return home. But I think I knew he never would. Then, when I found out that you were moving in, I came over and spiffed it up with a lick and a spit." She turned to study my face and added, "I hope you don't mind."

"Mind? Why would I mind?" I wanted to hug her in relief. No brewing storms, no callous remarks, just that unrelenting smile. "I'm just grateful that I won't be facing corners filled with cobwebs and mold growing on old furniture. I'm glad someone took care of it all these years instead of letting it go to ruin."

Then it hit me—how did she know I'd be moving in? The lawyer had promised he wouldn't tell anyone. So much for confidentiality.

May stopped in the hallway, where photographs lined the walls. People I didn't know, places I'd never been, but they were beautiful and melancholy and incredibly sad in a way I couldn't define.

I raised a finger and hesitantly traced the frame of one that stood out among the rest. Protected by glass, a man and woman were curled together on an iron settee in the middle of a garden.

"They loved each other very much, didn't they? Who were they?"

May gave me a gentle smile. "My brother, Daneen, and his wife, Ellen."

Jason's parents. My in-laws.

"You never got to meet them, did you?"

I gave her a sidelong glance, not sure of how much she knew. "I wanted to, but no . . . I never had the chance."

May reached out and tipped up my chin. "You are far too pale for such a pretty young woman." She dipped into one of the voluminous pockets on her apron and brought out an apple and tucked it in my hand. "You need some color in your cheeks to match that fiery hair of yours. This will help."

She pointed to another photograph. Daneen and Ellen stood in front of a lush garden. Overflowing baskets filled with tomatoes and lettuce, carrots and cucumbers, surrounded them. "Breakaway has many treasures. Daneen and Ellen were its rarest. They loved this farm. They loved their son. They never looked at the flaws in anything. *Or anyone.*"

What she left unsaid hung between us like thick fog.

I wondered just how much I could tell her. "Jason seldom spoke of his parents." It wasn't totally true, but I felt a sudden desire to spare her feelings.

"That, I do not doubt." She held my gaze. "Jason seldom divulged anything relating to his past. Come, let me show you the living room."

We entered the living room, and once again, light flooded the room at the touch of a switch. A velveteen sofa and love seat looked new, but the rest of the furniture stood ponderous, weighty oak, solid and stern. A bay window glittered as May drew open the floor-length drapes. A window seat, upholstered in the same green velvet as the curtains, overlooked the side yard, facing the trunk of an oak that had seen far more years than I.

A dizzy feeling that we were being watched hit me, but it was swept away in the next moment when I realized that I'd fallen in love with the house. I spun around, clapping my hands. "I never dreamed it would be so lovely!"

The room took a deep breath as a splash of sunlight filtered in through the sparkling glass, and the light transformed every corner. Newly potted ferns and ivies draped down from shining brass hooks on the ceiling, and I realized that May had brought them for me. Then I stopped, rooted to the floor, as I spotted a picture hanging low on the north wall.

The man in the photo was young, but there was no mistaking the face. Jason's eyes glittered at me with the same cruel assessment I'd known throughout my life with him. I pulled my sweater tighter, suddenly cold, and the scars on my throat began to itch again. I glanced over at May. She'd been watching me as I rubbed them gently. Flushing, I waited for her to comment.

"I'm sorry, Laurel," she murmured. "I should have taken that down. I just wasn't thinking. Please forgive me?"

Trembling, I reached out, stopping just short of touching the photograph. Would I ever be able to face his image without shaking? May silently stepped in front of me and turned the picture to face the wall. I slowly let out my breath. *Breathe deep, calm the soul.* A companion photo hung next to it, a man as fair as Jason had been dark, though somewhat older.

"Who's that?" I asked.

May's face lit up. "That was my son, Galen. Jason's cousin." Pride rang in her voice. "I miss him dreadfully."

"Was he older?" I asked, examining the photograph. The man's face was robust, but not red, and he had sandy blond hair gathered into a short braid that hung down his back. He sported a reddish beard and I found myself unable to look away. His eyes radiated the same gentle firmness as May's. Beneath her wrinkles, I could tell that May possessed the same definite bone structure. Not nearly as angular as Jason's.

May nodded. She fingered the portrait and her prints remained faintly on the glass. "Galen was six years older than Jason was." Her eyes sparkled. "He was nothing like his cousin. They were the sun and the moon. He died in this house." She glanced at her watch. "My word, I didn't realize so much time has passed. I've got pies in the oven." She edged towards the door. "I just wanted to meet you."

"How did you know I was here?" I walked her to the door.

May smiled and I suddenly felt exposed. Jason had called her a "nosy old bitch," and now I knew why, at least from his standpoint. She'd make keeping secrets as hard as keeping your hand out of the cookie jar, and Jason had kept a lot of skeletons locked in that dark closet that was his mind.

She laughed faintly. "I knew. I just knew. Galen and I never thought anyone in the family would ever live at Breakaway again. That's why he moved in here. We never told Jason." She gave me a keen look and added, "I'm pleased you're giving it a try. This house belongs to you . . . and you belong to it."

"You don't know how much I needed to hear that," I said, swallowing a sudden swell of tears. It had been so long since anybody had been nice to me, had acted like I wasn't tainted. I almost believed her.

"Words can be powerful allies. Or enemies." May glanced up at the sky. "It's going to be hot this afternoon. My garden can use the warmth."

"Let me walk you to the path. I need to bring in Circe."

"Circe?"

"My cat. She's been in the carrier for several hours. We took several breaks along the way, but I'm afraid she's probably fighting mad by now. She hates to travel."

"I don't blame her. Come, let's get her settled, then." As we headed toward my car, she said, "My Galen was a veterinarian. Did you know that?"

I shook my head. "I'm afraid not. Jason never said anything about his life here, or his family. He told me Breakaway Farm was a moldering dump."

"Jason had more problems than his parents wanted to admit," May said as we reached my Pathfinder. I had to pull out a couple of the suitcases first, but I finally had Circe in hand. May picked up the bag containing the new litter box and bag of litter.

I protested. "You don't have to do that—your pies, remember?"

"Laurel, I can carry an empty litter box. The pies will keep for another few minutes. They're huckleberry, by the way."

"Thank you," I said.

May led me to the half bath on the first floor. "Why don't you lock her in here until you get your unloading done? She'll be fine if you set up her box and fetch her some water."

Circe let out a yowl, staring indignantly from her cage.

With a laugh, May said, "What a pretty calico! And she's a lively one, I'll bet. There are lots of mice and shrews out here. She'll have fun hunting."

We put her in the bath and I unpacked her litter box and filled it, then set out food and water before walking May down the path.

As she passed the car, she pointed to my portfolio. "You paint, don't you? You don't have much else with you," she added.

I shook my head. "I travel light. Easier that way."

"Well, then, good-bye. I'll bring you over one of my pies." And, just like that, the fey woman vanished down a side path, quiet as a whisper.

HE COULD FEEL the cat's presence before he could find her. When he was hiding in the mirrors, he would travel from one to the next and so forth, and now he peeked out of the bathroom mirror to look at the calico, who stared up at him, eyes glowering, with a hiss.

"You may not pass," she said. "She's mine. I won't let you hurt her."

He laughed and a thousand chimes blew in the wind, low and reverberant. Inclining his head with respect, he said, "Mistress of Cats, little protector. In life, I tended to your kind. I mean no harm to you. What can you tell me about her?"

And Circe, her emerald eyes glinting in the light that filtered through the window, whispered one word, "Lonely." And then, pleading, "Don't hurt her."

The man smiled softly then, and the calico backed away, hunching down, hissing at the mirror. But he passed, and after a while, she curled up and went to sleep.

And he went back to waiting.

AFTER I FINISHED unloading the car, I let Circe out of the bathroom and dropped into a chair in the kitchen with a cup of peppermint tea. Luckily, the place was fully furnished—I wouldn't have to buy much.

As I relaxed, floating in the diffused light that flooded the room, the scent of peppermint drifted up to clear my mind. Finally, I forced myself to pull out my compact.

May hadn't asked, but there was no way she could have overlooked them. I ran my fingers along the fading lines that crisscrossed my throat.

How many times had I defended myself against the accusations that I'd asked for it?

And yet, inside, I could hear my own voice loudest of all. *If only you'd left early enough . . . if only you'd called for help . . .* The scars would fade from my throat in time, but they'd burn forever in my memory.

Wearily, I wandered into the living room, where I turned Jason's picture back around. The glittering man. How he'd first sparkled into my life! Suave, sophisticated, the mysterious stranger of all young girls' dreams, the dark knight who rushes in to sweep us away. I lifted the frame off the wall and stared deep into those eyes. And then I slammed it into the fireplace, smashing it to bits.

You're dead, I thought. *You're dead and you can't hurt me anymore.* But deep in my heart, I didn't really believe it.

HE REMAINED HIDDEN for a few days, watching her from mirror to mirror, keeping quiet, talking only to the cat. The calico had set up a cautious conversation with him. In return, he reached out of the mirrors, petted her tummy, offered her a chin scratch.

By the time he was ready to approach the woman, he had a pretty good idea of what had happened. Jason always had been a hardnosed son of a bitch, he'd been cruel and vindictive, and at times, downright dangerous. But Jason was dead, and cruel or not, had brought Galen the key to his manacles.

He tried to make sense of what his cousin told him, but so much seemed confusing. But from what he understood, the woman had killed Jason. And like his cousin or not, murder wasn't the most desirable option.

Circe told him a different story, but like all cats, she lived on a different time line. She seemed to think the mess went down during the blooming of the daffodils before the daffodils this time—in other words, a year ago, spring.

And so he watched Laurel from the mirrors in the house, watched her alone, and quietly turned away when he felt he was intruding on her private moments. She was beautiful, in an autumn sort of way. Cloaked in red hair and fair skin, Laurel reminded him of a woman made of burning leaves. But he could see the scars on her throat, and they made him wonder.

Jason kept silent on the matter.

. . . .

A NOISE CAUGHT my attention. That was one thing about Breakaway Farm—the house was filled with creaks and shudders and all the requisite noises that attend old houses. I'd gotten used to most of them, but now and then, I couldn't shake the feeling that I was being watched.

I put down my embroidery and listened. This noise had been loud enough to really hear. And it sounded like it was coming from my bedroom.

Circe was sitting on the rocking chair.

"You hear that, baby?"

She slowly turned her gaze to me and mewed. She'd been responsible for my rescue from Jason, knocking a vase within reach so I could grab hold of it and hit him once, twice, and the final third time that ended both his attempts to kill me and his life. She'd meowed in my ear, keeping me conscious till I managed to drag myself over to the phone to call 911.

There it was again—louder. Circe's ears twitched and she sat up, looking anxious. Even if it was just a squirrel or raccoon in the attic, I needed to know, so I picked up the baseball bat that I'd left in the corner of the room, and started upstairs.

As I approached my bedroom, I heard the noise again. The door was open and I crept inside, my cell phone in my pocket ready in case I needed to call the cops. Out here in the country, though, it would take them precious time to reach me. I had to learn how to take care of matters on my own.

The four-poster bed stood silent. The window was closed. Nothing looked out of place. Slowly, I lowered the bat and squinted in the dim light. The closet door was off its hinges—I'd removed it first thing, out of habit. The door to the master bath was open and I inched over, peeking inside. Nothing.

What the hell? Maybe it had just been the house. Maybe old houses settled more than I thought they did. Shrugging, I turned around and found myself facing the antique mirror that rested against one wall. I'd moved it away from my bed because something about it made me nervous.

A man stared back at me from my reflection.

Whirling, I raised the bat, but there was no one standing behind me. I jerked back to the mirror. Sure enough, he was still there, gazing at me from inside the glass. I slowly lowered the bat. What the hell was going on? Was I hallucinating? Overtired? *Or is it a ghost?* whispered a little voice in my mind.

Ghost. A ghost. I tried the word on my tongue as I gazed into the man's eyes. And then I recognized him from the photo in the living room. I was staring at May's son. Galen, who was long, long dead.

NOW THAT HE had her attention, how could he keep her from running scared? He pressed one hand against the glass and smiled softly. The last thing he wanted to do was chase her away. As he watched her struggle to believe, he noticed Circe saunter up to her mistress. The cat casually leaped onto the vanity and stretched up, her front paws leaning against the frame of the mirror. She gazed into the mirror at him, her luminous eyes almond shaped and glowing, and then let out a hiss and lightly leaped into Laurel's arms.

Laurel stared at him, then at the cat in her arms. She whispered something—he couldn't fully hear, being stuck in the mirror—but when she looked at him again, her gaze was soft, and a flicker of a smile rested on her lips. She shifted the cat to her left arm and raised her right hand, slowly bringing it up to meet his on the other side of the glass.

A shiver raced through him—a whisper of song on the wind. It was enough for one night. He flashed her a pale smile, then faded from sight.

AT FIRST, I only saw him in the mirror, but as I got used to his presence, Galen began to show up in other places. I'd turn around and he'd be in the corner of the kitchen. I'd be out in the garden and see him watching from the attic window. He never left the house, though, and I had the feeling he was trapped.

Circe didn't like him, but cats and spirits didn't mix, so I wasn't too worried. She followed me around the house, seldom leaving my side at night.

As the weeks went by, I kept meaning to broach the subject with May, but I wasn't sure how to begin. *Hey, I see your dead son rambling around my house . . . What gives with that?* just didn't cut it. And whenever May came over, Galen made himself scarce.

Meanwhile, I pumped her with questions. If Galen was going to hang around my house, I wanted to know as much as I could about the ghostly man who always had a cheerful smile for me.

"How did Galen die?" I asked one day after we'd been talking about the renovations he'd made on the house.

She pressed her lips together. "The doctor . . . the doctor said he had a heart attack. But Galen was strong, he was in shape and kept his health up. One day . . ." Her voice cracked, but she waved away the tissue I offered her. "One day, I came over to see why he hadn't shown up for breakfast. It was the morning after Halloween. His body was on the floor in the bedroom. He . . . just died."

"I'm sorry," I whispered, wondering if that was why he'd come back. Maybe he wanted May to know something. "What was he like?"

May sniffed back her tears as she picked up the rolling pin. She was attempting to teach me how to make pie crust. Baking wasn't one of my strong suits, but with a tree full of apples growing ripe in the side yard, it just seemed wrong to let them go to waste.

"He was a good man," she finally said. "He was the son every mother dreams of having. Strong, handsome, good hearted, loved animals. He never had a date because all the girls wanted to *just be friends*. They'd cry on his shoulder about the men who treated them badly, then go right back for more abuse."

She shook her head. "I'll never understand," she added, then stopped abruptly, looking at me. "I'm sorry . . ."

I stared at the pie crust as she gently flipped it over the rolling pin, then spread it over the deep pie dish. How could I explain? I'd been explaining for months to people . . . and making excuses for years to myself.

"Sometimes . . . you believe what you're told. That nobody else will ever want you. That you're worthless. You believe it because you grow up hearing it over and over. Jason was a god in my eyes. He acted—he told me—he was doing me a favor by loving me. None of my mother's string of boyfriends were role models, and I was so shy that nobody else ever asked me out. How could I avoid falling for a man who I thought could actually love me? Who promised to love me forever?"

I busied myself with the teakettle, then gave up and looked at her bleakly. "It ended the day after our honeymoon. And I was so embarrassed, I could never tell anyone just how bad our marriage was."

May laid a gentle hand on my arm. "I know, child. I know. I understand."

"Not all of us are strong," I whispered, dropping several tea bags in the chintz pot. "Not all of us know how to be strong."

After that, May came over a lot. She taught me how to bake. She strolled with me through the gardens and showed me which were weeds and which would blossom into flowers come spring. And always, always in the background, Galen hovered at the edge of my vision.

At night, I talked to him. Sometimes he showed himself, others not, but I always knew he was there. I'd tell him about my day while I folded laundry or brought out my paints or thumbed through the newspaper. And meanwhile, I did research on ghosts to find out just what I was dealing with.

But for all my research, I still couldn't figure out what Galen wanted. He wouldn't talk to me—I didn't even know if he could—and he never ventured outside. If he wanted to resolve some lingering issue with his mother, he would have been falling all over himself to appear when she came over. All the books did was to confirm that some ghosts were benign, others weren't, and that some might just be memories trapped in a space-time continuum.

But as the weeks wore on, I did know one thing for certain: I enjoyed his company. Galen was the perfect roommate—undemanding, quiet, and there every night. And he really listened to me—even though I didn't know if he could actually hear me.

Eventually, I began to feel more than just friendship . . . enough to start undressing in front of the antique mirror where he appeared in my bedroom. On a morbid note, it occurred to me that I was probably standing right where he had when he'd died, but I pushed the thought away. And when he stared at me as I let my clothes drop to the ground, I made it worth the look.

HE HAD HER, and he knew he had her. Jason had been right—she was pliable. And before long, he'd have his freedom. The house had held him chained for years. But he always knew there was one way out. He didn't dare show himself to his mother—she might offer herself and that would never do. He'd never be able to live with the guilt. But this girl . . . this woman . . . she would make it possible for him to slip out from behind the mirror. To walk into the light.

He had to win her trust, had to convince her that he was safe. And so he listened to her, night and day, and no one was the wiser.

Except for the cat.

Circe planted herself on Laurel's lap or on the floor between them whenever he showed up. Whatever the case, he wasn't afraid. There was no way she could expose him, even though she could see right through his smiles.

Gradually, Laurel began to let down her guard. Galen found himself mesmerized by the sight of her as she stood naked, caressing herself through the dark sultry nights. Autumn wore on and instead of growing more excited about his impending release, he began to dread the turn of the days.

Each night, he hesitated a little bit more. The sound of her voice, static-ridden though it may be, filled him with the urge to smile. Galen began to live for the evenings when they could spend time together.

At the end of each day, they bid each other good night with hands pressed against the glass, touching through the veils. And Galen began to question his plan, because there was something in Laurel's eyes that gave him pause, that made him think that maybe she really could love him. And no woman had ever fallen for him before.

HALLOWEEN.

I stood by the window, watching the sun slowly lower itself below the treeline. The season was turning, autumn had arrived. May was due over tomorrow, we were going huckleberry picking and she was going to teach me how to make jam. As I took a deep breath, a tangy chill settled into my lungs, and I felt incredibly sad. The smell of wood smoke and crackling leaves reminded me of some lurking sorrow. Just what it was—I didn't know, but whatever it was, it hovered in the shadows.

I turned back to the bed. Circe was sitting there, staring at me with her brilliant green eyes. She let out a little chirp and I sat beside her, scratching her under the chin. Her eyes were closed—*cat bliss*—and I let out a long sigh, looking over at the mirror.

Galen was late tonight. He usually appeared an hour or so before I went to sleep and we spent the time together, quietly pressing hands through the mirror or I would read to him, wondering if he could hear me. Right now, I was reading to him from Tennyson and was set to read *The Lady of Shalott* next.

Circe suddenly hissed, her hackles rising as she stared at the mirror, poised for a fight. I slowly stood, wondering whether Galen was coming. Even though I knew she didn't like him, she'd never acted like this before.

I slowly approached the mirror, and there he was, standing, his hand against the glass. He looked upset, and I leaned closer, bringing my hand up to the cool glass.

"Is something wrong?" I stared into his eyes, my hand against his. "What's wrong?"

He stared at me, his gaze fastened on mine, as the clock chimed the hour. At the first stroke of midnight, the mirror began to melt as his hand closed over mine. Startled, I screamed, as Circe leaped into my other arm.

The looking glass vanished and I became Alice.

GALEN SHOOK HIS head, dazed. Had it really happened? Was he free from the mirror? Could he move on, out of the house, to whatever afterlife waited for him? And then memory hit. He let out sharp gasp.

No . . . no . . . please no. Don't let it be true. His heart spoke before his mind and he turned toward the mirror, dreading what he knew he would see.

There, behind the glass, pounding against it, stood Laurel, Circe at her feet. Her body and the cat's lay in front of the mirror, near him, both seizing.

I'm free suddenly became mingled with *I just killed the best thing that ever happened to me.*

Galen shook his head. "No . . . no . . . please . . ." It came out a whimper, lost in the silence of All Hallow's night. It came out a scream from the back of his throat.

"Laurel! Laurel!" He tried to pound on the mirror but here he was spirit, unable to touch the glass except . . . except for one way. "Please, tell me I didn't do this to you . . ."

And then he stopped. The clock was chiming the final strokes of midnight. He slammed his hand against the pane and motioned for Laurel to do the same. A look of terror in her eyes, she obeyed. As their hands met, he could feel her fingers sliding through the glass. Behind her, he caught a glimpse of Jason, watching them, seething.

"You can't have her!" With all his strength, Galen yanked Laurel by the wrist and she tumbled out, back into her body, Circe following suit. And just as quickly, he was swept into the mirror, his spirit captured once more.

The clock fell silent. Midnight was over. The veils between the worlds had closed for another year and he was still trapped, but this time, it was his choice. He'd made the decision that his own captor chose not to make.

Galen turned as his cousin came up behind him. There would be no forgiveness. Jason had been whispering in his ear too long. Galen let out a single laugh and as the mists swirled, he grappled Jason, who slipped out of his grasp and faded from sight.

"You didn't win," Galen whispered. "You won't *ever* win, because I'll always watch out for her. As long as she lives in this house, I'll be there to watch over her!"

I WOKE UP on the floor, aching and feeling bruised. What the hell had happened? As I rubbed my head, vague images drifted through my mind. Touching the glass, feeling Galen's delight as he traded places with me . . .

But if that was true . . . then what was I doing sitting on the floor? Circe was sitting next to me, nosing me with her sandpaper tongue. I scratched her between the ears.

"Hey, baby, what happened? Did I pass out?" Maybe I was more tired than I thought.

She stared at me, unblinking, then walked over to the mirror. As she reached up to scratch it, she yowled. Startled, I fell forward, knocking the mirror to the floor. The glass broke into shards, and I leaped away to avoid getting cut. Circe raced off, her tail high in the air.

"It's okay, baby. It's okay—it's just an old mirror." But as I looked for the dustpan and broom, an odd feeling settled in my stomach. I looked back at the mirror. The nerves were gone.

I walked into the bedroom and swept up the glass. For a moment, I thought I saw Galen's image in the broken shards, but then it vanished. Once my floor was free from glass slivers and the broken frame, I headed into the bathroom to brush my teeth. As I looked into the mirror, a mist formed on the other side and there he was. My beloved. I pressed my hand against the glass.

"Galen," I whispered. "I wish there was a way we could touch."

He gazed back sadly, and pressed his hand against the glass on the other side.

Diana Gabaldon

International bestseller Diana Gabaldon is a winner of the Quill Award and of the Corine International Award for fiction. She's the author of the hugely popular Outlander series, including Cross Stitch, Dragonfly in Amber, Voyager, Drums of Autumn, The Fiery Cross, A Breath of Snow and Ashes, *and* An Echo in the Bone. *Her historical series about the strange adventures of Lord John Grey include the novels* Lord John and the Private Matter; Lord John and the Brotherhood of the Blade; *and a collection of Lord John stories,* Lord John and the Hand of Devils. *The* Outlandish Companion *is a nonfiction guidebook and commentary to the Outlander series. Her most recent book is a graphic novel titled* The Exile, *a new story based on* Outlander.

Here she gives us the bittersweet tale of a man torn out of his proper time and place who will go to almost any length, and endure any hardship, to make it home again.

A Leaf on the Wind of All Hallows

It was two weeks yet to Hallowe'en, but the gremlins were already at work. Jerry MacKenzie turned Dolly II onto the runway—full-throttle, shoulder-hunched, blood-thumping, already halfway up Green leader's arse—pulled back on the stick, and got a choking shudder instead of the giddy lift of takeoff. Alarmed, he eased back, but before he could try again, there was a bang that made him jerk by reflex, smacking his head against the Perspex. It hadn't been a bullet, though; the off tire had blown, and a sickening tilt looped them off the runway, bumping and jolting into the grass.

There was a strong smell of petrol, and Jerry popped the Spitfire's hood and hopped out in panic, envisioning imminent incineration, just as the last plane of Green flight roared past him and took wing, its engine fading to a buzz within seconds.

A mechanic was pelting down from the hangar to see what the trouble was, but Jerry'd already opened Dolly's belly and the trouble was plain: The fuel line was punctured. Well, thank Christ he hadn't got into the air with it, that was one thing, but he grabbed the line to see how bad the puncture was, and it came apart in his hands and soaked his sleeve nearly to the shoulder with high-test petrol. Good job the mechanic hadn't come loping up with a lit cigarette in his mouth.

He rolled out from under the plane, sneezing, and Gregory the mechanic stepped over him.

"Not flying her today, mate," Greg said, squatting down to look up into the engine, and shaking his head at what he saw.

"Aye, tell me something I don't know." He held his soaked sleeve gingerly away from his body. "How long to fix her?"

Greg shrugged, eyes squinted against the cold wind as he surveyed Dolly's guts.

"Half an hour for the tire. You'll maybe have her back up tomorrow, if the fuel line's the only engine trouble. Anything else we should be looking at?"

"Aye, the left wing-gun trigger sticks sometimes. Gie' us a bit o' grease, maybe?"

"I'll see what the canteen's got in the way of leftover dripping. You best hit the showers, Mac. You're turning blue."

He was shivering, right enough, the rapidly evaporating petrol wicking his body heat away like candle smoke. Still, he lingered for a moment, watching as the mechanic poked and prodded, whistling through his teeth.

"Go on, then," Greg said in feigned exasperation, backing out of the engine and seeing Jerry still there. "I'll take good care of her."

"Aye, I know. I just—aye, thanks." Adrenaline from the aborted flight was still surging through him, thwarted reflexes making him twitch. He walked away, suppressing the urge to look back over his shoulder at his wounded plane.

JERRY CAME OUT of the pilots' WC half an hour later, eyes stinging with soap and petrol, backbone knotted. Half his mind was on Dolly, the other half with his mates. Blue and Green were up this morning, Red and Yellow resting. Green flight would be out over Flamborough Head by now, hunting.

He swallowed, still restless, dry-mouthed by proxy, and went to fetch a cup of tea from the canteen. That was a mistake; he heard the gremlins laughing as soon as he walked in and saw Sailor Malan.

Malan was Group Captain and a decent bloke overall. South African, a great tactician—and the most ferocious, most persistent air fighter Jerry'd seen yet. Rat terriers weren't in it. Which was why he felt a beetle skitter briefly down his spine when Malan's deep-set eyes fixed on him.

"Lieutenant!" Malan rose from his seat, smiling. "The very man I had in mind!"

The devil he had, Jerry thought, arranging his face into a look of respectful expectancy. Malan couldn't have heard about Dolly's spot of bother yet, and without that, Jerry would have scrambled with A flight on their way to hunt 109s over Flamborough Head. Malan hadn't been looking for Jerry; he just thought he'd do, for whatever job was up. And the fact that the Group Captain had called him by his rank, rather than his name, meant it probably wasn't a job anyone would volunteer for.

He didn't have time to worry about what that might be, though; Malan was introducing the other man, a tallish chap in army uniform with dark hair and a pleasant, if sharp, look about him. Eyes like a good sheepdog, he thought, nodding in reply to Captain Randall's greeting. Kindly, maybe, but he won't miss much.

"Randall's come over from Ops at Ealing," Sailor was saying over his shoulder. He hadn't waited for them to exchange polite chat, but was already leading them out across the tarmac, heading for the Flight Command offices. Jerry grimaced and followed, casting a longing glance downfield at Dolly, who was being towed ignominiously into the hangar. The rag doll painted on her nose was blurred, the black curls partially dissolved by weather and spilled petrol. Well, he'd touch it up later, when he'd heard the details of whatever horrible job the stranger had brought.

His gaze rested resentfully on Randall's neck, and the man turned suddenly, glancing back over his shoulder as though he'd felt the stress of Jerry's regard. Jerry felt a qualm in the pit of his stomach, as half-recognized observations—the lack of insignia on the uniform, that air of confidence peculiar to men who kept secrets—gelled with the look in the stranger's eye.

Ops at Ealing, my Aunt Fanny, he thought. He wasn't even surprised, as Sailor waved Randall through the door, to hear the Group Captain lean close and murmur in his ear, "Careful—he's a funny bugger."

Jerry nodded, stomach tightening. Malan didn't mean Captain Randall was either humorous or a Freemason. "Funny bugger" in this context meant only one thing. MI6.

CAPTAIN RANDALL *WAS* from the secret arm of British Intelligence. He made no bones about it, once Malan had deposited them in a vacant office and left them to it.

"We're wanting a pilot—a good pilot"—he added with a faint smile—"to fly solo reconnaissance. A new project. Very special."

"Solo? Where?" Jerry asked warily. Spitfires normally flew in four-plane flights, or in larger configurations, all the way up to an entire squadron, sixteen planes. In formation, they could cover one another to some extent against the heavier Henckels and Messerschmitts. But they seldom flew alone by choice.

"I'll tell you that a bit later. First—are you fit, do you think?"

Jerry reared back a bit at that, stung. What did this bloody boffin think he—then he caught a glance at his reflection in the windowpane. Eyes red as a mad boar's, his wet hair sticking up in spikes, a fresh red bruise spreading on his forehead and his blouson stuck to him in damp patches where he hadn't bothered to dry off before dressing.

"Extremely fit," he snapped. "Sir."

Randall lifted a hand half an inch, dismissing the need for sirs.

"I meant your knee," he said mildly.

"Oh," Jerry said, disconcerted. "That. Aye, it's fine."

He'd taken two bullets through his right knee a year before, when he'd dived after a 109 and neglected to see another one that popped out of nowhere behind him and peppered his arse. On fire, but terrified of bailing out into a sky filled with smoke, bullets, and random explosions, he'd ridden his burning plane down, both of them screaming as they fell out of the sky, Dolly I's metal skin so hot it had seared his left forearm through his jacket, his right foot squelching in the blood that filled his boot as he stamped the pedal. Made it, though, and had been on the sick and hurt list for two months. He still limped very noticeably, but he didn't regret his smashed patella; he'd had his second month's sick leave at home—and wee Roger had come along nine months later.

He smiled broadly at thought of his lad, and Randall smiled back in involuntary response.

"Good," he said. "You're all right to fly a long mission, then?"

Jerry shrugged. "How long can it be in a Spitfire? Unless you've thought up a way to refuel in the air." He'd meant that as a joke, and was further disconcerted to see Randall's lips purse a little, as though thinking whether to tell him they *had*.

"It is a Spitfire ye mean me to fly?" he asked, suddenly uncertain. Christ, what if it was one of the experimental birds they heard about now and again? His skin prickled with a combination of fear and excitement. But Randall nodded.

"Oh, yes, certainly. Nothing else is maneuverable enough, and there may be a good bit of ducking and dodging. What we've done is to take a Spitfire II, remove one pair of wing guns, and refit it with a pair of cameras."

"One pair?"

Again that slight pursing of lips before Randall replied.

"You might need the second pair of guns."

"Oh. Aye. Well, then . . ."

The immediate notion, as Randall explained it, was for Jerry to go to Northumberland, where he'd spend two weeks being trained in the use of the wing cameras, taking pictures of selected bits of landscape at different altitudes. And where he'd work with a support team who were meant to be trained in keeping the cameras functioning in bad weather. They'd teach him how to get the film out without ruining it, just in case he had to. After which . . .

"I can't tell you yet exactly where you'll be going," Randall had said. His manner through the conversation had been intent, but friendly, joking now and then. Now all trace of joviality had vanished; he was dead serious. "Eastern Europe is all I can say just now."

Jerry felt his inside hollow out a little and took a deep breath to fill the empty space. He could say no. But he'd signed up to be an RAF flier, and that's what he was.

"Aye, right. Will I—maybe see my wife once, before I go, then?"

Randall's face softened a little at that, and Jerry saw the captain's thumb touch his own gold wedding ring in reflex.

"I think that can be arranged."

MARJORIE MACKENZIE—DOLLY to her husband—opened the blackout curtains. No more than an inch . . . well, two inches. It wouldn't matter; the inside of the little flat was dark as the inside of a coal scuttle. London outside was equally dark; she knew the curtains were open only because she felt the cold glass of the window through the narrow crack. She leaned close, breathing on the glass, and felt the moisture of her breath condense, cool near her face. Couldn't see the mist, but felt the squeak of her fingertip on the glass as she quickly drew a small heart there, the letter J inside.

It faded at once, of course, but that didn't matter; the charm would be there when the light came in, invisible but there, standing between her husband and the sky.

When the light came, it would fall just so, across his pillow. She'd see his sleeping face in the light: the jackstraw hair, the fading bruise on his temple, the deep-set eyes, closed in innocence. He looked so young, asleep. Almost as young as he really was. Only twenty-two; too young to have such lines in his face. She touched the corner of her mouth, but couldn't feel the crease the mirror showed her—her mouth was swollen, tender, and the ball of her thumb ran across her lower lip, lightly, to and fro.

What else, what else? What more could she do for him? He'd left her with something of himself. Perhaps there would be another baby—something he gave her, but something she gave him, as well. Another baby. Another child to raise alone?

"Even so," she whispered, her mouth tightening, face raw from hours of stubbled kissing; neither of them had been able to wait for him to shave. "Even so."

At least he'd got to see Roger. Hold his little boy—and have said little boy sick up milk all down the back of his shirt. Jerry'd yelped in surprise, but hadn't let her take Roger back; he'd held his son and petted him until the wee mannie fell asleep, only then laying him down in his basket and stripping off the stained shirt before coming to her.

It was cold in the room, and she hugged herself. She was wearing nothing but Jerry's string vest—he thought she looked erotic in it—"lewd," he said, approving, his Highland accent making the word sound really dirty—and the thought made her smile. The thin cotton clung to her breasts, true enough, and her nipples poked out something scandalous, if only from the chill.

She wanted to go crawl in next to him, longing for his warmth, longing to keep touching him for as long as they had. He'd need to go at eight, to catch the train back; it would barely be light then. Some puritanical impulse of denial kept her hovering there, though, cold and wakeful in the dark. She felt as though if she denied herself, her desire, offered that denial as sacrifice, it would strengthen the magic, help to keep him safe and bring him back. God knew what a minister would say to that bit of superstition, and her tingling mouth twisted in self-mockery. And doubt.

Still, she sat in the dark, waiting for the cold blue light of the dawn that would take him.

Baby Roger put an end to her dithering, though; babies did. He rustled in his basket, making the little waking-up grunts that presaged an outraged roar at the discovery of a wet nappy and an empty stomach, and she hurried across the tiny room to his basket, breasts swinging heavy, already letting down her milk. She wanted to keep him from waking Jerry, but stubbed her toe on the spindly chair and sent it over with a bang.

There was an explosion of bedclothes as Jerry sprang up with a loud "FUCK!" that drowned her own muffled "damn!" and Roger topped them both with a shriek like an air-raid siren. Like clockwork, old Mrs. Munns in the next flat thumped indignantly on the thin wall.

Jerry's naked shape crossed the room in a bound. He pounded furiously on the partition with his fist, making the wallboard quiver and boom like a drum. He paused, fist still raised, waiting. Roger had stopped screeching, impressed by the racket.

Dead silence from the other side of the wall, and Marjorie pressed her mouth against Roger's round little head to muffle her giggling. He smelled of baby scent and fresh pee, and she cuddled him like a large hot-water bottle, his immediate warmth and need making her notions of watching over her men in the lonely cold seem silly.

Jerry gave a satisfied grunt and came across to her.

"Ha," he said, and kissed her.

"What d'ye think you are?" she whispered, leaning into him. "A gorilla?"

"Yeah," he whispered back, taking her hand and pressing it against him. "Want to see my banana?"

"*Dzień dobry.*"

Jerry halted in the act of lowering himself into a chair, and stared at a smiling Frank Randall.

"Oh, aye," he said. "Like that, is it? *Pierdolić matka.*" It meant, "Fuck your mother," in Polish, and Randall, taken by surprise, broke out laughing.

"Like that," he agreed. He had a wodge of papers with him, official forms, all sorts, the bumf as the pilots called it—Jerry recognized the one you signed that named who your pension went to, and the one about what to do with your body if there was one and anyone had time to bother. He'd done all that when he signed up, but they made you do it again, if you went on special service. He ignored the forms, though, eyes fixed instead on the maps Randall had brought.

"And here's me thinkin' you and Malan picked me for my bonny face," he drawled, exaggerating his accent. He sat and leaned back, affecting casualness. "It is Poland, then?" So it hadn't been coincidence, after all—or only the coincidence of *Dolly*'s mishap sending him into the building early. In a way, that was comforting; it wasn't the bloody Hand of Fate tapping him on the shoulder by puncturing the fuel line. The Hand of Fate had been in it a good bit earlier, putting him in Green flight with Andrej Kolodziewicz.

Andrej was a real good bloke, a good friend. He'd copped it a month before, spiraling up away from a Messerschmitt. Maybe he'd been blinded by the sun, maybe just looking over the wrong shoulder. Left wing shot to hell, and he'd spiraled right back down and into the ground. Jerry hadn't seen the crash, but he'd heard about it. And got drunk on vodka with Andrej's brother after.

"Poland," Randall agreed. "Malan says you can carry on a conversation in Polish. That true?"

"I can order a drink, start a fight, or ask directions. Any of that of use?"

"The last one might be," Randall said, very dry. "But we'll hope it doesn't come to that."

The MI6 agent had pushed aside the forms and unrolled the maps. Despite himself, Jerry leaned forward, drawn as by a magnet. They were official maps, but with markings made by hand—circles, Xs.

"It's like this," Randall said, flattening the maps with both hands. "The Nazis have had labor camps in Poland for the last two years, but it's not common knowledge among the public—either home or abroad. It would be very helpful to the war effort if it *were* common knowledge. Not just the camps' existence, but the kind of thing that goes on there." A shadow crossed the dark, lean face—anger, Jerry thought, intrigued. Apparently, Mr. MI6 knew what kinds of things went on there, and he wondered how.

"If we want it widely known and widely talked about—and we do—we need documentary evidence," Randall said matter-of-factly. "Photographs."

There'd be four of them, he said, four Spitfire pilots. A flight—but they wouldn't fly together. Each one of them would have a specific target, geographically separate, but all to be hit on the same day.

"The camps are guarded, but not with anti-aircraft ordnance. There are towers, though, machine guns." And Jerry didn't need telling that a machine gun was just as effective in someone's hands as it was from an enemy plane. To take the sort of pictures Randall wanted would mean coming in low—low enough to risk being shot from the towers. His only advantage would be the benefit of surprise; the guards might spot him, but they wouldn't be expecting him to come diving out of the sky for a low pass just above the camp.

"Don't try for more than one pass, unless the cameras malfunction. Better to have fewer pictures than none at all."

"Yes, sir." He'd reverted to "sir," as Group Captain Malan was present at the meeting, silent but listening intently. Got to keep up appearances.

"Here's the list of targets you'll practice on in Northumberland. Get as close as you think reasonable, without risking—" Randall's face did change at that, breaking into a wry smile. "Get as close as you can manage with a chance of coming back, all right? The cameras may be worth even more than you are."

That got a faint chuckle from Malan. Pilots—especially trained pilots—were valuable. The RAF had plenty of planes now—but nowhere near enough pilots to fly them.

He'd be taught to use the wing cameras—and to unload the film safely. If he was shot down but was still alive and the plane didn't burn, he was to get the film out and try to get it back over the border.

"Hence the Polish." Randall ran a hand through his hair and gave Jerry a crooked smile. "If you have to walk out, you may need to ask directions." They had two Polish-speaking pilots, he said—Poles who'd volunteered, and an Englishman with a few words of the language, like Jerry.

"And it is a volunteer mission, let me reiterate."

"Aye, I know," Jerry said irritably. "Said I'd go, didn't I? Sir."

"You did." Randall looked at him for a moment, dark eyes unreadable, then lowered his gaze to the maps again. "Thanks," he said softly.

THE CANOPY SNICKED shut over his head. It was a dank, damp Northumberland day, and his breath condensed on the inside of the Perspex hood within seconds. He leaned forward to wipe it away, emitting a sharp yelp as several strands of his hair were ripped out. He'd forgotten to duck. Again. He shoved the canopy release with a muttered oath and the light brown strands caught in the seam where the Perspex closed flew away, caught up by the wind. He closed the canopy again, crouching, and waiting automatically for the signal for takeoff.

The signalman wigwagged him and he turned up the throttle, feeling the plane begin to move.

He touched his pocket automatically, whispering, "Love you, Dolly," under his breath. Everyone had his little ritual, those last few moments before takeoff. For Jerry MacKenzie, it was his wife's face and his lucky stone that usually settled the worms in his belly. She'd found it in a rocky hill on the Isle of Lewis, where they'd spent their brief honeymoon—a rough sapphire, she said, very rare.

"Like you," he'd said, and kissed her.

No need for worms just now, but it wasn't a ritual if you only did it sometimes, was it? And even if it wasn't going to be combat today, he'd need to be paying attention.

He went up in slow circles, getting the feel of the new plane, sniffing to get her scent. He wished they'd let him fly Dolly II, her seat stained with his sweat, the familiar dent in the console where he'd slammed his fist in exultation at a kill—but they'd already modified this one with the wing cameras and the latest thing in night-sights. It didn't do to get attached to the planes, anyway; they were almost as fragile as the men flying them—though the parts could be reused.

No matter; he'd sneaked out to the hanger the evening before and done a quick rag doll on the nose to make it his. He'd know Dolly III well enough by the time they went into Poland.

He dived, pulled up sharp, and did Dutch rolls for a bit, wigwagging through the cloud layer, then complete rolls and Immelmanns, all the while reciting Malan's Rules to focus his mind and keep from getting airsick.

The Rules were posted in every RAF barracks now, the Ten Commandments, the fliers called them—and not as a joke.

TEN OF MY RULES FOR AIR FIGHTING, the poster said in bold black type. Jerry knew them by heart.

"'Wait until you see the whites of his eyes,'" he chanted under his breath. "'Fire short bursts of one to two seconds only when your sights are definitely "ON."'" He glanced at his sights, suffering a moment's disorientation. The camera wizard had relocated them. Shite.

"'Whilst shooting think of nothing else, brace the whole of your body: have both hands on the stick: concentrate on your ring sight.'" Well, away to fuck, then. The buttons that operated the camera weren't on the stick; they were on a box connected to a wire that ran out the window; the box itself was strapped to his knee. He'd be bloody looking out the window anyway, not using sights—unless things went wrong and he had to use the guns. In which case . . .

"'Always keep a sharp lookout. Keep your finger out.'" Aye, right, that one was still good.

"'Height gives you the initiative.'" Not in this case. He'd be flying low, under the radar, and not be looking for a fight. Always the chance one might find him, though. If any German craft found him flying solo in Poland, his best chance was likely to head straight for the sun and fall in. That thought made him smile.

"'Always turn and face the attack.'" He snorted and flexed his bad knee, which ached with the cold. Aye, if you saw it coming in time.

"'Make your decisions promptly. It is better to act quickly even though your tactics are not the best.'" He'd learned that one fast. His body often was moving before his brain had even notified his consciousness that he'd seen something. Nothing to see just now, nor did he expect to, but he kept looking by reflex.

"'Never fly straight and level for more than thirty seconds in the combat area.'" Definitely out. Straight and level was just what he was going to have to do. And slowly.

"'When diving to attack always leave a proportion of your formation above to act as a top guard.'" Irrelevant; he wouldn't have a formation—and that was a thought that gave him the cold grue. He'd be completely alone; no help coming if he got into bother.

"'INITIATIVE, AGGRESSION, AIR DISCIPLINE, and TEAM WORK are words that MEAN something in Air Fighting.'" Yeah, they did. What meant something in reconnaissance? Stealth, Speed, and Bloody Good Luck, more like. He took a deep breath, and dived, shouting the last of the Ten Commandments so it echoed in his Perspex shell.

"'Go in quickly—Punch hard—GET OUT!'"

"Rubber-necking," they called it, but Jerry usually ended a day's flying feeling as though he'd been cast in concrete from the shoulder blades up. He bent his head forward now, ferociously massaging the base of his skull to ease the growing ache. He'd been practicing since dawn, and it was nearly teatime. *Bull-bearings, set, for the use of pilots, one*, he thought. Ought to add that to the standard equipment list. He shook his head like a wet dog, hunched his shoulders, groaning, then resumed the sector by sector scan of the sky around him that every pilot did religiously, three hundred and sixty degrees, every moment in the air. All the live ones, anyway.

Dolly'd given him a white silk scarf as a parting present. He didn't know how she'd managed the money for it and she wouldn't let him ask, just settled it round his neck inside his flight jacket. Somebody'd told her the Spitfire pilots all wore them, to save the constant collar-chafing, and she meant him to have one. It felt nice, he'd admit that. Made him think of her touch when she'd put it on him. He pushed the thought hastily aside; the last thing he could afford to do was start thinking about his wife, if he ever hoped to get back to her. And he did mean to get back to her.

Where was that bugger? Had he given up?

No, he'd not; a dark spot popped out from behind a bank of cloud just over his left shoulder and dived for his tail. Jerry turned, a hard, high spiral, up and into the same clouds, the other after him like stink on shite. They played at dodgem for a few moments, in and out of the drifting clouds—he had the advantage in altitude, could play the coming-out-of-the-sun trick, if there were any sun, but it was autumn in Northumberland, there hadn't been any sun in days . . .

Gone. He heard the buzzing of the other plane, faintly, for a moment—or thought he had. Hard to tell above the dull roar of his own engine. Gone, though; he wasn't where Jerry'd expected him to be.

"Oh, like that, is it?" He kept on looking, ten degrees of sky every second, it was the only way to be sure you didn't miss any— A glimpse of something dark and his heart jerked along with his hand. Up and away. It was gone then, the black speck, but he went on climbing, slowly now, looking. Wouldn't do to get too low, and he wanted to keep the altitude . . .

The cloud was thin here, drifting waves of mist, but getting thicker. He saw a solid-looking bank of cloud moving slowly in from the west, but still a good distance away. It was cold, too; his face was chilled. He might be picking up ice if he went too hi—there.

The other plane, closer and higher than he'd expected. The other pilot spotted him at the same moment and came roaring down on him, too close to avoid. He didn't try.

"Aye, wait for it, ye wee bugger," he murmured, hand tight on the stick. One second, two, almost on him—and he buried the stick in his balls, jerked it hard left, turned neatly over, and went off in a long, looping series of barrel rolls that put him right away out of range.

His radio crackled and he heard Paul Rakoczy chortling through his hairy nose.

"*Pierdolić matka!* Where you learn that, you Scotch fucker?"

"At my mammy's tit, *dupek*," he replied, grinning. "Buy me a drink, and I'll teach it to ye."

A burst of static obscured the end of an obscene Polish remark, and Rakoczy flew off with a wigwag of farewell. Ah, well. Enough sky-larking then; back to the fucking cameras.

Jerry rolled his head, worked his shoulders, and stretched as well as could be managed in the confines of a II's cockpit—it had minor improvements over the Spitfire I, but roominess wasn't one of them— had a glance at the wings for ice—no, that was all right—and turned farther inland.

It was too soon to worry over it, but his right hand found the trigger that operated the cameras. His fingers twiddled anxiously over the buttons, checking, rechecking. He was getting used to them, but they didn't work like the gun triggers; he didn't have them wired in to his reflexes yet. Didn't like the feeling, either. Tiny things, like typewriter keys, not the snug feel of the gun triggers.

He'd only had the right-hand ones since yesterday; before that, he'd been flying a plane with the buttons on the left. Much discussion with Flight and the MI6 button-boffin, whether it was better to stay with the right, as he'd had practice already, or change for the sake of his cack-handedness. When they'd finally got round to asking him which he wanted, it had been too late in the day to fix it straight off. So he'd been given a couple of hours' extra flying time today, to mess about with the new fixup.

Right, there it was. The bumpy gray line that cut through the yellowing fields of Northumberland like a perforation, same as you might tear the countryside along it, separating North from South as neat as tearing a piece of paper. Bet the emperor Hadrian wished it was that easy, he thought, grinning as he swooped down along the line of the ancient wall.

The cameras made a loud *clunk-clunk* noise when they fired. *Clunk-clunk, clunk-clunk!* Okay, sashay out, bank over, come down . . . *clunk-clunk, clunk-clunk* . . . he didn't like the noise, not the same satisfaction as the vicious short *Brrpt!* of his wing guns. Made him feel wrong, like something gone with the engine . . . aye, there it was coming up, his goal for the moment.

Mile-castle 37.

A stone rectangle, attached to Hadrian's Wall like a snail on a leaf. The old Roman legions had made these small, neat forts to house the garrisons that guarded the wall. Nothing left now but the outline of the foundation, but it made a good target.

He circled once, calculating, then dived and roared over it at an altitude of maybe fifty feet, cameras clunking like an army of stampeding robots. Pulled up sharp and hared off, circling high and fast, pulling out to run for the imagined border, circling up again . . . and all the time his heart thumped and the sweat ran down his sides, imagining what it would be like when the real day came.

Midafternoon, it would be, like this. The winter light just going, but still enough to see clearly. He'd circle, find an angle that would let him cross the whole camp and please God, one that would let him come out of the sun. And then he'd go in.

One pass, Randall had said. Don't risk more than one—unless the cameras malfunction.

The bloody things did malfunction, roughly every third pass. The buttons were slippery under his fingers. Sometimes they worked on the next try, sometimes they didn't.

If they didn't work on the first pass over the camp, or didn't work often enough, he'd have to try again.

"*Niech to szlag,*" he muttered, Fuck the devil, and pressed the buttons again, one-two, one-two. "Gentle but firm, like you'd do it to a lady's privates," the boffin had told him, illustrating a brisk twiddle. He'd never thought of doing that . . . would Dolly like it? he wondered. And where exactly did you do it? Aye, well, women did come with a button, maybe that was it—but then, two fingers? . . . *Clunk-clunk. Clunk-clunk. Crunch.*

He reverted to English profanity, and smashed both buttons with his fist. One camera answered with a startled *clunk!*, but the other was silent.

He poked the button again and again, to no effect. "Bloody fucking arse-buggering . . ." He thought vaguely that he'd have to stop swearing once this was over and he was home again—bad example for the lad.

"FUCK!" he bellowed, and ripping the strap free of his leg, he picked up the box and hammered it on the edge of the seat, then slammed it back onto his thigh—visibly dented, he saw with grim satisfaction—and pressed the balky button.

Clunk, the camera answered meekly.

"Aye, well, then, just you remember that!" he said, and puffing in righteous indignation, gave the buttons a good jabbing.

He'd not been paying attention during this small temper tantrum, but had been circling upward—standard default for a Spitfire flier. He started back down for a fresh pass at the mile-castle, but within a minute or two, began to hear a knocking sound from the engine.

"No!" he said, and gave it more throttle. The knocking got louder; he could feel it vibrating through the fuselage. Then there was a loud *clang!* from the engine compartment right by his knee, and with horror he saw tiny droplets of oil spatter on the Perspex in front of his face. The engine stopped.

"Bloody, bloody . . ." He was too busy to find another word. His lovely agile fighter had suddenly become a very clumsy glider. He was going down and the only question was whether he'd find a relatively flat spot to crash in.

His hand groped automatically for the landing gear but then drew back—no time, belly-landing, where was the bottom? Jesus, he'd been distracted, hadn't seen that solid bank of cloud move in, it must have come faster than he. . . . Thoughts flitted through his mind, too fast for words. He glanced at the altimeter, but what it told him was of limited use, because he didn't know what the ground under him was like, crags, flat meadow, water? He hoped and prayed for a road, a grassy flat spot, anything short of—God, he was at five hundred feet and still in cloud!

"Christ!"

The ground appeared in a sudden burst of yellow and brown. He jerked the nose up, saw the rocks of a crag dead ahead, swerved, stalled, nose-dived, pulled back, pulled back, not enough, oh, God—

His first conscious thought was that he should have radioed base when the engine went.

"Stupid fucker," he mumbled. " 'Make your decisions promptly. It is better to act quickly even though your tactics are not the best.' Clot-heid."

He seemed to be lying on his side. That didn't seem right. He felt cautiously with one hand—grass and mud. What, had he been thrown clear of the plane?

He had. His head hurt badly, his knee much worse. He had to sit down on the matted wet grass for a bit, unable to think through the waves of pain that squeezed his head with each heartbeat.

It was nearly dark, and rising mist surrounded him. He breathed deep, sniffing the dank, cold air. It smelt of rot and old mangel-wurzels—but what it didn't smell of was petrol and burning fuselage.

Right. Maybe she hadn't caught fire when she crashed, then. If not, and if her radio was still working . . .

He staggered to his feet, nearly losing his balance from a sudden attack of vertigo, and turned in a slow circle, peering into the mist. There was nothing *but* mist to his left and behind him, but to his right, he made out two or three large, bulky shapes, standing upright.

Making his way slowly across the lumpy ground, he found that they were stones. Remnants of one of those prehistoric sites that littered the ground in northern Britain. Only three of the big stones were still standing, but he could see a few more, fallen or pushed over, lying like bodies in the darkening fog. He paused to vomit, holding on to one of the stones. Christ, his head was like to split! And he had a terrible buzzing in his ears . . . He pawed vaguely at his ear, thinking somehow he'd left his headset on, but felt nothing but a cold, wet ear.

He closed his eyes again, breathing hard, and leaned against the stone for support. The static in his ears was getting worse, accompanied by a sort of whine. Had he burst an eardrum? He forced himself to open his eyes, and was rewarded with the sight of a large dark irregular shape, well beyond the remains of the stone circle. Dolly!

The plane was barely visible, fading into the swirling dark, but that's what it had to be. Mostly intact, it looked like, though very much nose-down with her tail in the air—she must have plowed into the earth. He staggered on the rock-strewn ground, feeling the vertigo set in again, with a vengeance. He waved his arms, trying to keep his balance, but his head spun, and Christ, the bloody *noise* in his head . . . he couldn't think, oh, Jesus, he felt as if his bones were dissolv—

IT WAS FULL dark when he came to himself again, but the clouds had broken and a three-quarter moon shone in the deep black of a country sky. He moved, and groaned. Every bone in his body hurt—but none was broken. That was something, he told himself. His clothes were sodden with damp, he was starving, and his knee was so stiff he couldn't straighten his right leg all the way, but that was all right; he thought he could make shift to hobble as far as a road.

Oh, wait. Radio. Yes, he'd forgotten. If Dolly's radio was intact, he could . . .

He stared blankly at the open ground before him. He'd have sworn it was—but he must have got turned round in the dark and fog—no.

He turned quite round, three times, before he stopped, afraid of becoming dizzy again. The plane was gone.

It *was* gone. He was sure it had lain about fifty feet beyond that one stone, the tallest one; he'd taken note of it as a marker, to keep his bearings. He walked out to the spot where he was sure Dolly had come down, walked slowly round the stones in a wide circle, glancing to one side and then the other in growing confusion.

Not only was the plane gone—it didn't seem ever to have been there. There was no trace, no furrow in the thick meadow grass, let alone the kind of gouge in the earth that such a crash would have made. Had he been imagining its presence? Wishful thinking?

He shook his head to clear it—but in fact, it *was* clear. The buzzing and whining in his ears had stopped, and while he still had bruises and a mild headache, he was feeling much better. He walked slowly back around the stones, still looking, a growing sense of deep cold curling through his wame. It wasn't fucking there.

He woke in the morning without the slightest notion where he was. He was curled up on grass; that much came dimly to him, he could smell it. Grass that cattle had been grazing, because there was a large cowpat just by him, and fresh enough to smell that, too. He stretched out a leg, cautious. Then an arm. Rolled onto his back, and felt a hair better for having something solid under him, though the sky overhead was a dizzy void.

It was a soft, pale blue void, too. Not a trace of cloud.

How long . . . ? A jolt of alarm brought him up onto his knees, but a bright yellow stab of pain behind his eyes sat him down again, moaning and cursing breathlessly.

Once more. He waited till his breath was coming steady, then risked cracking one eye open . . .

Well, it was certainly still Northumbria, the northern part, where England's billowing fields crash onto the inhospitable rocks of Scotland.

He recognized the rolling hills, covered with sere grass and punctuated by towering rocks that shot straight up into sudden toothy crags. He swallowed, and rubbed both hands hard over his head and face, assuring himself he was still real. He didn't feel real. Even after he'd taken a careful count of fingers, toes, and private bits—counting the latter twice, just in case—he still felt that something important had been misplaced, torn off somehow, and left behind.

His ears still rang, rather like they did after a specially active trip. Why, though? What had he heard?

He found that he could move a little more easily now, and managed to look all round the sky, sector by sector. Nothing up there. No memory of anything up there. And yet the inside of his head buzzed and jangled, and the flesh on his body rippled with agitation. He chafed his arms, hard, to make it go.

Horripilation. That's the proper word for gooseflesh, Dolly'd told him that. She kept a little notebook and wrote down words she came across in her reading; she was a great one for the reading. She'd already got wee Roger sitting in her lap to be read to after tea, round-eyed as Bonzo at the colored pictures in his rag book.

Thought of his family got him up onto his feet, swaying, but all right now, better, yes, definitely better, though he still felt as though his skin didn't quite fit. The plane, where was that?

He looked round him. No plane was visible. Anywhere. Then it came back to him, with a lurch of the stomach. Real, it was real. He'd been sure in the night that he was dreaming or hallucinating, had lain down to recover himself, and must have fallen asleep. But he was awake now, no mistake; there was a bug of some kind down his back, and he slapped viciously to try to squash it.

His heart was pounding unpleasantly and his palms were sweating. He wiped them on his trousers and scanned the landscape. It wasn't flat, but neither did it offer much concealment. No trees, no bosky dells. There was a small lake off in the distance, he caught the shine of water— but if he'd ditched in water, surely to God he'd be wet?

Maybe he'd been unconscious long enough to dry out, he thought. Maybe he'd imagined that he'd seen the plane near the stones. Surely he couldn't have walked this far from the lake and forgotten it? He'd started walking toward the lake, out of sheer inability to think of anything more useful to do. Clearly time had passed; the sky had cleared like magic. Well, they'd have little trouble finding him, at least; they knew he was near the Wall. A truck should be along soon; he couldn't be more than two hours from the airfield.

"And a good thing, too," he muttered. He'd picked a specially Godforsaken spot to crash—there wasn't a farmhouse or a paddock anywhere in sight, not so much as a sniff of chimney smoke.

His head was becoming clearer now. He'd circle the lake—just in case—then head for the road. Might meet the support crew coming in.

"And tell them I've lost the bloody plane?" he asked himself aloud. "Aye, right. Come on, ye wee idjit, think! Now, where did ye see it last?"

HE WALKED FOR a long time. Slowly, because of the knee, but that began to feel easier after a while. His mind was not feeling easier. There was something wrong with the countryside. Granted, Northumbria was a ragged sort of place, but not *this* ragged. He'd found a road—but it wasn't the B road he'd seen from the air. It was a dirt track, pocked with stones and showing signs of being much traveled by hooved animals with a heavily fibrous diet.

Wished he hadn't thought of diet. His wame was flapping against his backbone. Thinking about breakfast was better than thinking about other things, though, and for a time, he amused himself by envisioning the powdered eggs and soggy toast he'd have got in the mess, then going on to the lavish breakfasts of his youth in the Highlands: huge bowls of steaming parritch, slices of black pudding fried in lard, bannocks with marmalade, gallons of hot strong tea . . .

An hour later, he found Hadrian's Wall. Hard to miss, even grown over with grass and all sorts like it was. It marched stolidly along, just like the Roman Legions who'd built it, stubbornly workmanlike, a gray seam stitching its way up hill and down dale, dividing the peaceful fields to the south from those marauding buggers up north. He grinned at the thought and sat down on the wall—it was less than a yard high, just here—to massage his knee.

He hadn't found the plane, or anything else, and was beginning to doubt his own sense of reality. He'd seen a fox, any number of rabbits, and a pheasant who'd nearly given him heart failure by bursting out from right under his feet. No people at all, though, and that was giving him a queer feeling in his water.

Aye, there was a war on, right enough, and many of the menfolk were gone—but the farmhouses hadn't been sacrificed to the war effort, had

they? The women were running the farms, feeding the nation, all that—
he'd heard the PM on the radio praising them for it only last week. So
where the bloody hell was everybody?

The sun was getting low in the sky when at last he saw a house. It
was flush against the Wall, and struck him somehow familiar, though
he knew he'd never seen it before. Stone-built and squat, but quite large,
with a ratty-looking thatch. There was smoke coming from the chimney,
though, and he limped toward it as fast as he could go.

There was a person outside—a woman in a ratty long dress and an
apron, feeding chickens. He shouted, and she looked up, her mouth falling open at the sight of him.

"Hey," he said, breathless from hurry. "I've had a crash. I need help.
Are ye on the phone, maybe?"

She didn't answer. She dropped the basket of chicken feed and ran
right away, round the corner of the house. He sighed in exasperation.
Well, maybe she'd gone to fetch her husband. He didn't see any sign of a
vehicle, not so much as a tractor, but maybe the man was—

The man was tall, stringy, bearded, and snaggle-toothed. He was also
dressed in dirty shirt and baggy short pants that showed his hairy legs
and bare feet—and accompanied by two other men in similar comic attire.
Jerry instantly interpreted the looks on their faces, and didn't stay to laugh.

"Hey, nay problem, mate," he said, backing up, hands raised. "I'm
off, right?"

They kept coming, slowly, spreading out to surround him. He hadn't
liked the looks of them to start with, and was liking them less by the
second. Hungry, they looked, with a speculative glitter in their eyes.

One of them said something to him, a question of some kind, but the
Northumbrian accent was too thick for him to catch more than a word.
"Who" was the word, and he hastily pulled his dog tags from the neck
of his blouson, waving the red and green disks at them. One of the men
smiled, but not in a nice way.

"Look," he said, still backing up. "I didna mean to—"

The man in the lead reached out a horny hand and took hold of his
forearm. He jerked back, but the man, instead of letting go, punched
him in the belly.

He could feel his mouth opening and shutting like a fish's, but no
air came in. He flailed wildly, but they all were on him then. They were
calling out to each other, and he didn't understand a word, but the intent
was plain as the nose he managed to butt with his head.

It was the only blow he landed. Within two minutes, he'd been efficiently beaten into pudding, had his pockets rifled, been stripped of his jacket and dog tags, frog-marched down the road and heaved bodily down a steep, rocky slope.

He rolled, bouncing from one outcrop to the next, until he managed to fling out an arm and grab on to a scrubby thornbush. He came to a scraping halt and lay with his face in a clump of heather, panting and thinking incongruously of taking Dolly to the pictures just before he'd joined up. They'd seen *The Wizard of Oz*, and he was beginning to feel creepily like the lass in that film—maybe it was the resemblance of the Northumbrians to scarecrows and lions.

"At least the fucking lion spoke English," he muttered, sitting up. "Jesus, now what?"

It occurred to him that it might be a good time to stop cursing and start praying.

London, two years later

SHE'D BEEN HOME from her work no more than five minutes. Just time to meet Roger's mad charge across the floor, shrieking "MUMMY!", she pretending to be staggered by his impact—not so much a pretense; he was getting big. Just time to call out to her own mum, hear the muffled reply from the kitchen, sniff hopefully for the comforting smell of tea and catch a tantalizing whiff of tinned sardines that made her mouth water—a rare treat.

Just time to sit down for what seemed the first time in days, and take off her high-heeled shoes, relief washing over her feet like seawater when the tide comes in. She noticed with dismay the hole in the heel of her stocking, though. Her last pair, too. She was just undoing her garter, thinking that she'd have to start using leg-tan like Maisie, drawing a careful seam up the back of each leg with an eyebrow pencil, when there came a knock at the door.

"Mrs. MacKenzie?" The man who stood at the door of her mother's flat was tall, a dark silhouette in the dimness of the hall, but she knew at once he was a soldier.

"Yes?" She couldn't help the leap of her heart, the clench of her stomach. She tried frantically to damp it down, deny it, the hope that had sprung up like a struck match. A mistake. There'd been a mistake. He hadn't been killed, he'd been lost somehow, maybe captured, and now they'd found hi—then she saw the small box in the soldier's hand and her legs gave way under her.

Her vision sparkled at the edges, and the stranger's face swam above her, blurred with concern. She could hear, though—hear her mum rush through from the kitchen, slippers slapping in her haste, voice raised in agitation. Heard the man's name, Captain Randall, Frank Randall. Hear Roger's small husky voice warm in her ear, saying "Mummy? Mummy?" in confusion.

Then she was on the swaybacked davenport, holding a cup of hot water that smelled of tea—they could only change the tea leaves once a week, and this was Friday, she thought irrelevantly. He should have come on Sunday, her mum was saying, they could have given him a decent cuppa. But perhaps he didn't work on Sundays?

Her mum had put Captain Randall in the best chair, near the electric fire, and had switched on two bars as a sign of hospitality. Her mother was chatting with the captain, holding Roger in her lap. Her son was more interested in the little box sitting on the tiny pie-crust table; he kept reaching for it, but his grandmother wouldn't let him have it. Marjorie recognized the intent look on his face. He wouldn't throw a fit—he hardly ever did—but he wouldn't give up, either.

He didn't look a lot like his father, save when he wanted something badly. She pulled herself up a bit, shaking her head to clear the dizziness, and Roger looked up at her, distracted by her movement. For an instant, she saw Jerry look out of his eyes, and the world swam afresh. She closed her own, though, and gulped her tea, scalding as it was.

Mum and Captain Randall had been talking politely, giving her time to recover herself. Did he have children of his own? Mum asked.

"No," he said, with what might have been a wistful look at wee Roger. "Not yet. I haven't seen my wife in two years."

"Better late than never," said a sharp voice, and she was surprised to discover that it was hers. She put down the cup, pulled up the loose stocking that had puddled round her ankle, and fixed Captain Randall with a look. "What have you brought me?" she said, trying for a tone of calm dignity. Didn't work; she sounded brittle as broken glass, even to her own ears.

Captain Randall eyed her cautiously, but took up the little box and held it out to her.

"It's Lieutenant MacKenzie's," he said. "An MID oakleaf cluster. Awarded posthumously for—"

With an effort, she pushed herself away, back into the cushions, shaking her head.

"I don't want it."

"Really, Marjorie!" Her mother was shocked.

"And I don't like that word. Pos—posth—don't say it."

She couldn't overcome the notion that Jerry was somehow inside the box—a notion that seemed dreadful at one moment, comforting the next. Captain Randall set it down, very slowly, as though it might blow up.

"I won't say it," he said gently. "May I say, though . . . I knew him. Your husband. Very briefly, but I did know him. I came with this myself, because I wanted to say to you how very brave he was."

"Brave." The word was like a pebble in her mouth. She wished she could spit it at him.

"Of course he was," her mother said firmly. "Hear that, Roger? Your dad was a good man, and he was a brave one. You won't forget that."

Roger was paying no attention, struggling to get down. His gran set him reluctantly on the floor and he lurched over to Captain Randall, taking a firm grip on the Captain's fresh-creased trousers with both hands—hands greasy, she saw, with sardine oil and toast crumbs. The captain's lips twitched, but he didn't try to detach Roger; just patted his head.

"Who's a good boy, then?" he asked.

"Fith," Roger said firmly. "Fith!"

Marjorie felt an incongruous impulse to laugh at the captain's puzzled expression, though it didn't touch the stone in her heart.

"It's his new word," she said. "Fish. He can't say 'sardine.'"

"Thar . . . DEEM!" Roger said, glaring at her. "Fitttthhhhh!"

The captain laughed out loud, and pulling out a handkerchief, carefully wiped the spittle off Roger's face, casually going on to wipe the grubby little paws as well.

"Of course it's a fish," he assured Roger. "You're a clever lad. And a big help to your mummy, I'm sure. Here, I've brought you something for your tea." He groped in the pocket of his coat and pulled out a small pot of jam. Strawberry jam. Marjorie's salivary glands contracted painfully. With the sugar rationing, she hadn't tasted jam in . . .

"He's a great help," her mother put in stoutly, determined to keep the conversation on a proper plane despite her daughter's peculiar behavior.

She avoided Marjorie's eye. "A lovely boy. His name's Roger."

"Yes, I know." He glanced at Marjorie, who'd made a brief movement. "Your husband told me. He was—"

"Brave. You told me." Suddenly something snapped. It was her half-hooked garter, but the pop of it made her sit up straight, fists clenched in the thin fabric of her skirt. "Brave," she repeated. "They're all brave, aren't they? Every single one. Even you—or are you?"

She heard her mother's gasp, but went on anyway, reckless.

"You all have to be brave and noble and—and—perfect, don't you? Because if you were weak, if there were any cracks, if anyone looked like being not quite the thing, you know—well, it might all fall apart, mightn't it? So none of you will, will you? Or if somebody did, the rest of you would cover it up. You won't ever not do something, no matter what it is, because you can't not do it, all the other chaps would think the worse of you, wouldn't they, and we can't have that, oh, no, we can't have that!"

Captain Randall was looking at her intently, his eyes dark with concern. Probably thought she was a nutter—probably she was, but what did it matter?

"Marjie, Marjie, love," her mother was murmuring, horribly embarrassed. "You oughn't to say such things to—"

"You made him do it, didn't you?" She was on her feet now, looming over the captain, making him look up at her. "He told me. He told me about you. You came and asked him to do—whatever it was that got him killed. Oh, don't trouble yourself, he didn't tell me your bloody precious secrets, not him, he wouldn't do that. He was a flier." She was panting with rage and had to stop to draw breath. Roger, she saw dimly, had shrunk into himself and was clinging to the captain's leg; Randall put an arm about the boy automatically, as though to shelter him from his mother's wrath. With an effort she made herself stop shouting, and to her horror, felt tears begin to course down her face.

"And now, all this time later, you come and bring me—and bring me . . ."

"Marjie." Her mother came up close beside her, her body warm and soft and comforting in her worn old pinny. She thrust a tea towel into Marjorie's hands, then moved between her daughter and the enemy, solid as a battleship.

"It's kind of you to've brought us this, Captain," Marjorie heard her saying, and felt her move away, bending to pick up the little box. Marjorie sat down blindly, pressing the tea towel to her face, hiding.

"Here, Roger, look. See how it opens? See how pretty? It's called—what did you say it was again, Captain? Oh, oakleaf cluster. Yes, that's right. Can you say 'medal,' Roger? Meh-dul. This is your dad's medal."

Roger didn't say anything. Probably scared stiff, poor little chap. She had to pull herself together. But she'd gone too far. She couldn't stop.

"He cried when he left me." She muttered the secret into the folds of the tea towel. "He didn't want to go." Her shoulders heaved with a convulsive, unexpected sob and she pressed the towel hard against her eyes, whispering to herself, "You said you'd come back, Jerry. You said you'd come *back*."

She stayed hidden behind her flour-sacking fortress, while renewed offers of tea were made—and to her vague surprise, accepted. She'd thought Captain Randall would seize the chance of her retreat to make his own. But he stayed, chatting calmly with her mother, talking slowly to Roger while her mother fetched the tea, ignoring her embarrassing performance entirely, keeping up a quiet, companionable presence in the shabby room.

The rattle and bustle of the tea tray's arrival gave her the opportunity to drop her cloth facade, and she meekly accepted a slice of toast spread with a thin scrape of margarine and a delectable spoonful of the strawberry jam.

"There, now," her mother said, looking on with approval. "You'll not have eaten anything since breakfast, I daresay. Enough to give anyone the wambles."

Marjorie shot her mother a look, but in fact it was true; she hadn't had any luncheon because Maisie was off with "female trouble"—a condition that afflicted her roughly every other week—and she'd had to mind the shop all day.

Conversation flowed comfortably around her, a soothing stream past an immoveable rock. Even Roger relaxed with the introduction of jam. He'd never tasted any before, and sniffed it curiously, took a cautious lick—and then took an enormous bite that left a red smear on his nose, his moss-green eyes round with wonder and delight. The little box, now open, sat on the pie-crust table, but no one spoke of it or looked in that direction.

After a decent interval, Captain Randall got up to go, giving Roger a shiny sixpence in parting. Feeling it the least she could do, Marjorie got up to see him out. Her stockings spiraled down her legs, and she kicked them off with contempt, walking bare-legged to the door. She heard her mother sigh behind her.

"Thank you," she said, opening the door for him. "I . . . appreciated—"

To her surprise, he stopped her, putting a hand on her arm.

"I've no particular right to say this to you—but I will," he said, low-voiced. "You're right; they're not all brave. Most of them—of us—we're just . . . there, and we do our best. Most of the time," he added, and the corner of his mouth lifted slightly, though she couldn't tell whether it was in humor or bitterness.

"But your husband—" He closed his eyes for a moment and said, "*'The bravest are surely those who have the clearest vision of what is before them, glory and danger alike, and yet notwithstanding, go out to meet it.'* He did that, every day, for a long time."

"You sent him, though," she said, her voice as low as his. "You did."

His smile was bleak.

"I've done such things every day . . . for a long time."

The door closed quietly behind him, and she stood there swaying, eyes closed, feeling the draft come under it, chilling her bare feet. It was well into the autumn now, and the dark was smudging the windows, though it was just past teatime.

I've done what I do every day for a long time, too, she thought. *But they don't call it brave when you don't have a choice.*

Her mother was moving through the flat, muttering to herself as she closed the curtains. Or not so much to herself.

"He liked her. Anyone could see that. So kind, coming himself to bring the medal and all. And how does she act? Like a cat that's had its tail stepped on, all claws and caterwauling, that's how. How does she ever expect a man to—"

"I don't want a man," Marjorie said loudly. Her mother turned round, squat, solid, implacable.

"You need a man, Marjorie. And little Rog needs a father."

"He has a father," she said through her teeth. "Captain Randall has a wife. And I don't need anyone."

Anyone but Jerry.

Northumbria

HE LICKED HIS lips at the smell. Hot pastry, steaming, juicy meat. There was a row of fat little pasties ranged along the sill, covered with a clean cloth in case of birds, but showing plump and rounded through it, the odd spot of gravy soaking through the napkin.

His mouth watered so fiercely that his salivary glands ached and he had to massage the underside of his jaw to ease the pain.

It was the first house he'd seen in two days. Once he'd got out of the ravine, he'd circled well away from the mile-castle and eventually struck a small cluster of cottages, where the people were no more understandable, but did give him some food. That had lasted him a little while; beyond that, he'd been surviving on what he could glean from hedges and the odd vegetable patch. He'd found another hamlet, but the folk there had driven him away.

Once he'd got enough of a grip of himself to think clearly, it became obvious that he needed to go back to the standing stones. Whatever had happened to him had happened there, and if he really *was* somewhere in the past—and hard as he'd tried to find some alternative explanation, none was forthcoming—then his only chance of getting back where he belonged seemed to lie there, too.

He'd come well away from the drover's track, though, seeking food, and as the few people he met didn't understand him any more than he understood them, he'd had some difficulty in finding his way back to the Wall. He thought he was quite close, now, though—the ragged country was beginning to seem familiar, though perhaps that was only delusion.

Everything else had faded into unimportance, though, when he smelled food.

He circled the house at a cautious distance, checking for dogs. No dog. Aye, fine, then. He chose an approach from the side, out of view of any of the few windows. Darted swiftly from bush to plowshare to midden to house, and plastered himself against the gray stone wall, breathing hard—and breathing in that delicious, savory aroma. Shite, he was drooling. He wiped his sleeve hastily across his mouth, slithered round the corner, and reached out a hand.

As it happened, the farmstead did boast a dog, which had been attending its absent master in the barn. Both these worthies returning unexpectedly at this point, the dog at once spotted what it assumed to be jiggery-pokery taking place, and gave tongue in an altogether proper manner. Alerted in turn to felonious activity on his premises, the householder instantly joined the affray, armed with a wooden spade, with which he batted Jerry over the head.

As he staggered back against the wall of the house, he had just wit enough left to notice that the farmwife—now sticking out of her window and shrieking like the Glasgow Express—had knocked one of the pasties to the ground, where it was being devoured by the dog, who wore an expression of piety and rewarded virtue that Jerry found really offensive.

Then the farmer hit him again, and he stopped being offended.

IT WAS A well-built byre, the stones fitted carefully and mortared. He wore himself out with shouting and kicking at the door until his gammy leg gave way and he collapsed onto the earthen floor.

"Now bloody what?" he muttered. He was damp with sweat from his effort, but it was cold in the byre, with that penetrating damp cold peculiar to the British Isles, that seeps into your bones and makes the joints ache. His knee would give him fits in the morning. The air was cold, but saturated with the scent of manure and chilled urine. "Why would the bloody Jerries want the damn place?" he said, and sitting up, huddled into his shirt. It was going to be a frigging long night.

He got up onto his hands and knees and felt carefully round inside the byre, but there was nothing even faintly edible—only a scurf of moldy hay. Not even the rats would have that; the inside of the place was empty as a drum and silent as a church.

What had happened to the cows? he wondered. Dead of a plague, eaten, sold? Or maybe just not yet back from the summer pastures— though it was late in the year for that, surely.

He sat down again, back against the door, as the wood was marginally less cold than the stone walls. He'd thought about being captured in battle, made prisoner by the Germans—they all had, now and then, though chaps mostly didn't talk about it. He thought about POW camps, and those camps in Poland, the ones he'd been meant to photograph. Were they as bleak as this? Stupid thing to think of, really.

But he'd got to pass the time till morning one way or another, and there were lots of things he'd rather not think about just now. Like what would happen once morning came. He didn't think breakfast in bed was going to be part of it.

The wind was rising. Whining past the corners of the cow byre with a keening noise that set his teeth on edge. He still had his silk scarf; it had slipped down inside his shirt when the bandits in the mile-castle had attacked him. He fished it out now and wrapped it round his neck, for comfort, if not warmth.

He'd brought Dolly breakfast in bed now and then. She woke up slow and sleepy, and he loved the way she scooped her tangled curly black hair off her face, peering out slit-eyed, like a small, sweet mole blinking in the light. He'd sit her up and put the tray on the table beside her, and then he'd shuck his own clothes and crawl in bed, too, cuddling close to her soft, warm skin. Sometimes sliding down in the bed, and her pretending not to notice, sipping tea or putting marmite on her toast while he burrowed under the covers and found his way up through the cottony layers of sheets and nightie. He loved the smell of her, always, but especially when he'd made love to her the night before, and she bore the strong musky scent of him between her legs.

He shifted a little, roused by the memory, but the subsequent thought—that he might never see her again—quelled him at once.

Still thinking of Dolly, though, he put his hand automatically to his pocket, and was alarmed to find no lump there. He slapped at his thigh, but failed to find the small hard bulge of the sapphire. Could he have put it in the other pocket by mistake? He delved urgently, shoving both hands deep into his pockets. No stone—but there was something in his right-hand pocket. Something powdery, almost greasy . . . what the devil?

He brought his fingers out, peering as closely at them as he could, but it was too dark to see more than a vague outline of his hand, let alone anything on it. He rubbed his fingers gingerly together; it felt something like the thick soot that builds up inside a chimney.

"Jesus," he whispered, and put his fingers to his nose. There was a distinct smell of combustion. Not petrol-ish at all, but a scent of burning so intense he could taste it on the back of his tongue. Like something out of a volcano. What in the name of God Almighty could burn a rock—and leave the man who carried it alive?

The sort of thing he'd met among the standing stones, that was what.

He'd been doing all right with the not feeling too afraid until now, but . . . he swallowed hard, and sat down again, quietly.

"Now I lay me down to sleep," he whispered to the knees of his trousers. "I pray the Lord my soul to keep . . ."

He did in fact sleep eventually, in spite of the cold, from simple exhaustion. He was dreaming about wee Roger, who for some reason was a grown man now, but still holding his tiny blue bear, minuscule in a broad-palmed grasp. His son was speaking to him in the Gaelic, saying something urgent that he couldn't understand, and he was growing frustrated, telling Roger over and over for Christ's sake to speak English, couldn't he?

Then he heard another voice through the fog of sleep and realized that someone was in fact talking somewhere close by.

He jerked awake, struggling to grasp what was being said, and failing utterly. It took him several seconds to realize that whoever was speaking—there seemed to be two voices, hissing and muttering in argument—really was speaking in Gaelic.

He had only a smattering of it himself; his mother had had it, but—he was moving before he could complete the thought, panicked at the notion that potential assistance might get away.

"Hoy!" he bellowed, scrambling—or trying to scramble—to his feet. His much-abused knee wasn't having any, though, and gave way the instant he put weight on it, catapulting him facefirst toward the door.

He twisted as he fell and hit it with his shoulder. The booming thud put paid to the argument; the voices fell silent at once.

"Help! Help me!" he shouted, pounding on the door. "Help!"

"Will ye for God's sake hush your noise?" said a low, annoyed voice on the other side of the door. "Ye want to have them all down on us? Here, then, bring the light closer."

This last seemed to be addressed to the voice's companion, for a faint glow shone through the gap at the bottom of the door. There was a scraping noise as the bolt was drawn, and a faint grunt of effort, then a *thunk!* as the bolt was set down against the wall. The door swung open, and Jerry blinked in a sudden shaft of light as the slide of a lantern grated open.

He turned his head aside and closed his eyes for an instant, deliberate, as he would if flying at night and momentarily blinded by a flare or by the glow of his own exhaust. When he opened them again, the two men were in the cow byre with him, looking him over with open curiosity.

Biggish buggers, both of them, taller and broader than he was. One fair, one black-haired as Lucifer. They didn't look much alike, and yet he had the feeling that they might be related—some fleeting glimpse of bone, a similarity of expression, maybe.

"What's your name, mate?" said the dark chap, softly. Jerry felt the nip of wariness at his nape, even as he felt a thrill in the pit of his stomach. It was regular speech, perfectly understandable. A Scots accent, but—

"MacKenzie, J.W.," he said, straightening up to attention. "Lieutenant, Royal Air Force. Service number—"

An indescribable expression flitted across the dark bloke's face. An urge to laugh, of all bloody things, and a flare of excitement in his eyes— really striking eyes, a vivid green that flashed sudden in the light. None of that mattered to Jerry; what was important was that the man plainly knew. He *knew*.

"Who are you?" he asked, urgent. "Where d'ye come from?"

The two exchanged an unfathomable glance, and the other answered. "Inverness."

"Ye know what I mean!" He took a deep breath. *"When?"*

The two strangers were much of an age, but the fair one had plainly had a harder life; his face was deeply weathered and lined.

"A lang way from you," he said quietly, and despite his own agitation, Jerry heard the note of desolation in his voice. "From now. Lost."

Lost. Oh, God. But still—

"Jesus. And where are we now? Wh-when?"

"Northumbria," the dark man answered briefly, "and I don't bloody know for sure. Look, there's no time. If anyone hears us—"

"Aye, right. Let's go, then."

The air outside was wonderful after the smells of the cow byre, cold and full of dying heather and turned earth. He thought he could even smell the moon, a faint green sickle above the horizon; he tasted cheese at the thought, and his mouth watered. He wiped a trickle of saliva away, and hurried after his rescuers, hobbling as fast as he could.

The farmhouse was black, a squatty black blot on the landscape. The dark bloke grabbed him by the arm as he was about to go past it, quickly licked a finger and held it up to test the wind.

"The dogs," he explained in a whisper. "This way."

They circled the farmhouse at a cautious distance, and found themselves stumbling through a plowed field. Clods burst under Jerry's boots as he hurried to keep up, lurching on his bad knee with every step.

"Where we going?" he panted, when he thought it safe to speak.

"We're taking ye back to the stones near the lake," the dark man said tersely. "That has to be where ye came through." The fair one just snorted, as though this wasn't his notion—but he didn't argue.

Hope flared up in Jerry like a bonfire. They knew what the stones were, how it worked. They'd show him how to get back!

"How—how did ye find me?" He could hardly breathe, such a pace they kept up, but had to know. The lantern was shut and he couldn't see their faces, but the dark man made a muffled sound that might have been a laugh.

"I met an auld wifey wearing your dog tags. Very proud of them, she was."

"Ye've got them?" Jerry gasped.

"Nay, she wouldna give them up." It was the fair man, sounding definitely amused. "Told us where she'd got them, though, and we followed your trail backward. Hey!" He caught Jerry's elbow, just as his foot twisted out from under him. The sound of a barking dog broke the night—some way away, but distinct. The fair man's hand clenched tight on his arm. "Come on, then—hurry!"

Jerry had a bad stitch in his side, and his knee was all but useless by the time the little group of stones came in sight, a pale huddle in the light of the waning moon. Still, he was surprised at how near the stones were to the farmhouse; he must have circled round more than he thought in his wanderings.

"Right," said the dark man, coming to an abrupt halt. "This is where we leave you."

"Ye do?" Jerry panted. "But—but you—"

"When ye came . . . through. Did ye have anything on you? A gemstone, any jewelry?"

"Aye," Jerry said, bewildered. "I had a raw sapphire in my pocket. But it's gone. It's like it . . ."

"Like it burned up," the blond man finished for him, grim-voiced. "Aye. Well, so?" This last was clearly addressed to the dark man, who hesitated. Jerry couldn't see his face, but his whole body spoke of indecision. He wasn't one to dither, though—he stuck a hand into the leather pouch at his waist, pulled something out, and pressed it into Jerry's hand. It was faintly warm from the man's body, and hard in his palm. A small stone of some kind. Faceted, like the stone in a ring.

"Take this; it's a good one. When ye go through"—the dark man was speaking urgently to him—"think about your wife, about Marjorie. Think hard; see her in your mind's eye, and walk straight through. Whatever the hell ye do, though, don't think about your son. Just your wife."

"What?" Jerry was gobsmacked. "How the bloody hell do you know my wife's name? And where've ye heard about my son?"

"It doesn't matter," the man said, and Jerry saw the motion as he turned his head to look back over his shoulder.

"Damn," said the fair one, softly. "They're coming. There's a light."

There was; a single light, bobbing evenly over the ground, as it would if someone carried it. But look as he might, Jerry could see no one behind it, and a violent shiver ran over him.

"*Tannasg,*" said the other man under his breath. Jerry knew that word well enough—spirit, it meant. And usually an ill-disposed one. A haunt.

"Aye, maybe." The dark man's voice was calm. "And maybe not. It's near Samhain, after all. Either way—ye need to go, man, and now. Remember, think of your wife."

Jerry swallowed, his hand closing tight around the stone.

"Aye. Aye . . . right. Thanks, then," he added awkwardly, and heard the breath of a rueful laugh from the dark man.

"Nay bother, mate," he said. And with that, they were both off, making their way across the stubbled meadow, two lumbering shapes in the moonlight.

Heart thumping in his ears, Jerry turned toward the stones. They looked just like they'd looked before. Just stones. But the echo of what he'd heard in there . . . he swallowed. It wasn't like there was much choice.

"Dolly," he whispered, trying to summon up a vision of his wife. "Dolly. Dolly, help me!"

He took a hesitant step toward the stones. Another. One more. Then nearly bit his tongue off as a hand clamped down on his shoulder. He whirled, fist up, but the dark man's other hand seized his wrist.

"I love you," the dark man said, his voice fierce. Then he was gone again, with the *shoof-shoof* sounds of boots in dry grass, leaving Jerry with his mouth agape.

He caught the other man's voice from the darkness, irritated, half-amused. He spoke differently than the dark man, a much thicker accent, but Jerry understood him without difficulty.

"Why did ye tell him a daft thing like that?"

And the dark one's reply, soft-spoken, in a tone that terrified him more than anything had so far.

"Because he isn't going to make it back. It's the only chance I'll ever have. Come on."

THE DAY WAS dawning when he came to himself again, and the world was quiet. No birds sang and the air was cold with the chill of November and winter coming on. When he could stand up, he went to look, shaky as a newborn lamb.

The plane wasn't there, but there was still a deep gouge in the earth where it had been. Not raw earth, though—furred over with grass and meadow plants—not just furred, he saw, limping over to have a closer look. Matted. Dead stalks from earlier years' growth.

If he'd been where he thought he'd been, if he'd truly gone . . . back . . . then he'd come forward again, but not to the same place he'd left. How long? A year, two? He sat down on the grass, too drained to stand up any longer. He felt as though he'd walked every second of the time between then and now.

He'd done what the green-eyed stranger had said. Concentrated fiercely on Dolly. But he hadn't been able to keep from thinking of wee Roger, not altogether. How could he? The picture he had most vividly of Dolly was her holding the lad, close against her breast; that's what he'd seen. And yet he'd made it. He thought he'd made it. Maybe.

What might have happened? he wondered. There hadn't been time to ask. There'd been no time to hesitate, either; more lights had come bobbing across the dark, with uncouth Northumbrian shouts behind them, hunting him, and he'd hurled himself into the midst of the standing stones and things went pear-shaped again, even worse. He hoped the strangers who'd rescued him had got away.

Lost, the fair man had said, and even now, the word went through him like a bit of jagged metal. He swallowed.

He thought he wasn't where he had been, but was he still lost, himself? Where was he now? Or rather, when?

He stayed for a bit, gathering his strength. In a few minutes, though, he heard a familiar sound—the low growl of engines, and the swish of tires on asphalt. He swallowed hard, and standing up, turned away from the stones, toward the road.

HE WAS LUCKY—for once, he thought wryly. There was a line of troop transports passing, and he swung aboard one without difficulty. The soldiers looked startled at his appearance—he was rumpled and stained, bruised and torn about and with a two-week beard—but they instantly assumed he'd been off on a tear and was now trying to sneak back to his base without being detected. They laughed and nudged him knowingly, but were sympathetic, and when he confessed he was skint, had a quick whip-round for enough cash to buy a train ticket from Salisbury, where the transport was headed.

He did his best to smile and go along with the ragging, but soon enough they tired of him and turned to their own conversations, and he was allowed to sit swaying on the bench, feeling the thrum of the engine through his legs, surrounded by the comfortable presence of comrades.

"Hey, mate," he said casually to the young soldier beside him. "What year is it?"

The boy—he couldn't be more than seventeen, and Jerry felt the weight of the five years between them as though they were fifty—looked at him wide-eyed, then whooped with laughter.

"What've you been having to drink, Dad? Bring any away with you?"

That led to more ragging, and he didn't try asking again.

Did it matter?

HE REMEMBERED ALMOST nothing of the journey from Salisbury to London. People looked at him oddly, but no one tried to stop him. It didn't matter; nothing mattered but getting to Dolly. Everything else could wait.

London was a shock. There was bomb damage everywhere. Streets were scattered with shattered glass from shop windows, glinting in the pale sun, other streets blocked off by barriers. Here and there a stark black notice: Do Not Enter—UNEXPLODED BOMB.

He made his way from St. Pancras on foot, needing to see, his heart rising into his throat fit to choke him as he did see what had been done. After a while, he stopped seeing the details, perceiving bomb craters and debris only as blocks to his progress, things stopping him from reaching home.

And then he did reach home.

The rubble had been pushed off the street into a heap, but not taken away. Great blackened lumps of shattered stone and concrete lay like a cairn where Montrose Terrace had once stood.

All the blood in his heart stopped dead, congealed by the sight. He groped, pawing mindlessly for the wrought-iron railing to keep himself from falling, but it wasn't there.

Of course not, his mind said, quite calmly. It's gone for the war, hasn't it? Melted down, made into planes. Bombs.

His knee gave way without warning, and he fell, landing hard on both knees, not feeling the impact, the crunch of pain from his badly mended kneecap quite drowned out by the small blunt voice inside his head.

Too late. Ye went too far.

"Mr. MacKenzie, Mr. MacKenzie!" He blinked at the blurred thing above him, not understanding what it was. Something tugged at him, though, and he breathed, the rush of air in his chest ragged and strange.

"Sit up, Mr. MacKenzie, do." The anxious voice was still there, and hands—yes, it was hands—tugging at his arm. He shook his head, screwed his eyes shut hard, then opened them again, and the round thing became the houndlike face of old Mr. Wardlaw, who kept the corner shop.

"Ah, there you are." The old man's voice was relieved, and the wrinkles in his baggy old face relaxed their anxious lines. "Had a bad turn, did you?"

"I—" Speech was beyond him, but he flapped his hand at the wreckage. He didn't think he was crying, but his face was wet. The wrinkles in Wardlaw's face creased deeper in concern; then the old grocer realized what he meant, and his face lit up.

"Oh, dear!" he said. "Oh, no! No, no, no—they're all right, sir. Your family's all right! Did you hear me?" he asked anxiously. "Can you breathe? Had I best fetch you some salts, do you think?"

It took Jerry several tries to make it to his feet, hampered both by his knee and by Mr. Wardlaw's fumbling attempts to help him, but by the time he'd got all the way up, he'd regained the power of speech.

"Where?" he gasped. "Where are they?"

"Why your missus took the little boy and went to stay with her mother sometime after you left. I don't recall quite where she said. . . ." Mr. Wardlaw turned, gesturing vaguely in the direction of the river. "Camberwell, was it?"

"Bethnal Green." Jerry's mind had come back, though it felt still as though it was a pebble rolling round the rim of some bottomless abyss, its balance uncertain. He tried to dust himself off, but his hands were shaking. "She lives in Bethnal Green. You're sure—you're sure, man?"

"Yes, yes." The grocer was altogether relieved, smiling and nodding so hard that his jowls trembled. "She left—must be more than a year ago, soon after she—soon after she . . ." The old man's smile faded abruptly and his mouth slowly opened, a flabby dark hole of horror.

"But you're dead, Mr. MacKenzie," he whispered, backing away, hands held up before him. "Oh, God. You're dead."

. . . .

"THE FUCK I am, the fuck I am, the *fuck* I am!" He caught sight of a woman's startled face and stopped abruptly, gulping air like a landed fish. He'd been weaving down the shattered street, fists pumping, limping and staggering, muttering his private motto under his breath like the Hail Marys of a rosary. Maybe not as far under his breath as he'd thought.

He stopped, leaning against the marble front of the Bank of England, panting. He was streaming with sweat and the right leg of his trousers was heavily streaked with dried blood from the fall. His knee was throbbing in time with his heart, his face, his hands, his thoughts. *They're alive. So am I.*

The woman he'd startled was down the street, talking to a policeman; she turned, pointing at him. He straightened up at once, squaring his shoulders. Braced his knee and gritted his teeth, forcing it to bear his weight as he strode down the street, officerlike. The very last thing he wanted just now was to be taken up as drunk.

He marched past the policeman, nodding politely, touching his forehead in lieu of cap. The policeman looked taken aback, made to speak but couldn't quite decide what to say, and a moment later, Jerry was round the corner and away.

It was getting dark. There weren't many cabs in this area at the best of times—none at all, now, and he hadn't any money, anyway. The Tube. If the lines were open, it was the fastest way to Bethnal Green. And surely he could cadge the fare from someone. Somehow. He went back to limping, grimly determined. He had to reach Bethnal Green by dark.

IT WAS SO much changed. Like the rest of London. Houses damaged, halfway repaired, abandoned, others no more than a blackened depression or a heap of rubble. The air was thick with coal dust, stone dust, and the smells of paraffin and cooking grease, the brutal, acrid smell of cordite.

Half the streets had no signs, and he wasn't so familiar with Bethnal Green to begin with. He'd visited Dolly's mother just twice, once when they went to tell her they'd run off and got married—she hadn't been best pleased, Mrs. Wakefield, but she'd put a good face on it, even if the face had a lemon-sucking look to it.

The second time had been when he signed up with the RAF; he'd gone alone to tell her, to ask her to look after Dolly while he was gone. Dolly's mother had gone white. She knew as well as he did what the life expectancy was for fliers. But she'd told him she was proud of him, and held his hand tight for a long moment before she let him leave, saying only, "Come back, Jeremiah. She needs you."

He soldiered on, skirting craters in the street, asking his way. It was nearly full dark now; he couldn't be on the streets much longer. His anxiety began to ease a little as he started to see things he knew, though. Close, he was getting close.

And then the sirens began, and people began to pour out of the houses.

He was being buffeted by the crowd, borne down the street as much by their barely controlled panic as by their physical impact. There was shouting, people calling for separated family members, wardens bellowing directions, waving their torches, their flat white helmets pale as mushrooms in the gloom. Above it, through it, the air-raid siren pierced him like a sharpened wire, thrust him down the street on its spike, ramming him into others likewise skewered by fright.

The tide of it swept round the next corner and he saw the red circle with its blue line over the entrance to the Tube station, lit up by a warden's flashlight. He was sucked in, propelled through sudden bright lights, hurtling down the stair, the next, onto a platform, deep into the earth, into safety. And all the time the whoop and moan of the sirens still filling the air, barely muffled by the dirt above.

There were wardens moving among the crowd, pushing people back against the walls, into the tunnels, away from the edge of the track. He brushed up against a woman with two toddlers, picked one—a little girl with round eyes and a blue teddy bear—out of her arms and turned his shoulder into the crowd, making a way for them. He found a small space in a tunnel mouth, pushed the woman into it and gave her back the little girl. Her mouth moved in thanks, but he couldn't hear her above the noise of the crowd, the sirens, the creaking, the—

There was a sudden monstrous thud from above that shook the station, and the whole crowd was struck silent, every eye on the high arched ceiling above them.

The tiles were white, and as they looked, a dark crack appeared suddenly between two rows of them. A gasp rose from the crowd, louder than the sirens. The crack seemed to stop, to hesitate—and then it zigzagged suddenly, parting the tiles, in different directions.

He looked down from the growing crack, to see who was below it—the people still on the stair. The crowd at the bottom was too thick to move, everyone stopped still by horror. And then he saw her, partway up the stair.

Dolly. *She's cut her hair*, he thought. It was short and curly, black as soot—black as the hair of the little boy she held in her arms, close against her, sheltering him. Her face was set, jaw clenched. And then she turned a bit, and saw him.

Her face went blank for an instant and then flared like a lit match, with a radiant joy that struck him in the heart and flamed through his being.

There was a much louder *thud!* from above, and a scream of terror rose from the crowd, louder, much louder than the sirens. Despite the shrieking, he could hear the fine rattle, like rain, as dirt began to pour from the crack above. He shoved with all his might, but couldn't get past, couldn't reach them. Dolly looked up, and he saw her jaw set hard again, her eyes blaze with determination. She shoved the man in front of her, who stumbled and fell down a step, squashing into the people in front of him. She swung Roger down into the little space she'd made, and with a twist of shoulders and the heave of her whole body, hurled the little boy up, over the rail—toward Jerry.

He saw what she was doing and was already leaning, pushing forward, straining to reach . . . the boy struck him high in the chest like a lump of concrete, little head smashing painfully into Jerry's face, knocking his head back. He had one arm round the child, falling back on the people behind him, struggling to find his footing, get a firmer hold—and then something gave way in the crowd around him, he staggered into an open space, and then his knee gave way and he plunged over the lip of the track.

He didn't hear the crack of his head against the rail or the screams of the people above; it was all lost in a roar like the end of the world as the roof over the stair fell in.

THE LITTLE BOY was still as death, but he wasn't dead; Jerry could feel his heart beat, thumping fast against his own chest. It was all he could feel. Poor little bugger must have had his wind knocked out.

People had stopped screaming, but there was still shouting, calling out. There was a strange silence underneath all the racket. His blood had stopped pounding through his head, his own heart no longer hammering. Perhaps that was it.

The silence underneath felt alive, somehow. Peaceful, but like sunlight on water, moving, glittering. He could still hear the noises above the silence, feet running, anxious voices, bangs and creakings—but he was sinking gently into the silence, the noises grew distant, though he could still hear voices.

"Is that one—?"

"Nay, he's gone—look at his head, poor chap, caved in something horrid. The boy's well enough, I think, just bumps and scratches. Here, lad, come up . . . no, no, let go now. It's all right, just let go. Let me pick you up, yes, that's good, it's all right now, hush, hush, there's a good boy . . ."

"What a look on that bloke's face—I never saw anything like—"

"Here, take the little chap. I'll see if the bloke's got any identification."

"Come on, big man, yeah, that's it, that's it, come with me. Hush now, it's all right. It's all right . . . Is that your daddy, then?"

"No tags, no service book. Funny, that. He's RAF, though, isn't he? AWOL, d'ye think?"

He could hear Dolly laughing at that, felt her hand stroke his hair. He smiled and turned his head to see her smiling back, the radiant joy spreading round her like rings in shining water . . .

"Rafe! The rest of it's going! Run! *Run!*"

AUTHOR'S NOTE

Before y'all get tangled up in your underwear about it being All Hallow's Eve when Jeremiah leaves, and "nearly Samhain (aka All Hallow's Eve)" when he returns—bear in mind that Great Britain changed from the Julian to the Gregorian calendar in 1752, this resulting in a "loss" of twelve days. And for those of you who'd like to know more about the two men who rescue him, more of their story can be found in *An Echo in the Bone.*